More praise for *Memories of the F*

"A meditation, by turns inspired and bemusing, upon the remembrance (and reclamation) of things past and the inevitable victory of time over memory."
—*The Washington Post Book World*

"Read this book as you would take the baths at Hot Springs. Slide into the water and let Updike float you hither and thither through place and time. Updike has the ability to evoke the micro-epochs that fascinate us. He can bring to life what seem to those of us who have lived them the vital differences between the decades of our lives.
—*Chicago Tribune*

"An exploration of a modern American terrain of desire, guilt, and moral ambiguity that he has made distinctly his own. . . . Updike is really pursuing the indeterminacy of memory, digging as best he can *beneath* official accounts—and our own self-deception—to find the heart's place in history.
—*The New York Times Book Review*

"*Memories of the Ford Administration* is full of Updike's finely tuned observations, his marvelously apt metaphors. It contains many valuable insights, many clever passages that cry out to be quoted. . . . A mixture of trenchant wit and terminal sadness. It is a novel to be read and appreciated."
—*St. Louis Post-Dispatch*

"A metaphor of fire, symbol of passion and revolution, flickers through Updike's novel, leading us to wonder whether Alfred, like his hero, will be subjected to the cleansing fire of violence."

—*New York*

"In *Memories of the Ford Administration,* Updike writes in the voice of the Devil, conveying the bleakest vision of the world in the cheeriest, most lascivious manner."

—*Worth*

"Vintage Updike, who always supplies humor and entertainment, both intellectual and grossly physical."

—*BookPage*

"A virtuoso performance . . . Updike writes with droll wit and sly observation, serving up a meditation on history hidden in an erotic comedy. This should stand in the Updike oeuvre where *Pale Fire* does in that of Nabokov.

—*Library Journal*

"Irony, whimsy, supple prose, pungent imagery, penetrating social observation, and a focus on his protagonist's libido are the familiar elements Updike brings to his book. . . . Social history of a high order."

—*Publishers Weekly* (starred review)

"A witty look back at the amorphous morality and seductive pleasures of the mid-seventies American scene . . . This story Updike mixes rather ingeniously with a historical narrative based on the life of President James Buchanan, the Gerald Ford of [the] nineteenth century. . . . Part of the fascination in reading him is the sense, even at this late date, that we have yet to be able to pin him down.

—*Mirabella*

MEMORIES OF THE
FORD ADMINISTRATION

Also by John Updike

John Updike

MEMORIES
OF THE FORD
ADMINISTRATION

A NOVEL

Fawcett Books • *New York*

Published by The Ballantine Publishing Group

www.ballantinebooks.com

Library of Congress Catalog Card Number: 96-96665

ISBN 0-449-91211-6

This edition published by arrangement with Alfred A. Knopf, Inc.

Manufactured in the United States of America

First Ballantine Books Mass Market Edition: November 1993
First Ballantine Books Trade Paperback Edition: August 1996

10 9 8 7 6 5 4 3 2

I am well aware that the reader does not require information, but I, on the other hand, feel impelled to give it to him.

—ROUSSEAU, *The Confessions*

Man in his essence is the memory [or "memorial," *Gedächtnis*] of Being, but of ~~Being~~.*

—HEIDEGGER, *The Question of Being*

* As quoted in the preface to *Of Grammatology*, by Jacques Derrida, by the translator from the French, Gayatri Chakravorty Spivak, who supplied the refinement in brackets and presumably the translation from the German, which coincides in this sentence (but not everywhere) with that of Jean T. Wilde and William Kluback.

MEMORIES OF THE
FORD ADMINISTRATION

From: Alfred L. Clayton, A.B. '58, Ph.D. '62
  To: Northern New England Association of American
       Historians, Putney, Vermont
  Re: Requested Memories and Impressions of the
       Presidential Administration of Gerald R. Ford
       (1974–77), for Written Symposium on Same to Be
       Published in NNEAAH's Triquarterly Journal,
       Retrospect

I REMEMBER I was sitting among my abandoned children
watching television when Nixon resigned. My wife was out
on a date, and had asked me to babysit. We had been separated
since June. This was, of course, August. Nixon, with his bulgy
face and his menacing, slipped-cog manner, seemed about to
cry. The children and I had never seen a President resign
before; nobody in the history of the United States had ever
seen that.

Our impressions—well, who can tell what the impressions
of children are? Andrew was fifteen, Buzzy just thirteen,
Daphne a plump and vulnerable eleven. For them, who had

been historically conscious ten years at the most, this resignation was not so epochal, perhaps. The late Sixties and early Seventies had produced so much in the way of bizarre headlines and queer television that they were probably less struck than I was. Spiro Agnew had himself resigned not many months before; Gerald Ford was thus our only non-elected President, unless you count Joe Tumulty in the wake of Wilson's stroke or James G. Blaine during the summer when poor Garfield was being slowly slain by the medical science of 1881, while Chester Arthur (thought to be corrupt, though he was an excellent fisherman and could recite yards of Robert Burns with a perfect Scots accent) hid in New York City from the exalted office he would finally accede to. If my children were like me, they were relieved to have a national scandal distract us from the scandal that sat like a clammy great frog, smelling of the swamp of irrecoverable loss, in the bosom of our family: my defection, my absence from the daily routine after dominating all the years of their brief lives with my presence, my coming and going, my rising and setting, my comforting and disciplining; my driving them to school and summer camp, to the beach and the mountains, to Maine and Massachusetts; my spelling of their mother in her dishevelled duties from breakfast to bedtime, from diaper-changing to, lately, sitting nervously in the passenger's seat while Andrew enjoyed his newly acquired driver's permit. I was the lonely only child of an elderly Republican couple, and fatherhood had been a marvel to me, an astonishing amusement; my teaching schedule at Wayward Junior College, then an all-female junior college beside the once-beautiful Wayward River here in southernmost New Hampshire, permitted an almost constant paternity, or it might be more accurate to say a fraternity—a coming-and-going facetious chumminess more like an elder brother's than like a progenitor's. Lacking siblings, I had, with my wife's offhand compliance, created them. Born in 1936, in northern

Vermont, where the mountains begin to flatten out and slouch toward Canada, I was named by my staunch parents after that year's affable but unsuccessful candidate against Roosevelt, and became a father at the mere age of twenty-two, my first year in graduate school. The obstetrician, a stout woman wearing a lime-green skullcap, emerged from the depths of Cambridge City Hospital, wiped her hands like a butcher on his bloody apron, and shook mine with the stern words, "You have a son." Buzzy followed when I was twenty-five and still not a Ph.D., and dear Daphne—the smallest at birth, a mere seven pounds ten, and the brightest-eyed ever after—two years later still, in 1963, the autumn Kennedy was shot and the second fall term of my first instructorship, at verdant and frosty Dartmouth. Salad days! Days of blameless leafing out! I had all the equipment of manhood except a grown man's attitude. My queen, my palely freckled and red-headed bride, still had her waist then, her lissome milky legs, and an indolent willingness to try anything. Lyndon Johnson's supercharged Sixties were about to break upon us like a psychedelic thunderstorm. We reined in our fertility, and hunkered down for happiness.

[*Retrospect* editors: Don't chop up my paragraphs into mechanical ten-line lengths. I am taking your symposium seriously, and some thoughts will run long as rivers in thaw, and others will snap off like icicles. Let me do the snapping, please.]

So I sat among my children less like a villain than like a fourth victim, another child of the gathering darkness (why did Nixon wait until the evening to quit? to avoid looking like a daytime soap opera?) and of the hurt and headless nation. This pose, of my being one more hapless inhabitant of our domestic desolation rather than the author of it, was in fact convenient for us all, freeing my children to like me still and to welcome my visits from my ascetic little bachelor pad across the river, in the quintessentially depressed industrial city of Adams—a one-mill hamlet renamed in 1797, honoring the harassed second President, a local boy of sorts—and to enjoy as best they could their visits to me and the meager entertainments Adams afforded: a bowling alley, a lakeside beach of imported sand, a Chinese restaurant where Daphne once got a fortune cookie without a fortune slip in it and burst into tears, thinking it meant she was about to die, and one surviving movie house in the depleted downtown, of the marqueed, velvety, rococo-lobbied type that in small cities everywhere was fast disappearing, passing to boarded-up, graffitiferous extinction through a lurid twilight as a triple-X triple-feature sex cinema. (Sex still had a good name during the Ford Administration. Betty Ford had been a footloose dancer for Martha Graham and announced at the outset of the administration that she and Gerald intended to keep sleeping in the same bed. Their children came and went in the headlines with lives that bore little more looking into than the lives of most young adults. In those years one-night stands, bathhouses, sex shops abounded. Venereal disease was an easily erased mistake. Syphilis, the clap—no problem. Crabs, the rather cute plague of Sixties crash pads, had moved on as urban rents went up, and herpes' welts and blisters had yet to inflict their intimate sting. The paradise of the flesh was at hand. What had been unthinkable under Eisenhower and racy under Kennedy had become, under Ford, almost compulsory. Except that people were going crazy, as they had in ancient Rome, either from too much sex or from lead in the plumbing. Ford, a former hunk, got to women in a way Nixon hadn't. Twice, I seem to remember, within a few weeks' time, a female went after him with a gun; Squeaky Fromme was too spaced to pull the trigger, and Sara Jane Moore missed at close range. [*Retrospect* eds.: Check facts? Whole parenthesis might come out, if there are space pressures. But you *asked* for impressions.] I had no television in my exiguous fourth-floor digs—a long room where I had rigged a desk of two filing cabinets and a hollow door, and a square room almost completely filled by a double bed, each room with one window overlooking a narrow side street in the shadow of a deserted textile mill—and was dependent for news upon the hourly summaries and rare special bulletins on the area's only classical-musical station, WADM, plus headlines glimpsed on other people's newspapers, and out-of-date newsmagazines in the waiting rooms of dentists, lawyers, opticians, etc., consulted during the twenty-nine months of the Ford Administration.) In that dear dying movie house, whose name was Rialto, with its razored plush seats and flaking gilt cherubs, my three fuzzy-headed cherubs and I saw *The Godfather: Part II* and *Jaws.* Both terrified me and Daphne, though the boys poohpoohed us. By the time of *Jaws* Andrew was big enough, with a driver's license, to be humiliated by going to the movies with his father. And though *Jaws* packed them in, up into the raised loge seats and the precipitous balcony, the Rialto's fate was sealed; within months it went X-rated.

Snap.

As I sat there watching Nixon resign I had the illusion that the house we were in, a big Victorian with a mansard roof, a finished third floor, and a view from the upper windows of the yellow-brick smokestacks of the college heating plant, was still mine; its books, a collection beginning with our college textbooks, felt like mine, and its furniture, a child-abused hodgepodge of airfoam-slab sofas and butterfly chairs with canvas slings and wobbly Danish end tables and chrome-legged low easy chairs draped on their threadbare arms with paisley bandanas and tasselled shawls, felt still like mine, along with the cat hairs on the sofa and the dustballs under it, the almost-empty liquor bottles in the pantry and the tattered Japanese-paper balls that did here and there for lampshades, all of it in our wedded style, my wife's and mine, a unisex style whose foundation was lightly laid in late-Fifties academia and then ornamented and weathered in the heats and sweats of Sixties fringe-radicalism. I had left my wife but not our marriage, its texture and mind-set, and it was far from dawned upon me that this house, this hairy fringy nest she and I had together accumulated one twig at a time, not to mention these three hatchlings so trustfully and helplessly and silently gathered here beside me in the flickering light of one man's exploding ambition and dream (he was resigning, Nixon explained, for the good of the nation and not out of any personal inclination: "I have never been a quitter," he shakily said, scowling. "To leave office before my term is completed is opposed to every instinct in my body")—that this house was gone, cast off, as lost to my life as my childhood home in the hamlet of Hayes, my college rooms in Middlebury, our graduate-student quarters in Cambridge in a brick apartment building down Kirkland Street from the then-Germanic Museum, or the little apple-green Cape-and-a-half, our first bona-fide house, with a yard, a basement, and a letter slot, that the university rented to us in Hanover, right off Route 120, a stone's throw from the Orozco murals. In this living room I was, in truth, on a par with a televised image—a temporary visitant, an epiphenomenon.

[*Retrospect:* Sorry about all the decor. But decor is part of life, woven inextricably into our memories and impressions. When I first received NNEAAH's kind and flattering request to contribute to its written symposium, I ventured to the library and flipped through a few reference books, the kind of instant history that comes from compiling old headlines, and was struck by how much news is death, pure and simple. In these transition months of 1974, who wasn't dying? Chet Huntley and Georges Pompidou, Juan Perón and Earl Warren, Duke Ellington and Martin Luther King Jr.'s mother, Walter Lippmann and Jack Benny, with Generalissimo Franco seriously ailing and Evel Knievel far from well. Evel Knievel failed to ride a rocket across a canyon in Idaho; Pompidou was reported as saying, "Every politician *(Tous les politiciens)* has his problems *(ont leurs problèmes).* Nixon has Watergate *(Nixon a Watergate),* and I am going to die *(et je vais mourir.)*" Surely, *Retrospect* editors, you don't want this sort of thing, which any sophomore with access to a microfilm reader that hasn't broken its fan belt can tote up for you. You want *living* memories and impressions: the untampered-with testimony of those of us fortunate enough to have survived, unlike those named above, the Ford Administration. I was greatly moved, the other night, by a twitchy black-and-white film from 1913 of the survivors of Pickett's charge, meeting as old men on the Gettysburg battlefield fifty years later. The Southerners pretended to charge again, hobbling forward on canes, and the Northerners scrambled out from behind the stone wall on Cemetery Ridge and embraced them. Tears, laughter. Young killers into dear old men. Enough time slides by, we're all history, right? And if you want to feel *really* sick, NNEAAH, think of the time that will keep sliding by after you're dead. After *we're* dead, I should say. If I've misjudged my assignment, please trim this response to suit your editorial requirements.]

Memory has a spottiness, as if the film was sprinkled with developer instead of immersed in it. And then as in an optical illusion the eye makes what it can of the spots. The Queen of Disorder came back around midnight, let's say. It was August, a muggy month in our river valley, but summer was already pulling in at the edges, with all the lawns parched and the cicadas in full cry. She must have been wearing a little pale-flowered cotton dress on her generous but still lithe figure, with shoelace shoulder straps, and it must have crossed my mind that she had taken this dress off that night and then put it back on to come home. *Home*—she had suffered some losses but kept that word, that reality. "How were the kids?" she would have asked.

"Good. Sweet. We watched Nixon and tried to play Mille Bornes until Daphne got cranky."

Daphne's mother shrugged off a little loose-knit white sweater hung around her shoulders like a cape. The freckles on her bare shoulders were clustered thick enough to simulate a tan. Glancing at a corner of the ceiling as if a cobweb there had suddenly taken her interest, she asked, a bit timidly, "They talk?"

"No," I said.

"Even after Daphne went to bed? The boys?"

"*No*, Norma. What is there to say? I let them watch *Hawaii Five-O* with me and then tucked them in. I did prayers with Daphne but the boys told me you've quit the prayers."

"Have I?" she asked, turning her head to look at another cobweb. Her hair was the color of a dried—the health-food stores say sulphured—apricot held up to the light, and kinky, so that even when ironed hair had been the thing, along with sandalwood love beads and dirty bare feet, Norma had had a woolly look. I pictured her hair spread out on a pillow like spilled pillow stuffing and her date's meaty hands digging into its abundance. An abundance below, too, gingery, tingly, and in her armpits in those barefoot years when it was fashionable not to shave. Her shins then had become scratchy like a man's chin. I had grown a beard that came in thin and goatish. We used to go skinnydipping with friends at a lake up above Hanover and, stoned enough to feel the walls of my being transparent like those of a jellyfish, and to imagine we were all one big loving family, I had turned to a woman on the sand beside me and must have somehow begged for a compliment on Norma's generous figure, for I remember this other woman's dry sarcastic voice cutting through my shimmering jellyfish walls: *I'm so happy for you, Alf.* "It just seemed hypocritical," my Queen of Disorder said, "with us the way we are. Nothing sacred, and all."

"How *was* Ben?" Benjamin Wadleigh had been her date. Chairman of the music department, head of the Choral Society, a tall topheavy man with big puffy white hands that plunged into a piano's keys as if into mud, squeezing, kneading. He was recently separated from his tiny wife, Wendy, and a long-time admirer of my bushy, milky-skinned, big-breasted mate. "Where do you two *do* it, at eleven at night?"

"We use the woods," she said, in such a way I couldn't tell if she were joking. "Or the back of his station wagon. Necessity is the mother, et cetera. Want a drink?" She was drifting toward the pantry with all its nearly empty bottles. The two cats, hearing her voice, had come out of where they had been hiding during my stay, and rubbed around her legs in a purring braid, a furry double helix, of affection. I was allergic to cat dander and tended to kick at the creatures when they sidled close. Their purrs made me aware again of the throbbing background of cicada song—a sound like no other, which the brain in radio fashion can tune in and out.

"No way," I said, rising from my Danish easy chair. It had a cracked teak arm I had always been regluing when I lived here. I tried to brush tenacious cat hairs from the seat of my pants. I had new loyalties: my dark-eyed mistress watched my connubial visits like a hawk, and expected minute-by-minute accountings. "I'm trying to lead an orderly life," I explained, not unapologetically.

"Is that what it is?" Two inches of silvery pale-green vermouth, near enough the color of her eyes, had appeared in her hand, in a smeared orange-juice glass she had fished unwashed from the dishwasher. She bent her face and voice toward me and said, "Alf, you *must* talk to them, they're confused and hurt and always after me with questions—'What didn't he like about us?' 'Can she really be that great?' 'Won't he ever get it out of his system and come back?' "

I resented her trying to mar with female talkiness the manly silence, the smooth scar tissue, the boys and I had grown over my defection.

"The boys, especially," she went on. "Daphne's the healthiest, because she's so open and still childlike. But the boys—I don't know what's going on in their heads. They're very considerate of me, tiptoeing around as if I'm sick, not blaming me for doing this stupid thing of losing you, trying to do all the jobs around the place that you used to do . . ."

She would let her sentences trail off, inviting her conversational partner to be creative. Her canvases, when she found time to paint, were always left unfinished, like Cézanne's. A blank corner or two left for Miss Manners. Her own face, too, was generally left blank, without even lipstick as makeup. When she attempted mascara, she looked like a little girl gotten up as a witch. In the silly Sixties, she went in for pigtails, and to make a special effect, for a party, she would do one half of her hair in a braid and let the other half bush out. Her hair—have I made this clear?—was not exactly curly, it was *wiggly,* and in tint not exactly dried-apricot orange but paler, so that her pubic hair did not so much contrast with her flesh as seem to render it in a slightly different shade. Now, with Ben's lively juices still swimming in her, she was bringing home to me—filling in with color the dim black-and-white hollow haunted feeling with which I had watched Nixon on television—the feeling of *shame,* shame as a bottomless inner deepening, a palpable atmosphere slowing and thickening one's limbs as the gravity on Saturn would, shame my new planet, since my defection, leaving my house hollow and (that Anglo-Saxon word of desolate import) *hlafordleas,* lordless. But, as with many of her actions, Norma disdained completion. Having brought me to the point where I wanted to crawl up the stairs and awaken my children and beg their forgiveness, she glanced down at the cracked and oft-glued arm of the chair I had vacated and idly asked, "What were you reading?"

I had left a book splayed on the arm. It was *Slavery Defended: The Views of the Old South*, edited by Eric L. McKitrick. "An anthology of pro-slavery views before the Civil War," I explained. "Some of the arguments are quite ingenious, and compassionate. The slaveholders weren't all bad."

"Slaveholders never think so," she said. I felt in this a feminist edge, newly sharpened by my bad and typically male behavior. She softened it with, "Is this still about Buchanan?"

For the last ten years of our life together I had been trying in my spare time and vacations to write some kind of biographical—historical/psychological, lyrical/elegiacal, the sort of thing Jonathan Spence does with the Chinese—opus on James Buchanan, the fifteenth President of the United States. New Hampshire's own, Franklin Pierce, had been the fourteenth, but his Ambassador to England, and then his successor in the Presidential hot seat, had caught the corner of my eye. The only bachelor President, the most elderly up to Eisenhower, the last President to wear a stock, and the last of the doughface accommodators, before the North-South war swept accommodation away. A big fellow, six feet tall, with mismatching eyes, a tilt to his head, and a stiffish courtliness that won my heart. He projected a certain vaporous largeness, the largeness of ambivalence, where Pierce had the narrowing New England mind, gloomy as an old flint arrowhead. Buchanan's mind, people complained he couldn't make it up, and I liked that. There is a civilized heroism to indecision—"the best lack all conviction," etc. He and his niece Harriet Lane ran the spiffiest White House since Dolley Madison's, and I liked that, too. I felt lighter when I thought about him. The old gent was so *gallant*, there in the trembling shade of the Civil War. You know how it is, fellow historians—you look for a little patch not trod too hard by other footsteps, where maybe you can grow a few sweetpeas. My efforts, neverending as research led to more research, and even more research led back to forgetfulness and definitive awareness that historical truth is forever elusive, had begun at about the time we had decided, after Daphne's wide-eyed arrival on earth, that for their sake and ours we had had enough children. This was a wise decision, but also a pity, for Norma and I had a natural flair for producing children; our sperm and ova clicked even while our libidos slid right past one another, and the busywork of pregnancy, birth, nursing, and training toddlers gave us the shared sensation of being an ongoing concern.

"Still," I had to admit. My attempt at extending our family to include a bouncing book had proved painfully slow and thus far futile. Perhaps Buchanan was the cause of our breakup: I hoped that a change of life might shake free the dilatory, feebly kicking old fetus I had been carrying within me for a decade.

"Maybe you should give up and try somebody else," the Queen of Disorder wickedly, if diffidently, suggested. "He's too dreary."

"He's *not* dreary," I monogamously insisted. "I *love* him."

Somehow—I knew it would—this stung her; her cheeks showed some pink in the room's sickly, tasselled lamplight. Her blush made her eyes seem greener. In her hurt she sipped the glinting vermouth. I wondered if she had been kidding about her and Ben. She exuded that faint hayey smell women have in summer.

"You missed Nixon's resigning," I told her.

"We heard some of it on the car radio."

On the way to the woods, or wherever. Ben was living in one of the Wayward girls' dormitories, where guests were forbidden after ten. "We all watched it together," I said, conjuring up a domestic unity that hadn't quite existed. "It was sad."

"Why?" Norma was a down-the-line liberal. "The only sad thing is it puts that idiot Ford in office."

"Ben says he's an idiot?"

"*I* say."

"You know," I said, "darling, you ought to be careful in the woods. There's poison ivy, not to mention snakes."

She pushed back from her forehead a piece of her untidy wiggly hair and blew upward, as if that would keep it in place. She glanced at the corners of the ceiling again but with a different, less searching quality now; I knew her well enough to see her mind deciding that this homecoming had nothing more in it for her. She was tired and ready for bed. She tossed off the last of the vermouth and said, "You be careful, too. There's lots of mancatchers out there."

NOTHING SHE SAID was ever not somewhat true. One of my memories of the Ford years—indeed, the one that has next priority in this accounting, elbowing its way to the head of the line—is of a wet cunt nipping, as it were, at the small of my back as a naked woman settled herself astride my waist to give me an allegedly relaxing shoulder rub. The rub was some kind of reward, a therapeutic interlude in our two-person orgy, yet I have never really liked massages, not really believing in the chiropractic theory behind them, and the sensation, as if of a large French kiss, down toward where my ass divided, made me internally shudder. The fault is mine, my squeamish generation's. Men born later than the Truman Administration and subjected since early adolescence to open beaver shots in national magazines and to childbirth documentaries that spare the TV viewer nary a contraction will scarcely credit our innocence, inherited from our fathers and their fathers before them, concerning female genitalia. The two sets of lips, major and minor. The *frilly* look of it, climaxing in a little puckering wave of flesh around the clitoris. Its livid, oysterish, scarcely endurable complexity, which all but gynecologists used to spare themselves, along with the visual ordeal of parturition. Close your eyes and take the plunge, was the philosophy in olden days, and vacate the site as quickly as possible. Nine months later, responsible fatherhood would begin. *You have a son.* Those were dark ages, when everything was done in the dark, like spermatozoa blindly snaking up the Fallopian tube to the egg. No more: the cunt is no mere fur-rimmed absence in binary opposition to the phallic presence, it is itself a presence, a signified, with an aggressive anatomy of its own. If it is good enough to mop up the ache of an erection, it is good enough to lay down an icy bit of slime on the seducer's love-flushed skin.

The woman was not, strange to tell, the lady of my dreams, the woman for whom I had left my wife; it was little Wendy Wadleigh, having appeared at my dusty apartment in Adams on I forget what excuse, possibly some kind of reverse-twist consultation about Norma's relationship with her own estranged spouse, big-headed Ben. I had never quite warmed to Wendy; her legs were too short, her center of gravity was too low, her Debbie Reynolds–style energy was too indiscriminate, the cornflower blue of her eyes too eager and bright. She jogged, she cooked macrobiotic, she played the viola, she tutored dyslexics, she coached the Wayward girls in hockey and lacrosse, she swam at the school pool every day, she wore her pale hair in a shiny little athletic "flip." But in those far-off Ford days it was assumed that any man and woman alone in a room with a lock on the door were duty-bound to fuck. Hardly half an hour into her visit had come the quick drawing of the khaki shades, the latching of the door's burglar chain for double security, the knocking of the phone off the hook and the smothering of its automatic squawk beneath a pillow stolen from the suddenly pivotal bed. My rooms in Adams, as stated above [see page 6–7] numbered two, plus a kitchen the size of a bathroom and a bathroom the size of a closet. The two windows' view was of the back of a factory where a few bluish lights kept watch over long, empty floors still bearing the ghostly footprints of machinery gone south. By pressing one's face against a pane one could see past the side of a projecting neon restaurant sign two doors away toward a street corner where pre-Japanese autos dragged their rusty lengths through a stoplight. On this main street, tiny people flickered past the mirror-framed entrance to a shoe store that was always threatening final closure. To minimize distraction, I turned off WADM, where somebody's symphony was repetitively working up to a thunderous dismissal of that particular movement's themes. Am I alone in thinking of classical music as very slow in saying what it's getting at? All that passionate searching, and it ends by discovering the tonic where it began. I never listen to it, except when between worlds—driving in the car, or during those transitional Ford years.

In the sudden shades-down gloom, Wendy, suppressing her natural tendency to chatter, rapidly undressed down to her white underwear, which glowed like the soft strips of daylight below the canvas shades' brown hems. I did the same, mirroring her semi-abandon, keeping on my underpants for now, as if hesitating to unbandage a flaming wound. The ornate etiquette of screwing a woman for the first time! Does the lady expect a condom? Should one offer the use of the bathroom, and use it oneself, as before an extended auto trip? Are there any surface blemishes or peculiarities to be explained, lest they give alarm, or should we let the flesh speak for itself? The awkwardness takes us back to childhood, when one knows no accepted forms. In this abrupt closeness a subtle but immensely actual novelty—in odor, in texture, in erotic slant, and in estimated experience and expectation—looms like an intimidating cliff. Though I had held Wendy in my arms at many a college dance, and in the groping latter stages of many a faculty get-together, when the host, to prolong the already distended evening, fishes out a forgotten Billy Eckstine LP, her body was basically strange to me. Her skin, the broad patch of it between her bra and panties, felt cooler than I had expected, and harder in its curves, especially the adjacent two of her prominent rump. I allowed myself the unprecedented liberty of caressing these, through the silken sheath of her underpants, more bikini than I was accustomed to. It was considerate and perhaps cunning of Wendy to keep her underwear on; as a woman of my generation, she understood, as an undergraduate would not have, my need to be sheltered from too blindingly sudden an exposure to the glories of the female body, and the stimulus that underwear would be for me, with my long gradualist history of forbidden glimpses, up a skirt or through a blouse armhole, and of back-seat grapplings with resistant elastics and snaps. Or—why make a maneuver of it?—she herself felt shy, and her sense of etiquette dictated reserving to a later stage of our session removal, by trembling hands working in partnership, of these last garments. For though this was 1974, we had not been born to its freedoms but brought to them through the timidity and tabus of earlier eras. Even the late Sixties had an innocence, an oh-boy *Barbarella* forced cheer, counting off orgasms like the petals of a daisy, which the thoroughly experienced Ford epoch lacked. Each era simultaneously holds, in the personalities of its citizens, an absorption into mainstream life of previous social frontiers and an exhaustion of the energy that propelled recent breakthroughs and defiances. College kids had already pulled back from revolution and dharma, afraid of finding no place within the slumping economy and of getting shot in futile protest as at Kent State. The late-Fifties hippies were now leathery old carpenters and shepherdesses, child-ridden and LSD-addled, holed up in corners of a factitious rural America. We lay a while kissing, Wendy Wadleigh and I—heavy-petting, as they quaintly used to call it—warming each other up, her mouth getting looser and moister, her body in the warps of erotic space seeming to become a kind of tilted vessel funnelling saliva and spiritual energy through her mouth into mine, right down to my toes as they curled up into the arches of her feet. I began to float in love's hyperspace; my fingers spelunked their way past the elastic panty-band to the parabolic curves of her aluminum-smooth buttocks and the velvety dimple high between, she arched her back to increase the angle of provocation and our white and gleaming under-things fell from our bodies with a few pokes of her thumbs, like tangerine peels.

[*Retrospect* eds.: All this strictly should be in the pluperfect, since the narrative begins post-coitally: ". . . and our white and gleaming underthings had fallen from our bodies with a few pokes, etc." Adjust if you think crucial. Also, an alternative image for the last might be ". . . popped from our bodies like the pods of impatiens seeds." If our readers can be trusted to know how impatiens seeds act.]

I don't think Wendy had a climax, though her breathing apparatus expressed a lot of ravishment, and her eyes changed color wonderfully, their blue becoming inky at the moment of my entry, and she moved her hips with a great deal of energetic purpose. Not used to her brand of wetness, amazed to be inside her, I no doubt came too soon. That was another elementary fact it took me time to learn: cunts are as individual as faces, and seating oneself inside a new one is a violent chemical event. Her wetness had become so extreme I kept slipping, like a man in smooth-soled boots on a mudbank, and even before my last throb of ejaculation I was starting to resent this whole act of intercourse, which had been less than half, I felt, my idea.

So, when after some friendly chatter two inches from my face there in my bed she got up on her knees and gave me a backrub like some therapeutic Amazon, I was in no loving mood, and my ooze of resentment like frozen amber has preserved the sensation for nigh onto seventeen years. She was presuming to expand our acquaintanceship into uxorial physical services, when I was still married to one wife and had another—the Perfect Wife—lined up waiting. I itched to buck, to toss off this witchy incubus moistly riding my back, and yet, though sullenly, sank into submission beneath her health-club ministrations, distracted no doubt by a dozen worries—that my perfect and future wife was trying to reach me through the phone that was off the hook, or that one of my abandoned children had drowned in the river or fallen through the ice (the season of this incident is unclear; some bias in my recollecting machinery wants to make it winter, with icicles on the fire escape and boots and mittens among Wendy's castoffs), or that I have forgotten an appointment over at Wayward with one of my feather-headed tutees, or that I should be correcting term papers or working at my book, my precious nagging hopeless book. For we forget, as we tote up our lives in terms of copulations, how framed and squeezed the act is by less exalted realities—by appointments and anxieties, by the cooking smells arising from the floor below and the rumbling of one's hungry stomach, by the changes of light and obscure pressures of the day as the afternoon ebbs on the yellowing wallpaper into the gray fuzz of lost time. The day is shot, we say, as of a lackadaisical execution. And all the while behind the sun-dried brown shade near one's head (subdivided like a graham cracker by the sash rails and mullions) the great sky brims with its unnoticed towers of luminous, boiling cloud. No, only in retrospect, *Retrospect,* are our amorous encounters ideal, freed of inconvenience. Yet, when all sides concede that fucking Wendy Wadleigh was the last thing I should have been doing, given my carefully worked-out life plan, it remains to extol the marvellous change her eyes would undergo upon what the legal experts call penetration, not just this first time but every time thereafter. I have written *cornflower blue* but like all color attributions it is a linguistic confection, by which perhaps I, no botanist, mean merely to evoke their petalled quality, the foliation of blue within their irises, that at the moment of nether entry would become religious, supernaturally *fond*—three-dimensional, you could say*—the widened pupils drillholes into infinity while tawny flecks were hoisted up from their matrix of shining gel like sparks in a hologram. This carnal union *pleased* her, her eyes declared, and, however distracted and pussy-whipped one felt, one could not but swoon a little.

"Your muscles are so tense," she said of my back. "Relax, Alfred." She spoke my full name as if there were a joke in it.

"I'm trying. But I keep wondering what the hell we're doing. You and I."

"We're being loving," Wendy said, shyly, sensing that I was full of complaints and rebukes, which only post-coital politeness was keeping in. "People need *loving,* and if their spouses don't give it to them they seek it elsewhere."

"Yeah, but, sweet Wendy—"

"You have Genevieve as well as Norma?" she finished for me, supplying the names of the two poles of my not untypical (in the bedevilled Ford era) dilemma.

"Something like that," I admitted, my face sinking deeper into the pillow. Her thumbs and finger-pads were really going after my trapezii, especially up at the creaky corner where the

---

*Think: if we *were* members of a two-dimensional world, creatures pencilled onto a universal paper, how would we conceive of the third dimension? By strained metaphoric conjurations, like these of mine above. If we were dogs, how would we imagine mathematics? Yet there would be a few inklings—the hazy awareness, for instance, that the two paws we usually see are not all the paws we have, and that two and two might make something like four. It is important, for modern man especially, as we reach the limits of physics and astronomy, to be aware that there truly may be phenomena beyond the borders of his ability to make mental pictures—to conceive of the inconceivable as a valid enough category.

triangle of muscle ties into the acromial end of the clavicle. Whenever she lifted up to put her little plump weight into it, the wet kiss lower on my back went away, returning when her hands moved lower down, to the latissimae dorsi. I was beginning to like it. "Nice," I grudgingly admitted.

"See," she said, reading my mind, that aggravating way women do. "Just accept, Alfred. No complications. No commitments. Seize the day, as Saul Bellow says. Let me give you the gift of me. What else would you like me to do? You have some things you'd like me to do?"

"Don't you have to go home, Wendy? Aren't your kids coming back from school soon?"

"Ben's covering. He wanted to do some work around the house. He's going stir crazy in that dorm. I told him I was going shopping in Portsmouth. There are some new dress shops."

"Norma says he and she make love in the woods," I complained.

"That bother you?" Push. Pinch. "Why should it?" Lift. Kiss. She was a seesaw.

"It seems uncivilized," I said.

"You haven't answered my question."

"Which question?" She was lulling me, ratcheting me down into my reptile brain. I was so relaxed I had drooled on the pillow, darkening the cotton case in the shape of South America. Bodily fluids had no deadly viral dimension in the dear old Ford days; one dabbled and frolicked in them without trying to picture the microscopic galaxies within, the squadrons of spherical space ships knobby with keys for fatally unlocking our cell walls. The rhythm of Wendy's ass, dribbling my own sperm, squeezing up and down on top of mine, was proving contagious; I felt desire trickling back, against the gravity of my better judgment.

"What else you'd like me to do," she answered.

Deciding to counterattack, lest my manhood be rocked entirely away, I twisted over, forcing wider the triangle between her round white thighs. Smooth moon-colored thighs, with a fringe of small platinum hairs where her shaving stopped, and the oval gleam of a vaccination scar. Her eyes again changed, observing the restart of my erection. The phallic entity emitted a sour saline smell. "There *is* something," I confided to my uninvited drop-in from the moon.

"What, lover?" How polite she was. How anxious to do the right thing. What did she see in me? A non-husband, I supposed. There is a wonderful weight of grievances non-spouses are out from under.

"Sit on my face. Sit." My voice sounded hoarse. I was thirsty, thirsty for forgetfulness, for a smaller world. I wanted to be negated by her vulva.

Wendy's eager-to-please face, with its girlish plump cheeks and womanish crow's feet and hopeful eyes and mussed blond flip, underwent a hesitation, a rapid rethinking, a touch of fright at being here with this gruff stranger. "Oh darling," she stalled. "I'm all goopy down there."

"Well, in for a penny, in for a pound," I said, or should have said, or seem now as I write this to have said, debonairly. I wormed my body down toward her as, straddling my chest, her thrusting muff the no-color of pewter, she waddled on her knees upward on the swaying, complaining bed.

The bed, let me tell you, had been my first marital bed, an ascetically simple steel frame and box spring and foam mattress purchased at a warehouse store in Keene. Retired in favor of a stylish redwood box bought at Cambridge's Furniture in Parts, it had been stored up on the third floor in the Wayward house; I had been allowed (Norma in the crunch proved quite possessive and not as disorderly as I would have liked in sorting out our common property) to take it when I moved, along with two old folding director's chairs, a doughnut-shaped foam-rubber reading chair covered in crumbling Naugahyde, a gate-leg table I had inherited when my mother moved to Florida, a patchily threadbare Oriental rug from the same source, my door-top desk and supporting filing cabinets, a spotty gilt-framed mirror the Queen of Disorder had never liked the way she looked in, several of her unfinished paintings to remember her by, and a cardboard carton full of random plates and cups and cutlery and kitchen equipment, including a wonderfully useless old-fashioned conical potato-masher with its perforated conical "female" complement. The Perfect Wife pointed out to me that I was being used as a trashman. I could have trucked it all myself, in my gallant Corvair convertible—a by now rusting and shimmying relic of the Sixties, shaped like a bath-tub with a rear-end engine—but for the bed and a green fold-out sofa, as heavy with its hinged inner works as a piece of cast-iron machinery, that dated back to our Dartmouth days. Stallworth and Sons, who handle most of the college's moving, sent their smallest truck for the little trip across the river, and old Gus Stallworth himself came along, with one of his sons. Gus must have been seventy, but he could still hold up his end of a metal-webbed Hide-a-Bed or a full four-drawer filing cabinet without taking the wet cigar butt from his mouth. A life-time of lifting had compacted his inner organs and made him dense as an ingot. His sons were taller, with more air and still-fermenting malt in them, but the same leaden patience with inanimate things characterized all their professional movements, in and out of the collapsing home and up the ramp into the truck body with its pads and ropes and resonant empti-ness. It was terrible, to watch them plod back and forth non-committally, pulling my meager furnishings, my sticky Olivetti, my olive-drab typing table, my gooseneck lamp, my cartons of scrambled research notes, out of what was becom-ing, with each subtraction, Norma's house. The Stallworths had moved us in but eight brief years ago this coming August.

My wife and children couldn't bear to watch my departure, and had left the premises. I was alone with the Stallworths, suppressing my desire to cry out something like "No, *stop,* it's all a mistake, a crazy overreaching, I belong *here,* these things belong here, embedded in the mothering disorder, gathering dustballs and cat hair, blamelessly sunk in domestic torpor and psychosexual compromise!" Father and son plodded on, grunting and muttering, in clothes the color of cement, slaves to the erotic whims of the educated classes.

Norma let me take only the books connected with my work, including the little library on James Buchanan I had collected—the twelve volumes in dreary green, reprinted by Antiquarian Press, of *The Works of James Buchanan, Comprising His Speeches, State Papers, and Private Correspondence,* as edited by John Bassett Moore; a darling little chunky copy, with embossed brown cover, water stains, and tissue-protected engraved portrait, of R. G. Horton's campaign biography of 1857; the two maroon volumes, again a photocopy reprint, of Curtis's biography of 1883, fetched forth by Harriet Lane Johnston's fervent desire to see her uncle done justice; Philip Gerald Auchampaugh's scattered, defensive *James Buchanan and His Cabinet on the Eve of Secession,* a dove-gray paperback; Philip Shriver Klein's biography *President James Buchanan,* unrivalled since 1962, in a Scotch-taped jacket of sprightly blue and white, decorated with the seal of the United States; also decorated with this seal, and a number of other patriotic designs, a precious copy, bound in faded black, of the 835-page report of the Covode Investigation, printed and widely distributed as anti-Buchanan propaganda in 1860, by the House of Representatives; pre–Civil War histories by Allan Nevins, Roy Franklin Nichols, Avery Craven, Bruce Catton, and Kenneth M. Stampp; biographies in aggressive modern jackets of such figures as Stephen Douglas, Buchanan's *bête noire,* and John Slidell, his *éminence grise*; pamphlets and booklets concerning Wheatland and old Lancaster; bushels, in liquor boxes deprived of their dividers, of notes upon which indecipherability was growing like a species of moss; and in several boxes emptied of clean typing paper my often-commenced, ever-ramifying, and never-completed book. It was not exactly a biography (Klein had done that definitively, though I had often wished that he, with his unique accumulation of information, had elected to write *the more extensive work* his preface tells us he had originally intended) but a tracing of a design, a transaction, the curious long wrestle between God and Buchanan, who, burned early in life by a flare of violence, devoted his whole cunning and assiduous career thereafter to avoiding further heat, and yet was burned at the end, as the Union exploded under him. The gods are bigger than we are, was to be the moral. They kill us for their sport.

My book began with Buchanan's pious and fearful upbringing in a log cabin, at a trading post, Stony Batter, in the mountainous middle of Pennsylvania, so lonely a spot that his mother, legend went, hung a bell about the child's neck lest he wander too far into the forest and become lost. Down from that wooded fastness—*a wild and gloomy gorge*, Klein poetically puts it, *hemmed in on all but the eastern side by towering hills and now far removed from any center of commercial activity*—the family, enlarged by the arrival, after Jamie in 1791, of five girls, descended to civilization, to a farm in the little town, solidly Scotch Presbyterian, of Mercersburg. The future President's father, also called James, was locally considered a hard man, who gave credit at the store he kept but never extended it. *"The more you know of mankind," he would say,* Klein says, *"the more you will distrust them."* A big grim businessman, like Kafka's father—a sheltering insensitive mountain of a father. The boy's mother, *née* Elizabeth Speer, was, like many a mother in the biography of a successful man, sensitive, spiritual, fond of poetry. She could recite *with ease,* her son wrote in an autobiographical sketch, *passages from Milton, Pope, Young, Cowper, and Thomson.* Klein writes, on unstated authority, *Her ambition was to get to Heaven; her life a quiet acceptance of every event.* She was young James's first tutor; then he attended, at the age of six, the Old Stone Academy in Mercersburg. Mercersburg's Presbyterian pastor, Dr. John King, of whom Buchanan was later to write he had *never known any human being for whom* [he] *felt greater reverence,* urged that the boy be sent, at the age of sixteen, to Dickinson College, in Carlisle, though James Buchanan, Sr., claimed to need his eldest's help in the store and on the farm. Mother hoped that Jamie would enter the ministry but Father advocated preparation for the law.

Buchanan entered Dickinson's junior class in 1807, with nineteen others. (How sweetly the smallness of the numbers speaks for the youth of our nation, a mere Atlantic apron of cultivation and settlement upon the immense land the coming century would see plundered!) The college was struggling, *in a wretched condition,* Buchanan confided to his self-sketch; *and I have often since regretted that I had not been sent to some other institution. There was no efficient discipline, and the young men did pretty much as they pleased. To be a sober, plodding, industrious youth was to incur the ridicule of the mass of the students. Without much natural tendency to become dissipated, and chiefly from the example of others, and in order to be considered a clever and spirited youth, I engaged in every sort of extravagance and mischief in which the greatest* [illegible] *of the college indulged.* On a Sunday morning in September, before James was to return for his senior year, a letter arrived which his father opened and, without a word, passed on to him; it was from Dr. Davidson, the principal of Dickinson, saying that, but *for the respect which the faculty entertained for my father, I would have been expelled from college on account of disorderly conduct. That they had borne with me as best they could until that period; but that they would not receive me again, and that the letter was written to save him the mortification of sending me back and having me rejected.* The mortification! The shame! The kindly Dr. King, a Dickinson trustee, intervened, giving James *a gentle lecture— the more efficient on that account*[—] and pledging himself to Dr. Davidson on the young man's behalf; Buchanan was accepted back for his senior year, and graduated in 1809.

The boy and the college, however, still had difficulties. *At the public examination, previous to the commencement, I answered every question without difficulty which was propounded to me.* He thought he deserved highest honors; the Dickinson faculty, however, awarded him none, *assigning as a reason for rejecting my claims that it would have a bad tendency to confer an honor of the college upon a student who had shewn so little respect as I had done for the rules of the college and for the professors. I have scarcely ever been so much mortified at any occurrence of my life as at this disappointment.*

Dare we dawdle a moment longer by the embers of Buchanan's formative years, as rather delectably recalled by himself? An especially intimate and lively passage attempts to animate his relation with his mother. *For her sons,* he wrote in retrospect (probably well before 1828, for though the sketch ends there, it exists in several installments and tones, including an off-putting leap into the third person), *as they successively grew up, she was a delightful and instructive companion. She would argue with them, and often gain the victory; ridicule them in any folly or eccentricity; excite their ambition, by presenting to them in glowing colors men who had been useful to their country or their kind, as objects of imitation, and enter into all their joys and sorrows.* More intimately still: *I have often myself, during the vacations at school and college, sat down in the kitchen and whilst she was at the wash tub, entirely from choice, have spent hours pleasantly and instructively conversing with her.* We sniff here the comforting pungence of lye and the invigorating tang of heterosexual debate. What woman henceforth will entertain, ridicule, inspire, empathize as this one did? Is it not the biological cruelty of mothers to leave, so to speak, too big a hole? Buchanan all his life was to manifest conspicuous pleasure in the company of women, bantering with Southern politicians' witty wives right to the moment of secession. And his loyalty to his Southern advisers, long after their advice had become duplicitous, has a flavor of the Dickinson episode—a wish *to be considered a clever and spirited youth*, one of the guys. The wish to be liked, the wish to be great: they can co-exist in one heart, but do not inevitably harmonize. Anti-oedipally, he left college *feeling but little attachment towards the Alma Mater.*

He apprenticed in law to James Hopkins, of Lancaster. Thus he came east; he crossed the Susquehanna, by ferry. There would soon be a bridge, between Columbia and Wrightsville; a lawsuit involving its financing In the wake of the Panic of 1819 would distract him from his courtship of Ann Coleman, and its burning in 1863 possibly saved his house from being razed by Lee's army. But these contingencies are in the future, not yet history. Lancaster, with six thousand inhabitants, considered itself a metropolis, the biggest inland city in the United States. The nation's first turnpike, a gravelled, stump-free road from Lancaster to Philadelphia, had been opened by its private promoters the year Buchanan was born born at a western stage of the Great Wagon Road which the turnpike improved and replaced. Eighteen years later, he arrived in Lancaster to learn the law. *I determined that if severe application would make me a good lawyer, I should not fail in this particular; and I can say, with truth, that I have never known a harder student than I was at that period of my life. I studied law, and nothing but law, or what was essentially connected with it. I took pains to understand thoroughly, as far as I was capable, everything which I read; and in order to fix it upon my memory and give myself the habit of extempore speaking, I almost every evening took a lonely walk and embodied the ideas which I had acquired during the day in my own language.*

A lonely walk. A bell about his neck in the forest. An Elysian landscape wherein one could declaim aloud to oneself and not be heard. When Hopkins' preceptorship ended early in 1812, and Buchanan turned twenty-one, he went west, against his father's advice, by horseback, to Elizabethtown, Kentucky, to investigate a tract of land to which his father had a partial, disputed title. Had he stayed, would he have become a Clay, a Lincoln? Possibly, that summer, he encountered Thomas Lincoln, who, according to Klein (Buchanan's autobiography says nothing of this excursion), *lived near Elizabethtown and was on the court docket for some land-title cases at this time.* Lincoln might very well have had in tow his three-year-old son, Abraham. When he himself was three, Buchanan very likely saw George Washington passing through Cove Gap on his way to squelch the Whiskey Rebellion. From President Washington to President Lincoln in one patriotic lifetime. The Elizabethtown land case had been in litigation since 1803, and Kentucky already had plenty of lawyers. Years later, Ben Hardin recalled Buchanan's telling him *I went there full of the big impression I was to make—and whom do you suppose I met? There was Henry Clay! John Pope, John Allan, John Rowan, Felix Grundy—why, sir, they were giants, and I was only a pigmy. Next day I packed my trunk and came back to Lancaster—that was big enough for me.*

He was admitted to the Lancaster bar on November 17, 1812. He hung out his shingle on East King Street, advertising himself in the papers on February 20, 1813, as being available *two doors above Mr. Dutchman's Inn, and nearly opposite to the Farmers Bank.* He was appointed, young as he was, prosecutor for Lebanon County, eliciting a letter from his overbearing father advising him to show *compassion & humanity for the poor*

creatures against whom you may be engaged. In 1813 he made
$938. In 1814 he made $1,096. He and *the town's jovial 400-
pound prothonotary, John Passmore,* bought the office building
on East King Street, which included a tavern. Four hundred
pounds: another giant. Giants were common in that miniature
America—a trick of scale, perhaps. After Jackson, an irascible
giant, they thinned out. Polk was "Little Hickory." Douglas
was "The Little Giant." Lincoln obtained gianthood but by
taking giant woes upon himself; it was a gigantism of suffering,
reinforced by chronic constipation, depression, and fits of
noble prose. Buchanan was six feet tall, a goodly size but in
human scale. In 1814, at a Fourth of July barbecue, he gave a
rousing speech denouncing Madison's bungling of the current
war against the British. James Madison was a true giant, but
physically too small for the fact to be universally recognized.
Buchanan was the president of the local Washington Association, an organization for young Federalists; Madison was, of
course, a Democratic-Republican, of the awkwardly named
opposition party born of Jefferson's resistance to what he felt
were monarchical, unduly centralist, anti-democratic, anti-
republican, and anti-French tendencies in the Washington Administration. Democratic-Republicans would rather make war
on Great Britain than on Napoleon. The Federalists nominated Buchanan for state Assemblyman The day after his
nomination news arrived that the British had burned Washington. The young office-seeker's first campaign duty, then, was
to volunteer in the general mobilization and march to the
defense of Baltimore. His company, calling itself the "Lancaster County Dragoons," was beseeched for volunteers for a
secret mission; he volunteered, and their secret mission proved
to be not fighting the British but stealing sixty horses from the
residents of the countryside, *always preferring to take them from
Quakers,* says Klein, not citing his source. The lowly mission
was accomplished; the British withdrew from Baltimore, hav-

ing inspired the lyrics for "The Star-Spangled Banner." The dragoons were disbanded; Buchanan came home and was elected Assemblyman. In Lancaster the Federalists always won but their fortunes, sagging lately, were restored by anti-war sentiments. Buchanan's full-of-advice father wrote him: *Perhaps your going to the Legislature may be to your advantage & it may be otherwise.* If his father had been less advisory, would Buchanan have been a stronger man, leaning less on others? Would he have been less secretive? He hid his thoughts from even his Cabinet, it was said of his time in the White House. Parents do pry. Our first lies are to them. Buchanan did his duties in Harrisburg. *A tall, broad-shouldered young man with wavy blond hair, blue eyes, and fine features* (Klein), he gave his maiden speech on February 1, 1815, against conscription and Philadelphia's privileged set, championing the West against the East and the poor against the rich. He was told he should become a Democrat. A friendly Democrat, William Beale, state Senator from Mifflin County, *called upon me, and urged me strongly during this session to change my party name, and be called a Democrat, stating that I would have no occasion to change my principles. In that event, he said he would venture to predict that, should I live, I would become President of the United States.* To demonstrate his Federalism Buchanan gave another Fourth of July speech in Lancaster, attacking the Democrats as *demagogues* and *factionaries* and *friends of the French,* possessed by *blackest ingratitude* and *diabolic passions.* He got re-elected but the speech created an enmity among the Jeffersonians that lasted all his political life. Even his *rabidly pro-Federalist father thought his attack was too severe,* and Buchanan allowed, *There are many sentiments in this oration which I regret,* but goes on in his memoir to quote cherished bits, such as this of the citizens aroused by the British invasion: *They rushed upon their enemies with a hallowed fury which the hireling soldiers of Britain could never feel. They taught our foe that the soil of freedom would always be the grave of its invaders.*

The rules forbade running for Assemblyman a third time. He was out of politics. He thought of going to Philadelphia to practice and his father talked him out of it. He had a bilious fever; he was prone all his long life to illnesses of stress. Staying in Lancaster, he worked at the law. A local judge judged of him, *He was cut out by nature for a great lawyer, and I think was spoiled by fortune when she made him a statesman.* In the years 1816–18 he thrice successfully defended the Federalist-appointed judge Walter Franklin against impeachment charges brought by the Democratic legislature, arguing the case with what a witness called *great ingenuity, eloquence, and address.* He based his case on the United States Constitution and its separation of powers. He was always to take a lawyer's careful approach to government, seeking shelter within the Constitution. That the Constitution, like the Judeo-Christian Deity, encompassed ambiguities and mysteries—invitations to men to improvise—was not borne in upon him. He was, we might imagine, in the infatuated stage of what was to be described, on the floor of the Cincinnati Convention in 1856, as a consummated marriage: *Ever since James Buchanan was a marrying man, he has been wedded to the Constitution, and in Pennsylvania we do not allow bigamy!*

His income rose from $2,246 in 1815 to $7,915 in 1818. He was a rising young man, still in his twenties, not only a Mason but a Junior Warden, and then a Worshipful Master. He achieved entry to Lancaster's highest social circles. Candlelit balls in the great room of the White Swan Inn, starlit sleigh rides through the wooded farmland—harness bells jingling, horse flanks steaming, young faces tingling, hands entwining beneath the heaped furs and buffalo robes. The stars overhead in their frosted robe of eternity, a lit house and hot punch and mince cakes at their destination, one of the ironmasters' stone mansions. Buchanan's partner at law, Molton Rogers, son of the Governor of Delaware, began courting Eliza Jacobs, daughter of Cyrus Jacobs, the master of Pool Forge. Rogers suggested that Buck join them some evening as an escort for Ann Coleman, Eliza's cousin. Their mothers were sisters, daughters of James Old of Reading. Jacobs and Robert Coleman had alike labored for Old and alike wooed a daughter. Jacobs fancied himself a rough-cut farmer and stayed on his Pool Forge acres, near Churchtown. Coleman had citified ambitions and had moved his large family, the same year young Jamie had begun his preceptorship with Hopkins, to an imposing brick town house within a half-block of Lancaster's Centre Square. Coleman had been Old's accountant, and had become an associate judge, a church warden, a trustee of Dickinson College. Marital ambition had no higher to climb, in this Pennsylvania countryside, than an ironmaster's daughter. Klein, a considerable extrapolator, says of Ann, *A willowy, black-haired girl with dark, lustrous eyes, she was by turns proud and self-willed, tender and affectionate, quiet and introspective, or giddy and wild.* His "James Buchanan and Ann Coleman" (*Lancaster County Historical Society Journal*, Vol. LIX, No. 1, 1955), in which he gives John Passmore's weight as *450* pounds, expresses it thus: *She was by all accounts a slim, black-haired beauty with dark, lustrous eyes in which one might read wonder, doubt, or haughtiness as the mood suited.* Her portrait, which hangs now in the master bedroom at Wheatland, her frustrated lover's restored home—a national shrine with costumed guides and postcards for sale—tells us little of this except the black hair. She has a long nose and lace collar and a stray ringlet on her forehead, and even in the stiff style of early-nineteenth-century portraiture she seems a little too alert-eyed and high-browed, a bit menacingly apprehensive beneath the high arch of her long brows; her shapely small mouth is poised as if on the cusp of a querulous remark. Klein goes on, in his high-stepping style, *That she remained unmarried at twenty-three may have been because she was emotionally unstable, but more likely it was due to the stubborn insistence of her parents that she make an advantageous marriage.* Her father was not only the richest man in Lancaster County but one of the richest in these young United States. Yet why would he or, by some accounts, her mother object to Buchanan, who was already a man of substance and reputation, as full of propriety and promise as a plum is full of juice?

Here we come to history's outer darkness, where my book was to take on its peculiar life. For a long time, on the safe excuse of further research, I circled, fiddled, held fearfully back, until a deconstructionist arrived in the English department—a certain Brent Mueller, who while landlocked at some Midwestern teachers' college had deconstructed Chaucer right down to the ground, and also left Langland with hardly a leg to stand on. Brent, a pleasant enough, rapid-speaking fellow with the clammy white skin of the library-bound and the stiff beige hair of a shaving brush, explained to me that all history consists simply of texts: there is no Platonically ideal history apart from texts, and texts are inevitably indefinite, self-contradictory, and doomed to a final aporia.

So why not *my* text, added to all the others? I leaped in. I began, I should say, to leap in, to overcome my mistaken reverence for the knowable actual versus supposition or fiction, my illusory distinction between fact and fancy. Here, dear NNEAAH and editors of *Retrospect,* in continuance of my faithful if prolonged answer to your inquiry, is a section of my text, composed under the benign overarch of the Ford Administration, and no doubt partaking of some of that Administration's intellectual currents.

In the middle of September of 1819, under a late-summer sky of a powdery blue, in the rose-red little city of Lancaster, Pennsylvania—incorporated as a city just the previous year, and within the past decade the very capital of the common-wealth—a tall fair man and a thin dark woman shorter than he but tall for her sex could have been seen walking together along East King Street with all outward signs of affection and attachment. They moved—her face frequently upturned to-ward his, till instinctive decorum dictated she again lower her eyes, and his head somewhat curiously tilted and given to an occasional twitch, as if making a minor readjustment of per-spective or as if better to hear the murmuring words of his vivacious and intense companion—past arrays of three- and four-story buildings built of brick or closely cut limestone, some heightened by dormers and decorated by wooden mer-chants' signs carved and painted to simulate the forms of lions and stags, leopards and eagles, Indian chiefs and European kings and other such of the emblems that once haunted New World dreams. The gentleman wore a russet frock coat with claw-hammer tails and an ivory-colored silk waistcoat embroi-dered along the button-tape, a white shirt with upstanding collar, and a loosely but studiously tied linen cravat. His tight-fitting buckskin breeches descended into jockey boots of black leather, with downturned buff cuffs. The lady's dress of dotted lawn was high-waisted in the Empire style, tied beneath her breasts with a tasselled pink gown-cord. Over it she wore a grape-colored cape of light cloth trimmed in black velvet. A gauzy frill wreathed her throat; a small cockleshell-shaped bon-net of close-woven straw, with a pleated taffeta ribbon, de-fended her face from the sun, here in this latitude but a half-degree north of the Mason-Dixon Line; in addition, she carried a lime-green parasol of moiré silk. This enviable couple were James Buchanan, one of Lancaster's leading bachelors, an accomplished lawyer and experienced politician, and Ann Coleman, the city's pre-eminent unmarried heiress. They had become engaged this summer, so their public appearance together was the opposite of scandalous. The parrot-bright signboards, the dimpled small windowlights of the basking brick housefronts, the subdued glisten of the slightly hazy day could be imagined to be smiling down upon them.

Buchanan, having overcome his customary reluctance to exchange the security of his heaped desk for the uncertainties of the wider world, had departed his office on East King Street—two doors down from the Dutchman's Inn, where he had found lodgings when first arrived in Lancaster nearly ten years ago—and had called for Ann at the Coleman town house in the next block, at the corner of Christian Street. In this latitude, at this hour of five o'clock, as Ann looked up toward the steady, gentle, finicking, rather high-pitched voice emanating from her escort, she saw the sun—its daily arc levelling toward the equinox above the roofs, shingled in slate or split cedar—blocked by his large head. A chill gripped her heart at this eclipse, with the reflection that this imposing man, who had taken her eye when, at the age of thirteen, herself newly moved to Lancaster, she had watched him from the upstairs parlor windows, a long-legged youth with a dutiful, obedient, ambitious hurry to him, striding to the Court House in Centre Square in the service of James Hopkins, his preceptor at law—that this man was truly a shadow, an opaque phantom looming abruptly large in her life. Two seasons ago, he had been a mere name, a dim figure in the gossip of her friends, the Jenkinses and Jacobses, spoken of with warmth and respect and yet a hint of sly amusement, whether layable to some eccentricity of Buchanan's person or to the inferiority of his self-made, hardfisted father's antecedents was not clear. Though a legal and political eminence, he lacked, in Lancaster County terms, real wealth or status. Now it seemed she had conjured this shadow up, in something like three dimensions, through a weakness of her will, a crack in her self-esteem. Since childhood Ann had battled waves of obscurely caused distemper—a pettishness, a sense of unjust confinement, a nagging disorientation some-times severe enough to keep her in bed. The reality around her, like a bread lacking the ingredient needed to make it rise, did not seem real enough, though other people appeared to be fully, even passionately engaged in its show of reward and punishment, failure and success.

Her fiancé was favoring her with the details of a pending lawsuit, of great importance, for it threatened the existence of the Columbia Bridge Company, which had so recently erected, at the site of the old Wright's ferry, the first span across the mighty Susquehanna River, an internal improvement crucial to the commonwealth's and indeed the nation's western devel-opment. "A threat to this company," he said, "is a jeopardy not only to the public weal but to the private fortunes of our friends, for William Jenkins and his Farmers Bank are heavily invested in the company's continuing to thrive. I foresee, my dear Ann, if Jenkins favors me with the grave responsibility of fending off this potentially ruinous suit, many hours in my office this autumn and more than one tedious journey to the courts in Philadelphia."

What was he trying to tell her? That, having attained the promise of her hand, he must abandon her for men's business? By encouraging his suit, in despite of doubts voiced within her family and her circle of female friends, she had exposed herself to ridicule, and his duty now was to stand near her, as a solemn safeguard of the wisdom of her choice.

They had turned back from her doorway eastward on King Street, pausing on the corner of South Duke. On the unpaved streets, their reddish earth packed to a dusty smoothness by the accelerated traffic of summer, buggies passed almost silently, the black-painted spokes of their high wheels shimmering to disks of semi-transparency, and the trotting horses' fetlocks angulating like ratcheted clock parts, faster than the eye could follow. The sidewalks, away from the paving stones rimming the cobbles of Centre Square, were boards irregularly laid, and the young couple's heels rang on these thick planks pit-sawed from giants of oak and ash and walnut within Penn's great woods.

"Am I to take this speech to mean," Ann asked, softening her voice so that his head deferentially leaned lower, "that I must prepare myself for large remissions in your attendance? Having endured," she went on, regretting the petulant edge she heard in her own voice, yet finding its total suppression impossible to achieve, "your long visit to your family in Mercersburg this August, followed by a bachelor holiday at Bedford Springs, I had hoped we might be much together in the coming social season. My parents crave to know you better; my sisters and brothers wish always to have their good opinions of you confirmed."

He slightly flushed, and coolly smiled. "That is, to have, you are too gracious to say, the unflattering opinions that reach their ears dispelled." His posture straightened; he stared ahead; Ann allowed this demonstration of wounded dignity to pass her notice in silence. Their leisurely pace, rendered a bit crabwise by their sideways attentiveness, carried them past Demuth's Tobacco Shop, its signboard since 1770 a carven bewigged dandy holding an open snuff-box, and the inn named the William Pitt, Earl of Chatham, which even at this early hour was buzzing, behind its drawn shutters, of the evening mood. Across the street, another inn, the Leopard, emitted its own growl of growing merriment, and high up under the left eave of the—in the reduced scale of a North American settlement—grand stone façade of the Bausman house, a small sculpted face, known locally as the Eavesdropper, smilingly stared toward the conversing couple with blank stone eyes.

"Dear Ann, I must *work,*" Buchanan protested. "I must improve my lot to such a station that our wedding, if not precisely between equals by the world's crass standards, is close enough to quell comment. Your brother Edward has been all too disposed to give ear to those who slander me as seeking your fortune. He has welcomed the poison into your family, and furthers its spread in the town."

There was a subdued fire in this man, Ann reflected, that might warm them both, if she fan it gently. "Edward is not well," she explained simply. "In his infirmity and rage at his own body, he vexes matters that do not concern him. He and Thomas, being just above me in age, and my constant play-mates once Harriet died, imagine I am still theirs to control, and no man who proposed to be more than brother to me would please them."

"They scorn me and provoke me," Buchanan went on, for-going some of his usual circumspection and showing, she felt, an unbecoming womanish pitch of complaint, "and encourage your father in his dislike."

The vigor of his petulance heightened the color of his face—a plump face, with an extra chin softly cradled in the wings of his upstanding collar and with dents of an almost infantile dulcity at the corners of his lips—and imparted a slightly alarming rolling aspect to his eyes, which were a clear pale blue but mismatched by a cast in the left, which led it to wander outwards and to gaze, it seemed, past her head to interests beyond. At times he frightened her with what he saw and what he didn't; he did not realize, in the case at hand, that it was her mother more than her father who had objected to their engagement. "He's not a *man,*" her mother had pro-nounced more than once, pinching shut her toothless mouth on the verdict. "Such a popinjay wouldn't have lasted an hour at my father's furnace." There was something in these iron people, Ann had been made aware, that stiffened at the approach of her swain with his artful, patient, silvery voice. Buchanan, in love with his own poeticizing mother, didn't see that a woman could be as stout an enemy as a man.

Conscious of concealing some of the truth, Ann bantered with him. "My father is an iron man," she said. "He does not easily bend. He had fixed his hopes for me upon the son of another ironmaster, so the merged forges could beat out more muskets for the next revolution."

"And out of blood more dollars for the Coleman fortune," Buchanan said, unnecessarily, for a shamed awareness of the violent source of her family's wealth had been implicit in her self-mocking words. For all his legal canniness, Ann thought, this man had a streak of obtuseness, a patch of dead caution, that prevented him from grasping, as can many coarser men—such as the men in her family—a situation at a glance, and from travelling instantly across a chain of argumentation to the firm ground of a conclusion. Instead, he must test each step, as if earth is all treacherous, and when he did contend on one side, as in his speeches against the Democrats, it was with a shrill excess, as though not convinced of his own sincerity. Her family's slights, which she had done all she could to hide from him, rankled because he was too willing to detect, with his double vision, a truth behind them. "At last Sunday's dinner at Colebrookdale," he complained, "you heard him bait me, albeit jocosely, on the matter of my disciplinary infractions at Dickinson, having as trustee made himself privy to the details—misdemeanors of a dozen years ago, and the stiff-necked faculty as much at fault as myself! And he unreasonably associates me with that auction prank of Jasper's, and implies impropriety in my election wager with Molton."

Ann interrupted this gust of grievances. "My father means to suggest that you have enjoyed a fair portion of tavern soci-

ety, and that a prospective son-in-law might reconcile himself
to enjoying less. And I do agree, Jim. Call me selfish, but I want
you with me every minute you can spare from your ambitions.
I have pinned my life to yours." She took his arm to descend
the curb; his big body, more corpulent and silkily clad than that
of the long-legged legal apprentice she had spied from her
window, was comforting in its mute mass, like that of a saddled
horse in the instant before she felt herself lifted up from the
mounting stool onto its trembling, warm-blooded back.

They had turned, in their stroll, right at the corner of Lime
Street, away from the traffic and the taverns, past the home, at
the bottom of the down-sloping block, of Jacob Eichholtz, the
portraitist, whose loving brush fixed in paints the fleshy visages
of Lancaster's leading citizens, and toward the cemetery
known as Woodward Hill, where, a half-century hence, Buchanan would be laid, with a civic pomp that he had specifically forbidden in his will, a document in which he also exactly
designed and inscribed his own tombstone. But today he was
alive, alive, and Ann, too, who would lie not long hence in St.
James Episcopal Churchyard at Orange and Duke streets; their
living, well-clad bodies were linked in luxurious promenade
beneath the red oaks and shivering poplars and straight-
trunked hickories. Hickory Town had been the homely name
whereby Lancaster was first known to white men, ninety years
ago. The arboreal foliage had not yet turned, though the dry
kiss of sap-ebb was upon it, and a few early fallen leaves scraped
beneath the couple's advancing boots—his buckled, hers laced.
They talked merrily of Jasper Slaymaker's prank, his and John
Reynolds', pulling up in their gig at public auction and shouting out a bid and racing away, not knowing they had been
recognized. The auctioneer in all solemnity knocked down
their taunt as the winning bid and declared them the owners
of a hotel and obsolete ferryboat line in Columbia, to the tune

of six thousand seven hundred dollars—to Buchanan a healthy year's wages, to Ann a laughing matter.

Dust dulled their boot-tips as the board sidewalks yielded to a path of worn earth that ran along the iron fence of the burial ground. Simple round-topped markers, of slate and a soft soap-white dolomite, stood erect within, the oldest of them bearing names already weathering into oblivion. The proximate quiet of the cemetery soothed our strollers; in their intervals of conversational silence could be heard the chirring of cicadas, laying the summer to rest, and the calls of birds quickening their activity as the day's heat gently withdrew. A prospect of uninterrupted shade appeared, beneath the arches of elm boughs silently striving for light and air. Ann folded her silken parasol with a snap.

As if released by the closing of the catch, Buchanan resumed his complaint, in a voice tense with self-pleading: "Your father thinks I bend too much. Disliking my maiden speech in the Assembly as too proximate to the Democratic creed, he liked no better my Fourth of July attack upon the last administration for its French-inspired demagoguery, its wanton destruction of the national bank and, with it, all restraints on credit. Ever since partaking of radicalism at Princeton, Madison has had a passion for the godless doctrines of French rationality; he took us into a disastrous war as little better than Napoleon's cat's-paw. Monroe, though a blander cup of tea, has been poured from the same Paris pot; his wife and daughter Eliza Hay have turned Washington into a veritable Versailles of backbiting and empty etiquette. This continent was meant to be an escape from Europe, not a provincial imitation of it. Like all the sound men of Lancaster, I am a Federalist to the bone, in the conservative and balanced style of the deathless Washington. Property rights, but not rule by the rich. Personal rights, but not radical mobocracy and incessant revolution. Washington's noble example and the beautifully wrought balances of the Constitution indicate the same middle path between impractical extremes, and if for following this path—sometimes broad, and sometimes painfully narrow—I must be the object of calumny and cheap ridicule from all sides, from men of iron as well as men of straw, so be it," he went on, a sideways glance at his companion asking acknowledgment of his sly allusion to the Colemans. "Thank God in His Providence," Buchanan concluded, "that with my second term in the Assembly I am forever finished with public office; my wife will never be exposed, dearest Ann, to the humiliations and manifold thanklessness of politics."

"Are you indeed finished with public office? I sense in you a quest for the widest audience, a will more subtle than my father's but no less relentless."

"Rest assured: the domain of local law, and the domestic hearth ruled by you, will form sphere enough for me and my moderate abilities. There is a rapacity," he went on, relaxed and thoughtful with her to a degree she could not but observe with gratification, "and a growing coarseness to public life whose tenor I detest. As these colonies grow westward, and the coastal cities become richer, and more various in their immigrants, the common man in his natural greed and low appetites becomes the index of measure; the gentility of the founders is running thin. Little Maddy was the last of the original creative spirits, and Monroe will be the last President in knee breeches. The present era of good feeling is but a lull before the storm, when the West must declare itself to be a child either of the North or of the South. Eleven slave states, eleven free, and Missouri. The Missouri question is a reef upon which the whole ship, so bravely patched and launched, may split in two; our American problem is, we have land and climate enough for a number of nations, and seek to be only one."

"Perhaps," Ann offered, in keeping with the new freedom

of intercourse his largeness of assertion invited, in a realm beyond the regions of petty quarrel and divergent loyalty, "my family but wait for more fervent signs of affection and trust from you. My father is more nakedly self-made than yourself, and my brother Edward is tormented by his curse of doubtful health."

"Once we are securely wed," Buchanan affirmed, pressing the hand of hers resting upon his arm with his free hand, while maintaining with two gloved fingertips his grip upon a slender walking stick, its silver knob in the shape of a fox's smiling head, "the flow of good will shall be less forced. A settled deed argues for its own acceptance; an established union dictates its terms for peace. Until our marriage, we are vulnerable to interference. Your family's claim to loyalty inevitably distresses you; their call upon your affections dates back to your infancy, where my claims are but newly placed, and rest unsteadily upon matters of seemingly voluntary choice."

Seemingly because of his Presbyterian fatalism, that saw all glimmering moments caught in an inflexible web of divine predestination? The Colemans were of the Episcopal church, removed from Papism and Puritan gloom both. "And when shall we arrive at this blessed established state?" Ann asked, her own voice tense and rising. "We are not young; you were all of twenty-eight this April, and next month I will be twenty-three. The girl-friends of my childhood are already all wed. The strictest propriety does not ask that we wait longer than a season or two more."

"The season cannot be this fall," he stated, suddenly firm, with that impenetrable bluntness lawyers can muster. "This Columbia Bridge Company tangle, added to other concerns of my practice, will take all but a few of my hours; the financial distress Monroe and his Yankee Richelieu, Quincy Adams, have allowed to fall upon the nation has made work for lawyers if no one else."

"Oh"—an exclamation of disappointment escaped her lips. "Must I spend another winter as a spinster?" She felt her heart sink at the prospect of gray wet weeks and months still closeted with her parents, while her five brothers and four sisters, the living remainder of fourteen births, haunted the house, coming and going, George with death already in his jaundiced and skeletal face, Edward arrogant and sardonic in his smoldering fury of unhealth, Thomas more playful in his authority over the sister just beneath him in the chain of births, all with their prating wives, women as complacent as dough, while her silly sister Sarah, the fourteenth child, wide-eyed and giddy at the onset of womanhood, professed to be in love with what she fancied to call God. All of these kin, it seemed to Ann, implied, in their tactful avoidances as well as in open teasing and quarrel, disapproval of her marital choice, and through their coughs and courtesies and heavy family odor they sifted upon her head a drizzle of foreboding, an unspoken opinion that this tall smooth speaker of many politic words was not what he gaudily seemed, in his russet tailcoat and impeccably tied cravat, but was instead treacherous, a finagler, a twister in pursuit of her fortune and the Coleman connection, and less than a man. *He's not a man.* He was some other kind of creature, a half-man, a chimera bred of these changing modern times, a pretender, so that her betrothal had a doomed flavor, a taste of mistakenness that tightened her throat and at idle moments of the day threatened to pinch tears from her eyes, sharpened her words with ill temper, and bade her imagine pity and concern in the faces of those in the house who loved her, including the servants and the children of her older siblings. Her imagination was steeped for long idle hours in the hectic substances of books—romances and rhymed effusions quickly printed in Philadelphia and Baltimore from English texts hurried like contraband to these artless shores—and imaginings flared within her in strange heated waves, so that after an afternoon dreaming another's dream in the upstairs parlor she distrusted her thoughts and even the reports of her senses, which without actual distortion came to her overlaid by a cold dim quality, like moonlight, of illusion. Even now, in this outdoor moment, underneath the many green trembling leaves and beside the iron fence cast in a pattern of circles and spears, the man beside her, leaning down in expectance of her response to his blunt demand for delay, appeared to loom with an illusionary thinness, like a large occluding emblem of painted tin, of less thickness than King Street's signboards and the tombstones of slate in the burying ground. They represented people, these stone silhouettes, once as alive as she, Ann thought, and many younger than she—her sister Harriet had been younger—and now dead in their coffins, rotting into bits like those starved lambs whose stiff matted bodies crows tear at in the tall pasture-grass, cawing. A line occurred to her from a poem of Lord Byron's of a fascinating morbidity, from a slender edition of *The Prisoner of Chillon and Other Poems of 1816* into whose burgundy-red covers the acid sweat of her fingers during the summer past had worn ovals of a paler red, *I had a dream, which was not all a dream,* and then another, *The bright sun was extinguished.* Ann wanted to scream. Buchanan's static image filled the field of her vision, leaning toward her respectfully, tenderly, regretfully, in the wake of his forked offer of allegiance and absence—his tidy curvaceous nimble lips, his ponderous possessive face, his touchingly mismatched eyes, his rising crest of oak-colored hair. Claws clamped her heart; beaks tore at it. *Happy were those,* came to her amid the waves of heat, of unreality, *who dwelt within the eye / Of the volcanoes, and their mountain-torch.* She felt trapped within the coffin of a book. This man was a single stiff page. She feared the book was about to slam shut on her, though for him it would go on and on, through foreign lands and ever higher offices, a saga of endurance. *Ships sailorless lay rotting on the sea*—how terrible, poets should not be allowed to frighten young women like that, perhaps in England, among the gentry, where life was all a game, but not here, here in these forested States, where life was simple and hard and serious, on land just lately seized from the savage redmen and soaked with their blood, as the turning leaves each year demonstrated. Still Buchanan hung there, speechless, waiting for a sign of her love, her loyalty though he must be much away from Lancaster on legal business. Perhaps the hot waves within her were magnifying time, subdividing each moment of this hazed warm late afternoon, late in summer, late in the day, with its narrow bird-chirps and minutely veined elm leaves overhead.

> *The winds were wither'd in the stagnant air,*
> *And the clouds perish'd; Darkness had no need*
> *Of aid from them—She was the Universe.*

The upstairs front parlor, where Ann found the peace to be alone with her books, the clatter of King Street noticeable only when two drunken men began to shout together, the air fragrant of cold ashes and furniture wax and stale potpourri and sun-warmed plush, had fallen away, the very walls with their wallpaper of red stripes and blue-and-gold medallions had fallen away dizzyingly, when she read these last words, their terror collected in the mysterious *She* with its Godlike capital letter. A world without clouds, without winds—but of course, the world within the coffin would lack everything.

Buchanan, politely troubled by her silence, sensing her disturbance if not her premonition, presumed to touch again the back of her hand, her four pink-nailed fingers where they rested on the cloth of his coatsleeve, and at this touch she took on flesh again, she took on life, her heart moving her blood through the supple conduits of her tall young body, maintaining in her slender skull the polychrome light of consciousness. Her universe shrank to these soft, familiar environs, and her condition to that of a woman on the verge of married life, soon

to have a house of her own, with waxed furniture, and respectful servants, and crackling fires in the fireplaces, and windows
to keep clean with vinegar and water as Mother directed her
maids to do, a cup of vinegar to every bucket of water. It was
Byron's dreadful vision now that seemed illusory, a dream
indeed. Talking and walking at a slower pace, as if together
recovering from a slight case of ague, Buchanan and Ann made
their sauntering way north on South Queen Street to Centre
Square, as candles were beginning to be lit in the dusky rear
rooms of the staid houses of brick and limestone, then right a
half-block to the Coleman residence, where Ginger, a manu-
mitted black slave said to have had an Onondaga grandmother,
served them Cantonese tea, sailed to them through three
oceans, with a side glass of peach brandy, brewed by North
Carolina Moravians, for the gentleman.

I ALSO REMEMBER, not exactly from the Ford years but
from Nixon's last Presidential April [*Retrospect* eds.: CK but
Easter '74 April 14th by my perpetual calendar], stamped as
sharply on my memory as a tin weathervane, the silhouette of
the Perfect Wife, Genevieve Mueller, as she stood, in a smart
spring outfit consisting of a boxy hound's-tooth-checked jacket
and pleated white wool skirt, on the street in front of her house
in Wayward under the giant surviving elm there on the corner.
She was poised to cross over to her own front door, we had
made no plans to meet, I just happened to have run in the car
to the town's three-store (gas station, grocery *cum* minimal
hardware, and drugstore also stocking newspapers, magazines,
paperbacks, plastic toys, and tennis balls) downtown for the
Sunday paper and circled back toward my house by way of her
house, an early-nineteenth-century former farmhouse, clap-

boarded and painted pumpkin yellow, with rust-brown shutters and trim, and set back from the road by a breadth of front
lawn and some struggling azaleas, a modest symmetrical house
made majestic for me by the extravagant extent of my longing
and covetousness. Many the night, swinging out of my most
direct path home after dropping off a babysitter, I had thought
of Genevieve lying in there asleep in the arms of that methodical Midwestern deconstructionist and nearly wept with envy
at the imagined bliss concealed by their darkened upstairs windows. Since those nights of barren yearning—my arc of auto-
motive divagation described in snow and spring rain, under
summer's thick canopy of leafiness and then the recklessly
spilled salt of stars glimpsed through nets of disencumbered
twigs—she and I had suddenly, recently managed, under cover
of the bustle of an academic community, to make contact, to
confess our mutual discontents, to make love, to fall in love, to
exchange feverish pledges whose exact meaning and circum-
stantial redemption remained cloudy in my mind. This cloudi-
ness was to be rapidly dispersed. I braked to a stop, exhilarated
not only by the sight of my beloved's perfect figure, so trim
and compact and smartly stamped, in its black-and-white
checks, on the tender surface of the sacred morning, beneath
the persistent elm's great vase-shape mistily brimming with
pale-chartreuse buds, but by the resinous eager tang of spring
in the air, inviting me to be, late-thirtysomething though I was,
eternally young. I was full of the sap of recent sexual conquest.
Life felt sweet. Genevieve was wearing high heels, in two
sharply contrasting tones, and all around her Nature, too, was
standing on tiptoe. With one of her unsmiling stares—her eyes
were the deep brown of black coffee, in a face of luminous
unblemished pallor, with a slight bony arch to her long-
nostrilled nose—she came around to the driver's side of my car,
my [see page 24] piratical, debonairly unsafe, gallantly rusted

Corvair. My top was down. [I would write, "She stepped off the curb and came around to the, etc." except that the informal town of Wayward, like the Lancaster of my imagining, was short on curbs and sidewalks, and had none here, where the elm tree's roots would in any case have posed a problem for the pavers.]

"I told him," she said.

"You told him?" I repeated inanely. I could not tell if the smell of fear—electric, like that of ozone—was mine or hers. "You told him what?" I did not have to ask who the "him" was.

"About us."

I could not stop thinking of how lovely Genevieve looked, there in the feathery sunlight underneath the elm, on an Easter morning when the whole town seemed to have been cleared, as if for shooting a movie—not another car in sight, not a bird cackling to clutter the sound track. She kept looking down the street, as if toward the director.

"You *did?*" Now my voice did sound sick. My whole world, disorderly or not, had been pulled out from under me.

Her focus slightly changed, shortened, to take in my face. The sunlight had that white sharp quality it has in the spring, before the leaves come out. Each pebble on the street, gritty with the past winter's sand and salt, threw a crescent-shaped shadow. My mind crackled with irrelevant thoughts, such as what a pleasant spacious country America was, with its freedoms and single-family homes, and that I should have received this fatal news in a more dignified position than sitting here helpless in my jaunty old bathtub of a horseless carriage. Genevieve was speaking very rapidly, rather breathlessly. "Was that wrong? He's been sensing something lately, and we got to talking last night, and he was so innocent, it seemed cruel not to tell him. Wasn't that right?"

I loved her so much, she looked so perfect, her face just

tly wider than ideal, like a child's, that I foolishly smiled and nodded, feeling fuzzy all through, like the elm. "And what did he say?"

"Well," she said, and looked over me and my car down toward the street, toward the center of town. She was obviously dressed for church, and perhaps he was coming from church, with their two little girls. It was hard to picture him as a churchman, even on Easter morning, since his professional career was based upon the exposure of meaningless binaries and empty signifiers. "We said many things. We were up until three, hashing over our whole marriage. But basically he said, Fine, if that's what I want and if you'll marry me."

The Perfect Wife. Mine. It was locked in. I was on my way to Paradise. I felt rushed, a bit, like the good thief on the cross. Still, it was a direction. All I had to do was dispose of my own wife and children. They had been deconstructed, but didn't know it yet. I would have to tell them. The wife, the kids. It was a not uncommon crisis in this historical era, yet there is a difference between an event viewed statistically, as it transpired among people who are absorbed into a historical continuum, and the same event taken personally, as a unique and irreversible transformation in one's singular life, with reverberations travelling through one's whole identity, to the limits of personal time. Since history always posits *more* time, backwards and forwards, in that respect it is *less* serious than a single, non-extendable life.

The Perfect Wife and her imperfect husband had come to the college three years before. They were seven or eight years younger than we, and the departments, small as the college is, don't instantly mingle. But as time went on I had opportunity enough to observe her, and to judge her a jewel beyond price. I took note of her faultless figure, the breasts and hips emphatic but every ounce under control, and her exquisite, if slightly mannish, clothes, and her crisp but tender nurture of her two little girls, one of whom was a comically exact copy of her, in her husband's pallid coloring, while the other, with Gene-vieve's black eyes, brows, and hair, had a considerable portion of Brent's dogmatic angularity, jutting jaw, and furrowed, troubled, skeptical forehead. At the Wayward College indoor pool, during faculty-use hours, Genevieve was as neat a nymph as a trademark artist ever penned, favoring a square-cornered swimcap of white rubber and a black single-piece bathing suit more stunning in its professional severity than any belly-baring bikini. At faculty parties, she was the model of woolen-clad, single-braceleted correctitude, alertly receptive while conversing with the President in her lavender upswept hair and regal purple muu-muu (the President, not Genevieve), amiably reserved and faintly teasing with the gangling young instructors and their giggly common-law brides, and cheer-fully frontal with her husband's academic equals. Me, I usually viewed her in profile, admiring her pursed considering lips, her single flashing eye beneath the dense clot of curved lashes, and her scarcely perceptible nasal curve, which I saw as Mediterra-nean, a genetic trace inherited from the fabled age of matriar-chal queendoms, of calmly murderous white goddesses. We at first avoided one another at these gatherings; there was a dan-gerous magnetism both felt from the start. Her conversation, when we dared politely talk, seemed a bit flat, factual, and (with my wife's wandering indirections as background noise) unsubtle; but I blamed this on mental contamination by her husband, with his pugnacious monosyllable of a monicker and his boyish thrust of stiff beige hair above his slanting forehead. He was contentious, dismissive, cocky, and a great hit with the students; he played to them with a televisable glibness and catered to their blank, TV-scoured brains by dismissing on their behalf the full canon of Western masterpieces, every one of them (except *Wuthering Heights* and the autobiography of Frederick Douglass) a relic of centuries of white male oppression, to be touched as gingerly as radioactive garbage. In faculty meetings he spoke, though less than half a generation younger than I, with the brash authority of the New Thinking; gray heads bowed and made way, in this quaint institution devoted to the interim care of well-bred, well-off girls en route from their fathers to their husbands, for "studies" whose ideal texts were the diaries, where they could be found, of black female slaves. He was active, dynamic, persuasive, and committed. He took teaching *too* seriously, it seemed to me—as a species of political activity, as an opportunity for the exercise of power, even while decrying the white male power of bygone generations. Never mind; I invited him to be my opponent at tennis and squash, as a way of drawing closer to his wife. (Genevieve in tennis whites! With a heartbreaking little black hem to her socklets!! Her backhand was even better than her forehand, and after we became lovers she confided to me that she had been a natural left-hander, made over into a rightie by the penmanship instructors of a regressive, nun-run private school in lower Wisconsin.) When it came to dinner at their home, I marvelled at her impeccable housewifery, her gourmet cooking, her poignantly staged presentation of her little girls, in not only clean pastel gowns but miniature satiny bed-jackets, for their good nights to the guests. She had managed to instill in her household a European sense of children as graceful adornments to the parents, as opposed to our ugly American democratic style, with even an infant given his noisy vote in all proceedings. As to decor, in my own house there was simply too much—too many pictures on the wall, too many worn-out rugs overlapping on the floor, too much carelessly inherited furniture, too many shawls and cats shedding threads and hairs on the sofa cushions, too many half-empty bottles in the pantry and half-read books piled up everywhere, even in the bathrooms—whereas here there was just enough of books, tables, vases, chairs, a cool sufficiency with poverty's clean lines, a prosperity short of surfeit. Even the grounds around their modest home, on a street of older houses unevenly redeemed from Depression-era decay, some having replaced the original clapboards with shingles and some with aluminum siding, showed Genevieve's will toward order—the flower beds weed-free, the ornamental plantings bark-mulched. And when it came at last to lovemaking, on the hard floors and rented couches that adultery utilizes *faute de mieux,* hers was quick, firm, adventurous, definitive. There was none of that female maze and endocrinal grievance I had to work through with the Queen of Disorder. I pictured my wife's psychosexual insides as a tidal swamp where a narrow path wound past giant nodding cattails and hidden egret-nests, with a slip into indifference gaping on both sides; Genevieve's entrails were in comparison city streets, straight, broad, and zippy. If she had been in the least disappointing in this regard, I might not have found myself at this pebbly elm-shadow-striped corner, facing a fait accompli.

If you'll marry me. They had cut a deal. They were a team, a pair of scissors. Snip here, snip there. The second thread was mine, a sensitive loose end.

The world had changed complexion; in an instant, the intoxicating spring air had become a wet hot washrag pressed against my face—the pressure of the actual, the mortal, the numinously serious. I didn't know what to say, there with her perfection, so black and white, so anxious and unsmiling, before me. She spoke again, her eyes wider, as if to take into accounting some new margin to me. "Did I do the wrong thing? I thought we had agreed."

We had agreed we were in love, lovely, too lovely ever to lose each other. I just wasn't quite ready for the agreement's translation into practical terms, into legal action involving realtors, judges, mellifluous lawyers, abandoned children. Yet I had no heart to say so, no heart but to say comfortingly, she being the child in sight, "No, that was right. It sounds as though you were very honest and brave."

She tensely, tersely nodded, tucking that admitted fact away. I was giving myself away by inches.

"Where is Brent now?"

"He's at church," Genevieve answered. "The communion line was huge, and I said I'll walk home to get the lamb roast in. They'll probably swing by the drugstore for the paper."

She glanced at me for a response, but I was silently smiling with an absurd élan, the fruit of too many Hollywood movies viewed in adolescence. When in crisis, double the cool. Cary, Gary, Alan, Errol. Meanwhile my stomach seemed to be swallowing me through an enormous trapdoor.

"I was going to call you tomorrow at your office. He said he wouldn't move out until school was over. We won't tell the girls until then so as not to ruin their grades. So you have until June to tell Norma."

My part was all written; I was a character in their play. "I didn't know Brent went to church," I said.

"Only once a year, as a favor to me and the girls."

"He loves you."

"He says so." A flicker of something—in the air, on my face—brought the forward momentum of her smoothly working brain to a small halt. "Do you want to back out?" she asked, in a voice moved up a notch in volume, for clarity. "You may, Alf." Her voice dipped into tenderness, just as a gauzy cloud overhead dimmed the white sunshine of this day that had left winter behind. "You mustn't do what feels wrong to you."

"*You* and *I* feel right," I tried weakly to explain. "It's just that *it*—"

"It's too much," she finished for me. "It *is* a lot. I think I'll go ahead with my side in any case; he and I have gone too far."

He and I—the phrase made my blood fizz with jealousy. And the thought of Genevieve's freeing herself to roam the Ford era's sexual jungle was intolerable, in the totally eclipsing way that the thought of death is. I would have this woman if it killed me, I resolved. And no matter who else it killed. "You and he are going to keep living together till June?" I asked.

She blinked; her lashes on a Sunday morning were not so long and clotted as in party makeup. Each lash was distinct, giving her a starry-eyed look. "That was his proposal," she said.

"You two are going to keep fucking?"

"Are you and Norma?"

"I haven't told her yet. The situations aren't parallel. We don't fuck that much anyway. We think about it, and drift away. You and that prick really do it. You really just upped and told him about us. I can't believe it." I couldn't believe, either, that I was showing this anger; but having committed myself, just then, to die for her if necessary gave me the right.

The Perfect Wife's chin, level with my eyes, was shaped like the tip of a valentine or slightly blunted shovel and held a small depression, too shallow to be called a dimple; now this evanescent shadow began to tremble. I had stung her, already exhausted by her session with Brent, to tears. And Easter morning wasn't going to hold its breath forever: A back door somewhere slammed. A bird, descended from the dinosaurs, issued several clauses of a long territorial proclamation. My foot lightly raced my engine. Brent was about to turn the corner in their military-tan Peugeot, armed with two little girls in frilly dresses. Theirs, too, was a nuclear family I was smashing. I felt sick to the point of self-extinction but the day with its hard-to-believe old message kept buoying me up, in my hollowing new knowledge. I was the new man, called into being. "Sorry," I said to Genevieve, of my outburst. The sight of her face—its pearl-like clarity of skin and faintly childish breadth—often stirred in me a paternal gravity, a Gregory Peck–like timbre of sorrowing masculinity. "Everything's fine.

I love you. I'm glad you told. Somebody had to get the ball rolling. Be brave, darling. I'd love to be your husband." And I myself rolled off, moving homeward at half-speed through Wayward's familiar streets, wobbly pocked salt-peppered streets like an old pair of corduroy trousers, worn to the warp and weft above the knees, that you put on morning after morning, your change and wallet already in the pockets.

With the apparition of feminine perfection out of sight behind the corner, I could imagine myself back to normal, a pleasant pagan family man carrying home to a house already littered with our culture's bulletins this Sunday's *Manchester Union-Leader* and *New York Times*, deliciously loaded with Nixon's ramifying deceptions: grand jury, Judge Sirica, Leon Jaworski, House Judiciary Committee, and furthermore he owed half a million in underpaid taxes. I must tell Norma I was leaving her, Norma and the children. But when? Our life together was so full of appointments and engagements. Just this afternoon, I had promised to take Andy and Buzzy, and Daphne if she bawled loud enough when we told her it was too adult, to something sinister called *Chinatown*, and later that afternoon we were invited for cocktails and heavy hors d'oeuvres (meaning we could stay deep into the night, sufficiently fed) to the Wadleighs'. All the music department would be there, and some of the prize music students, exotic as alpacas with their long necks and golden brushed hair, and a smattering from the other departments, and we would all get nicely enlightened and *gemütlich* on Jim Beam bourbon and Gallo white wine, with semi-surreptitious intakes on a communal toke of fascistically banned pot, and big-headed Ben would begin to play one of his several pianos, as if with three or four furious hands, there in the Wadleighs' glass-and-redwood modern domicile, built with Wendy's money (her mother had been a Sears, or maybe a Roebuck) high above the river, and the students would shyly get out their guitars and in sweet thready voices sing the protest songs that had outlasted America's Vietnam involvement, and who could miss such a party? Not me. I wondered if the Muellers would be there, and if Genevieve, *mia promessa sposa*, would give me any kind of a betrothed glance. As I imperfectly remember, they were, and she didn't. Not a glance. The perfect pretender.

THE TWELVE HOURS' CARRIAGE RIDE from Philadelphia still jolted queasily in Buchanan's bones, further stiffened by the damp chill of late November, as, darkness having already descended, he climbed the six granite steps to William Jenkins' front door. Beneath its semi-circular fanlight, between its sidelights of leaded clear glass, the door was freshly painted black in the latest Lancaster style, setting off quite brilliantly the polished brass knocker in the shape of a mermaid suspended head down, her bare breasts doing the knocking: a fanciful conceit from which the gentleman's hand instinctively flinched, accustomed to calling at this house though he was.

The Jenkinses' house stood on South Duke Street, halfway between the Colemans' mansion and Buchanan's bachelor rooms, and it seemed convenient and wise, weary as he was in his jolted bones and his overused eyes and throat from four days of legal investigation and disputation in the pestilentially congested City of Brotherly Love, to give his client hopeful news before betaking himself to East King Street, the comfort of a solitary glass of Madeira, and, after a quick and simple supper fetched up to his quarters by the serving girl, to the Colemans' for a politic evening call. There were some emotional fences to mend, Buchanan realized. The fall of 1819 had been trying for his fiancée as well as for the nation; his repeated absences upon matters of business had worn upon Ann's nervous and—an unsympathetic observer might have said—much-indulged disposition. He did not, himself, mind her need for indulgence, any more than a man minds a skittish temper and rolling eye in a finely bred trotter; it savored, to him, of luxury—a luxurious self-regard encouraged by society, as confirmation of her high position, which would merge, once they were married, with his own.

Yet anticipation of the company of Ann's falsely welcoming parents, along with that of Sarah, her seventeen-year-old sister, who would be unduly and persistently curious about the glamorous details of the metropolis—which the lawyer had been too professionally occupied to sample, but for a bolted meal at a crowded inn and, to clear his head, an evening stroll along Market Street, past the Presidential mansion from which it had been Washington's wont to set out in a cream-colored French coach, ornamented with cupids and flowers—and perhaps that of brother Edward, saturnine and inflexibly correct, suppressing his cough and any words of overt disapproval while his gaze smoldered in the corner within the leaping shadows cast by the Colemans' fish-oil lamps, did not, this anticipation, relieve his inner chill: better to warm himself a moment at the Jenkinses', where his welcome was sincere, forged of long acquaintance, and his attendance carried a clear pecuniary value. A brownish light still figured in the westward sky. Low clouds spit a few dry flakes of early snow. From the semicircular stone porch that formed the sixth step he saw that it was bright within; though the Jenkinses' fortunes were presently shaky, they burned the best quality of candles, spermaceti, and had lately acquired an Argand lamp, an ingenious Swiss device, impossible to surpass for illumination, with a glass chimney and a clockwork pump for steadily supplying oil to the circular wick.

Mary Jenkins came herself to the door, her round face framed in a lace cap with ruchings. "Dear Mr. Buchanan, come in! Mr. Jenkins is gone for the night with his ailing mother at Windsor Forge, but my sister Grace is here to console me, and now you! Please do come meet her."

He hesitated, the icy touch of the naked mermaid still tingling in his fingertips, even through his gloves' thin kid, and the farmhouses and stubbled fields and darkling woods numbly appraised through his carriage window still somehow smeared on his vision, proof of a burgeoning national vastness despite the financial panic, which had flooded the market with so much unwanted property that even sheriffs' fees could not be realized. "I—I had meant merely to acquaint your good husband with the progress of the Columbia Bridge Company suit, before proceeding to recuperate from nearly a week's absence in Philadelphia."

"Recuperate here—we were just sitting in the parlor, too lazy to move. We'll warm up the teapot again. Or would a cordial better repay your long journey? Grace," she called from the foyer, into the radiant parlor, "who has come calling but the very man in Lancaster I wanted you most to meet!"

Buchanan's timorous advance, tall beaver hat in hand, into the sitting room discovered, in a certain mist of historicity, an enchantress sitting on a rose-colored sofa with a serpentine back.

Or perhaps, to give recorded history its due, she had been upstairs, and, in the words of the most vivid, if anonymous and unreliable, account of this incident, *Straining her ears to distinguish the voices that came from a downstairs room, Miss Hubley was pleasantly surprised to know that Mr. Buchanan was the caller at the home, and her sense of curiosity, no less than a well-defined personal interest in the caller, manifested itself in a very concrete way.*

Hurriedly completing the most tempting toilet that suggested itself to her emotional temperament, Grace Hubley left her bedroom and entered history. *Buchanan and his associate* [a phantom only this telling evokes; surely not Molton Rogers, off courting Eliza Jacobs, who was to die in childbirth in three brief years, nor the fabulously fat John Passmore, who by 1819 was in fact the Mayor of Lancaster, the little city's first] *were suddenly surprised to hear a gentle footstep on the stair, a swishing of well-set silks and then to be confronted with the charming young lady as she presented herself to the admiring visitor.*

Young: Grace Hubley was born on April 27, 1787, making her thirty-two, four days shy of four years older than James Buchanan, and two years older than her sister Mary. So the siren breast exuded the ripe charm of superior experience. In the words of the account, a newspaper article neatly mounted but unascribed in the archives of the Buchanan Foundation at Wheatland, *Her culture was further heightened by a period of life spent with relatives in Philadelphia, who introduced her into the social whirl of the city and brought her into close intimate contact with the noted hostesses and gentlemen of that day.* That day, this day, be they as they may, a man's heart beats quicker at the sight of a strange and comely woman, bathed in a light that seems her own. She was fairer than her sister, and the Hubley roundness of face was not yet worn into creased complacence by the satisfactions and cares of the wedded state. Clustered candles, their spotty web of light extended by tin sconces inset with oval mirrors, filled the dainty high-ceilinged room with a fragrance that felt to come from afar, from the sea, a seaweedy sweetness not merely sweet but august, an august incense conveying marine mystery. Buchanan had never viewed the ocean, merely read of its crossing in voyagers' tales and Shakespeare's *Tempest* and seen, in Philadelphia, the two great rivers, the Schuylkill and the yet mightier Delaware, swelling as they neared their rendezvous with the mother of waters. Excursions to the Chesapeake Bay were not uncommon among the prosperous youth of Lancaster, but he was so new to their set, and so industrious in the maintenance of his achieved status, that he had not yet ventured to the shore. The healing mountain waters of Bedford Springs cooled his summer enough, away from the fragrant debris of the tides, the lavish reach of sands, the colossal heedlessness of the endless waves, whose infinity mocks our consciousness.

"My sister, Miss Grace Hubley," Mary Jenkins was saying through his daze of enchantment. A small fire, the size of a cat, purred in the fireplace. The grouped and reflected candles gave off additional warmth enough to allow Miss Hubley to display, it appeared to the visitor, a generous amount of skin, among the curves of a loosely arranged and resplendent shawl. "And this is Mr. James Buchanan, Junior—a former state Assembly-man and a lawyer whose counsel on many matters is treasured by Mr. Jenkins."

The fresh face in the room appeared radiant, in the shifting web of radiance. Miss Hubley's hair, the same pale brown as Buchanan's, was done up in a taut nest of braids behind, with ringlets falling free about her face, from a glossy central parting striking in its straight perfection. Her long eyebrows had an inquisitive arch, and her lightly tinted mouth expressed a cushioned pleasure in itself and its flirtatious workings a world of temperament removed from Ann's angular, impatient lips. When Miss Hubley spoke, it was with an enchanting Southern mulling of the words. "Oh," she said, "one does not have to be in the Jenkins household many hours to hear tell of Mr. Buchanan. He is the man to be watched, in Lancaster."

"I am a diligent lad from the Tuscaroras, Miss Hubley, and claim to be no more than that. In the glitter of this gracious city, I cast a dull but faithful gleam." Yet he seated himself—in an armless oval-seated side chair with tapered curved legs whose neo-Grecian fluting was echoed in the rails of the back, which had a lyre-shaped splat—near the end of the damask-covered pink Chippendale sofa where Grace Hubley shimmeringly perched. An iridescent silk shawl of Persian pattern, such

Oriental fabrics being fashionable in Europe ever since Napoleon's Egyptian foray, permitted glimpses in the warm candlelight of her plump shoulders' ivory skin and of the powdered embonpoint the décolletage of her high-waisted gown of *well-set silks* revealed. He bent low, placing his beaver hat, with its own fashionable iridescence, between his boots, his Philadelphia boots, of a thinner black leather than his Lancaster boots, their tops cut diagonally in the hussar style.

"You disclaim, to elicit flattery," his new companion gaily accused him. "You have lost your mountain manners, if ever you had them."

"My dear mother is a woman of some graces, who loved the old poets as well as the Bible, and my father a man of sufficient means to send me to college, though he missed my strong back on his farm. He began on the road to prosperity as the sack-handler in a frontier trading post; in his youth in County Donegal, his own father had deserted him, and when the dust of our Revolution settled he quit his dependency on his dead mother's brother, and sailed." Lest this self-description which he impulsively confided seem boastful, he added, "But the simple Christian virtues remain my standard of success, and when my second term in the Assembly ended three years ago last June, I with great pleasure surrendered all political ambition."

Mary Jenkins loyally protested, "Yet the Judge Franklin case has kept you in the public eye, and there is talk," she explained to her sister, giving their guest the dignity of the third person, "of the Federalists putting up Mr. Buchanan for the national Congress in next year's election. And just the other day he and Mr. Jenkins and James Hopkins were appointed to form a committee to advise our Congressman on the question of slavery in Missouri."

Buchanan hastened to disclaim, "Lancaster is a small city,

Miss Hubley, and a few dogs must bark on many street corners."

"I assume you will advise to vote *against* extending slavery; I think it wicked, *wicked,* the way those planters want to spread their devilish institution over all of God's terrain!"

Such fire of opinion, the tongue and heart outracing reason, attracted Buchanan, and alarmed him. "We do so advise, Miss Hubley, though in terms less fervently couched than your own. Myself, since the Constitution undeniably sanctions slavery, I see no recourse but accommodation with it *pro tempore.* A geographical compromise, such as rumor suggests Senator Clay will soon propose, to maintain the balance of power within the Senate, would, I am convinced, allay the sectional competition that has heavily contributed to the present panic of selling and suing. For unless the spirit of compromise and mediation prevail, this young nation may divide in three, New England pulling one way and the South the other, and the states of middling disposition shall be left as ports without a nation to supply their commerce. Disunited, our fair States may become each as trivial as Bavarian princedoms!"

Grace said, theatrically addressing her sister, "Oh, I *do* adore men, the sensible way they put one thing against another. Myself, Mr. Buchanan, I cannot calmly *think* on the fate of those poor enslaved darkies, the manner in which not only the men in the fields are abused but the colored ladies also—I can*not,* it is a weakness of my nature, I cannot contemplate such wrongs without my heart rising up and yearning to smite those monstrous slavedrivers into the Hades that will be their everlasting abode!"

Buchanan tut-tutted, "Come now, the peculiar institution presents more sides than that. You speak as a soldier's daughter, Miss Hubley, but here in peaceable Pennsylvania we take a less absolute view. The slavedrivers, for one, are themselves driven, by circumstances they did not create. Chattel slavery, though I, too, deplore its abuses, is as old as warfare, and to be preferred to massacre. In some societies, such as that of ancient Greece, the contract between master and slave allowed the latter considerable advantages, and our Southern brethren maintain that without the institution's paternal guidance the negro would perish of his natural sloth and inability. At present, our friends in the South see their share of the national fortune dwindling; much of the urgency would be removed from the territorial question, it is my belief, if new territories— to the south of the South, so to speak—were to be mercifully removed"—he made a nimble snatching gesture, startling both members of his little audience—"from the crumbling dominions of the moribund Spanish crown. Cuba, Texas, Chihuahua, California—all begging to be plucked."

He settled back, pleasantly conscious of the breast-fluttering impression his masculine aggressiveness had made. Now he directed his attention, with a characteristic twist of his head, specifically toward Mrs. Jenkins, who had remained standing, held upright by the strands of hostessly duty. "But I mustn't tarry, delightful though tarrying be," he said. "Inform Mr. Jenkins, if you will, that the Columbia Bridge Company matter took some hopeful turns under my prodding, and if he wishes to be apprised of their nature, and of the distance I estimate we have left to travel, he will find me in my chambers tomorrow all day."

"I will indeed inform him," the excellent wife agreed. "But please, Mr. Buchanan, you shame me by not letting me offer you a beverage, and then a spot of supper. My sister and I were to sit down to a simple meal—salt-pork roast, fried potatoes, dried succotash, and peach-and-raisin pie. It would brighten our dull fare if you could join us, and would keep you out of the taverns for an evening."

"People exaggerate my tavern attendance, even in my unattached days," Buchanan said, in mock rebuke, and with a jerk of his head rested his vision on Miss Hubley's alabaster upper chest, bare of any locket or sign of affection pledged. His attachment to Ann nagged at him awkwardly; he should be speeding from this house and presenting at the Colemans' door live evidence of his safe return from Philadelphia.

"Oh, *do* stay with us," Grace Hubley chimed. "It would be a kindness even after you are gone, for sisters continually need something to gossip about."

Between folded wings of peacock-shimmery Persian silk, the woman's powdered skin glowed in his imperfect vision, which needed for focus constant small adjustments of his head. "I would be honored to serve as helpless fodder for your sororal interchange," he pronounced, "but there can be no question of imposing my presence for the length of a meal. I will, Mrs. Jenkins," he announced, relaxing into conviviality, "upon your kind urging have tea to keep Miss Hubley company, and a thimbleful of port to keep company with the tea."

When Mrs. Jenkins, to arrange these new provisions, left the room, its glittering glow seemed to intensify; the purring blaze in the fireplace—its mantel in the form of a Grecian temple carved with fluted pillars and classic entablature of which the frieze was decorated with acanthus garlands in bas-relief—added its flickers and flares to the eddying web of candlelight. Cocking her head in unconscious imitation of Buchanan's own, Miss Hubley said prettily, since he had referred to his attached state, "I have heard the most wonderful things concerning Miss Coleman. She is as original as she is beautiful, and her family of an unchallenged prominence."

"The Colemans are seldom challenged, it is true," he said, permitting himself the manner if not the substance of irony in such a serious connection. "Even at the age of seventy-one, the Judge keeps a good grip on his interests, and his grown sons greatly extend his influence."

"Mary tells me all Lancaster thinks you are a knight errant to brave the Coleman castle and carry away the languishing princess." When this apparition laughed, the shadowed space between her breasts changed shape. Her voice formed cushions in the air, into which Buchanan sank gratefully after days of nasal legal prating in an oppressive metropolis.

"She would not languish long, were this particular knight to take a fatal lance."

Grace Hubley thoughtfully pursed her plump, self-pleasing lips. "It makes a woman unsteady, perhaps, to have too many attractions; it prevents in her mind the resigned contentment of a concluded bargain." Here she spoke, less mischievously than usual, from experience, absorbed and foreshadowed: we are told *Grace Hubley was a young woman of three negative romances, not including the part she played in the Buchanan-Coleman episode. Thrice engaged to be married, misfortune and a fickleness of temperament ordained her ultimately to spinsterhood.*

Buchanan, too, may have suffered from a surfeit of attractiveness. A decade later, he excited the Washington journalist Anne Royall to gush, in the third volume of her *Black Book* (1828–29), *No description that the most talented writer could give, can convey an idea of Mr. Buchanan; he is quite a young man (and a batchelor, ladies) with a stout handsome person; his face is large and fair, his eyes, a soft blue, one of which he often shuts, and has a habit of turning his head to one side.* He had been his mother's first son and, with the death of his older sister, Mary, in the year he was born, her eldest child. Five sisters followed, four of them surviving to form playmates and an audience. His capacity for basking in female approval was essentially bottomless, and Ann Coleman's good opinion had to it a certain bottom, reinforced by her family. Grace Hubley, in turn, we are told, possessed *a beauty and vivaciousness of disposition that made her the pet adorable of her acquaintance.* Her feathery banter was to his vanity, we might conceive, as a deep barrel of sifted flour is to a man's forearm. He stirred her, he took her tinge. The shadows the Colemans cast in his head were dispersed by the light of *this social conversation very adroitly guided by the keen objective mind of Miss Hubley. Golden minutes fled by on winged feet.* As the embrace of the November evening tightened around them, and the windows of the tall sitting room with its fine provincial furniture gave back only tremulous amber reflections of the lights burning within, and Mary Jenkins absented herself to supervise details of the impending meal, possibly the conversation between these two strangers, the *pet adorable* and the favorite son, whose ages flanked the turning point of thirty, deepened in intimacy and dared probe the innermost source of consolation and anxiety harbored by Americans of the early nineteenth century, the strenuous maintenance of which so remarkably consumed and yet also supplied their energy—the Christian faith. Struck by her repeated righteous rejection of black slavery in all its forms, indeed scandalized by her airy, quick-tongued condemnation of an institution so extensively and venerably bound up in the nation's laws of property and means of production, he ventured, "Miss Hubley, I envy you the clarity of your views. God's design, it is evident, presents no riddles to your vision."

"What riddles there are, Mr. Buchanan, I leave to the Lord to solve." By this hour her own sipping had moved from tea to a brandy cordial in a tulip-shaped glass, and a certain rosy warmth and confident languor broadened her gestures, beneath the loosening exotic length of Persian shawl.

He inclined his *stout handsome person* forward from the delicate lyre-back chair with fluted legs, so that his vision won for its field slightly more of the radiant expanse of Miss Hubley's bosom. "May I ask—" He hesitated. "I ask in all respectfulness, with full solemnity—have you known, then, an inner experience of election, that supports this lovely certainty of yours?"

She adjusted her shawl, to achieve an inch more concealment, then relaxed into self-exposition, saying, "I would not express it in so political a phrase—but for as long as I can remember, I have sensibly felt the closeness of the Lord. He looks over me—He approves of me—He rebukes me—He enjoys me."

"Ah, I *do* envy you. My own mother could not speak with a more serene assurance."

"But is not this true of everyone, Mr. Buchanan? At least, of the white and educated race?"

"You ask, I cannot answer," admitted the future statesman, lowering his gaze in an approach to shame. "My own sad case may be singular. Parson and evangelist and deacon all alike speak of some necessary factual encounter, some near-sensory experience of Jesus, which I cannot in unhappy honesty wring from hours of prayer, or find even in my memories of childhood. The forest surrounding Stony Batter, the curses of the drovers and the misery of their animals, even the bland and randomly changing temper of the skies above seemed then to bespeak an inscrutable indifference, the cool tenor of which no intensity of yearning on my part could alter. The Presbyterian faith teaches of foreordained election and its opposite; can it be, I must ask myself, that my deadness of heart in this regard is sign of some eternal negation—an incurable absence of the quality, grace, which your very name proclaims?"

She had held her attitude of repose, one silken sleeve posed along the restless mahogany curve of the sofa's back, with a deliberate patience, sensing that this greatly endowed and yet spiritually lamed man was attempting a declaration of, for him, dangerous depth. Quickly moving her posed arm to make, with the other, a clench of earnestness in her lap, she mirrored the tilt of his body toward hers and said in a lowered but still singing voice, "It is not a woman's way, Mr. Buchanan, to make an issue of doubt. Helpless we are born, helpless we die, and betweentimes we live at the mercy of those who are stronger. It is not our task to quarrel with God. Yet life is good, evidently; earth's abundance and glory are but the outward validation of the love we feel flowing, without stint, from within. There are truths beyond the reach of reason. Surely Miss Coleman, to the degree of intimacy that is already your privilege, relieves your uncertainties, and charms away your doubts."

"Alas, Miss Hubley, and in the strictest confidence, not only does she herself doubt; she mocks. She is a headlong reader of Lord Byron's bombastic and cynical scribblings, and I fear has some sympathy for the most vicious anti-principles of the European anarchists!"

"But how can that be? Her family is the richest in Lancaster!"

"You cite as objection the very cause. Only luxury can afford ruinous thoughts. Luxury, and poverty beyond redemption."

Grace Hubley sat back, thinking that she had gone as far with this initial interview as was practicable; she was aware of hunger clashing with brandy in her stomach, and of a certain weariness this man even in his splendor and susceptibility inspired. He lacked true masculine spontaneity, that possibility of cruelty which brings the final alertness, the last voluptuous rounding, to feminine interest. "Well," she said in a flattened tone of conclusion and provisional withdrawal, "there are many Christian women, of sound and regular views, who would welcome your attentions, Mr. Buchanan, and throw a soothing light upon the matter of your election." Having so long waxed flirtatious, she relaxed into theological admonition, continuing, "I fear you vex with your mind what only spirit can decide. You must not bargain with God, as you do with other men of substance. God is not substantial in this sense. He cannot be bargained with. He allows us freedom only to accept or reject Him. Accept Him, sir, simply, without cavil, as a woman does—a woman, of course, of sound disposition and normal attitude."

Before this insinuation at Ann Coleman could quite register, another sound woman, stout and dutiful Mary Jenkins, appeared; the golden minutes had fled by, *the evening dinner hour was at hand. Despite her profuse invitations Buchanan desisted from partaking.* He reclaimed his beaver hat and the dove-gray gloves folded within it, stood erect with a creak of his travelled knees, and informed the vision in silk—who wore in his sight yet some aspect of a foe, a combatant in the implicative battles of sexual negotiation—"I will strive to accept your advice, Miss Hubley. This chance encounter has been not merely pleasurable but instructive. Shall it occur again, I wonder?"

"If the Lord wills," she said prettily, confident that it would.

But it did not; events whirled the possibility away. If Grace Hubley is viewed, under a loving but stern Providence, as the source of Buchanan's impending misfortune, and of a neurosis that decades later disabled his Presidency and plunged our nation into its bloodiest war, then she deserved to be punished. Not only did she live unwed but she died violently, in utmost pain. *As she grew older in life, and thrice had broken engagements that would have brought her respected husbands, she devoted most of her energies to the entertainment of her friends, many of whom were as light-hearted and blithe as she, too, had been. It was on the return from chaperoning a party of young people from the historic old hotel at Wabank that she met her death. Standing with her back to an open-grate fire, in an unsuspecting moment a spark lit upon her dress, and before help could be called she was seared most terribly over the body and died in pitiful agony in a few hours.* The date, thanks to a tombstone, is known: November 19, 1861. The Union disasters at Bull Run and Ball's Bluff were already history; her death was a match-flare within a spreading conflagration. But surely Grace Hubley did not, after Buchanan *desisted from partaking of dinner with the Jenkins family, and hurriedly departed to his home, where he enjoyed his own solitary meal and performed his toilet for his appointment that evening with his fiancée,* execute the melodramatic perfidy described:

Hardly had he left the Jenkins house, when Miss Hubley slipped to her boudoir and hastily penned a note to Miss Coleman that was "the most unkindest cut of all" to the delicate, sensitive nature of the woman who received it. It was short and concise, telling that Mr Buchanan had stopped at the Jenkins home to see her and "that they had spent a very pleasant afternoon together."

Nay, rather than believe such outright and useless malice one would cling to the muffled but musical sentence with which George Ticknor Curtis disposed of the scandal in his authorized (by Buchanan's younger brother Edward and his niece Harriet Lane Johnston) *Life* of 1883: *It is now known that the separation of the lovers originated in a misunderstanding, on the part of the lady, of a very small matter, exaggerated by giddy and indiscreet tongues, working on a peculiarly sensitive nature.* Whose tongues? Jenkins tongues, Rogers tongues, Jacobs, Reynolds, Boyd, Shippen, Slaymaker? A town has many tongues, and twice as many eyes and ears.

Curtis knew more than he told, but he had not seen the packet of mementos so precious to Buchanan that the careful old man dispatched them to a New York bank for safekeeping when Pennsylvania, and Wheatland with its reviled occupant, were menaced by an invasion of Confederate troops. In his retirement, the former President had been shown a gossipping article on the Ann Coleman incident, and, in Curtis's words, *He then said, with deep emotion, that there were papers and relics which he had religiously preserved, then in a sealed package in a place of deposit in the city of New York, which would explain the trivial origin of this separation. His executors found these papers inclosed and sealed separately from all others, and with a direction upon them in his handwriting, that they were to be destroyed without being read. They obeyed the injunction, and burnt the package without breaking the seal.*

Another burning, and not from a stray spark. Why did he religiously preserve these papers and relics, if the executors were truly to burn them? Surely he wanted us—posterity, to whom he would be history—to know the facts of the matter. *Mr. Buchanan had a habit of preserving nearly everything that came into his hands.* Curtis was the third chosen biographer, and the first not to be overwhelmed by the mass of Buchanan papers. The initial choice, Mr. William B. Reed of Philadelphia, *a personal friend . . . in whom he had great confidence,* was appointed in Buchanan's will, *but was prevented by private misfortune from doing anything more than to examine Mr. Buchanan's voluminous papers.* Edward and Harriet, eager to have their brother and uncle vindicated and explained, found another writer. *After Mr. Reed had surrendered the task which he had undertaken, the papers were placed in the hands of the late Judge John Cadwallader of Philadelphia, another personal friend of the President. This gentleman died before he had begun to write the proposed work.* Curtis, a New Englander, Harvard graduate, and lawyer turned professional writer, who had never met Buchanan, persevered, in patient legalistic fashion. He had written a fuller account of the Coleman incident, and showed it to Samuel L. M. Barlow, his friend and Buchanan's, for approval. Barlow, would you believe, did not approve: he wrote Curtis, *I am clearly of the opinion that you should not print any considerable portion of what you have written on the subject of his engagement to Miss Coleman. . . . In this view Mrs. Barlow agrees fully.* Oh, Mrs. Barlow, what a toad you are, lurking in the garden of history!

We are left, like our hero, in the dark. Night came to the so-called city of Lancaster as decisively as to a village. Only the taverns in and around Centre Square cast much light through their windows onto the sidewalks of rough planking, which thudded hollowly beneath the heels of Buchanan's hastening boots. The tilted attic roof of blue-black clouds at whose eaves a brown sunset had wanly peeped now was breaking up, disclosing spatterings of dry cold stars. The afternoon's feeble spittings of snow had yielded to crystalline air tasting of woodsmoke, fresh horse dung, and evening ale. He could see his breath before his face. Guilt of an unformulated and foreboding sort revolved in his stomach with what it sourly contained of tea, port, Lititz pretzels, and a lonely supper. *It has never been ascertained just whether or no Buchanan was received by his fiancée that evening. If he was, the dullest of imaginations can readily picture the chill that must have characterized the greeting. Considering the modest, sensitive nature of the young woman, it seems improbable that she could have faced the torture of a meeting.* From whatever direction he approached the Coleman house, its façade was dark; its front door felt closed to him. The panes of its parlor windows held only light reflected from afar, like the residue of liquid that is left in a emptied dish. The future statesman hesitated outside, divided between longing for a lamp of recognition to flare within Ann's house and a certain fear of the same flare, and at last retired, his dignity and weariness intact, to his bachelor lodgings.

THERE YOU HAVE my attempt, *Retrospect* editors, to work into the fabric of reconstruction the indeterminacy of events. As in physics, the more minutely we approach them, the stranger facts become, with leaps and contradictions of indecipherable quanta. All we have are documents, which do not agree. Was there, we might legitimately ask, ever an actual afternoon when Buchanan met Grace Hubley? We first hear of it in an article, maddeningly undated and somewhat edited in quotation by Klein, written by Blanche Nevin, a daughter of the Reverend John W. Nevin—an intimate of Buchanan's seven years of retirement and the deliverer of the President's funeral sermon in 1868—and of Martha Jenkins Nevin, whose father had been William Jenkins' brother Robert. In other words, Blanche Nevin's mother had been Mary Jenkins' and Grace Hubley's niece-in-law; her account has the authenticity of family lore. *Some time after the engagement had been announced, Mr. Buchanan was obliged to go out of town on a business trip. He returned in a few days and casually dropped in to see . . .* [ellipses not mine] *Mrs. William Jenkins, with whose husband he was on terms of intimate friendship. With her was staying her sister, Miss Grace Hubley, . . .* [see bracketed disclaimer above] a *pretty and charming young* [for *young* see discussion on page 62] *lady. From this innocent call the whole trouble arose. A young lady* [a different *young lady,* presumably] *told Miss Coleman of it and thereby excited her jealousy. She was indignant that he should visit anyone before coming to her. On the spur of the moment she penned an angry note and released him from his engagement. The note was handed to him while he was in the Court House. Persons who saw him receive it remarked afterward that they noticed him turn pale when he read it. Mr. Buchanan was a proud man. The large fortune of his lady was to him only another barrier to his trying to persuade her to reconsider her rejection of himself.*

For that matter, was there ever a Ford Administration? Evidence for its existence seems to be scanty. I have been doing some sneak objective research, though you ask for memories and impressions, both subjective. The hit songs of the years 1974–76 apparently were

> "Seasons in the Sun"
> "The Most Beautiful Girl"
> "The Streak"
> "Please, Mister Postman"
> "Mandy"

"Top of the World"
"Just You and Me"
"Rhinestone Cowboy"
"Fame"
"Best of My Love"
"Laughter in the Rain"
"The Hustle"
"Have You Never Been Mellow?"
"One of These Nights"
"Jive Talkin' "
"Silly Love Songs"
"Black Water"
"Don't Go Breakin' My Heart"
"Play That Funky Music"
"A Fifth of Beethoven"
"Shake Your Booty"
"Breaking Up Is Hard to Do"
"Love Is Alive"
"Sara Smile"
"Get Closer"

I don't recall hearing any of them. Whenever I turned on the radio, WADM was pouring out J. S. Bach's merry tintinnabulations or the surging cotton candy of P. I. Tchaikovsky, the inventor of sound-track music. No, wait—"Don't Go Breakin' My Heart" rings a faint bell, I can almost hum it, and the same goes for "Breaking Up Is Hard to Do," if it's not the same song. In fact, all twenty-five titles give me the uneasy sensation of being the same song. The top non-fiction bestsellers of those years were *All the President's Men, More Joy: Lovemaking Companion to the Joy of Sex, You Can Profit from a Monetary Crisis, Angels: God's Secret Agents, Winning Through Intimidation, Sylvia Porter's Money Book, Total Fitness in 30 Minutes a Week, Blind Ambition: The White House Years, The Grass Is Always Greener over the Septic Tank,* and *The Hite*

Report: I read none of them. Fiction, too, evaded my ken; the multitudes but not I revelled in the dramatized information of such chunky, univerbal titles as *Jaws, Shōgun, Ragtime, Trinity, Centennial,* and *1876,* or in the wistful escapism of *All Things Bright and Beautiful* and *Watership Down,* which was, I seem very imperfectly to recall, somehow about rabbits. The top TV shows were *All in the Family, Happy Days,* and *Laverne and Shirley*: I never watched them, having no TV set in my furtive digs. I would half-hear the interrupting news bulletins on WADM whenever some woman would take a shot at Ford or Ford took a shot at the Cambodians—Cambodia being the heart of the world's darkness in these years—but otherwise the only news that concerned me was what came over the telephone and up the stairs.

The longer I stayed in my burrow over in Adams, the more visitors I attracted. I was a kind of vacuum nature, especially female nature, abhorred. Students would drop by unannounced: I remember the rasp of my buzzer, the tremulous girlish voice stammering her excuses into the rusty speaker below in the little foyer strewn with advertising handouts and misdelivered mail, my hasty cleanup of dropped underwear and dirty dishes while this student climbed the uncarpeted flights of stairs, her young heart beating like a caged bluebird. These Wayward girls all had cars, not just cars but convertibles in the fall and spring and four-wheel-drive squarebacks in the blizzard season; for them it was no great trick to drive over the bridge and find my place behind the old shoe factory—undone by Italian imports and fractionally given over to little electronics outfits all hoping to become the next Apple—less than a block off the half-boarded-up main shopping drag, called Federal Avenue on the drawing board when the town, little more than a mill, inn, and waterfall when it was named in 1797, was laid out in the 1830's, under the second Adams's supplanter Jackson, as an ideal industrialopolis. The city was a worker's paradise on paper—the proud main drag ending at the main textile factory's gates; a parallel grand residential boulevard with a mall down the middle like Park Avenue and a big flat Common in between. At the center of a symmetrical web of walks stood a bandstand and a monument to the two Federalist Presidents, Washington and Adams, with a pair of night-gowned beauties who were not Martha and Abigail but the abstract houris of the Republic, Liberty and Equality, in these fallen times much decorated with polychrome graffiti, spray-painted pudenda, invitations to FUCK ME and SUCK MY COCK, and the like. The Jacksonian mapmakers hadn't quite foreseen the Irish and then the Poles who would replace the Yankee farm girls at the idyllic looms and lasts, or the Hispanics and Asians that had appeared in these recent decades in such bewil-dering numbers, with their rapid languages and Old World predilection for crimes of passion. But the city has stretched its grid toward the surrounding hills to make more neighbor-hoods, and put up bi-lingual signs in the welfare office, and hired more dark-skinned counsellors at the high school, and allows the Common to be used for fiestas on saints' days. Is this the place, *Retrospect* editors, for me to confess my basic opti-mism and even exhilaration in regard to the American process? The torch still shines, attracting moths of every shade. Live free or stay home.

Which student was it? My core memory, or impression, generating a radiant halo of verbalization, is of the push of her breast on the back of my arm, above the elbow, as we looked together at her term paper, there by the window with the friable brown shade like a graham cracker, near my desk with its litter of James Buchananiana. Waxy photocopies and scrib-bled index cards and overdue library books—the disorder sick-ened me, but I had hopes of pulling out of it a clean narrative thread that would some day gleam in the sun like a taut fish-ing line.

This unmistakable nudge of lipid tissue was one more bit of confusion I didn't need. I wanted to step forward, releasing my upper arm from the pressure, but, pinned by my desk chair, I could only lean away, an evasive tactic she easily countered by edging her feet, in their canvas sneakers—this was before the era of bulky, many-ply running shoes and after the heyday of Pappagallo ballerina slippers—a few inches closer to my loafers. "Miss Arthrop"—let us call her Jennifer Arthrop, at a grab—"you don't have to stand so close."

"I can't *see*, Professor Clayton, if I don't. I brought only my sunglasses." Nearsightedness in women, I suppose, is favored by evolution; men are charmed by it, a vision that focuses on the cooking pot, the sewing needle, and immediate male needs. It would be fatal to hunting prowess, however, and in men it must persist through the genes of social parasites.

The document in my hands, a sheaf of $8\frac{1}{2}''$-by-$11''$ paper covered, back then, with erratic rows of manually typed characters, eludes the eyes of memory, but let us say, donning the corrective lenses of invention, that it was entitled "Protestant-Christian Mythicization as an Enforcer of Male-Aggressive Foreign Policy in the Administrations of William McKinley and Theodore Roosevelt." Fifteen pages, double-spaced, a term paper for extra credit, from one of my better students. Miss Arthrop came from Connecticut, where her father was a communications-company executive and her mother ran a gift shop. Her excuse for showing up in my divorcing man's hideout was the slight lateness of her paper, which was due Friday and by Monday would be decisively late and doomed to be docked one grade. Today was Sunday, a gray area. Her admirably firm breast renewed its pressure on the back of my sensitive arm, in its thin shirtsleeve. In desperation I moved away, an awkward half-twist, around my swivel chair toward the window, my knees inches from the spiny, dusty radiator, the half-raised shade revealing the day to be, in the downward space between my building and the factory, a gloomy one. My maneuver left Miss Arthrop standing in her full sweater at the corner of my desk, blinking, suggesting a caryatid from whose head the weighty entablature had been abruptly removed. The sweater was striped and shaggy, as if she were just back from a ski trip. Perhaps she was. Perhaps, when I raised the shade, a row of dripping icicle tips sparkled into view.

Walking nervously about a little, to keep my distance and to conceal and stifle the involuntary beginnings of an erection, I riffled through her paper's pages. McKinley a fervent Ohio Methodist. Mother hoped he would become a minister. His famous description to a delegation of Methodists in 1898 of going down on his knees to the Almighty and coming to the decision to possess the Philippines. Sexual significance of going down on one's knees. Contemporary cartoons portraying Philippines as lightly clad maiden being taken from senile Spanish king by virile U.S. figure. McKinley's confessing, *And then I went to bed, and went to sleep and slept soundly,* as if after coitus. Vaginal innuendo of Dewey Bay. Feminine images of Samoa (divided with Germany in 1899) and Hawaii, whose annexation was pushed by McKinley's Assistant Secretary of the Navy Theodore Roosevelt. Zoftig Queen Liliuokalani. Blatant phallocentrism of Roosevelt's Big Stick. Insistent binaries of his public discourse: hard/soft, strong/weak, bold/timid, square/round. *Be like the soldier and the hunter.* Sexist characterization of Latin (soft-weak-round) country of Colombia, reluctant to cede canal rights (virginity): *You could no more make an agreement with the Colombian rulers than you could nail currant jelly to the wall.* Evident sexual symbols of nailing jelly and dredging canal. Miss Arthrop's deconstruction was getting me excited. TR's desire to de-phallusize (Miss Arthrop's word) William Howard Taft, his former protégé turned ingrate and foe, with the homoerotic announcement *I am stripped to the buff.* His seeing the U.S. itself (Colombia by

another name) as a woman, to be "controlled," like his celebrated liberated daughter, Alice: *I can be President of the United
States or I can control Alice. I cannot possibly do both.*

I had perused many such papers before, but never with the
solemnly watchful authoress and I a few strides from my un-
made bed. The trouble with systematic feminism is that it
heightens rather than dampens one's phallocentricity. It makes
more difficult the sexual forgetting we depend upon for decent
everyday social intercourse. I couldn't keep my eyes off her
breasts, the rounded shelf of them within the fuzzy sweater,
and the curve of her hip, which we shall dress for this remembrance in elasticized ski pants. There was something unkempt
and doughy about late-adolescent girls that usually, mercifully,
kept them from being attractive to me; against the age-old
abstract ideal of the *jeune fille* stood the disconcerting par-
ticularity of every instance, the unique female individual with
a chin too sharp, some baby fat still to lose, a dreadful vulgar
near-childish voice, or an unairbrushed pimple beside her
slightly bulbous nose. Their minds, probed, revealed ungainly
abysses that sent me scurrying back from the edge.

In that far-off Ford era—a benighted, innocent time—the
college had, believe it or not, no announced policy on fornication between faculty and students. In the Sixties, indeed, gentle and knowing defloration had been understood by some of
the younger, less married faculty gallants as an extracurricular
service they were being salaried to perform. By barbaric standards derived from a rural or tribal world of numb animality,
females of eighteen had reached consensual age, and good luck
to them. The social experiment that had begun in bohemia and
continued in communes and culminated in co-ed dormitories
had discovered what pre-Gutenbergian societies already knew:
sex, like eating, has a limit; a point of saturation can be reached,
and all the screwing in the world will not rattle bank foundations or bring down the walls of the Pentagon. The earth only

seems to move. Puritanism had overstated the gravity of the matter. The United States of the Ford era had absorbed the punch of widespread fornication and found itself still walking and talking, disappointingly enough. So there was no consolidated prohibition, nor likelihood of a subsequent rape or sexual-harassment suit, to prevent me from elaborating on Miss Arthrop's nudge. There were only the scattered contraindications of my formal vows to the Queen of Disorder, given in a very low Congregational church service, and my informal vows of deathless fealty to the Perfect Wife, given in many a heated darkness, and the nagging aftertaste of several incidental nibbles at Wendy Wadleigh, plus my inkling that this dogged, slightly pasty girl with the weekend submission was not quite what she seemed. She was, speaking of unideal *jeunes filles*, ten or fifteen pounds on the heavy side—not that the Ford era, as I remember it, had anything like the horror of overweight evinced in the anti-inflationary Reagan years or in the Coolidge-Hoover period of ascetic Prohibition.

Stalling, sorely tempted for all of the above reservations to launch myself on this little chubby uncharted sea, I asked her, "Why do you think, Miss Arthrop, Cuba was never annexed, either in the wake of the Spanish-American War or earlier, prior to the Civil War, when filibusters were all over Central America and the Ostend Manifesto, in 1854, urged that Cuba be either purchased from Spain or, that failing, taken by force?"

She moved a step away from the icicle-fringed window, so that her entire side—thigh, haunch, thick waist, and soft shoulder—took a long lick of light, and her eyes, now in bars of icicle-shadow, had a melting look. These nearsighted, unbespectacled eyes, in her plump face, seemed watery and small yet held an appeal, the call of uncharted salt waters, taken with a breeze of willingness emanating from her shaggy striped sweater, her tight forest-green ski pants, her dingy Tretorn tennis shoes, which the Wayward girls wore summer and winter, in sunshine or slush. "Who was Ostend?" she asked, in a soft, croaky voice, as if her vocal cords were dried out by the heat of my room. The radiator valve had broken and could not be turned off; on all but the coldest nights I left the bedroom window open a few inches.

"It was a port in Belgium," I said professorially, matching her step with a backwards one of my own, edging my pelvis behind the curved edge of my reading chair, that giant brown doughnut of airfoam and Naugahyde [see pp. 23–4], "where the three United States Ministers to France, Spain, and Great Britain met to discuss the matter of Cuba. The Minister to Great Britain at that time was James Buchanan."

"Who was James Buchanan?" Miss Arthrop asked.

That tore it. Even though, to be fair, the course of mine she was enrolled in (winter term, three credits) was "The Long Post-Bellum: 1865 to 1914," this revelation of ignorance so abysmal quite quelled her siren's song. Further, the revelation was accompanied by a flicker of weird possibility: she had been sent. She hadn't learned all her post-structuralist cant in any class of mine. She was Brent Mueller's—what? Pupil, disciple, conquest, cat's-paw. She had been sent by him to tempt me into betraying his wife, my perfect love. Cold-blooded wickedness! While my mind was spinning, I told her, "The fifteenth President of the United States, just before Lincoln. Born 1791, also in a log cabin. But you haven't answered my question. In your own terms of phallic aggression, and given that the American South wanted Cuba both as an extension of slave territory and to prevent its becoming another black republic like Haiti, why didn't Manifest Destiny—a phrase first used, as you know, in 1845, by the journalist John L. O'Sullivan—gobble it up?"

"I don't know" was all she could say, all I wanted her to say. I had unwomaned her—clapped her into the chastity belt of student inferiority.

"Look at Cuba's shape," I instructed her. "Talk about *phallic*. And what are its main product? *Cigars*. TR already had his Big Stick, and if there's one thing one big stick hates, it's another. We could have spared ourselves Castro, if Cuba had just been shaped like the Virgin Islands."

The abovesigned is not entirely sure, at this distance of time (but far less time, I may point out, than elapsed between the ministry of Jesus and the composition of the earliest Gospels), that he spoke quite so wittily, with so quick a command of New World geopolitics, but the fending feeling is authentic, and the reality of this child's sexual aggression, and the momentous way in which her presence transformed my paltry apartment, turning it into a moral arena, a theater of combat in which the door lock and window shade and fake-leather modernist chair all acquired tactical significance. The enemy of my new life had sent this spy to undermine the purity of my position. I was sacrificing my imperfect, though well-settled, marriage for a perfect, though as yet undeveloped, one. Letting this teen-ager (or twenty-year-old, at best) undress and be pierced by my aroused flesh would be a severe and distinct mistake, even if messing with students were not generally poor policy. How can you give a bad grade to a good lay? How can you take respectful lecture notes when the old guy is only so-so in bed?

Yet these my perceptions did not make it easier to evict this feminine intruder from my quarters. She seemed to gain corporeality with every passing minute. The possibility that she was the robotic sex-slave of Brent Mueller, with his taut, aerobically exercised body and brain stocked with the latest academic chic, and had come to me from this cunning cuckold's couch with duplicitous intent gave her blobby budding womanhood, as it were, some anatomy. Danger added its sharp musk to her bland aroma of willingness, of openness to what the situation might bring. I broke into a fine sweat of wanting.

To *see* those bulky breasts, firm as muscle on her stocky body in its ski togs, with ruddy nipples and rosy areolae, and to touch those mute haunches and buttocks, with fingers curled to scrape my nails in a torturer's exquisite refinement of epidermal delight . . . Only feverish pedantic prattle staved off my desire to leap forward into the heavily baited trap. "I myself have always been struck," I said, trying to keep my breathing under control (I get asthmatic in tight situations), "by the rather sweetly hysterical quality of what McKinley revealed of himself to that delegation of Methodists. He had a nurturing, vulnerable side, McKinley, and I don't say that just because he was assassinated, which is a cheap way to get sympathy. His wife, Ida, was a *dreadful* trial to him—she fell apart after her mother and two daughters died within a few years of each other. She became an epileptic; she would throw a fit in the middle of a state dinner. When he saw one coming on, dear President McKinley would jump up, drop a napkin over her face to hide its hideous contortions, and carry her out of the room. Furthermore, she was a possessive, querulous bitch. When he was Governor of Ohio she made him wave to her from his office window with a handkerchief every day at three o'clock. A man who stuck it out with Ida can't be all evil and phallic, do you think? As to Roosevelt—well, he was compensating. He had been asthmatic and puny as a child—like me, as a matter of fact—and spoke in a rather high, effeminate voice. What I'd love some student to do for me some day is write about effeminacy in the Presidency—the President as national mother. Like LBJ—he loved us all in sorrow, protest though we did. The *most* motherly, of course, was the one who sent the most American boys to their deaths—Lincoln."

Jennifer's pale roundish face had gone as fuzzy as her sweater; the fading light of this winter afternoon was making me, too, feel nearsighted. "Phallic isn't all bad," she said, making one more stab at being seductive, at carrying out that child-exploiting fiend Brent Mueller's perfidious errand.

"Like dirt," I said, "in the right place."

"Beg your pardon, Professor Clayton?"

"A saying you're too young to know," I said. "Dirt is just matter in the wrong place."

"My mother is *always* saying that," she said. "I just couldn't hear you exactly—"

"—with the light fading the way it is," I finished for her. "Tell me about your mother. She runs a gift shop. Do you want to live her life?"

"Not exactly, I guess." These young unformed minds, they hit on a word, in this case "exactly," and can't stop using it, until another theme word comes along. "She got married when she was twenty."

"Don't you make that mistake, Jennifer. What I want you to do when you graduate from Wayward is take your credits and get a BA at a good four-year college, preferably co-ed. A single-sex school like this is an anachronism—women don't need to banish men out to another planet to achieve person-hood. A *cruel* anachronism—it puts too much stress on the opposite-sex faculty members."

It was cruel of God, had He existed, to put unformed minds in such formed bodies. Jennifer preened, seeming to pour her-self upward, so that her breasts within her sweater strained to rise, as if full of helium. "Don't you want I should stay and have a drinky-poo?" In the Ford era, scandalously, the legal drinking age in all six New England states was a mere eigh-teen. "Or maybe cookies and milk?" she added, in kittenish parody of any thought of mine that she was too young for all this and alcohol, too.

"Good heavens, my dear girl, no," I responded, becoming in counter-parody dithery and elderly. "People might talk.

You don't want your reputation ruined. Can't that still happen? Isn't there still a marriage market out there, at least a black market? These digs are grown-up territory, I have no idea how you found them."

"Professor Mueller—" she began, and then saw her mistake.

"He did, did he? Aha. Tell your buddy Brent for me to keep his little aporias over on his side of the river, please."

"What's an aporia?"

"A dead end. Not you, Jennifer, but this particular maneuver of your mentor's. The bastard's trying to steal his wife back." Her face, sinking out of sight as winter lowered the lid on the narrow space between my windows and the factory, was clean of any expression. "I look forward to reading your paper—we'll consider Sunday Friday, so you'll get full credit. Think about what I said about Presidents as mothers. When all this fuss about sexism is over, we'll be able to sit down together and see that men and women are just like Tweedledee and Tweedledum. With what Jacques Derrida calls a *différance*. Not to be confused with what Nietzsche calls *ressentiment.*"

Impossibly literary, you say? Remember, *Retrospect* eds., I was hyperstimulated; my skin was tingling, my pulse was well over a hundred. I wanted to put myself into right relation with this girl, to take up her two-breasted challenge, to peel her bulky sweater up over her head, tousling her curly locks and exposing to what was left of daylight the secretly supportive stitching of her bra, and to let myself be, in the time-honored fashion, de-phallusized. We are, each man and woman, doors that open to disclose an Oz, an alternate universe of emerald forests and ruby reception rooms.

Jennifer Arthrop did seem baffled. Our encounter had reached its aporia. My sexually stimulated skittishness must have looked to her like kidding, a professor's supercilious dismissal when in all good faith she had volunteered to be my blue angel, egg yolk running down my face while I crowed like a rooster. Yet, too, there was a stir of relief in her brutish blurred features as I gingerly worked her toward the door. I hadn't so much as laid a finger on her, as the phrase goes. I slipped the chain and bolt and exposed a widening slice of uncarpeted hall landing and rickety wooden railing. I ached all over, as another goes. More phrases: Last chance. Money in the bank. In for a penny, in for a pound. The public be damned. An opportunity missed is worth a stitch in the bush. My guest stepped onto the landing quickly, as if ducking into cold water, clutching her blue parka, retrieved from my brown doughnut chair, in her arms, against her flattened breasts. She had been let off the hook, the sexual hook. I said, in a fatherly burr, rubbing my rejection in, "Take care, Miss Arthrop. There's ice on the outside steps. My landlord is a crippled miser who lives in Massachusetts."

As she descended the clattering stairs, I heard Jennifer humming, to taunt me back, "Don't Go Breakin' My Heart."

[OR, IN ANOTHER PART of the emerald forest:]

Buchanan was in the Court House by nine o'clock that gray morning in late November. A note was handed to him. He read it and turned pale.

Perhaps the whole Court House, built in 1787 to replace the one that burned in 1784, turned pale. Through the Palladian windows of its upstairs reference library, where the handwritten, canvas-bound judgments and appeals were pulled from sagging pine shelves and lay about carelessly splayed and abandoned on oak reading tables, the sun showed as a sore white spot in the drearily overcast sky. The clerks, messengers, and fellow lawyers in Buchanan's vicinity, not to mention that populace of cadgers and adaptable hirelings who collect wherever momentous business is being conducted, turned pale in sympathy, recognizing this moment as a critical one, with historical ramifications. The letter was written on stationery of blue wove paper, in Ann Coleman's large impatient handwriting, with crossings to the "t"s and finishing strokes to the terminal "e"s whose emotional vehemence had ruthlessly splayed the goose quill.

My dear James Buchanan:

Indications mount that your regard for me is less warm and sincere than the solemn pledge of marriage demands. I have been informed, alas from a source I cannot doubt, that while I at my home around the corner joyously awaited your return from Philadelphia, you paid a prolonged call upon Mrs. William Jenkins and her sister, Miss Grace Hubley—a sociable call prolonged past dark, to the hour of supper.

Consulting with my parents, I asked that the lamps of welcome in our house be snuffed. I have not slept, and write you now by morning light. This instance of your neglect, though not, it might be said, grievous by itself, confirms in an unignorable manner the many intimations of indifference I have this fall received from you. When I sought to express my feelings of abandonment, you pled preoccupation with the quantity of new legal business occasioned by the national distress, and I composed myself to be, for this interval, accessory to your ambition. Undoubtingly I scorned those voices close to me insisting that the object of your regard was not my welfare but my riches.

Your earnestness, your industry, your reticence, even your intervals of melancholy and self-distrust—such seemed to me the proper costume of a man's soul, a soul that might merge with mine, providing shelter to my frailty and substance to my longings. I opened to you as to none other—for each bud flowereth but once. With what dreadful fatality, then, with what terror and shame, have these autumnal months borne in upon me the conclusion that my warmth accosts in you a deceptive coolness as unalterable as the mask of death. Had my affection been received by you as a treasure confided, and not as an adornment bestowed, you would not be flaunting your new prestige before the sisters Hubley nor flirting about Lancaster in the dozens of sprightly incidents obliging gossip reports to me. Did you truly love me, your bones of their gravity would have torn you from such unfaithful lightness!

I foresee your protestations, your skillful arguments. I hear your voice plead circumstance and good intentions. Believe me, the barrier to our united happiness lies fixed. Our engagement is broken. I shall return to your rooms on King Street all the effects, epistolary and material, of our attachment, and will look for the mutual return of mine, to my home but a few steps away. I do not wish, nor, since you claim to be a gentleman, do I expect, to meet you, as more than a nodding acquaintance, again.

> *In sincere sorrow,*
> *Ann Caroline Coleman*

Her full name, to add to the insult of *claim to be a gentleman.* Yet on a separate, smaller piece of paper, tinted rose, as keepsake or partial retraction, a few lines of poetry copied in her hand:

> *"How should I greet thee?—*
> *With silence and tears."*

> *"My soft heart refused to discover*
> *The faults which so many could find"*

> *"Oh! snatched away in beauty's bloom,*
> *On thee shall press no ponderous tomb;*
> *But on thy turf shall roses rear*
> *Their leaves, the earliest of the year;*
> *And the wild cypress wave in tender gloom."*

"For the sword outwears its sheath,
And the soul wears out the breast,
And the heart must pause to breathe,
And Love itself have rest."

Thanks to this last, much-quoted stanza Buchanan was able to recognize these fragments as from the profane works of that aristocratic scribbler Lord Byron, who had inclined so many susceptible young hearts to apostasy and melancholy posing. Of Ann's wayward habits, her weakness for the candied poison of this satirical and corrupt acolyte of the tyrant Napoleon had struck him as the least charming, and the most needful to be discouraged once she had been his lawful wife. The United States were no place for foppish anarchy. When he thought of his mother's hard life at Stony Batter—the laundry-boiling, the chicken-gutting, the eye-stinging stenches of woodsmoke and lye and the carrion of drying pelts, the tumult of horses and hound dogs outside the open cabin door, the thump and skidding of barrels and crates and the drovers' foul language from which neither her ears nor his as a child could be shielded, and the pious poetry of Milton and measured lines of Pope with which she exercised her sweet voice in a moment of evening quiet, by the flutter of a kindle-light stuck between the stones of the fireplace—when he thought of this in contrast with Ann's pampered and pettish existence he had to suppress a certain indignation, it was true. Yet now these verses were offered to him as a last thin bridge across an abyss of separation, and had something plaintive and adhesive about them inviting him, even as she decreed his abolition, to resume pursuit. Well, he would give her flouncing anger a few days to cool, and the tongues of Lancaster to cease wagging, and then see about crossing this bridge. Buchanan was a proud man. He had not marched to Baltimore in 1812 and in a downpour seized horses for the Third Cavalry—he had not as a lone rider made his way through Kentucky's dark and bloody ground and back—he had not three times outwitted the Democrat enemies of Judge Franklin in the state legislature to go begging forgiveness from this ironmaster's daughter. He had excited her affection, he was certain, and the female soul, conservative by nature, does not quickly turn from an established love. A few days' delay in response could do him no harm. *Sufficient unto the day is the evil thereof,* his mother had more than once quoted to soothe his youthful hurts.

All this, in a few seconds' reaction, on the level of conscious estimation and calculation. But underneath, a sickening sliding. His color was the pallor of a man who had consumed a bad oyster an hour before, or who had just been summoned to a deadly duel. The humiliation. The shame. How could they not meet and he not be cut off from all the bright circles of Lancaster society? All around him, through the rectilinear streets of a town without privacy, there were ears anxious to hear, lips ready to crow. His reputation was destroyed by this repudiation. A gloomy acid taste, a hatred for all the iron Colemans, rose at the back of his throat and had to be swallowed back, there amid the library shelves, the splayed books, the slowly resumed activity, as his pallor ebbed. Why would God give him this slap? It felt in his heart like the thud of a keg of cut nails falling from the back of a Conestoga wagon, splitting the staves and leaving a dent in the earth as deep as a tin water dipper. God had not struck him so hard since 1808, when his father opened the letter from Dickinson. Then, too, a terrible taste and disbelief had arisen in the back of his throat. Before that, there had been the death of baby Elizabeth. That was in 1801. They had moved to Mercersburg by then, and his father had a farm as well as a store. His new sister—he already had three—slept in a rocking cradle in a corner of his mother's room. Looking down at her day by day, wondering why her bed always smelled like the straw when the stable hadn't been cleaned, little Jamie watched his sister fight for breath within the cradle. Her bright blue eyes looked angry, sinking into her face, in their orbits of bone, as her cheeks grew lean and creased. She looked less and less like a baby and more like an old person, or an old angry monkey. Her hands curled on her chest and her eyes got dull as drops of candlewax, and there came a morning when she was waxy all over, and the spark of life had gone to Heaven to join the soul of his sister Mary, who had died the year he was born as if to give him room. Elizabeth was his mother's name, as his name was his father's. Elizabeth's angry blue mouth, with its dry squawks and yellow spit-up, had become triangular, a sharp hole leading downward to nothing, and something terrible—the adamant No that God could pronounce—entered her brother's stomach like a stone, like the fall of a keg of nails. That very day, it seemed in his faulty memory, his mother in her sorrow had baked buttery sweet corn cakes, as if to reward the other of her children— Jamie and Jane and Maria and Sarah—for continuing to live.

I REMEMBER, or seem to, a moment—it must have been at least a year into the Ford Administration, since it bespeaks an advanced state of domestic rearrangement—when Genevieve and I tucked her two little girls into bed on a futon spread on the living-room floor of my apartment in Adams. The girls, Laura and Susan, were nine and six. The Perfect Wife and I had cooked them a perfect children's dinner—well-done hamburgers, unfrozen peas and French fries, and popsicles for dessert, let's say—in my closet of a kitchen, with its hidden troops of roaches that would parade forth at night. We all played some sort of board game—I forget the details, it was based on the fuzzy zoömorphs of *Sesame Street,* and involved spinning a dial that kept sticking at the same slice of directive pie—and put the girls to bed and then went to bed ourselves. Just as if we were really married and formed a legitimate family.

Tears start up at so pretty and perilous a memory. The girls gravely stared up at us, their glossy bangs brushed to a glow— Laura had her father's sandy-brown hair, Susan her mother's straight pure black, almost Chinese in luster—and their eyes shared the wide-awake look of the little pet dolls and stuffed animals tucked beneath the L. L. Bean puff with them. Laura clutched a plastic glamour-girl with spun-glass hair and long stiff pink plastic legs, and Susan a limp lamb with dirty wool. Matter in the wrong place. Their being there, on my floor, blew, as a phrase of the era went, my mind. Simultaneously host and interloper, destroyer and nurturer, I fussed over technicalities. Would they be too warm, with the radiator I couldn't turn off? I'd leave the window open a crack. Should I leave the bathroom light on, so they could find it in the dark? I would, but I'd close the door all but a crack, so the light wouldn't shine in their faces. Would the sound of city traffic and the flickering neon sign of the restaurant keep them awake? I'd lower the shade and maybe close the window entirely, then. "Your mommy and I will be right in that other room, in case you need us for anything."

"You can close your door," Laura told me, with what I imagined was precocious understanding of our need for privacy. Perhaps in retrospect it was her need to stop my fussing.

I laughed in complicity. "Thanks, Laura, but there *is* no door, funnily enough. There isn't room to swing a door, the bed takes up all of the bedroom, and there's the radiator on this side, so somebody who lived here before me took the door off the hinges and threw it away."

"Wasn't that against the law?" little Susan asked.

"You mean," I said, "like taking the little ticket off a pillow?"

The two girls stared up at me in silence, not seeing the joke.

But I was a new factor in their lives, and they wanted to be careful, respectful.

Where was their real, their validated, father? It comes to me: he was up in the mountains, skiing. The faculty couples had taken pity on him, and he was always being invited places— sailing, skiing, three days of tennis camp. He was Mr. Popular. On this occasion, while we mice played, he was with, I am almost certain, the Wadleighs. They had gotten back together, after a year of outside skirmishes and consultation with finan- cial advisers; her money had worked its way into their marital interstices like a tenacious glue; he had too many pianos to move out. In addition to their modernist house above the river they owned a condo in a postmodern complex above Conway, near Wildcat. So Brent was tearing up the slopes with the Wadleighs while his perfect wife and I were playing house in the slums of Adams. Not slums, exactly, since the entire city, some would say, was a slum. Only the boldest of our Wayward girls ever crossed the bridge alone, to buy snowboots or have her typewriter repaired, and it was a roguish date indeed who took one of them barhopping through the string of ethnic cafés threaded among the all-but-abandoned mills.

From the teetering height of my corrupt adulthood I gazed down at the staring small girls. Laura, with Brent's coarse beige hair, had more of Genevieve's delicacy of feature—the sloe eyes, the starry eyelashes, the high-arched nose with its pinched nostrils—and Susan's black hair, silkier even than her mother's, framed a brow and jaw prominent and squared off like Brent's. But, then, Genevieve's jaw did not recede, either; her chin was spade-shaped [Eds.: Have I said this?], with a delicious kissable flat spot, almost a dent, smaller than a dime, in the center. In fact the girls were still unformed and traces of their parents eddied within a pure potentiality that con- fronted me with a strong sense of separate identity, of genetic synthesis hurled forward into a world that would eventually leave me behind. But for now I towered over them. The girls had always been friendly, if shy, with me; to them I was a man who had come to comfort and entertain their mother in the vacuum their father had left. I was taken for the cure where in truth I was the malady. This deception, which I could not practice on my own, older children, saddened yet gratified me; in this embarrassing time of transition the only unblaming eyes turned upon me belonged to the two persons I had most injured. More guilty-making still, they were charming pre-adolescent miniatures of my mistress and lacked any of the awkward hormonal overdrive and overweight beginning to afflict my Daphne, who had turned twelve since I had left.

"Sweet dreams, guys," I said to my tiny guests, my future stepdaughters, and, villain though I was, I didn't quite have the effrontery, or the physical elasticity, to bend down and kiss them good night. I retired to the kitchen's penitential space to wash the dishes while the Perfect Mother kneeled on the futon between the girls and murmured to them the day's last reassurances, ending with a sweet, wispy lullaby and prayer. She said prayers with them, a fact I found as exciting as the breadth of her spread derrière as she bowed low, mingling her hair with her daughters'.

How far I had moved into a new self! My own children a mile distant going to bed without prayers, in a hollow cold house made huge by its lack of a resident man, and I posing as a paternal angel here in my overheated lair, my male fulfillment purchased at the cost of a blighting blow to all these budding lives. It gave my stomach abrasive butterflies that had rubbed its lining raw. The round white dishes, coming clean one by one in the watery suds of the porcelain sink, where in a few hours the cockroaches would hold their nocturnal rally, belonged to a different universe from myself; I could never come clean.

And yet . . . domestic/erotic rearrangements like this happened all the time. The Queen of Disorder was no saint. With Ben Wadleigh stuffed back for the while into his marriage with Wendy, my own wife disappeared into the night on the arm of a variety of beaux, including, the children told me in scandalized tones, a lunk much younger than herself, who claimed to be a carpenter, and we all knew what that meant in the Ford era—it meant dropout, it meant hippie, it meant upper-class kid who had fried his brain on drugs. Norma had agreed in principle to a divorce, but in her disorderly way was languidly slow about taking legal steps, and I didn't have the heart to hurry her. It was enough that, living with the children, she looked worse in their eyes than I did, a prodigal out of sight over in Adams, showing up at the house now and then to devour the fatted calf.

When the plates were all stacked in the rubber-coated rack like ceramic baleen, behind a shark's grin of washed silver, I stepped stealthily back into the dimmed living room and met Genevieve's image halfway. Her slightly wide face, her slender hands to which her wedding ring still clung, the triangle of white wool turtleneck in the V of her black cashmere sweater floated in the jagged shadows of the room like dry spots in an overinked newspaper halftone. [*Retrospect* eds: if too many similes, delete some, much as the heartless mother birds of some species allow the weaker chicks to be pushed from the nest by the stronger.] Embracing Genevieve, I was always slightly shocked by how real she was—the bony plates of her back, the muscular volume of her thorax, the ovoid solid of her head with its volatile, vulnerable, avid facial components. We kissed always as if erasing some regret that might otherwise be spoken. We kissed at this moment lightly, since her girls were presumably still awake and watching. We had a third of a bottle of white wine left over from dinner; we took it and the two wineglasses drying in the rack into the bedroom. Since there was no other furniture in the room, we sat together on the bed; since there was no door, we kept our voices low. City lights, including the flickering neon up the street, below sill level, filled the narrow room with swatches of overheard (as it were) luminosity, doubled in complexity by the half-drawn shade.

"What's the matter, Alf?" she asked softly. "You seem so sad."

"I'm not sad," I lied, knowing the truth would eventually out, just as our underpants would come off, "just being quiet. Your girls were so sweet, tonight. They trust me." Speaking in husky lowered voices changed the quality of our statements, gave them urgency; we were uttering passwords in a *film noir*.

Her smile added its glimmer to the room, beneath her eyeball whites with their highlights. I could never imagine how people could, with their naked thumbs, gouge out others' eyeballs, though the event has ample historical verification. "Why wouldn't they? You're very trustworthy."

She was often a little in advance with her assertions; she meant that I would become trustworthy, when I was their legal stepfather. "Ask my own children about that," I blurted.

Her smile glimmered out, but not dangerously. She had been here before. "You're supporting them," she argued. "You visit them. You visit them a lot, and I never complain." Her recitation had a lilt to it, like the lullaby she sang the girls, night after night. She stepped up the tempo. "You give them nearly all your money, and you're being very patient with their mother. You're being saintly, Alf."

I had to laugh at this last, though the shadow-pits of her eye sockets, the bone cups holding their vulnerable plums, were brimmingly solemn. The soreness in my stomach was easing. The good old talking cure. "My children are sweet, too," I said. "They never accuse me, or ask me how come." This was not quite true: lately Daphne, the baby of the three but a woman in bud, had begun to probe the issues that the two boys stoically ignored.

Genevieve took a fresh tack, in a *voce* no longer so *sotto*. Her mother's instinct told her her girls were asleep. "They don't *have* to ask, Alf. They could see the way their mother treated you. You were lower than the cats in that household hierarchy. Everybody at Wayward could see it; it was one of the first things people on the faculty gossipped with us about when we came here, how disempowering of you Norma was."

My husbandly instinct was to defend Norma, to explain that I had felt no great pain, that it takes two to disempower, that we had evolved a style together, since our laid-back Cambridge days, of mutual benign neglect; but since the Perfect Mistress was spending the night, wifelily enough, and deserved a husband's consideration from me, I suppressed this instinct with a sip of our leftover wine. "What else did the faculty say about us?" I asked.

Genevieve didn't quite like this thrust of my curiosity, as exploiting her uncharacteristic lapse of discretion, but she had to play along, for the same reasons I was trying to keep smooth our perilous attempt tonight at playing house. At the center of our scandal, with centrifugal spouses, we were stuck with each other as surely as the principals of an arranged marriage. She said reluctantly, "They said what a gifted artist Norma was, and what a pity she never finished a canvas, and how brilliant you were, and what a shame that you could never finish your book on Buchanan."

I expected her to go on, as the Queen of Disorder would have, wanderingly pursuing her thoughts to a provocative aporia or a trailing-off that, by our old habits, chimed stimulatingly with an unspoken intuition of mine. But this new woman's style was to stop when she had nothing clear and certain to say. It put more of a conversational burden on me than I was accustomed to. I volunteered, "I probably don't *want* to finish it. I'm scared of being separated from him."

"From Buchanan?" she said, in genuine surprise. We could still surprise each other; that was nice.

"Yes. I love him," I said, feeling the wine, and hoping I wasn't boozily slipping into rubbing her too much the wrong way. But how could she be jealous of a long-dead man? Dust, he was now, in Woodward Hill Cemetery, dust and bones and bits of skin, like a mylodon.

Her smile appeared and disappeared quickly, signalling woman-warmth beneath the surface of the room's dimness, a dimness splotched with bluish and yellowish patches of light from nighttime Adams. "*Is* he lovable?" she sensibly asked.

"Not very," I admitted, then backtracked, "but yes, very. He was stiff and conscientious and cautious. His Presidential addresses are so dry you could learn to hate him. But then you don't, you get to feel a mind underneath the words, making sense, trying to pull off a balancing act. All these nineteenth-century people made sense, in a way we can't any more. They still had a language you could build with. But anybody," I went on, placing a preliminary hand on the small of her back, its little pad of buttock-fat pushed upward by her posture as she sat, legs crossed yoga-style, on my bed, "can love a lovable person. The challenge is, for the historian, to love the unlovable. He was scared of the world, Buchanan. He thought it was out to get him, and it was. He was right. He tried to keep peace. That whole decade of Presidents did, Fillmore and Pierce and Buchanan—try, I mean—and they suc*ceed*ed, they *did* keep the South placated, and in the Union, which was important, since if war had come in 1850 instead of 1860, the outcome might have been very different; the South had all its assets in place— the military tradition, the great officers, the down-home patri-otism, King Cotton—and the North still needed to grow. And precious little thanks they've got from history for it—the doughface Presidents. History loves blood. It loves the great blood-spillers. Poor Buchanan was ahead of his time, trying to bring mankind up a notch, out of the blood. On the other hand, you'd have to say, he loved power, that spidery kind of power politicians had back then, just a few of them pulling all the strings; he was Polk's Secretary of State, and Polk was *not* afraid to spill blood. The way the two of them jockeyed Mexico into war was really rather shameful, and tricky, too, since the Mexican government kept changing, you could almost say there was no government to make war on. Neither was Jackson, of course, afraid of blood. Buchanan became a Jacksonian, because Jackson was *the* force, the only force really, once the aristocrats fizzled out with Quincy Adams; a whole political party, the Whigs, rose up with no point to it at all except being against *him*, Jackson; they took the name Whig to imply that Jackson was a Tory. King Andrew, they called him. The Whigs have a sadness to them; their great men, Webster and Clay, never got to be President and the two Presidents they did elect, Harrison and Taylor, were both generals who died almost as soon as they got into office; it was like a curse. Buchanan became a Jacksonian for his own political survival, but Jackson made him nervous, the same way God did. It was a locker-room kind of thing, the way I picture it; to show his contempt Jackson sent him to Russia. That's what you did with political friends you didn't like, you made them Minister to Russia. You put them in the icebox. A lot of Pennsylvanians got to be Ambassador to Russia, because in national politics nobody ever knew quite what to do with Pennsylvania; it was enormous, it sat there in the middle of everything, the Keystone State supposedly, but it couldn't seem to get an act together. Henry Adams says somewhere Pennsylvania was so busy being the ideal American state it never distinguished its interests from those of the whole Union. The reason," I wound up, my hand having found its way down into her dear little underpants, silky, her skin silky, too, my hand the meat of a silk sandwich, "I can't finish the damn Buchanan book is that I have too much to say, and yet nothing really new. Just the old facts, churned up again."

"You could deconstruct them," she suggested, my backrub warming her voice, making it more languid.

I resented her reference to her husband's dark art. "I don't know how," I said. "As I understand it, if you deconstruct history you take away its reality, its guilt, and for me its guilt is the most important thing about it—guilt and shame, I mean, as a final substratum of human reality."

"Is that what I mean to you?" she asked, smiling, lulled by my hand, which was now two hands, the left nestling itself into the split lap her yoga posture made. "Guilt and shame? That's so sad, Alf. That's not at all what you're taught when you're raised Catholic. God came down and died to save us. The world is His gift, given twice. Enjoy it."

"I do, I do. How *is* our friend Brent?" I asked, a bit cruelly, as if she had mentioned him.

"The same. Very matter-of-fact. A little cold since I turned down his last offer." He kept making her offers; the last one, that if she would return to him he would give up his teaching post and take her away from Wayward. He had said, Genevieve had reported, that this was what I wanted also, her going away, though it was impossible for me to say so. She had asked me, over the phone, sounding frightened, if this was true. It was true, a certain relief had touched me at the thought of him whirling her off, but I said No, it certainly was not, and this was true also. The thought of her vanishing from my life hit me with a thud that obliterated all else: let the world crash and burn instead, with all our children in it.

"What's with him and the Wadleighs?" I asked.

"I wouldn't dare ask," she said, rather dryly. She stiffened her back and lifted my left hand from her lap, where it had found its way up a silken length of thigh to the crotch of her underpants, which felt damp. "Nothing, I'm sure. Brent is very straight. Don't forget, we're both from the square old Midwest. Once we were married, it never occurred to him to be unfaithful. It made him terribly easy to fool," she went on to confess. "I felt so *guilty.*"

I liked that: I wanted her to share my guilt. It disturbed me that she saw us as engaged, step by step, in a reasonable transition, with Brent and Norma as obstacles not insurmountable. It made for a certain lack of resonance in her perfection. Perhaps perfection does not resonate. I had never told her of my experience with Jennifer Arthrop and of my sensation that the girl was Brent's doxy and delegate, sent to entrap me.

She had removed my hand for a reason. "Let me check if the girls are asleep," she said, reverting to a conspiratorial whisper. She left the bed and I luxuriated in the certainty of her return. I could see her shadow bending low over the girls; I heard her making efficient noises in the kitchen, improving on my tidying up, and then the bathroom toilet flushed. The bathroom was reached through the kitchen, an arrangement that concentrated the plumbing and left the rest of the apartment free for the higher human functions. I nearly dozed in my contentment, wound around with the audible strands of our temporary cohabitation. Laura or Susan stirred in her sleep, moaning distinctly the words, "Bad dog," and somewhere far off in Adams a police siren soothingly ululated. Not our problem. Somebody else's mess.

My temporary wife startled me by returning to our bed-filled bedroom electrically naked, her immaculate whiteness slashed by shadows cast by windowlight. She carried against her breasts the folded clothes she had shed; her pubic triangle pierced her pallor as if die-punched. She was sturdy, Genevieve, with shoulders a shade squarer and wider than on most women, and breasts like a Greek statue's, wide-spaced and firm, neither big nor small, with nipples that stiffened and puckered in erotic response so amusingly she sometimes caressed them herself, to get the effect, teasing them with her fingertips in and out of my lips as they hardened. In the room's cubist shuffle of dark and light her shoulder blades and pelvis crests showed edges, so her nudity had a structure, a knit, a poignance of anatomy like that of a clumsily carved Eve huddling forward clutching a giant fig leaf on a medieval portal. But to my touch she was all silky and ferny, a branching tree of yielding surprises, queenly in her skin's broad gleam, girlish in her compliant acrobatics, a perfect blend of attentive nerve and rounded muscle, with this something solid to her, almost as of a man more finely made, so that I had the sense, always, of being *met.* Fully met, somehow, though here in this shadowy chamber, while we suppressed our noises lest we wake her girls, what I saw were bright pieces—the curve of a buttock, the teeth of her open mouth, the glint of her ring on her hand on my erect prick.

"Darling," I breathed. "Do me a favor."

"What, darling?"

"Take off your wedding ring."

She hesitated. "Why?"

I gripped her skull to put my lips tight against her ear. Her fine black hair brushed stickily against my mouth, the underside of my nose. "So you'll be totally naked. So you'll be totally mine. This way you're half his."

She shook her head like a dog, to free her ear from my lips, her skull from my hands. She stared at me and said, in an indolent, neutral voice, "Well, as long as you let Norma keep stalling the divorce you're half hers."

"She's a*greed.* She's *get*ting it. She's just slow. Jesus, let her be." Anger had risen in me, curdling the love-juice. Even in the midst of our lovemaking Genevieve was pressing our bargain. I tried to pull off her ring. She bent her face to our hands and bit my finger, hard. I pulled my fist away and swung it into her side, below the ribs, where the body is soft and undefended and liquid, a collection of squids, snails, and jellyfish. She rolled away with a muffled grunt but then spread her legs and without words bid me to get on top of her and fuck. She came quickly, one beat ahead of me, as if to put me in my place. I poured what felt like a river into her hot insides. No condoms then, no fear of the microscopic. The dangers were all macrocosmic, vague and huge; Brent's psychological presence felt to me like a mountain. At his base we lay spent, and slippery with little rivers of complex molecules. Her wedding ring was still on. I wondered if I didn't like her best that way, gold-shackled to another man while I pumped her perfect cunt full. As stated above [page 22], in the Ford era, bodily fluids were still sacred and pure. I drowsily wanted to drink all of Genevieve—the dew on her upper lip and along the hairline, the bitter swamp of her armpits, the slick lake of her belly, the sweat of her feet. I suppose I wanted to drink my own sperm out of her, where she was goopy, in Wendy's word. I recall another woman, somewhere in the tangle under Ford, crying out, as I uncoiled and kissed her mouth after muff-diving for a goodly while, "I'm kissing my own cunt!" These are deep waters, where we meet ourselves coming at us wearing scuba-gear.

Sorry, *Retrospect*. I didn't mean to rattle on in this unprintable way. I meant to end the passage with the word "met," italicized. My mistress, Brent Mueller's wife, squarely met me in those spottily lit sexual catacombs celebrated (see *Romeo and Juliet*) for missed appointments.

ANN COLEMAN—gone to Philadelphia! Overwrought, red-nostrilled with the beginnings of a cold, she boarded the stage-coach for the arduous day-long journey along the turnpike early on the morning of Saturday, December 4th. The coming day was yet only an unhealthy blush low in the eastward sky, a crack of sallow light beneath a great dome of darkness to which stars still clung, like specks of frozen dew, though the moon had fled. Raw damp cold snatched at her hands, her ankles. Her skin felt hypersensitive; she possibly had a fever, to go with the sniffles. Her head felt peculiar—its sharp perceptions detached from herself, like a spectator from a show. The earth was hard with frost, and at the landing stage outside the White Swan Hotel, phenomena—the creaking undercarriage of the coach caked in frozen mud; the slamming doors decorated with the images of English racehorses within oval frames; the nervous scraping shoes of the real, harness-scarred horses; even the angry shouts in German of the coachman to the baggage-handlers, mere boys prodded from their warm beds by hope of a few pennies—sounded loud and cumbersome and out of control. Her younger sister, Sarah, was with Ann: this is history, as is the scarcely believable fact that Sarah, six years in the future, was to meet her death in Philadelphia at Ann's present age of twenty-three, under circumstances uncannily similar. Whatever Robert Coleman's proportional part, in relation to his wife's Berks County prejudices and the flighty moods of his high-strung daughter, in the breaking of Ann's engagement to the handsome, industrious young lawyer from Mercersburg, it was Coleman alone who, six years later, banished from Sarah's life the Reverend William Augustus Muhlenberg, for no greater sin than the young clergyman's insisting, as early as 1822, upon holding evening services at St.

James Episcopal Church. In those days prosperous men, white, Protestant, and land-owning, rolled across lesser lives like barrels loaded to the bursting of their staves with a self-righteousness thick as molasses.

Born the last day of July in 1802, Sarah was but seventeen in 1819, all rosy cheeks and babbling lips between her bonnet and the bow of her silken bonnet-strings. She was developing a pretty mouth, Ann observed, the upper lip bent above the lower with the soft protuberant fit of a snapdragon that opens when you pinch it. A shallow dimple came and went in Sarah's cheek as her lips gushed chatter and visible vapor. She was the chubbier sister, her hair curlier, her mind frothier and more pliant; her cheeks red, her eyes bright as if with tears, she was excited to silliness by this adventure, a visit to their sister Margaret, who lived in a grand brick town house on Chestnut Street with her husband, Judge Joseph Hemphill, known across the jocular commonwealth as "Single-Speech Hemphill," because his maiden speech in the Seventh U.S. Congress proved to be also his last. The young ladies from Lancaster were to shop, and visit the theatre, and, the weather and their dispositions permitting, promenade among the splendid Georgian buildings testifying to Philadelphia's colonial prominence and the decade when it served as the nation's capital. Gaslights,* and throngs in fancy attire, and shops stocked with European finery! Their father has concocted this pleasure-trip to distract Ann from her grief and grievance, Sarah realizes, but dimly, so dazed is she by the vision of Philadelphia, by the endlessly various and promising adult life opening up behind

---

*Installed in Philadelphia's New Theatre in 1816, their first commercial use in America. Their very first use had occurred ten years earlier, when David Melville, of Newport, Rhode Island, bravely utilized gas to light his home and the street directly in front. Across the water, London first publicly installed gas in 1807, and Paris adopted it for street lighting in 1818.

the immediate prospect. Not for her, this morning, the stone in Ann's belly, the sick despair. Even as the cold of the dark December morning drives the older sister's hands deeper into her muff of marten fur, a hollow unease within Ann shades toward nausea and faintness. Perhaps she is pregnant—but no, this is not history, it is idle rumor. Buchanan was a virgin—our only virgin President! Ann is rendering him such, demasculating him forever, at this moment, as she sets her foot in the carriage that is bearing her out of his life, and out of history.

Their valises are loaded into the coach. Perhaps it was still a hulking, springless stage wagon, with canvas top and open sides and crude bench seats; but I would rather hand my ladies up into a new-fangled so-called Concord coach, its egglike shape inspired by the "tallyho" coaches depicted in British Regency prints, with high, wide-tired wheels to negotiate stumps and boulders left in the roadway. To cushion some of the shocks the "rocker-bottom" body was hung on "thorough-braces"—multi-ply leather straps that caused the coach body to nod and sway back and forth *like the violent pitching of a vessel,* one traveller recorded, *with a strong wind ahead.* Seasickness was inevitable, even for passengers less frail and morose than Ann Coleman, and even if by rare good fortune none of her fellow passengers, as the mileposts lumbered by, required the comfort of tobacco within the closed carriage, or smelled cheesily of the need of a bath, or belched the fumes of half-digested ale. The sixty-nine miles from Lancaster to Philadelphia constituted an ordeal, albeit in a Concord coach made prettily of white oak, upholstered in silk, and painted on its inside panels with mythological subjects, beguiling the jostling captives of the journey with the pink apparitions, amid blue billows and white columns, of Eros and Psyche, Venus and Mars, Artemis and Actaeon. Ann arrived in Philadelphia sicker than when she had mounted the carriage in Lancaster's Centre Square. Her nose ran steadily; her temples ached; the back of her throat felt raw; her brow felt hot to her older sister's hand. Ann was shivering, in an era when any chill might presage a disease that would run a fatal course, and she went immediately to bed.

And yet, four days afterwards, on the 8th of December, she was promenading on the streets of Philadelphia and encountered a friend of the Coleman family, Judge Thomas Kittera, who was to write in his diary the next day, *At noon yesterday I met this young lady on the street, in the vigour of health, and but a few hours after[,] her friends were mourning her death. She had been engaged to be married, and some unpleasant misunderstanding occurring, the match was broken off. This circumstance was preying on her mind. In the afternoon she was laboring under a fit of hysterics; in the evening she was so little indisposed that her sister visited the theatre. After night she was attacked with strong hysterical convulsions, which induced the family to send for physicians, who thought this would soon go off, as it did; but her pulse gradually weakened until midnight, when she died. Dr. Chapman, who spoke with Dr. Physick, says it is the first instance he ever knew of hysteria producing death. To affectionate parents sixty miles off what dreadful intelligence—to a younger sister whose evening was spent in mirth and folly, what a lesson of wisdom does it teach. Beloved and admired by all who knew her, in the prime of life, with all the advantages of education, beauty and wealth, in a moment she has been cut off.*

This is the document, this diary entry, which George Ticknor Curtis transcribed into his notes from a lost original, and omitted, with his tedious discretion, to quote in his published biography. Yet it is history, Judge Kittera's paragraph. It survived the holocaust of documents that still rages—documents shredded, pulped, compacted, abandoned to the cleaning crew, bulldozed deep in green plastic bags, mercilessly churned in the incessant cosmic forgetting. Judge Kittera's paragraph, preserved among Curtis's notes at the Historical Society of

Pennsylvania, throws a watery light, as if one of those water bowls which were used in the era before ground glass as lenses, to magnify candlelight and vision both, has been interposed between the weak sun of that December noon and these silhouetted young female figures posing on the blue-and-brown cobbles of the nation's most populous city. Were their arms full of new-bought items with which to dazzle the Lancaster provincials? Were they accompanied by servants, from the Hemphill household?—for that matter, would Judge Robert Coleman [how many judges there seem to be in this tale, a veritable choir of them!], the richest man in Lancaster, have sent his precious daughters off without an escort?—an obese old Lutheran duenna, say, with a pink wart at the corner of her upper lip, under black mustache-wisps, and dropsical ankles and the start of a goiter, and a sighing sort of philosophy that masks nihilism in pious resignation. *Life is full of disappointments,* she tells her wards wearily, and *Sufficient unto the day is the evil thereof,* feeding the patient pabulum of the old to the appetitive young. If she was along on this trip, she left no trace on the record; household servants were as abundant and as beneath notice in that age as appliances are in this: there may come an energy-starved post-petroleum age that cannot imagine our constant sliding in and out of automobiles, our unthinking daily flicking of a dozen powerful switches. Yet from the record, the perishable record, can be recovered, amid so much eternal shadow, the exact entertainments that betranced Sarah on the fatal night: she saw the celebrated Joseph Jefferson, grandfather of a namesake to become more celebrated yet, and a Mr. and Mrs. Bartley performing in a play, *Grecian Daughter*; also Collins' "Ode on the Passions," and the comic opera *Adopted Child.* The historical record can also be made to yield the full name of the unlikely Dr. Physick mentioned above: Philip Syng Physick (1768–1837), in 1819 professor of anatomy at the University of Pennsylvania, and a famously deft and mercifully quick performer of hemorrhoidectomies, tonsillectomies, and lithotomies.

["Ode on the Passions"! I should supply, out of my own spent passions, the hysteria—Ann's uniquely, in Dr. Chapman's experience, fatal hysteria. Her father as a heavy onrolling barrel of righteous molasses has already been evoked. To this add crackling clouds of claustrophobia that does not know itself as feminist. She is squeezed on all sides by patriarchal prohibitions and directives, and the oppressive broad envisioned faces of her mother (a complacent mixture of iron and dough, an obtuse Old face) and her haughty brother Edward, these family faces lowering upon her as if she is a baby in a crib and pressing the air out of her chest, plus the mental picture of Buchanan's inscrutable askance face and prim white cravat and russet frock coat suggesting, as at the moment by the cemetery fence this past September (see page 47), a thin painted cutout of tin leaning above her, a feelingless tilted wall she cannot get through, she can*not*: an appalled vision, on a transcendental plane where her consciousness intersects with ours of her, of herself, trapped here in Philadelphia away from the comforting matrix of ruddy dusty Lancaster, as discardable, as doomed to the cosmic forgetting, a minor historical figure, with but one little footnoted life to contribute to the avalanche of recorded events, one glimmering moment in the careless desperate cascade of Mankind's enormous annals—no, this is too much *my* terror, my hysteria—my h(i)st(o)ria, the deconstructionists might say, if they, too, and their anti-life con(tra)ceptions were not now becoming at last passé and universally de(r)rided.

[Into this void where history leaves off I must thrust *something*. Perhaps a little Byron, whose verses Ann has sipped like a fatal nectar—let us say the final, swelling stanza of his "Epistle to Augusta," written in 1816 (as gaslights were being installed in the New Theatre) but not published until 1830, a year and a decade too late for Ann:

> For thee, my own sweet sister, in thy heart
> I know myself secure, as thou in mine;
> We were and are—I am, even as thou art—
> Beings who ne'er each other can resign;
> It is the same, together or apart,
> From life's commencement to its slow decline
> We are entwined—let death come slow or fast,
> The tie which bound the first endures the last!

[Or perhaps:]

Returning to the Hemphill house, and finding that Margaret had gone out on a domestic errand, Ann made her way upstairs to the bedroom allotted to her for her stay; but, unable to compose her mind, she sought out her younger sister, Sarah, in the room adjoining. She knocked, and a voice welcomed her from within. Entering the room, which overlooked the front of the house as Ann's overlooked the back, gave her the momentary illusion of escaping the dreary tumult captive within her skull; the sight of the seventeen-year-old, sitting pertly on the windowseat with her knees drawn up, gazing down at the urban abundance of street traffic, of carriages and barrows, of gentlemen in tall silk hats and peddlers in wool caps pulled close to their heads with tied earflaps, recalled Ann to the fact there there was more, vastly more, to the world than her own romantic plight, with its constant inner thrumming of near-panic, as the ticking minutes sealed into permanency an insufferable, an impossible, an *insulting* loss.

Her sister's fresh and guileless face, shining in the afterglow of some reverie, was like a crack of light at the bottom of the door of a closet in which she had been locked as punishment for a deed whose wickedness she could not understand.

"Dreaming of your prince, dear Sally?" The Ann who

talked, who brightly teased and lent her animation to the little
scenes of family life, was like a parallel self who carried on
while the real Ann, the heartsick and affronted Ann, sank ever
more drowningly into irrational despair. Her fever had retreated but left in its wake a dry cough and a stronger sense
of no longer being quite herself.

"Studying what a great deal of curious people there are in
the world!" her sister responded. "Perhaps the people in Lancaster are as curious, but one sees them every day."

"Yes, whom did I meet right on Walnut Street but Judge
Kittera? You remember him?—such a slow-speaking, pontifical Polonius. For the sake of our family connections, I endeavored to put a good face on the encounter."

"Was that difficult?" Back in Lancaster, Sarah might not
have asked so direct and pert a question, but here in strange
environs, in the house of a sister enough older to be their
mother, their status drew nearer to equality. Also, Ann in her
dreary passion looked to Sarah for cheer, for rays from the land
of the living, and the maturing child, sensing this, was accord-
ingly flattered and emboldened.

"No," Ann conceded. She became didactic, feeling Sarah
to have been stimulated by the great city to a hunger for
those social graces whose absence causes so keen an embarrassment to the untutored but whose acquisition, facilitating
that human intercourse whose usual fruit is disappointment,
comforts hardly at all. "When you put on a manner, the
heart to a degree follows. That is why women, Sally, must
always be gay and courteous, even among themselves. It was
a grateful relief, in truth, to discourse with one who knew
nothing of my disgrace, and who saw me as I once was, with
all possibilities still before me."

Sarah rose to the invitation to protest. "Surely there was
nothing to disgrace you in your action of breaking the engage-

ment with Mr. Buchanan. No one in Lancaster would dare to think so."

Ann sat of weariness upon her sister's bed. "But everyone thinks it disgraceful that I encouraged the suit of a man so patently unworthy, so uncaring, so vicious. The Jenkinses especially must call me a fool. And I concur in their verdict. Against all the good advice of my parents and brothers I married my heart to a phantom, a pretender, and now my heart cannot quick enough break the contract." A satisfying heat enveloped her eyes, and tears needed blinking back.

"Ann, surely you are unfair to Mr. Buchanan. It is your prerogative, but you are unfair. His fault, if fault it was, was excessively scrupulous attention to professional duty; if he has another fault, he is too kind to all sides, being as courteous to his barber and bootblack as to his social equals."

"Being kind all around is no kindness to me, if I languish neglected while he charms the town." Thinking this utterance too stiff a lesson, for the soft clay before her, in proper female pridefulness, Ann explained, "It was not simply his dalliance with the elderly Miss Hubley; it was a thousand signs of veneered indifference, even as he professed eternal devotion to me. His last offense merely confirmed all the rest. As my father asserts, and as many gentlemen of substance privately agree, this man knows no devotion but to his own self-interest. His father notoriously rose by sharp practice and his father before him deserted his family back in County Donegal."

"I have never had a lover," Sarah said, blushing and gazing down again upon the traffic of Chestnut Street, her near-childish profile grave in the gray windowlight, "but I thought Mr. Buchanan as enamored of you as his cautious nature permitted. He is no pirate or poet; he lacks even our father's fire; but there was a benevolence to him that would have worn well."

"Why, you are pontifical as well, little Sally! All those sermons of Dr. Clarkson's I thought you were dreaming through have gone to your brain, and to your tongue." Sarah was pious, more tenderly than her parents' conventional devotions would have demanded. She had been much affected by the recent demolition of the old stone St. James Church, with its rotting pews and royal mementos, and excited by the prospect of a new and more glorious edifice, to whose erection her father was the greatest contributor.

"You mustn't mock my faithfulness," the girl carefully replied, with a flash of independent poise that Ann even in her distraction had to admire. "Did you love the church as I do, you might be more steady in your affections, and less hasty in your treatment of Mr. Buchanan."

"Stop saying his name! I *am* steady, so steady my spirits are sunk beneath this break, though my head and all its advisers know it to be best."

"Perhaps the heart knows better than the head."

"Don't torment me with that possibility—I am in torment enough!"

At this outbreak Sarah rose from the windowseat and embraced her sister, lightly, with an inflection almost motherly, mixed with a younger sister's shyness. "The break can be repaired," she urged. "The day after tomorrow, we return, and the whole matter may have acquired a different mood. Mr. Buchanan will be true; he can see that you acted to please Papa more than yourself. When Papa has cooled, he will relent, and give you back your happiness. He has no just reason to block your engagement; many a father in Lancaster would rejoice to see his daughter betrothed to such a worthy man."

"Why hasn't he followed me here, if he is so true?"

Sarah knew which man was meant, amid this forest of male pronouns. "*You* have rejected *him*," she pointed out. "It has become a test of prides, yours against his. Yours is a woman's pride, and it should yield."

"Who taught you such doctrine? Why should a woman always be the one to yield?"

"Yielding is part of our natures, since our calling is not to fight wars but to nurture families. Mama often yields to Papa, and loses nothing by it. Indeed, she gains, in coin of his gratitude, and in spiritual capital."

"Mr. Buchanan"—Ann pronounced the name firmly, as if trying its syllables on again—"is not Papa, nor am I Mama, though we are both ironmasters' daughters."

Her sister's cheek dimpled. "Your iron is more finely wrought, so you have sought a more refined mate, and now you have spurned him for not being heavy enough."

Ann's fingertips kneaded her high rounded forehead, with its single stray ringlet. "Sally, all your admonitions are giving me a most terrible *mal de tête*. The fever I caught in the coach keeps returning in fits. Last night, I slept hardly at all, unable to stop my mind from churning. It is not so easy to undo things as you suggest. Papa still forgives you everything, as one does a child; me he will forgive nothing, nothing that embarrasses him in the public eye, as this engagement and its outcome has. Really, I must hide my head; I think I will let you and the Hemphills enjoy the theatricals tonight without my gloomy company."

"Oh, Annie—it's Mr. Jefferson, with his funny English accent! And Collins' 'Passions,' set to music! 'Exulting, trembling, raging, panting,' " she quoted, for comic effect.

Ann granted her a smile, but wanly. These heated waves of disquiet had commenced within her again, waves that seemed to signal a derangement, a seasickness of the soul. "I *will* go rest now, dear Sally. When Margaret returns, please tell her I am asleep, and pray that it be true."

> *With woeful measures wan Despair*
> *Low sullen sounds his grief beguil'd;*
> *A solemn, strange, and mingled air;*
> *'Twas sad by fits, by starts was wild.*

The same untrustworthy source that retailed with a unique anecdotal richness the chance meeting with Grace Hubley a few weeks before raises the possibility that Buchanan did pursue Ann. *One account of the tragedy that seems to have the quality of authenticity claims that before her death Buchanan received a note from his fiancee to come to Philadelphia to see her.*

And so the story runs that he prepared post-haste to make the journey. Ordering his horse and gig in readiness, Buchanan soon was on his way down the Philadelphia and Lancaster pike.

One by one the historic taverns that dotted the historic King's highway was [sic] *passed, and few were the stops made that eventful morning, which Buchanan believed was speeding him on his way to a reconciliation with Ann Coleman.*

By dinner hour the "Half-Way House" at Downingtown was reached and the journey halted a brief period for the meal. Dinner was over and Buchanan stood slightly apart from the other patrons of the inn staring out into the streets where the feeble street lamps were beginning to glow.

Strange day, to pass from morning to dinner hour so quickly, with only the halfway point reached. Surely by dinner hour the lone rider had reached his destination, the Hemphill house in Philadelphia, and, after the appropriate ceremonies at the door, in which a lover's urgency brushed aside an elder sister's protective hesitancy and a brother-in-law's guarded reservations, Buchanan found the form that was the object of his passions prostrate upon a couch, irresistibly attired in the filmy Empire style, with a full-length shawl to ward off a chill from the velvet-curtained window.

"I have come," he said simply. He looked magnificent, in his voluminous travelling cloak, with his tall figure and his large fair head tilted slightly forward at an attentive angle, to correct the almost non-existent flaw in his vision.

"I wrote my imploring note," she explained, in a faint yet distinct voice, "because my heart demanded justice for itself. I was wrong, wrong to be jealous of your entirely decorous call upon the Jenkinses. I have been wrong to let my parents' and brothers' sullen disfavor color my own emotional complexion. My affections have one rightful owner, James Buchanan, and he is you."

"And I have been wrong," Buchanan stated with thrilling warmth and timbre, as his impressive and graceful figure swooped to perch on a corner of the couch, covered in embossed wool moreen, where the curve of her muslin-veiled hip permitted some few inches of perching room, "to allow my pursuit of legal eminence to remove me from your side, and to dilute the constant attendance to which our announced attachment absolutely entitled you. If you were, dear angel, to favor me by renewing that attachment—the object of fervent prayers that have risen unceasingly from my breast since your harsh first note and your abrupt departure from Lancaster— I would abandon every ambition but that of serving your happiness."

"My happiness resides," Ann stated, lifting up her torso's gentle weight on the prop of a pink and shapely elbow, "nowhere but in pleasing you, and in winning the right to your attendance when the press of your duties permits."

They embraced, in an ardent compaction of cloth and hair and underlying flesh, of December cold borne in the folds of his costume and of bodily fever lingering in her delicate limbs, and repledged mutual fidelity. Henceforth he devoted himself to a discreet local practice—wills, bankruptcy, and land disputes—that rarely transported him beyond the rectilinear circuits of central Lancaster, and whose moderate remunerations were handsomely supplemented by portions of the Coleman fortune as it fell, under the melancholy necessities of death, to the heirs; genially Buchanan devoted himself to catering to the whims and passions of his increasingly plump and complacent wife, as their connubial blessings mounted to the number of seven—three boys and four girls, all well favored of feature and all miraculously spared, in the uncertain medical climate of the time, any fatal malady. The lacuna in local Federalist-party circles that Buchanan's withdrawal from active politics occasioned was quickly repaired; Edward Coleman, Ann's inimical brother, was significantly placated by his election to the national Congress in 1820 and a rapid advancement to the ranks of Senator and, crowningly, to the post of Grand Minister Plenipotentiary to the Court of the Sultan of the Ottoman Empire. Stephen A. Douglas, the Little Giant from Illinois, became the fifteenth President of the United States in the election of 1856. With his fabled gift of close-reasoned oratory and bold yet tactful manner of dealing man to man, a son of the West cherished by the South and esteemed by the North, he recouped the contentious term of the weak-willed Pierce; Douglas managed to stifle the influence of abolitionist and fire-eater alike while superintending the passing of slavery, via the bloodless and infallible operations of popular suffrage, from the territories and the border states, along with the gradual abatement of the vainly agitated fugitive-slave question. Slavery, isolated in an arc of southernmost states while the burgeoning industrial and commercial prosperity of the Midwestern and Middle Atlantic regions pulled the nation forward, was recognized as an anomaly bound to fade away. Not only was it inhumane, it was economically disadvantageous; wage labor was cheaper and more scientific. In November of 1860, Douglas, who had given up alcohol and fatty red meats for a purifying diet of seafood and undercooked vegetables, had little trouble defeating both the Deep South's candidate, Senator Jefferson Davis, and the Republican aspirant, a little-known one-term Representative from Illinois, Abraham Lincoln. By the time of Douglas's Second Inaugural in 1861,

both the United States and Mr. and Mrs. James Buchanan—
forty years wed—had all but forgotten, as if dreamed in a
delirium, these moments when, in the music of the passions,
> *Next Anger rush'd; his eyes, on fire,*
> *In lightnings own'd his secret stings;*
> *In one rude clash he struck the lyre,*
> *And swept with hurried hand the strings.*

But no, the dream was true. Ann, retiring to her room at the
back of the house, which overlooked a damp little enclosed
garden still green with moss and ivy and sinister plants whose
verdancy seemed to ape vegetation in wax, grew worse. Her
spirits descended as the afternoon waned, as if draining away
with the thin slant sunlight that as the hands of the clock crept
between four and five winked its last, a lurid orange, in Philadelphia's thousands of westward-gazing panes. Her younger
sister's gentle yet acute chastisements persisted in her mind,
shifting form as she worried at them, remembered phrases
coming loose and taking on an independent, wormy life. More
than the imputation of selfishness she minded the implication
that she had been stupid, throwing away her best chance at
marriage because of some frivolous and malicious Lancaster
gossip; darker than the shadow of laughable miscalculation
loomed that of her dignity's permanent defacement, a sense of
being besmirched by forces that had obscurely enlisted her
impetuous and prideful will. She was a Coleman, and the Colemans knew their place, and their place was high; by allowing
Buchanan to touch her life with his own wistful, silvery, cautious, yet persistent and cunningly effective pursuit of her
hand she had been sunk into a shame of chaos, of *mad disquietude,* as a poem she could not erase from her mind expressed
it, with images of volcanos and cannibalism, *mutual hideousness,*
a turbulent muddy reality just beneath the glitter and comfort
of afternoon tea, *a lump of death, a chaos of hard clay.* She had

had a presence, a rôle, and now even her sister, just yesterday a child, felt free to judge her, to pity her even, in this sickening paralysis that had come upon her. Only God, the God above and beyond the quaint God Whom Sarah and their parents worshipped in that ruin of an old colonial church, could lift her situation up from this muck of disgrace: yet when Ann's mind and soliloquizing never-ceasing inner voice reached out to grasp this one all-powerful possible Redeemer her grip closed upon nothing, nothing but the silence of absence wrought by her old mocking spirit before Buchanan brought indecision and weakness into her life.

Alone in her room, she felt trapped in her own skull, a closed oval chamber maddeningly echoing with images she could not control or organize: her father's wide face, with its long thin mouth like the lips of a turtle and his powdered hair drawn back into a pigtail; her mother's like a wrinkled apple pinched heavy-lidded in the frilled netting of her lace bonnet; Buchanan's strange askance pale visage bent above her like a tavern board swinging out of reach, touched by winds but not by her hands or the caress of her voice. His gentle consideration, his innocent sociability, his gathering prestige—all were now lost to her, and when she asked why, instead of receiving an answer she met herself—willful and proud and careless, as Sarah had said—out walking to deliver an unforgivable letter, in a landscape *treeless, manless, lifeless.* Her life was over, like a throw of the dice that makes us surrender them. Ann's brain circled on its oval track and found no way out, no escape that would do her honor. At the window overlooking the dank green garden, an empty dark garden of frozen forms steeped in Philadelphia's habitual miasma, the daylight in its glassy rectangles turned slowly opaque, sunset orange becoming a sluggish brown tint; from two stories below, travelling up from the ground-floor windows, kitchen sounds quickened and clucked. She must have dozed, for she was watching herself, from a distance so close she admired the rosy texture of her cheek, as a child at Colebrookdale, running barefoot on the moist lawn after fireflies. She caught one, and as it lay with bent black wing, never to fly again, the golden pulsing of its abdomen lit up the creases of her palm.

Her sisters, first Sarah, then Margaret, looked in at her. The clicks of the latch sounded like the blows of a forge; the waves of heat within her had intensified their flutter; she was in a sweat, between her breasts and under her arms; the muslin of her dress was soaked; there was a horizon of nausea, and below the waist she had a strange numbness, a feeling of floating off. Their concerned sisterly words, the tea a servant brought, the stout maid, called Abigail, who helped her change into a dry chemise, were all less real than the race within her head, where the same few thoughts went round and round and created a tightening fury at her parents and her scorned suitor for trapping her within their narrow expectations, their fixed and selfish conceptions of the right life. She could not breathe. A rigidity among her ribs forced pain out her back, between her shoulder blades. When Margaret looked in the second time, a mere bluish shadow in the room's muddy light, Ann could only speak in brief utterances, between efforts of gathering breath, of scooping it up like water in a small flat spoon.

Margaret had grown broad with middle age and in a voice almost as positive as a man's announced that she and Mr. Hemphill had decided to send for their doctor, Dr. Chapman.

The thought of his attendance pleased Ann. Since childhood she liked it, at home, when the doctor visited, with his black bag, and invaded her bedroom, where no other strange man was welcome. When Margaret had left the room, Ann closed her eyes and was again at Colebrookdale, skimming through an endless milky June evening with Edward and Thomas and Harriet. Harriet died. She was only eleven. The doctor's visits did her no good. Death cannot be so bad, it happens to everyone. In her white dress, glimmering like the fireflies, her dead sister seems so free. Ann cannot believe Buchanan lets her suffer like this—that he condemns her to lie here locked into her angry decision, her frail skull held in a blacksmith's vise.

A servant girl brings a candle in. The flame in its curved glass shade appears faint, a guttering hollow at the center of the circles Ann's blurred vision spins. Perhaps she will go blind. People do. Just this afternoon, before meeting Judge Kittera, she had seen a blind man begging on Chestnut Street. The room's windows have gone dark, above the now invisible garden, its frozen green forms lurking under a whitening moss of frost. One of the evil plants has a trick of curling its leaves as tight as little cigars in the cold. The God Who says so often No can say No to sight as well. He gave us the miracle of sight, somehow contained in the pierced jelly of the eyeball, and He can take it away. There are many blind, as there are many poor. In Philadelphia she has been shocked by the beggars; you see none in Lancaster, just men who go from farm to farm for odd work, and sleep in the barns, wild animals of a human sort, avoiding your eye when you look at them.

Dr. Chapman has come: a commotion at the front door, a murmur of talk in the hall, a company of footsteps on the stairs. His shadow moves into the light of the candle placed on the high bedside table, with its concentric rings as of water disturbed, and is suddenly vivid, taking up space in front of her eyes—a large, carefully moving man with ginger-red hair pulled straight back from his broad forehead and tied at the back with a dirty ivory-colored ribbon. He stands above her with a comforting bulk, his embroidered waistcoat and carelessly tied jabot glimmering between long unbuttoned lapels of a rusty-scarlet cloth. He rests the backs of his knuckles upon her forehead, takes her damp wrist in his cool thick fingers, and stares a long thoughtful while into the pierced jelly of her eyes. "Fretting has made you feverish," he pronounces.

She tells him her breathing is difficult and describes her sensations of simultaneous numbness and heat. The panicked race, herself against herself, in her head, and her sense of some sourceless refusal and insult compressing her spirit unbearably. He seats himself beside her bed on a brocaded side chair that has been brought. Dr. Chapman is trying to be a father to her, she perceives through the ribbed blur of candlelight—as if a father's heaviness is not already part of her complaint. "Your frame is resisting some recent event," he tells her solemnly. "You must relax into God's hands. Repose within the inevitable is the *sine qua non* of the healthy soul."

"How do we know the inevitable, unless we strive to change it and fail?"

"Strive we all must, Miss Coleman; but we cannot overnight change our natures, or the nature of God's arrangements in this fallen world of clay. Mrs. Hemphill tells me you have lately met disappointment in a romantic attachment."

"It was I who pronounced the disappointment; the gentleman, I now think, has been misjudged."

Dr. Chapman likes hearing this; his thick hands lift from the knees of his old-fashioned breeches in a reflex of salutation, and then settle again, as his deep, unhurried voice states, "Then so inform him, when circumstances permit. Or do not, as Providence wills. You are young, and the young heart exaggerates—indeed, it must exaggerate, to propel the body into the great task before it. The task, I mean, of procreation, and all it entails of social establishment. Our flights of poesy and yearning work toward a practical end. We wish to make a place in the world, and to please our Father on high, Who commands His creatures to be fruitful and multiply. The fair sex especially has been burdened with the wish to be fruitful. But these matters of carnal affection, my many years of clinical observation suggest, work themselves out by internal imperative, and are not so much at the mercy of exterior chance as we suppose. I know the gentleman in question only by repute, and the repute is mostly to the good; but even a small qualm, on your part, at this initiatory stage, needs respecting, since the long years of marriage tend to magnify each of the couple to the other, like mites made horrific under the microscope. Qualms will come, but better later than sooner."

Reflecting, Ann supposes, upon a sour experience of his own, Dr. Chapman softly snorts, and raises his hands up on his fingertips upon the platform of his thick thighs, so that the elbows of his arms point outward. The features of his face, unevenly blanched by the candlelight, lift as if to say "Ah!," and then collapse back into briskness. "My dear young lady, I beg you, respect your own impulses and intuitions, and do not condemn your body to a war with your protesting spirit. To bring the two into more harmonious association, I will prescribe an anodyne. Have you had experience of laudanum?"

The exotic word in the doctor's sonorous pronunciation looms like an angel above their two consulting heads. She answers so softly he has to lean forward, his elbows pointing outward still farther. "Once or twice, some years ago, for a toothache, and more recently for the monthly distress, with its accompanying sharp temper."

"The elixir holds miraculous powers of ease," Dr. Chapman avows, glancing around at the cluster of concerned family forming one large shadow near the door. "It solidifies the bowels, erases pain, and dissolves the cankers of the soul." His voice has become more consciously beautiful and rounded. He produces from an unfolding bag of black leather a corked vial shaped like a small man of thin glass, with rounded shoulders and a pear-shaped head capped by the cork. The yellow tint within the liquor, as of suspended dust like the spinning golden flecks in the water of a muddy-bottomed spring, casts an amber glow on the physician's face as he holds the vial up to the candle. "The cure of Paracelsus," he intones. "Named by him after *laudere,* to give praise. But not compounded of gold dust and melted pearls as the rascal claimed. Tincture of opium, opium in alcohol. The dose must be exact. The drink holds peace but also a demon." The physician turns his head—his wiry ginger hair shows a halo of dancing filaments—and addresses the clump of shadows behind him. "Mrs. Hemphill, does this house contain a dropper, and a teaspoon?"

Scurryingly, these are fetched, and all in awed silence watch as the physician counts out the drops one by one into the spoon. "Eighteen, nineteen . . ." The shadows of his brows and nose restlessly change shape on his face; his concentrated, lidded irises are pricked by the reflected candle-flame; each hesitant sphericle from the dropper holds a spark for its trembling instant. ". . . twenty-four, twenty-five. And if the dose does not induce relaxation within the half-hour, twenty-five again. But no more upon that until morning," Dr. Chapman warns, almost savagely, uplifting that great haloed head, its upper lip split by shadow like a lion's. "Nervous stress untouched by such a dose is not amenable to chemistry. An excess—" Lest he alarm the patient, he halts himself, and in truth there is no need to complete the thought. In this era suicide by laudanum is a commonplace of hushed parlor gossip, even in innocent inland Lancaster, though its written report was generally suppressed by the superstitious journals of the time, to whom the taking of life was God's abundantly exercised prerogative. Ann from her infatuated reading of the living British poets would have been acquainted, no doubt, with the heretical charms of being snatched away in beauty's bloom, of emptying some dull opiate to the drains and sinking Lethe-wards.

The potent tawny liquid, forming by cohesion its tremulous mound in the spoon's small bowl, glints as a housemaid, freckled plump Abigail, lifts it toward Ann's parted lips. The doctor has surrendered the operation as too intimate for a man still as robust as he, upon a young patient so replete with attractions, though distraught. The coolness of the pewter couches the insistent push of the liquid. The servant tips up the spoon's handle, and Ann swallows. Alcohol's sweetish sting masks a foreign bitterness, an Asian hint of something forced unripe, of green poppy-heads slashed. The attentive doctor has observed the dose, and now stands up with a peculiar loud exhalation of finality, a habit of his at wretched bedsides where he has done all of the little that medicine of this era can do.

Civil courtesies follow, and promises to return on the morrow, and murmured details of a light domestic watch to be set about the patient. The crowd of family ebbs away. The little man-shaped vial remains on the high bedside table in the corner of Ann's vision. Sarah, too, remains in the room at first. She says, "I do hope, dear sister, no words of mine have added to your afflictions. I spoke more than I knew, and carelessly, not gauging the true depth of your misery."

"You heard the good Dr. Chapman," Ann responds, with a show of spirit. "Our impulses and intuitions must be yielded to, yours as well as mine."

"Not where my interest is so much less than yours, and so little of the consequences are mine. If I urged Mr. Buchanan back upon you, forgive me such interference. He would not want your health endangered, even if it mean his own doom."

Ann answers wearily, tired of reasoning on this topic. "In truth, I wonder if my unhappy mood doesn't stem merely from the exertions of travel, worsening this spell of ague, and from the contrast of the Hemphills' so very settled state with my own. I feel all the respectable Colemans condemning me. I chose Mr. Buchanan in spite of them, and then I have cut him off just as they were growing resigned. And he—he would have so enjoyed being one of us."

"We all want only your happiness, be it single or wedded."

"And what of *your* happiness, this very evening? You

mustn't miss the theatre; the curtain can't be more than an hour off. Do leave me, Sally."

"Oh, we couldn't dare go without you."

"Please, do; I would very much prefer it. Margaret and Mr. Hemphill have been long planning this outing, and it would humiliate me to take back to Lancaster the tale of how my poor nerves prevented you from enjoying your first night at the theatre. Perhaps the Hemphills can find a swain among their acquaintances, to sit beside you in my seat. Oh, do go, Sally, so I can rest. I feel the cure of Paracelsus working in me. An undeserved sense of well-being suffuses my limbs, and a bliss as if a knot inside me has been cut. Go enjoy Mr. Jefferson, and all those passions. As your elder sister, I com*mand* you."

"Then, if you command me, I will ask the Hemphills to prepare to go out," Sarah agrees, her eyes sparkling as if already bathed in the light in the theatre lamps; yet, training herself to the patience of womanhood, she sits some minutes more, as Ann's eyes close, and her breathing softly rasps on the deep-seated tides of self-forgetfulness.

Lethe-wards the drug takes Ann, but not safely through the night. She awakes with the candle burnt down by a finger's length in its curvaceous glass shade, and the shield-back side chair with the brocaded seat, where both Sarah and Dr. Chapman had sat, empty. The exposed brocaded pattern centers a blue rose, of a strange midnight blue, as of a cabbage that frost has blackened. Every sensory impression wears a haloed intensity. From the front of the downstairs, at the other extreme of the house, comes a murmur scarcely more articulate than the incessant prattle of a brook, yet with the intermittences and eager resumptions of human speech. Her sister and brother-in-law have gone out to the theatre, presumably, with Sarah. Those of their children still at home must be, like Ann, in bed. So this conversation must be the servants making themselves at home in the master's absence, or some guests to whom Ann was not introduced, or a conversation reverberating from an adjacent house on the street. The thought that Mr. Buchanan has come to plead his case and carry her off she suppresses, though her pulse races at the possibility, as too good to be true.

Heavy in every languid limb, her chemise damp from her unnatural sleep, Ann pushes herself from the warm bed and squats on the cold-lipped chamber pot, relieving her bladder in a stream whose pungence rises to her nostrils with the sharpness of horse stale. A sign of unhealth, so strong an odor. But perhaps it is the drugged enlargement of her senses that makes it strong. Her body in its febrility feels the chill of the room as an assault on her skin, against which her circulating blood cannot generate a defense. Involuntarily she shivers, so that her hands jump back and forth in the watery air. As her mind clears of its dreams—plausible dramas sinking rapidly into oblivion, leaving behind shreds that melt as her mind tries to grasp them: her father and mother present in the Jenkinses' front parlor on South Duke Street, her father holding a teacup poised beneath his double chin, the saucer several buttons below, her mother on the sofa in her lace cap, Ann feeling her breast bursting with pent-up rage, the handle of a riding crop long and leathery in her hand, all discussing some issue (there were others present, Slaymakers and Jacobses) involving Mr. Buchanan, how a prankish bid of his at an auction had caused all the banks in Lancaster to fail, and a terrible vastation of financial panic to fall upon the entire town, while she was crying that it had not been his fault, he had simply misjudged, in the eagerness of his desire to be accepted by his peers and fellow Masons; and then they were outdoors, or rather she was outdoors alone, in a little close place of frozen ferns and ivy and mossy bricks, all rising around her like the walls of a well, to a spot of sky no bigger than the moon, a man's cut-out shadow at the top, gazing silently down, and she tried to scream for help and the silence that emerged from her locked throat must have been what woke her so suddenly—as her mind clears, she sees the horror in her hopeless social humiliated situation. She remembers walking beside Buchanan so that they seemed a pretty couple limned in a fine print of Lancaster, formerly Hickory Town, and she cannot believe, yet must believe, that such a promenade will never occur again, and they will nevermore cut such a dual figure together. All sorts of plausible visions—herself as mistress of his house, a house finer than any of her vulgar, bullying father's houses, with a more European accent to the furnishings, and volumes of French, Rousseau and Voltaire, in a glass-fronted bookcase, and willows on a wide lawn leading down a soft dusty road—have vanished, without a trace.

She must change. This damp chemise will be her death. Where are all the others? Philadelphia feels deserted. *But two / Of an enormous city did survive, / And they were enemies.* She remembers flannel nightgowns folded on a shelf in the cedar closet of this room. She pulls off her chemise and steps to the blue window, as naked in the fireless chamber as a Greek slave of marble, and looks down into the mossy garden; its forms are motionless, scribbled with shadows cast by moonlight, colorless. The room's cold hugs her bare body; her teeth chatter and her slender arms twitch of their own. Why has she been abandoned? Shouldn't some servant have lit a fire? Frost ferns have begun to sprout in the corners of the panes. She slips the flannel gown over her head, over her dark long hair, and chases herself back to bed, to its clammy sweated sheets of Irish linen, a dim shadow scrabbling at her bare feet. These toes, we have not seen them before, the pale ankles, straight and strait, fed by pale-blue veins. Her body is in its prime, a woman's still firm as a girl's, perfect in its anatomy though wracked in its nerves, which are the veins of her spirit.

Back in bed, shivering and giddy, she feels the languor of the anodyne come and go in her limbs, mingled with a growing depression and agitated sense of helplessness. Some impassable issue of pride, a pure image of herself now forever stained, has blocked her thoughts, bounced them back into her brain, the crackling ambit of her head, where split shadows begin to revolve again. What a peace it would make if she were to sleep forever! What a revenge upon the world that has cornered her in this narrow space: the crowds of contending vain wills that hem her in would as one grieve the sudden absence in their midst, an absence suddenly pure and irreproachable, beyond rebuke and change.

Repose in God's hands, the good doctor had directed. Ann tries to imagine giant hands beneath her, gently cupped, the creases visible as if lit by a throbbing firefly. Yet if God's hands were really there, would innocent children ever perish? Her sister Harriet, and her brother Thomas Bird at the age of two, and brothers Stephen and Robert dead as young men, all gone to their graves like small birds fallen stiff-winged in winter on gravel garden paths. All is as Lord Byron said, a *mad disquietude.* How did it go?—*the wild birds shriek'd / And, terrified, did flutter on the ground, / And flap their useless wings; the wildest brutes / Came tame and tremulous; and vipers crawl'd / And twined themselves among the multitude.* Since Christ died crying out against God on the cross men have tried to believe in eternal light but ere this century began the French anarchs let the darkness in, and Adams and Washington and Tom Paine, too, in rebelling against a king ruling by divine right. Though they build a new St. James of money and stone to replace the old the darkness is here to stay, it is our element, our punishment for wanting to be free, like Adam and Eve at the bidding of the viper.

How can she sleep with her mind in such a dismal storm? She thinks of the blessèd surcease sealed into the little cloudy bottle, its nipped-in neck and impish cork of a hat. Sleep without it seems an impossible deed, like a cork staying under the water, like the sleep of a man to be hanged in the morning. Tomorrow morning and all its rattling chain of days dragging thereafter menace her mind with a kind of thunder. This pummelling in her head is spreading through her frame, a terrible pulsing, a sick fire vibrating in her veins. Her legs feel hot, and keep moving restlessly on their own, while the room's growing cold assaults her face and sends her hands skittering back under the covers. Where are the servants? She can no longer hear the running brook of conversation from far downstairs. Sarah and the Hemphills—can they still be at the theatre? Is there no end of empty vain entertainment? She must be her own servant. *Twenty-five drops:* that much more Dr. Chapman had allowed. Triumphantly, like a traveller arriving at the end of her journey, Ann worries off the cork. But she is unable, on the high bedside stand, to find the doctor's glass dropper, though the teaspoon is there, glinting, long in its handle, like the whip in her dream. With trembling, shivering hands she pours a small amount into the spoon's shallow bowl. She tries to remember how full the spoon was at her first dose, and rather than administer too little she pours the laudanum, which has the viscidity of pear juice, until its glinting mound of liquid cohesion finds its limit at the spoon's edge. She wills her hand not to shake. The thrashing in her head, a circular beating of crow's wings of thought, continues. She greets again the taste of veiled bitterness, and sees the wry face she catches herself making, as if a mirror faces her from somewhere in the bedroom. She carefully replaces the spoon and lets her head sink back into the two pillows, stuffed with goosedown. Her body is hideous, she thinks, like a long sinuous animal with which she is engaged in a struggle, an octopus of veins dangling down from the deceptive dark jewels of the eyes, the high white forehead where God sets His kiss of divine likeness. We are Godlike in our brows, but the brows of cows are broader still. The Hin-

doos worship cows, she has read, and the British missionaries
cannot make them stop, with all their Bibles.

Impatiently she waits for the languorous well-being, the
quelling of the fire in her veins, the cutting of inner knots to
arrive; it is slow. The problem of Buchanan refuses to subside,
but keeps rising up like a painted figure on a spring, his head
performing that little twisting motion to adjust his imperfect
eye. She had him, he loved her, she loved him, she pushed him
away. The world seems all very mechanical. You push a thing
down, and something else pops up. Her thoughts become masculine, leading her down bypaths of reasoning like the strained
shouted arguments of two lawyers arguing in court, on and on,
to no purpose but increasing their fees. She must unite with her
fiancé, is the decision, and she will begin tomorrow by setting
into backwards motion her flight from Lancaster and the
breach of her engagement. At the same time, she must have
rest, or will be quite unable to perform, to organize her life on
its new basis of bravery and loyalty to her husband-to-be. The
back of her mouth has a film on it, a bubble of slime that tickles,
and that her coughing does not loosen. Her skull feels thin as
a blown egg. She lifts her head from its depression in the damp
nest of down and gazes upon the homunculus of the bottle. He
is her friend, her only attendant. His body of glass is cool, but
the handle of the spoon is strangely warm. She is more profi-
cient now in loosening the cork. She is generous with herself,
as those who have loved her—her father, her mother, her suit-
ors, her sisters—would want her to be. *Miraculous powers of
ease.* When the dilatory Abigail at last enters the room, or Meg
and Sally come back from the theatre babbling of gaslights,
Ann does not want to be awakened. She wishes to be alone
with the images her mind is making, intimate images like the
flickering of a snake's tongue in one of her sinuses. Dreams, it
is sleep's dreams we wish to reach, the deep free flowing of
their images, on the far side of an oblivion we dread to cross

and from which our nerves pull back like the horse whose strong stale Ann had scented.

Now the divine presence is manifesting itself; the giant hand is sensibly beneath her, even to the grain of its warm skin; everything is as it should be, bathed in a triumphant love that knows no interruption. The sun shines night and day, though our globe keeps turning its face into darkness. How marvellous, Ann reflects, that a fact so blazingly obvious—God's tireless inexhaustible love—should be hidden from us in all but a few moments of our earthly lives. Thus, chinks in the walls of a cellar admit stark evidence of day. *The expansion of the benigner feelings incident to opium,* Thomas De Quincey is writing across the sea at about this time, *is no febrile access, no fugitive paroxysm; it is a healthy restoration to that state which the mind would naturally recover upon the removal of any deepseated irritation from pain that had disturbed and quarrelled with the impulses of a heart originally just and good.* Goodness and the lucid perception of goodness fill Ann like a magic liquid poured into a woman-shaped flask, and then like iron gone solid in its motionless mold of sand and clay.

[*Retrospect* editors: feel free to delete or improve this passage, assuming you have the space to print it. It gave me much trouble. Had my book ever been completed and published, it would have given me more. The present tense forced itself upon me, as a way of drawing closer to Ann—the anti-historical tense of perpetual motion, of resurrection. The De Quincey quote may be a mistake, but one's instinct with these paper dolls is to pin them to the bulletin board with tacks of contemporaneous quotation. Dr. Chapman may owe too much to Shakespeare's prating apothecaries, but I decided to ride with it, gleaming philters and all. I would rather have done without dialogue entirely—it makes her sound too reasonable, too unhysterical—yet there *had* to have been voices around her in her crisis. Would Ann in fact have been alone long enough to take the laudanum? In Judge Kittera's paragraph there is a curious progression of time: *in the evening . . . After night . . . until midnight, when she died.* How many witnesses attended, as *her pulse gradually weakened*? People in history are more alone than we think—General Wolfe, for instance, died not in the midst of Benjamin West's panorama but over by a little bush in a corner of the battlefield, attended by a mere two men. How sadly alone Marilyn Monroe was in her dazed last days, for all her celebrity and lovers in high places! I worried a lot about the room temperature. How cold might it have been, indoors in Philadelphia on December 8th? Not as cold as New Hampshire, but not Southern, either. Wood fires, at any rate, and not coal? The Franklin stove in widespread use at the time? But perhaps not in bedrooms, especially guest bedrooms? And anent the chamber pot, which *had* to have been there—would she squat down to it, like Molly Bloom, or would it have been more discreetly placed, in the elegant town house of One-Speech Hemphill, in a cabinet commode? In the DAR's collection of period rooms in Washington, I have seen a chamber pot that moved in and out of a commode on little brass casters. As you can see, I preferred Ann simply to squat. The touch of cold on her skin brought her to life for me. I began to fall in love with her then. I felt the very closest to her in that glimpse of her blue-veined bare foot, arching to hop itself back into bed. That foot *had* to have been there, that night—or did they all wear socks, or knitted footwarmers, or moccasins imitated from the redmen? On the matter of nightgowns, I discovered that the first historical mention of one is in connection with Anne Boleyn, who didn't live to be old, either.* I mean, I can

---

*Even as I write, dear fellow New Hampshire historians, a young lady of our state, exactly Ann Coleman's last age of twenty-three, one Pamela Smart, a high-school media counsellor, has been indicted and convicted of seducing (with the aid of a videotape of *9½ Weeks*, described in *Halliwell's Film Guide*

taste that foot—skinny shapely foot with its ankle, intricately functional in its tendons and capillaries and twenty-six bones (see *Gray's Anatomy:* seven tarsal, five metatarsal, and three in each phalange, except for only two in the big toes, an odd modification that makes possible the *à pointe* position in classical ballet), the blind armies of cells all wanting to live and carry on in bonded league their functions for another fifty years. I love that blue-veined foot. Live, Ann! Rewrite history!!]

The melodramatic yet perversely vivid account quoted above [pages 61 ff. and 118] goes on, with serene inaccuracy, having established Buchanan in a Downingtown inn, where the feeble street lamps were beginning to glow: *It was not yet dark, and a funeral was passing, evidently for Lancaster. Buchanan looked at it idly. "Who is dead?" he asked. None of the idlers knew, but a man coming in from the street to refresh himself at the bar said that the procession had stopped further uptown, and that the undertaker had told him it was Ann Coleman, a Lancaster girl, who had died in Philadelphia while she was visiting friends.*

When he heard it Buchanan groaned and grew white, but stood motionless staring out of the window into the gathering night that shut the dark procession in dusky gloom.

---

as a "Crash course in hot sex for those who wish to major in such studies") a fifteen-year-old student with the successful aim of getting him and his thuggish pals to murder her husband. She remained impassive during her trial, but in a subsequent hearing, as her late husband's aggrieved father prolongedly hectored her from the witness stand, she jumped up and in her thrilling young voice exclaimed, "Your Honor, I can't handle this." We all saw it on television; one had to love her for it. Her utterance brings me as close as I am apt to get to the truth of Ann Coleman's conjectured and disputed suicide: Your Honor, she couldn't handle it.

AN ESPECIALLY CONFUSED MEMORY from the Ford years—
probably their second winter, to judge by the weather and a
certain weariness that had settled over the situation—concerns
a visit by my mother to my old mansard-roofed, shawl-
bestrewn house in Wayward, where Norma and my children
still held out, in my guilty mind's eye an embattled and tattered
band of defenders within a doomed fort. Somehow, the Queen
of Disorder, in her style of ingenuous dishevelment, had set it
up that my mother would spend some nights there but since
she was *my* mother I owed it to all of them to be there, too.
It all made sense, when she explained it to me, and made no
sense when I explained it to Genevieve, who was horrified and
indignant. Each woman's reasoning seemed irresistible when
I was within her gravitational field, and quickly evaporated
when I free-floated—when I was, say, driving across the concrete bridge between Adams and Wayward, or pondering a
discarded *Oui* in a Federal Street laundromat, amid the slosh
of a hundred soiled underpants.

The inconvenient family occasion must have been, I can
only think, my mother's eightieth birthday. She had been born
when Cleveland was President the second time. *I* had been
born when she was all of forty-one and long resigned to a
childless but not unfulfilling career as a small-town fourth-
grade schoolteacher and faithful helpmeet to my father, who
with his two relatively disreputable brothers owned and oper-
ated a feed-and-grain-and-hardware business in my tiny native
town of Hayes, Vermont, north of Montpelier and south of
Mount Elmore. She did the accounts and helped out behind
the counter on Saturdays, though of course she couldn't handle
the sacks of horse feed. It was still half a horsedrawn world
when I was born, and remained so until after 1945. In my little

corner bedroom, with its scorched brown wallpaper and round black stovepipe (which, passing through on its way from the kitchen to the roof, provided my only heat), I would wake and fall asleep to the drowsy *clipclop* of the farmers' wagons come down from the surrounding hills, where cows stood stiff-legged in rocky pastures steep enough to become ski slopes. A single gas station, with a variety of brands of gasoline offered in a rusty row of glass-headed pumps, served all the internal-combustion engines in town, and herds of sheep were sometimes driven up the main street, swamping wheeled traffic. People kept chickens and put up fruit preserves until the Fifties, when I went off south to Middlebury College. By then, New Yorkers buying up old farmhouses for summer retreats and ski chalets began to control the landscape. Still, the city folks needed hardware, too—power mowers and chain saws and bushwhackers instead of scythes and hay rakes. If hay sales fell off, the pet food picked up. My father did all right to the end, and died the same year as John Kennedy, suddenly, though not as suddenly. His heart had been giving him warnings and carried him off in the middle of a barn dance; he and my mother had been members of the Hayes and Calais Hoedown Association since they had been young marrieds. The last words he heard on earth were "Do-si-do your partner." A beautiful marriage, and precocious, timorous I its single, unhoped-for fruit. Looking back on myself from the perspective of mid-life rebellion, I saw an elderly sort of child, dutiful but allergic to animals and ragweed and fond of huddling indoors next to my hot stovepipe. My mother retired from teaching a few years before my father dropped dead, and kept on at the feed store a few years more, before my uncles, deep into drink and private debt, decided to sell out to a skimobile dealer from Burlington. When they and their wives retired with their loot to Florida she went with them, disappointing me considerably: I had assumed she was as much a part of Hayes as the welded cannonballs beside the Civil War monument, and would never leave my father to sleep alone through the snowbound winters beneath the two-toned (rough and polished granite) marker with its single CLAYTON and its two first names, Theodore and Elvira, the latter expectantly blank in its terminal digits.

She had now been a widow for a dozen years. Up north, she had been as comfortably fat as an Eskimo, and at first Florida, where eating is the main physical recreation, had fattened her even further; she had grown paradoxically pale in the clammy, murmurous shelter of air-conditioned apartments. But now the anorexia of old age had whittled away some of the soft excess of those early retirement years, and her tint had become the glassy yellow-gray of the hardened tropical white; her Northern skin had acquired in Florida a lizardlike texture, deeply wrinkled nowhere but finely granulated all over.

If this was indeed her eightieth-birthday party, there must have been candles, and crêpe-paper hats and poppers, and shy little presents purchased on adolescent budgets and loosely wrapped by fumbling fingers. My mother's mountain dryness and her schoolteacherish airs had repelled the children when they were younger—they had preferred my father's false-front spirit of fun, the beady-eyed back-at-you boosterism of a small-town merchant. But with him gone over a decade, and me gone over a year, my three children had warmed to her, as a relic of a lost Norman Rockwell type of family. Her living so long seemed to acquire the selfless motive of sustaining their rôles as grandchildren, while an absent father and absent-minded mother had undermined their status as children.

"No, I have no idea why I've lived so long," let us suppose she said, in response to the obvious question from one of the children, probably the wide-eyed Daphne. She would have been pushing thirteen by now, and Buzzy still fourteen, and Andrew a year into his driver's license. He had driven to the airport in Boston to pick her up, and I was to drive her back the day after tomorrow, the length of her stay having been forced upon us by the terms of her economy plane ticket. Three days of family make-believe without so much as a glimpse of my real and perfect mate. My mother's presence lay heavy across my chest. She knew only that Norma and I were having "difficulties" and that I, like a fourth-grader running off to a corner of the schoolyard to get away from the other children, had moved across the river. " 'Too mean to die,' they used to say when I was a girl," she said.

"Oh *no!*" came the *pro forma* protest, as with shaky but practiced and determined hands she served up pieces of cake, using the slender palette knife that, in the disorder of my legal wife's kitchen, was the closest thing to a cake server.

"Oh *yes,*" my mother insisted to us, "and I even know *why* I'm so mean. When I was a little girl, I had this hair down to my waist, what they call chestnut, with a touch of red in it but nothing like as red as your mother's, and *my* mother used to do it all up every morning in these long, long braids that she would then wind around my head and fix with pins so tight I would go around all day feeling as if my scalp was going to lift right off my head. It *hurt.*"

The children abruptly laughed, at the prod of that last word.

"Didn't you ever tell your mother it hurt?" Buzzy asked. He was the most open of the children, the most—it hurt me to see—trustingly inquisitive. Andrew had his gathering armature of male equipment—his license and rock tapes, and girlie magazines and cigarettes tucked not quite out of sight in his room—and Daphne still had some cocoon of hopeful childish ignorance, but Buzzy had nothing to protect him from the facts of the world. Or do I mean to say that there was nothing to deflect my pained identification with him?

"Oh, I wouldn't have *dared,*" my mother asserted, "because that was the way people *did* things. When I was a little girl, people did things one way only, or they were driven *out*—they would leave and go to Ohio, or Michigan, or Montana, where it didn't matter what they did. They never came back." Behind her eyeglasses, whose frames, in Florida style, were shaped, of several glittering ersatz substances, to suggest butterfly wings, her reptilian old eyes went round in mock alarm, and her audience of children laughed half in fright.

> An' the Gobble-uns 'll git you
>> Ef you
>>> Don't
>>>> Watch
>>>>> Out!

went the refrain of a poem she used to read her fourth-graders, with just this expression on her face. "In my day," she concluded, "suffering was thought to be *good* for people."

Her discourse was aimed, I felt, at me. The Claytons didn't do things like run away from their families, even only a mile away. There had never been a divorce among the Claytons, or in her family, the Heebes: I had heard her say this often. And yet there was, too, in her discourse an undercurrent of forgiveness, a certain playful softness. Florida had made her more sociable than when my father had done enough socializing for two, and more tolerant. She watched television, its shameless talk shows and raunchy serials; she heard the horror stories of her fellow senior citizens, the tales of modern life. Rampant divorce, cohabitation without benefit of marriage rites, unapologetic homosexuality, promiscuous communes. Loyalty to spouse a joke, loyalty to nation a scandal. And now her son gone under to the tide of endless wanting. It was not in me to explain the paradox: I was leaving this marriage as a tribute to marriage, to create a perfect marriage. Not the most uxorious Methodist deacon in Hayes would be a stricter adherent of the old vows, once I got the right wife. I was a fervent supporter of marriage, just not of *my* marriage, my present marriage. In the meantime, there I sat, my own family's black sheep, being gently teased.

"Was that the way Daddy was as a little boy?" asked Daphne, her cheeks made rosy by surfeit of cake and candlelight. "Bad?"

"Why, *no,*" my mother emphatically proclaimed, directing her rounded stare down through the candlelight, where I sat in the place of a fourth child, she and Norma having taken the heads of the table. "He was a *good* boy, all the neighbors agreed. They seemed surprised, because I had *not* been thought to be a good girl—I couldn't explain how my braids had been pulling at my scalp and making me *wild.* I called your daddy my miracle child," my mother went on, "because, as you know, he came into being long after such a thing was thought seemly." Here her age had betrayed her language into an awkward quaintness; she swiftly read puzzlement on the faces of her audience of children and like a good schoolteacher clarified: "I was forty-one when he was born. His father and I were so afraid"—here she laughed, exposing the touching perfection of her dentures—"oh dear, the things people didn't know in those years, we were just bundles of superstition; we were afraid that because we weren't so young little Alfred would turn out weak and frail in his body. But look at him—a year short of forty and except for a gray hair here and there he could be your older brother!" They all admired me; I could even feel, in the corner of my vision, the Queen of Disorder turning her abstracted face toward me, where she sat at my elbow, at the head of the table I had deserted. "He used to suffer so with his asthma," my mother went on, rather piteously now, as if all at the table must share her maternal concern. "There were whole nights when his father and I took turns not sleeping, this poor child gasping like every breath might be his last; but the doctor said he'd outgrow it, and he has!" The children stared at me with amazement—a prize they had somehow lost. Andrew, I felt, felt sorry for me, being held up to view this way; a confluence of little painfulnesses led him to frown and avert his gaze downward, his brow dark under its straggle of uncombed, Seventies-length hair. I imagined him trying, through the interference of these other psyches, to strike with mine the solidarity of mature males, and yet being inwardly defeated by the undeniable insult of my defection. Or perhaps he was simply longing for a cigarette and a cruise in the Volvo, to check out what his pals were doing tonight.

My mother might have stopped talking if a child had spoken up, but none of us did, overwhelmed by the sore points her monologue touched, singing my praises. "Except he was always so mannerly, and responsible, and even kind to animals. In that way, it may be, your daddy was a fragile child. He used to come home in tears from watching the other boys and even some of the girls do the things children do—pull the legs off grasshoppers, and torture frogs with matches and such."

I wondered if that was my bond with Buchanan—a helpless standing by, while vitality performed its wanton deeds.

"And he *never* made the least bit of trouble for his father and me—got such good marks, and helped out in the store since when he was no higher than the counter top. We used to say sometimes it was as if we were the children, and this boy the grown-up. Honestly."

It was true, one of my first impressions had been that my parents, being so much older than the parents of my friends, shouldn't be tested with the usual childish unruliness, lest they sicken and cease to shelter me. My instinctive attitude to the whole world, struck in infancy, might be described as over-solicitous. Or conceited—imagining that everyone depended on me for happiness.

Was it a trick of vision, or was Norma's pale blur of a face stuck in the corner of my eye, fixed in contemplation of me,

seen afresh by my mother's adoring light? The old lady had at
last wound down, and lifted a forkful of birthday cake to her
open mouth. With a self-conscious scrape in his throat Andrew
pushed back to leave the table; his younger brother imitated the
gesture. Daphne's bright eyes dimmed and her rosy cheeks
paled as she realized the storytelling was over, taking with it
the warm illusion of a family intact through the generations.
Norma's face jumped alarmingly nearer the corner of my eye
and in a whisper insisted, "Talk to Buzzy; he's been getting
terrible school reports."

Then, how eerie it was, not to leave the house, with apologies
spoken and unspoken, but to stay, as if I were my younger,
monogamous self's ghost. While my mother finished her cake
and Norma lit a cigarette and poured herself another dab of
white wine, I helped Daphne clear the dishes, and in the kitchen
loudly admired a streaky watercolor of a horse she had painted,
pinned to the refrigerator door with magnets that looked just
like cookies—Oreos and, especially convincingly, chocolate
chips. She had begun to take riding lessons at a stable in the next
town, toward Seabrook. What would girls that age do without
horses? Society's engines of sublimation and education were
still running in my absence, on reduced, one-parent fuel. Andrew called me outdoors to move my '69 Corvair, my unsafe
bachelor chariot, so he could extricate from the driveway what
had become his and Norma's '72 Volvo. I went out without
putting on a coat; I shivered and told him, "Don't stay out late."

"I won't," he said, as if I still had some authority over him.
Our breaths made manly barks of vapor in the night air, there
by the massed brittle-leaved rhododendrons and the slanting
cellar bulkhead. The cellar was especially thick with guilt for
me, as if all my derelict household duties had settled there,
gathering dust and rust.

"How—" My breath hung suspended. "How is everybody
doing, do you think?"

He knew what I meant. "O.K.," he said. "We're adjusting."

His phrase put a chill into me, through the thickness of my cotton shirt. Was I adjusting, too? When big fingers came and pulled off the grasshopper's legs, did I merely shrug and smile now? Was I taking my revenge, at last, for all that premature tender-heartedness?

"Don't worry about it, Dad," Andrew told me. "Everything's cool. What a man's gotta do, he's gotta do. At least you're still around. Some of my friends' dads have cleared right out."

"It's a sad world," said I, feebly.

Andy, too, was underdressed for the cold, in the high-school baseball team's little green windbreaker (he played second base for the JVs), and he beat his arms across his chest, so his voice came out jiggling. "It's lonelier for Buzzy and Daphne; they can't get out yet, they're pretty much stuck with Mom after school. But they'll grow up, they'll get over it."

"They will?" It came out as a question, not an affirmation. "How about your mother? Lonely for her, too?"

I had worked myself up into wanting all the hard answers. What if the Gobble-uns did get me?

The boy looked away. "She gets out now and then. Dad, I got to run."

"She does? Where does she go? Who with?"

"Beats me. Some jerk or other. They're all odious."

This was a parting shot; we hung there, wondering if we should kiss, and decided against it. The Volvo door slammed. We had bought that station wagon the year of Nixon's landslide because it somehow showed you were a liberal, against Vietnam and for abortion and conservation, but it had always seemed to me to give a bumpy ride and mediocre mileage. I didn't miss it.

Back inside the house, I visited my mother where she had settled with a black cup of coffee—no decaf or watery herbal brew for her—in the library. She seemed small, huddled in the wing chair bought secondhand in Central Square in Cambridge, with its silvery-blue velvet worn white where my head and wrists had rubbed off all the nap. She was shrinking; her hands were packages of bones wrapped in mottled paper. All around her stood my old books, left over from college and graduate school, packed and unpacked and repeatedly arranged by me in orderly rows. Trevelyan and the Beards and Gibbon and Churchill, *Europe Since Napoleon* by Thomson and *History of Japan* by Sansom, *The Medieval Mind* by Taylor in two volumes and also in two *The Growth of the American Republic* by Morison and Commager—stately volumes bound in stamped cloth of ivy green or navy blue, word-palaces of whose contents I had retained little but the confidence that, if needs be, I could again tread the maze and find the chamber where the necessary information would be waiting like the gilded treasures encased in a seldom-visited, sleepily guarded museum room. Paperbacks like Cash's *The Mind of the South* and Braudel's *Capitalism and Material Life 1400–1800* varied with their livelier spines the chronological logic of the rows. Already, especially where my Buchanan project had plucked some volumes and left gaps, anomalous books had drifted in— the paperback mysteries the Queen of Disorder would read in bed, and slick-jacketed novels by Anne Tyler and Barbara Pym and Lois Gould, and alien tutelary tomes such as *What to Listen for in Music*, by Aaron Copland, and *A History of Western Music*, by one Donald Jay Grout, presumably left over from her involvement with the affable Ben Wadleigh. I itched to edit and rearrange these shelves, but I was not ready to replace what I had taken, nor were the books left mine to touch.

I said to my mother, with false cheer, "How're you holding up? Not every day a body turns eighty."

"Thank the Lord. I hope He doesn't afflict me with too many more birthdays."

"Don't *say* that, Mother. The children were enchanted to-night—we all were—by your liveliness, your wit, your gift of recall. Though you didn't have to work so hard selling my virtues; they don't need to be sold, they'd *like* to have me back."

"Norma, too?"

"Sure. At least I assume so." I had never doubted it—was there room to doubt?

"Well, then, what's the problem?"

"*I'm* the problem. I like it out there, out of this house. I'm moving my Buchanan book along at last. I'm getting my"—in the Ford era, though much was permitted, one didn't say "shit" to one's octogenarian mother—"act together."

Perhaps if I had said "shit" it would have brought us to a new level of frankness and intimacy. But Vermont proprieties still ruled our relationship, and she was feeling the weight of her eighty years. My mother sighed and said, "That Buchanan. I never knew anybody had a good word to say for him until you took him up. He tried to ship the whole country south, Republican gospel had it when I was a girl."

"A totally unfair charge," I said. "He tried to hold the country together was his only sin. But we New Englanders finally got our way, Mom. We got our war." I saw she wasn't following this, and told her, "Go to bed whenever you're ready. I have to go say good night to Buzzy."

As I climbed the familiar stairs, with its pair of creaking landings, I could hear Norma singing to Daphne, sweetly, if not as sweetly as Genevieve to her two daughters. A mezzo versus a coloratura. *A History of Western Music:* that rankled. Possibly the Wadleighs had reconstituted their marriage on the then-fashionable "open" basis. Wendy had come calling on me once or twice in the year past, letting one thing lead to another, and I had flattered myself that she was cheating on Ben; if he knew of these visits, it became, repulsively, as if I were fucking him, too. Sex is always to some extent group sex. *Odious,* in Andrew's sudden heartfelt word.

But Buzzy's room still had the pre-sexual aura—the posters of foreign cars and fighter planes, the plastic dinosaurs arranged in a row, the telescope trained upward out the window at the lifeless moon and inviolate stars, the smell of glue, of collecting and making, the smell the universe has when it is new to us. "Hi."

"Hi." His room was dark and he was already in bed. His voice came out of the darkness deeper than I remembered it.

"How's it going, fella?"

"O.K."

"Really?" Taking care not to kick over the telescope on its tripod, I made my way through his hobby-crammed room to his bed and sat on the edge. "Your mother told me you've been getting some bad reports at school. That shouldn't happen to you. You're smart."

Blue light from the winter night outside rested on his profile, with its short nose flattened at the bridge like a baby's; his hair, which in my mind's eye remained fixed at a crewcut he had had at age six and that made his head look round as a ball, in fact was quite long, like a Rolling Stone's, and in its greasy length rather repulsive. He could have been an untidy girl, but for his deep voice. "I'm not so smart."

"What makes you say that?"

He turned his face toward me; his babyish profile vanished. "At school, when we read, I can tell the other kids are getting more out of it than I am. And they're quicker."

"Really?" It was hard to come down out of my own exalted preoccupations—the sublime sex with Genevieve at the still center of our scandal, the obscure doom that gathered around black-haired, hot-blooded Ann Coleman one night late in

1819—and enter into the difficult small world of this male child, but I must, I must. "When have you last had your eyes checked?"

"A while ago. He said the right eye was sort of sleepy and maybe the next time I should get a prescription."

"Well, then," I said, too briskly. "We'll get you a prescription."

"Glasses'll make me look dumb," Buzzy protested.

"You'll only have to wear them when you read."

"Yeah." Dear child, thus quickly and meekly he had accepted the embarrassment of glasses, of a yoke slipped onto his face. Yet, braver and more realistic than I, he did not give up on his basic point. "I can see the words O.K., it's that they don't add up in my head—they're like scrambled."

"Well, there's such a thing as dyslexia, maybe we should have you tested. Some people's brains reverse the letters; it has nothing to do with general intelligence."

He respectfully considered this palliation I was offering him, but insisted, "I'm not smart. Andrew is smart. He gets things right away. Daphne, too, even though she's a girl. Not that that makes any difference." In the Ford era, it should in fairness be admitted, genuine attitudinal progress was being made against racism and sexism, especially in the minds of the middle-class young.

"You've always seemed smart to me," I told Buzzy. "All your collections and interests. You've always gotten good grades. Not top, but good." I, my mother would have been the first to proclaim, had always gotten top grades. And where had they brought me? To postgraduate work in adultery and child neglect.

"Until last year," he said. "Until the seventh grade, and now the eighth. You haven't been around."

He meant it mildly, factually, but it stunned me. The moonlight blue on the shreds of snow in the yard, seen through the twigs at Buzzy's window. A sense of gentle endless falling. A deeply serious wound in things which the world usually conspires to let us ignore. I had to say it: "Do you think that's the reason? Because I'm not here? If I came back, do you think you could concentrate on your reading better?"

He was quick to excuse me. "Naa. I don't think that much about it any more. A lot of the kids' parents have broke up."

"That's like saying everybody's starving makes your own stomach feel full." He smiled at this, I could see. My eyes had grown accustomed to the dark of his room. Forms had shapes, rounded into being by crescents of bluish light. "Buzzy," I said, "I'm sorry. Your mother and I—what can I say? We're trying to work things out for the rest of our lives. We both love you a lot. I feel rotten about this, rotten all the time."

"It has nothing to *do* with you, Dad. It's *my* problem."

His voice sounded stern, even. "Oh, baby." I wanted to rest my head on his chest, but distrusted the melodramatic impulse. Why should he, with everything else weighing on him, have to pity me? "You're so brave to say that. We'll get some tests done, and see if there's anything wrong with your reading skills." The academic phrase made me hear that I was copping out. He had raised a serious issue, he was trying to face a limit to his life, a something like death, and I should address it with him, this one night when I was here in the house again as an occupant. "There's different kinds of smartness," was all I could think to say. "You can be very sensitive and intuitive and artistic and not do very well on academic tests. Lots of great people, like Einstein and Edison, didn't do well at school. Not that I'm saying you won't do well; it's just there's more to life than school. None of us are as smart as we'd like to be, but what can you do? If we were smarter, we wouldn't be us."

He saw that I had done my best, that my vial of consolation had been emptied. "O.K.," he said, excusing me to go, and added, "Maybe I've just been being lazy. The stuff they have you read is so dumb, *Animal Farm* and like that, showing how lousy Communism is."

"I'm sure that's it," I said, rising in relief, he having found the way out for me. "Don't be lazy," I could say now. "Give your teachers a chance. They're people, too. They're trying. We're all in this together."

Together in this pitiful world, I meant. I had meant to say good night to Daphne, but her door was closed and no light showed beneath it. Downstairs, I said to Norma in the pantry, where she was pouring herself some vermouth, "Poor guy, I can't stand it. I've fucked up his head."

"Oh, don't be so self-centered."

"That's what *he* told me. But you're both just being sweet. Where's my mother?"

"Gone up. I had to steer her toward the stairs. She's in terrific shape, really, but then suddenly she's just had it."

"Me, too. I'm shaking. I feel so bad for Buzzy, so helpless. Let's get him some dyslexia tests."

"He's had them. Less than two years ago. They said he was fine. Have you really forgotten?"

"I can't remember everything. Let's get him tested again, and at least get him glasses, for Christ's sake. What kind of goof-off parent are you, anyway? Andy says you're out every night with jerks."

She looked at me oddly, coolly, as if I were shouting to get her attention. "He did not," she said. She was sure of him, she lived with him, I didn't. "He wouldn't say any such thing. You seem upset. How about a slosh?"

The ceiling of the pantry was very low and the overhead light pressed on our heads, carving downward shadows on our faces. Norma didn't wear lipstick, her lips were the same pale flesh as her chin and as the fingers holding up to her lips the glass of pale-green fluid. The only time she had ever had her hair done in a beauty parlor had been on a boat we took to

Europe the summer before she became pregnant with Andy, and the spray-set beehive made her so self-conscious she couldn't rest until she had swum it away in the ship's pool. Her lips in the harsh overhead light were colorless cushions of slightly cracked flesh. Her freckles this time of year had faded. There were areas—the nape of her neck, and the insides of her upper arms, and the sub-buttock sections she bared when opening her legs to me—where freckles never appeared. "Want to try out your old bed?" she lightly asked, glancing away from me toward a corner of the pantry shelves, where the dustiest teacups rested.

I did, but said, "Come *on*, Norma. I can't do it to her."

"You did it to me. *Are* doing it."

"After many a year. And it's not right. I'm trying to make everything right, let's just move on. Let me go back across the river. I'll be back here again in time for breakfast, I promise."

The Queen of Disorder in her artistic insouciance rarely became angry, but when she did, it frightened me. Her eyes, the color of her vermouth, suddenly developed red rims, and her lips tightened so the cracks in them doubled in number. "*No*, damn it. She's *your* mother, you stay here with her. I'll go to bed alone like I always do. Your virtue, if that's what it is, is safe with *me*, buster."

In haughty silence, her cheeks mottled with rage as my mother's hands had been mottled with age, she showed me to my room—her studio, a large space we had made of two small maid's rooms by breaking down the wall between them, early in the years of our ownership. I had been a jolly householder back then, friend to the sledgehammer and the plasterer's hawk. The space now was given over to Norma's painting and paintings; the walls, loaded with canvases, supported along the baseboards additional leaning sheaves, thick as collapsed dominoes, few of the paintings finished but all of them containing some passages of feathery offhand rightness, these areas often away from the

center, where she had worked less intensely. Where she concentrated, the paint got heavy and stiff. Some of the paintings
were fruit-and-vegetable still lifes, their subjects overtaken by
organic rot, and others showed vistas seen from the house, often
with the mullions of the window included, like the bars of a
cage. A few—relatively very few—were of the children,
painted unsmiling, with severed feet and uncompleted arms,
and two or three had taken up a new subject, Norma herself,
beheld in a mirror, wearing that furtive three-quarters glance
self-portraits have, whether by Van Gogh or Velázquez. It must
have been hard for her, who was always looking away, to gaze
steadfastly into her own evasive eyes. One canvas, painted
presumably in the summer, showed her nude from the waist
up—from a little below the waist, actually, though the pearly
blank of her lower belly, its glow built of the most ephemerally
faint blues and blue-greens and diluted ochres, was unfinished.
Even if she had finished, her pubic bush would have fallen
below the edge of the canvas. The whole room smelled strongly
of oils and turps. Though in so many ways relaxed, Norma had
been ever shy of my face between her legs, because of her smell;
but this more powerful smell bloomed wherever she painted.
My bed was to be an old airfoam-slab sofa left over from the
Kirkland Street apartment, *circa* 1960. Newer acquisitions of
furniture had chased it in here, where the cats and dogs used it
as a bed while their mistress painted and sipped her afternoons
away, into the dimness of dusk. Its rough gray fabric was
covered with animal hairs, as if to weave a second cloth; for the
night it had been made up in starchy lemon-colored sheets and
some old blankets fragrant, I discovered when I lay down upon
my narrow pallet, of mothballs.

I could not sleep. This I do remember. The sound of my
estranged wife's feet, first in shoes and then without, over my
head in our old bedroom, and the nostalgic pungence of her oily
paints all around me kept me awake with erotic possibilities

unseized and all the more attractive for that. I must have mastur-
bated, trying to be tidy and quiet about it, though the little
screwed-in tapered legs of the sofa had a distinct wobble and
squeak. The household animals, barred from a space they could
usually include in their roamings, mewed and rubbed and
scratched outside the closed door, and only reluctantly padded
away. The radiators, responding to the melancholy tidal sough-
ing of the furnace below, ticked and gurgled in a way to which
I had become unaccustomed. Around eleven-thirty, Andrew
came home, the Volvo in the driveway as loud as a gravel-
crusher, and his ransacking of the kitchen for a final snack as
tumultuous as the raid of an army platoon. Then, as the inhabitants of the house settled and the thermostat bid the furnace be
quiet, my room with its many windows grew chilly. Like Ann
Coleman, I wanted the servants to come and build a fire. There
were no shades on the tall staring panes and the moonlight fell
in in plangent rectangles. An owl down in the woods by the
river issued its sickly interrogative call, like some luminous
ectoplasm lumpily pouring. The sleep of the others in the
house, three generations all tied to me and all emotionally
deprived on my account, pressed down upon me as I gingerly
and then furiously twisted between the rumpling sheets and
sought harmony with the pillow, softer and flatter than the two
back in my shabby but accustomed rooms in Adams.

After an hour or two I found that not only could I not sleep,
I could not breathe. The wealth of animal hair and dander under
my nose had reawakened my childhood asthma. To those aller-
gens were added stabs of local unsilence (floor creaks, contraction in the cooling and heating system, scurries of nocturnal
rodentia in the walls, not to mention the whispers and muf-
fler-snorts of belated traffic from the winding streets of Wayward as our great honeycomb of nubile females dismissed its last
drones) and a panicked sense of *being in the wrong place*, of being
dirt as defined above [page 87]. The harder I tried to suck in

breath, the harder this normally unconscious feat became. My spine seemed to be closing with my sternum like the chamber walls in that horror-story of Poe's. Absurdly, in my panic and chilly sweat, I found myself reminded, speaking of dirt in the wrong place, of Jennifer Arthrop's visit a year before and wanted to fuck her, to finish the scene another way, a way that seemed more fitting than her awkward exit, and did so, in my head, while my hand performed wonders on my disbelieving, drowsy prick and my lungs, momentarily self-forgetful, supplied oxygen to my agitated organism.

But once the little bliss of ejaculation (and what a curious bliss it is—like turning a somersault, it seemed to me as a boy, or like meeting a giant in a narrow mountain tunnel where he has to hunch—a somehow *icy* sensation, in tight-knit adolescence) was the second time achieved, my respiratory distress returned, so badly I had to get out of bed, wrapping a mothbally blanket about me, and walk around the room inspecting Norma's paintings by cobalt-blue moonlight. Around three, exhausted and breathless to the point of insanity, I tiptoed forth and crept up the complaining stairs and down the long hall to my former bedroom. Its door was ajar, and I stood in its maw for a minute, listening to the rasp of my wife's deep sleep, sensing the infrared blob of her body warmth, but then thought of Genevieve, similarly asleep in another de-husbanded cell of our community, and wondered really what Norma could do for me at this point, self-drained as I genitally was, and self-exempted from restful wedlock. I made my way back downstairs, snubbing with a barefoot kick the wagging, purring advances of the awakened animals, and closed my door in the hope that my ghostly excursion would have quieted my spirit enough for it to squeeze past my laboring lungs into sleep. But it had not. My breathing got worse; my bones ached in an invisible bear-hug. I began to fear I really might smother— s(Mother), to deconstruct the crisis a little. Her presence, though unconscious, beneath this roof threw onto my moral condition a starker northern light than was usually shed among the friendly obfuscations of the college environment, where we all stood pre-acquitted by the great liberations of Rousseau, Nietzsche, Freud, and Marx, who to such universal amazement and relief had shifted villainy from the individual to the society. Not that my mother, herself an exile from the cozy simplicities of Hayes, was overtly judgmental; it was *her in me* that was condemning me to be garrotted, the traditional Spanish penalty for robbery, for being caught in the wrong house. I later tried to transfer my sensations of suffocating moral impossibility onto Ann Coleman, in a composition already quoted, and so have perhaps included enough about them in this semi-solicited bundle of memories, impressions, and aborted history.

After four o'clock, moving with the slow-motion efficiency of a zombie, I pantingly dressed myself, slipped from the darkened house into my dormant Corvair, and beneath a setting gibbous moon drove through unpopulated streets across the empty bridge to the hospital in Adams, lit up on its urban hillside like a sinking ship. Gasping, joking, bathing myself in humiliation as a chicken bathes in dust, I was processed by the night nurse and a poor unshaven interne in rumpled green scrubs. His giant yawns displayed a mouth of healthy yellow molars. He gave me a shot of adrenaline and, when my breathing had miraculously returned to the realm of possibility, a quite unnecessary EKG, the chilly gel of whose electric contacts I took to be his punishment for my waking him.

Released, I took in the view of spired Adams and inhaled God's misty air. The moonless dawn held a surprisingly busy stir of early traffic. I drove back to Wayward in time to share a cup of coffee with my mother, an early riser. I had picked up some doughnuts at a just-opening Korean bakery on Federal Street, and she was old-fashioned enough to see them as a delicacy and not a hazard to her health. She was all sympathy and fine fettle, as if my night of misery had restored her to active motherhood.

The groggy day crept by. I realized I had, by an underground procedure, passed from Norma's troubled realm to my mother's more ancient queendom. She settled me upstairs in her room, the guest room, in her temporary bed, an old cherry fourposter I had once mistakenly bid for and won at an auction in White River Junction, when we were furnishing our first house, the apple-green Cape-and-a-half in Hanover. As the day progressed, my mother brought me toast and tea in the intervals of my dozing, and displayed me to my children as a man who had suffered enough. Propped up on pillows, books and teacups scattered around my knees, I lay on the high mattress with that curious elevated feeling, of hollow triumph, which a sleepless night bestows. When not attending to me, the old lady was conducting negotiations in the kitchen with Norma. In mid-afternoon my mother announced, "We've decided to move me over to Adams, to your place. It may be the last chance I'll ever have to spend a night in a bachelor's quarters." So as darkness returned I returned with the source of my being to grubby, comfy Adams.

And here, before driving her the next morning to Logan Airport and the plane back to Tampa, I gave her my bed, polluted by more than one partner, and slept in deep comfort on the futon, still redolent of Genevieve's dulcet dark-eyed little girls' guiltless slumbers. My mother, too, slept well for a change. "I never liked to complain," she said the next morning, "but Norma's housekeeping has always made me nervous. You never know what you'll find in the kitchen drawers, or what animal's going to jump into bed with you." This was, as directly as she could give it, her blessing on my leaving. Nothing in nature, not even the expansive force of water as it turns into ice, is as relentless as a mother's love for a son. We had had a good time the night before, dopey as I was; we warmed up two

Stouffer's TV dinners and laid in a fresh supply of cinnamon doughnuts, and sat up talking about the old days in Hayes— nothing special, just the streets themselves, house by house, store by store, and what had happened to the people, most of them dead or moved away by now, faces and names with a storybook quality for me, my first experience of humanity. The muscular ogres clanging metal down at the garage, the hunchbacked dwarf who ran the notions shop, the widow's evil eye at the lace window of the unpainted frame house. When between us we recovered a lost name, or pictured together an all-but-forgotten house or storefront, we would laugh with sheer joy, having defeated time. These exertions of remembering made my mother younger; animated expressions flitted down from a vanished Vermont and alighted, girlish migrants, upon her sallow, granulated Florida face.

Retrospect, I would reinvent our conversation and fill in more details, but this episode, once I convulse in my estranged wife's fragrant studio, kidnap my mother, and filially install her in my tawdry love nest, belongs outside our assigned venue, the Gerald Ford era—its impact, significance, and influence. My mother and I properly belong to the Roosevelt administrations, particularly the second term, in which I learned to talk and navigate three-dimensional space and developed my sense of a solitary self distinct from her warm, nurturing body. By the time of the 1938 Congressional elections, in which the Republicans (it is sometimes forgotten) gained seventy-five seats in the House and seven in the Senate, I had, under her guidance, with the help of a bottle whose rubber nipple tasted artificial and sour and whose milk was either too hot or too cold, given up suckling. That, and my exit from her womb the month before Landon awoke and found himself to be a loser, presumably fortified me for all the weanings with which life abounds. And yet, when my mother died in 1978, in the hopeful early reign of the evangelical engineer Carter, I was taken unaware by what a loss it was. Who now would remember me as a Keds-shod boy padding along the brick sidewalks of our tilted, maple-shaded downtown? Who was left to share cinnamon doughnuts with me as if they were, far from "junk food," a gourmet treat? The dear soul had left me alone with my eventual death. The dead teach this great lesson, which we are loathe to learn: we too will die.

THE REST [apropos of JB] is history. Buchanan heard the news of Ann Coleman's death not at some fabulized Downingtown inn but in the place where he usually was during the late months of 1819, at the Court House in Lancaster's Centre Square, tending to business. Earlier that week, while Ann was recovering, under the Hemphills' care, from her flight by carriage to Philadelphia, he had succeeded in getting an out-of-court settlement of the Columbia Bridge Company case. Klein tells us, *It was a great triumph for him.* Alas, Buchanan's patient life's many triumphs—he never lost an election, for instance, whether for Pennsylvania Assemblyman or for U.S. Congressman, Senator, and President—were destined to be bitterly qualified. For much of December 6th (a Monday) he had been at the prothonotary's office, writing four times, in the spidery legible hand that would not much change in the all but fifty years to come, the words *December 6th 1819. I agree that the amount of the above award shall be collected in three equal instalments from its date with interest; but that if any of the said instalments shall remain unpaid for Twenty days after it shall be due then execution may be issued for the amount of said instalment.* Signed by *Christ. Bachman,* significant party to this inscrutable action, and by *James Buchanan* as *Atty for Pltfs.* What a relatively smug and composed young maestro of finicking legal procedures it was who penned those words, not once but four times, as we can see on two facing pages of the large ledger of that year's transactions kept by the Lancaster Historical Society! Four days later, on December 10th, Buchanan was writing to Robert Coleman, Ann's formidable and now deeply wounded father, *My dear Sir:*

You have lost a child, a dear, dear child. I have lost the only earthly object of my affections, without whom life now presents to me a dreary blank. My prospects are all cut off, and I feel that my happiness will be buried with her in the grave. It is now no time for explanation, but the time will come when you will discover that she, as well as I, have been much abused. God forgive the authors of it. My feelings of resentment against them, whoever they may be, are buried in the dust. I have now one request to make, and, for love of God and of your dear, departed daughter whom I loved infinitely more than any other human being could love, deny me not. Afford me the melancholy pleasure of seeing her body before its interment. I would not for the world be denied this request.

I might make another, but, from the misrepresentations which must have been made to you, I am almost afraid. I would like to follow her remains to the grave as a mourner. I would like to convince the world, and I hope yet to convince you, that she was infinitely dearer to me than life. I may sustain the shock of her death, but I feel that happiness has fled from me forever. The prayer which I make to God without ceasing is, that I yet may be able to show my veneration for the memory of my dear departed saint, by my respect and attachment for her surviving friends.

May Heaven bless you, and enable you to bear the shock with the fortitude of a Christian.

I am, forever, your sincere and grateful friend,

James Buchanan

This letter was sent by messenger and refused at the door. Unopened, it found its way into what Curtis ceremoniously calls *the private depositaries at Wheatland;* thus it escaped the fire Buchanan's executors submissively imposed upon his other preserved memorabilia of the unhappy Ann Coleman affair [see pp. 73–4]. Our impression upon reading this heartbroken effusion is not entirely favorable; there are too many *dear*s in it, and rather too political a wish *to convince the world,* by marching in her funeral train. It is, however, a Romeo's lament compared with the other supposed document from Buchanan's pen in these thunderstruck days, an obituary that appeared in the Lancaster *Journal* on December 11th:

Departed this life, on Thursday morning last, in the twenty-third year of her age, while on a visit to her friends in the city of Philadelphia, Miss Anne C. Coleman, daughter of Robert Coleman, Esquire, of this city. It rarely falls to our lot to shed a tear over the mortal remains of one so much and so deservedly beloved as was the deceased. She was everything which the fondest parents or fondest friend could have wished her to be. Although she was young and beautiful, and accomplished, and the smiles of fortune shone upon her, yet her native modesty and worth made her unconscious of her own attractions. Her heart was the seat of all the softer virtues which ennoble and dignify the character of woman. She has now gone to a world where in the bosom of her God she will be happy with congenial spirits. May the memory of her virtues be ever green in the hearts of her surviving friends. May her mild spirit, which on earth still breathes peace and good-will, be their guardian angel to preserve them from the faults to which she was ever a stranger—

" 'The spider's most attenuated thread
Is cord, is cable, to man's tender tie
On earthly bliss—it breaks at every breeze.' "

The quotation, in its curious double quotation marks, is unattributed but comes from Young's much-loved *Night Thoughts* (comp. 1742–45). The printer's devil from the *Journal*'s office, sent for the copy, recalled finding Buchanan *so disturbed by grief that he was unable to write the notice.* Lancaster in the wake of Ann* Coleman's death was swept by talk of her suicide and of Buchanan's culpability: *I believe that her friends now look upon him as her Murderer,* Hannah Cochran wrote to her husband on December 14th. Buchanan had taken refuge with Judge Walter Franklin, whom he had three times defended from impeachment, and who, in this fiercely small world, lived next to the Colemans' house on East King Street. Some think that Franklin wrote the obituary, Buchanan being too *disturbed by grief.* There is a florid touch to it, an upward reach, which does not seem quite like our earthbound hero, his imagination flattened like the "J" of his unvarying signature. In the obituary's notion that for all the smiles of fortune her native modesty *made her unconscious of her own attractions,* something actual in the case strives to break through; Curtis, who knew people who knew Ann, says that she was described to him *as a very beautiful girl, of singularly attractive and gentle disposition, but retiring and sensitive.* She was shy; was she also, as the Pennsylvania Dutch put it, "queer," that is, anti-social? We can no more easily conceive of Ann happy with congenial spirits in the bosom of God than Ann happy among the bucolic busybodies of old Lancaster. She resists, in the mind's eye, community. In the portrait of her that hangs in Buchanan's bedroom at Wheatland, her long nose seems willful, her wide stare not inviting, her one stray curl a touch distraught. Those born rich are harder to please than those born poor; Buchanan

---

*The obituary says "Anne," but the tombstone has it "Ann." I have chosen the name writ in stone.

all his long life acted delighted to be here, here in this vale of tears, a born crony and ballroom flirt, tickled to be consorting with his fellow mortals, be they the Czarina of Russia or the black barber in Lancaster who pronounced in eulogy, *Why, sir, he didn't know what it was to give a rough answer to man, woman, or child.* A humble pleasure in human society: it is an absurdity that tends to promote life, like a belief in God. Buchanan had it, and Ann didn't; in this they were like the fish and the bird of the fable who fell in love.

Hannah Cochran, in the same letter in which she reported that Buchanan was being called *Murderer,* tells her husband, *After Mr. Buchanan was denied his requests, he secluded himself for a few days and then sallied forth as bold as ever. It is now thought that this affair will lessen his Consequence in Lancaster as he is the whole conversation of the town.* However, he soon left town, presumably finding refuge with his family in Mercersburg; in a letter of December 20, 1819, Amos Ellmaker wrote him *to speak of the awful visitation of Providence that has fallen upon you, and how deeply I feel it. The thought of your situation has scarcely been absent from my mind ten days. I trust your restoration to your philosophy and courage, and to the elasticity of spirits natural to most young men. Yet time, the sovereign cure of all these, must intervene before much good can be done. The sun will shine again—though a man enveloped in gloom always thinks the darkness is to be eternal. Do you remember the Spanish anecdote? A lady, who had lost a favorite child, remained for months sunk in sullen sorrow and despair. Her confessor, one morning, visited her, and found her, as usual, immersed in gloom and grief. "What!" says he; "have you not forgiven God Almighty?" She rose, exerted herself, joined the world again, and became useful to herself and friends.* Ellmaker went on to advise, *I say to give full vent and unrestrained license to the feelings and thoughts natural in the case for a time—which time may be a week, two weeks, three weeks, as nature dictates—without scarcely a small effort during that time*

*to rise above the misfortune; then, when this time is past, to rouse,
to banish depressing thoughts, as far as possible, and engage most
industriously in business.*

For the elections of 1820, the Federalists of Lancaster needed
a candidate for the national Congress, and settled on Buchanan. Years later, in London, conversing with Samuel L. M.
Barlow, the same who was to advise Curtis to suppress most
of what he knew about the Coleman event, Buchanan gave his
willingness to run a coloring of diffidence and personal need·
*I never intended to engage in politics, but meant to follow my
profession strictly. But my prospects and plans were all changed by
a most sad event which happened at Lancaster when I was a young
man. As a distraction from my great grief, and because I saw that
through a political following I could secure the friends I then
needed, I accepted a nomination.* Yet he conducted the campaign
with vigor enough to win this ugly chastisement in a published
letter signed "Colebrook," in allusion to his recent tragedy if
not in actual identification of one of Ann's brothers: *Allow me
to congratulate you upon the notoriety you have acquired of late.
Formerly the smoothness of your looks and your habitual professions of moderation had led those who did not know you to suppose
you mild & temperate.*

The words italicized in the preceding pages constitute virtually all the surviving contemporary texts reflecting upon the
sudden death of Ann Caroline Coleman and James Buchanan's
behavior in the aftermath. The texts are like pieces of a puzzle
that only roughly fit. There are little irregular spaces between
them, and through these cracks, one feels, truth slips. History,
unlike fiction and physics, never quite jells; it is an armature
of rather randomly preserved verbal and physical remains
upon which historians slap wads of supposition in hopes of the
lumpy statue's coming to life. One of the joys of doing original
research is to observe how one's predecessor historians have
fudged their way across the very gaps, or fault-lines, that one

is in turn balked by. History in its jaggedness constantly tears at our smooth conceptions of human behavior. If Buchanan was so deeply stricken by grief, how then did he sally forth *as bold as ever*? In his next year of legal practice, 1820, he won from Judge Alexander L. Hayes of the Lancaster County Court the encomium that *he had never listened to an advocate who was equal to Mr. Buchanan, whether in clear & logical arguments to the Court, or in convincing appeals to the reason and sympathies of the jury.* If Buchanan was so disgraced by his fiancée's mysterious death, why was he chosen a few months later to run for Congress? He won the election and—a full year later, in December of 1821—went to Washington City to participate in the seventeenth Congress, and within three more years was an important enough player of the national game to be involved in another scandal, of a purely political sort.

I REMEMBER at some point in all this going to New York with Genevieve for a few days. Women love New York, God knows why. All those clothes in the windows, or the other women in their clothes on the streets. That buzz and rub of other presences which women need, in ballrooms or seraglios; that being on display. Perhaps amid the towering verticals and the rectilinear recessions of the Manhattan grid a woman feels *framed*, set off, mounted to admire. Genevieve looked so sunny and crisp and carefree and glowing, striding beside me as we walked up a little slope on Madison, a sloping block that holds at its crest the brownstone palace from whose two great wings once Cardinal Spellman and Bennett Cerf each directed their empires and where now, I believe, the queen of tax evasion has imposed a glitzy hotel, so sunny and crisp and carefree, I say, that I kissed her, kissed Genevieve right there, as we walked,

to her surprise. In New York, Nature reaches us from underneath, in the slope of the land once full of Dutch farms; they
can't quite pave away the slope, it is Nature, and we were
Nature, she and I, fresh from our lovemaking and showering
in the hotel room. Mine, this thirty-two-year-old woman was
mine, hundreds of miles away from Wayward and Adams and
the old brown slave of a river between, mine in some summery
bare-armed dress of hers, her black hair still damp from the
shower and glistening like snow with microscopic rainbows,
like fresh powder in the morning before the ski tracks pack it
and the blue shadows of the firs are still long, mine among these
millions of strangers, mated with me, and guilt-free. Live free
and die, our state motto could run. I kissed her. It was summer,
but not sticky. I want to make it the summer of the bicenten-
nial, near the epic day of the tall ships and the cloudless sky
that stretched from coast to coast, all our national troubles
having momentarily blown over, but that seems too close to the
end of the Ford era; more likely it was '75, perhaps a sparkling
interval in early fall, six seasons since the spring when in smart
checked woolens she had announced to me under the bud-
nubbly elm that she had told Brent and the skids to divorce
were greased. Surely since then we had earned our freedom—
our sexual secretions weighed out in children's tears, our scandal fading into the college wallpaper, our names inscribed as
Mr. and Mrs. Clayton in the hotel register. In those Ford-
dominated years the custom took hold in the castle keeps of
hotel management for a man to register and a mere plural
number of guests to be noted, whether he was accompanied by
another man, a foundling child, a tame kangaroo, or (as in my
case) a gorgeous woman; but I had gone whole hog, slashing
M/M in front of my name, making her mine legally, as she
soon would be, once Norma focused on her lawyer's appointments and Brent relaxed his clenched jaw. He and the two girls
were visiting his parents in Minnesota. They were sectarian

Lutherans of the strictest variety and had to be very gently led up to the facts of his dissolving marriage. Hence Genevieve was free to come with me to this Northeastern States' Historian's Association (NSHA) Conference—on "Cold-War Deformations of Developing-World Economies and Elites," if I remember the topic—held in a big hotel, on the Avenue of the Americas, with a sugary scent to its wall-to-wall carpeting and in its atrium lobby the largest chandelier outside of Leningrad. Genevieve and I stayed in a little hotel, on West Fifty-first Street, used mostly by Europeans on bargain tours, blocks away from the intellectual hubbub of my fellow academics, and I skipped most of the meetings, panels, debates, and well-received papers. Life must now and then be allowed to take precedence over history—else there will be no new history.

Genevieve looked pleased but not entirely by my impulsive kiss, so quickly delivered she had not had time to pucker her lips over the teeth of her smile. A tiny bubble of my saliva winked on one of her incisors, making an infinitesimal rainbow here in the sunshine, in the long slot of light the skyscrapers had let through onto this block of Madison. Then a diagonal shadow fell across our progress like a police barricade. Her smile had turned a shade uncertain. "Why did you do that?" She was very appearance-conscious, I tended to forget; she had been educated by nuns.

"You looked so adorable," I tried to explain. "I feel so proud to be with you." I was embarrassed. "You're perfect."

The shadow on her face was slow to lift. "Nobody's perfect."

"You are. For me at least." I was beginning to feel silly. Far above us, beneath a set of dissipating jet trails, a towering glass box had taken a bite out of the sun. Down here on the grid, amid the grit and greed, hundreds of grayish pedestrians hurried along, oblivious of our love, my kiss, her qualm. She entwined her hand with my arm and recomposed the moment, but I did not forget this revelation of imperfect fit, I being happier, fuller of us, than she.

What did we *do* those three days and nights of married life? What others do—ate, and slept, and went to a movie (*Tommy*, perhaps, of which I remember nothing but a gargantuan piano, a man on stilts, and Elton John in some very uncomfortable-looking costume) and a show (*The Wiz*, of which I mostly recall the numerous view-occluding Afros in the audience). On the last day we hurriedly bought souvenir presents for our five children, I-♥-NY rag dolls for her girls, rude T-shirts and Statue of Liberty snowballs for my mixed-sex trio, these last trinkets a pale echo of an enchanting miniature trylon and perisphere my parents had brought me, when I was four, from the 1939–40 World's Fair. It lit up, somehow, and had a curving ramp of many tiny bas-relief people, streaming into the future, which was now. No—which had never been. World war, Holocaust, cold war, oil spills, famine, massacre, serial killing, man the vermin of the planet: the innocent future I had seen in that glowing souvenir, with a helicopter in every garage, had never come.

How can I recapture, dear colleagues of the NNEAAH, for your written symposium, the numbing wonder and dizzying strangeness of being with another man's wife hour after hour? I had never tasted a hamburger before eating one with Genevieve in the coffee shop at the Plaza the evening we emerged, blinking in the six-o'clock sunlight, from a late-afternoon showing of loud and garish *Tommy* and, hand in hand, sauntered from the sexual carnival of Broadway, with its fat hookers in vinyl hotpants, over to the relative tranquillity of shopperless Fifth Avenue and on up to the edge of the Park. It cost, the hamburger, $6.50, which seemed a prodigious price back then, in that innocent era before Carter's inflation, and was too fat with meat and lettuce and sliced onion and tomato and bulky sesame-seed roll to squeeze between my jaws, the way a boy from Hayes had always eaten a hamburger. Charbroiled on the outside, raw as steak tartare on the inside, this hypertrophied Plaza version of a fast food had to be consumed with a fork and knife, piece by piece, as Genevieve showed me, her eloquent narrow hands themselves like expensive implements, her tan fingers tipped with pink polish paler than a blush. Encapsulated with her inside a preview of our marriage, legitimately at her side in these uncaring multitudes, I felt a continuous tremble in my chest, as if a bubble might pop. With the wonder of a caveman observing his first eclipse I watched her pairs of underpants, lacy and bikini and pastel, go from clean to dirty to clean again, hung to dry on the heated bathroom towel rack; once, when she was in the shower, I snatched a pair from where she had let them drop on the carpet and buried my nose in the faintly stained crotch, as if to imprint forever her musk upon my memory cells.

It was impossible, in the course of our three days, to avoid generating excrement, and we were both shy as cats without a sandbox to scratch. As I followed her into the bathroom in the mornings, my nostrils were struck by the chthonian afterscent, spicier than Norma's spoor, of what had just passed from one of her seven sacred orifices. (Two nostrils, two ears, and the remaining three do not include the bellybutton, a cul de sac.) There was something Platonic, like a triangle's chalk ghost upon a scrubbed blackboard, or like the idea of war that haunts a futile peace conference, about our passage, with sometimes averted eyes, through a haze of illicit intimacy. She kept the room thrillingly neat and yet at night would subconsciously scuttle all the way across the king-sized mattress to involve me in a panicked embrace, a claustrophobic tangle of sweaty limbs and tangled sheets. She slept naked, whereas I, after a near-Canadian childhood spent mostly under layers of blankets and quilts, needed some weight of cloth, of pajama tops or an undershirt at least, to make me feel safe enough to sleep. I suppose she slept naked with Brent, and this thought greatly pained me. They were just enough younger than Norma and I to have caught those Sixties liberations in their youth, instead of catching up to them retroactively, when hobbled with children and employment. In her sleep, which I had never before witnessed, Genevieve sweated, her sleek brunette skin rich in glands, and sometimes thrashed and moaned aloud, with touching infantile whimpering moans, as if her vital force, masked in daylight by a crisp bearing learned from nuns, was unmasked and tormenting her. Yet in the morning she could recall no nightmare, and when my concerned questioning persisted, she would stare at me with an intensified opacity in her coffee-dark eyes, as if I were trying to delve too deep and had offended some Gallic standard of decorum which even the penetrations and exposures of love did not suspend. Her maiden name had been Lavalliere; the notion of an ancestral Frenchness took possession of me, as I had freedom now to notice in her body the delicate traces of a Latin hairiness—the almost invisible dark wisps at the extremities of her upper lip, just above the slightly taut points where her mouth's orifice terminated, and the distinct shadow, manlike in its bluish glaze, where her armpits were kept shaved. I expressed the infatuated hope that, when we were married, she would let her underarm hair grow out, in two pungent tufts, butterfly-shaped in my mind's eye, and let her legs become as shaggy as a Gascogne peasant girl's, so that there would be, by these few multiplied black millimeters, that much more of her, a surplus produced at my bidding, as a sign of my possession. But she shuddered in my arms at the proposal; not even my most delirious transports were about to overwhelm her thoroughly American standards of personal hygiene. There were a number of these tiny collisions, moments unremarked by us but not unnoticed, when my amorous fantasies, which dated back to fantasies bred amid the ethnic simplicities of Hayes, where the "Canuck" girls from the far side of the disused tracks figured as dark and dirty mysteries, met something proudly otherwise in her. In fact she didn't come from the backwoods of northern New England but from the highly civilized town of Madison, Wisconsin, state capital and site of a university, where her father had been a professor of Romance languages.

We did best, in a way, out on the streets; here the racially plural energy of Manhattan, the giant ongoing recklessness of the megalopolitan venture, seemed to confirm our own recklessness and to bestow an oceanic blessing. Doormen, waiters, taxi drivers, panhandlers all smiled upon us as if we were, as indeed we *were*, one more couple in a worldwide species whose main means of perpetuation and easement of angst takes the form of couples—soigné, gray-suited couples belonging to the New York power structure; unwashed, denim-swaddled, love-beaded couples from the aging counterculture; clinging, punching, juvenile couples; black-white couples; Caucasian-Oriental couples; homosexual couples with arms looped low around each other's waists; ancient Jewish couples blinking in the sidewalk sunshine like turtles basking on a familiar rock. Outdoors, we felt normal, accepted. Indoors, in the narrow hotel room that in three days had become softened like a cheap shoe by the confined movements of self-conscious cohabitation, we became prey to talk like this:

"Don't you wish," Genevieve suddenly sighed, a few minutes after lovemaking, as if its fluids were turning sour inside her, "I would just go away or get run over by a bus so you could go back to Norma?"

"My God, no. Why would I wish that? I love you."

She gave me an absent-minded cool-lipped kiss for saying this, quick as an automatic genuflection, but pursued her thought, with an adorable knitting together of her dark, broad, Ali McGraw–ish brows. "I know, Alf, but isn't it a drag in a way? You had such a nice comfortable relaxed sort of life . . ."

"Speak for yourself."

". . . nice house, nice kids . . ."

"You, too."

". . . and to give it all up for a sexual passion seems . . ."

"What?"

". . . oh, you know . . ."

She trailed off, expecting me to take up the slack, to reassure her for the thousandth time. "But my passion isn't just sexual," I obediently said. "I love the way you look dressed as well as undressed. I love the way you keep house and mother your little girls. I love everything about you. You're perfect."

"Nobody's perfect. It makes me sad to hear you say that. It's as if I'm not real to you, the way Norma is."

"Is being real what Norma's problem is? I must say, life out of that house is bliss of a sort. I told you how, the night I got trapped there, I couldn't breathe."

"That made me sad, too, hearing all about that. That you let yourself be trapped, and then felt so conflicted. We've been at this too long, Alf, for you to still feel conflicted."

"Does one ever," I began to say, *not feel conflicted?*, but thought better of it, since Genevieve appeared, in her naked porcelain elegance (a bisque glaze of tan on her shoulders and arms), a shade fragile and brittle. Her lips were thinned and tightened by thought; her big eyes, their whites as pure as chips of china, studied my face without blinking. Having waited for me to finish my sentence, she pronounced my least favorite syllable.

"Brent," she said, "says he's ready to do the divorce any time, now that his parents pretty much know, and he thinks Norma is, too, now."

"What does he know about Norma?" I asked with languid scorn, lucky fellow as I was with this naked beauty beside me on the king-size bed.

"He sees her," Genevieve said, looking at me with slight

defiance, her upper lashes pressed against the socket's upper curve of bone as if painted there. "Didn't you know that? They've gone out together a couple of times."

"Gone out?" *Odious*, Andrew had said. Was this the beau he had meant? "How often?"

She backed off a few inches, there in the hotel's enormous bed, frightened of the intensity of my reaction. "I don't know. More than once. After all, they have a lot in common. They have us in common."

"Brent and Norma?" I said, trying to couple them in my mind, to picture it. "But she's older than he."

"That's a chauvinistic remark, Alf. Just a few years, like we have between us, the other way. Anyway, nobody's saying they have sex."

"But"—and I suppose this remark is characteristic of the Ford era—"what else would they have?"

"They'd talk," my exquisite mistress matter-of-factly said. "He's impressed," she went on. "He thinks she's finally getting her shit together."

I hated the phrase, its debased pop psychology. I resented his using it of my wife; I resented his thrusting it into my dear mistress's ear. But there was no denying it, Genevieve was not a virgin, physical or mental; she was familiar with *his* shit. They shared a style, an approach. The Perfect Wife implies the Perfect Couple; once again, as when conferring hastily under the feathery springtime elm with her in her smart checks while he approached from an unknown direction, I felt caught between them, pinched in the nutcracker they formed. Naked with me now, she had been naked with *him* night after night, his tight asshole nestled against the perfect triangle of her pussy. Pussies were triangular in the Ford era, before high-sided swim suits compelled women to shave their groins of all but a vertical strip of natural adornment.

Genevieve was watching me. Her opaque, expectant,

slightly defiant stare, above the peripheral gleam of her body in the tangled, sweated-up sheets, had been frozen I knew not how many seconds. "What kind of shit?" was all I at last could think to say, weakly. In my jealousy I was getting an erection.

"Oh, less hung up on you. Less dependent and hurt. Starting to take responsibility for her own life."

"By sleeping with your creep of a husband, that's taking responsibility?"

"Brent's never said they sleep together. But why shouldn't they? We set them free. Alf, it's not very flattering to me, that you're so upset."

"I'm not upset. Fuck 'em all." *Fuck you, too,* was in my mind.

"If she did go with a free man, so to speak, wouldn't that be better than one more tumble in the hay with Ben Wadleigh after he and Wendy have reconstituted their marriage on a perfectly sick basis?"

"Who's to say what's a sick basis? At least the Wadleigh kids go to sleep with both their parents under the same roof with them."

I was blaming her; she knew it. She shrugged those shoulders with their smooth bisque tan, so unlike Norma's carelessly distributed constellations of freckles. "I've *told* you," Genevieve said, "go back to her."

"I don't want to," I replied in a hardened voice. "I want to fuck you, actually."

"I see you do," she said dryly.

But on top of her, in her, I had to blurt, "But she's so artistic, and he's so un-!" *Deconstruction despises art, stripping away all its pretenses,* was my point, but this didn't seem the moment to develop it.

Her shrug this time was all internal, a subtle moist tightening that I thought of as a French trick. "Opposites attract," she said. "Look at us."

"Us! But we're exactly alike, for a man and a woman." I

believed this because our lovemaking melted us into one, one with the dark, a mass of blind sensation, her dear flexible and seven times receptive body firm and graceful, like curves my mind kept drawing in the pitch-black back of some cave, perhaps Plato's. Once, I remember, our two-backed beast with its single pounding heart and coating of perspiration twisted and crawled itself clear off the bed, so that we fell at the foot on a wad of tossed covers, and rather than rearrange herself on the mattress my perfect love partner tucked back her black hair so a gleam of face showed in the faint light from the street and found my prick with her mouth and despite my squeamish, chivalrous, insincere efforts to push her off relentlessly sucked and hand-pumped me into coming, into helplessly shooting off (like fireworks in a chaste Fifties movie as a metaphor for sex) into a warm wet dark that was her tidy little head. I could hear her smile as, having swallowed, she rested this head (was it heavier?) on my chest and murmured something about our being "all mixed up with each other." Though her aroused skill showed that she had done this for Brent and possibly others, the act felt like a singularity, a unique trip to the edge of self-obliteration by a woman possessed, her needs and mine fused. In retrospect it seems as though I came not in her mouth so much as in the *room*, the black space limited by eight unseen corners, my body being the only one present, Genevieve transformed for this interval into pure fierce spirit.

It wasn't that hotel room, with its green-striped wallpaper and *faux*-antique furniture and view of an Italian-restaurant awning on West Fifty-first Street. For her to be so transported by passion, so much a maenad, she had to have had an *idea* of me, like a groupie blowing a rock star. The longer we know another, the less of an idea we have; eventually all we have are facts. By the time of our New York trip, Genevieve and I knew each other a bit too well for her to gulp me up brainlessly, at the mucky bottom of the carnivorous sea, while I at an extrem-

ity of invertebrate bliss ran a trembling tentacle around and
around the crenelated waxy hole at the center of her rhythmi-
cally lifting ear. A certain cool efficiency, rather, floats to the
surface of my memory of our three-day marriage. I was struck
by the brusque way in which she repelled a black chambermaid
who, rapping her key on the door and then turning it in the
lock, had tried to enter our room one mid-morning when we
were making love. Luckily, the chain was drawn across; but
the girl, stupid perhaps, or stoned, kept pushing and rattling,
and Genevieve left the bed naked to tell her, crouching at the
opened crack, to go away and come back later. Her peremp-
tory voice pierced me, lying love-dazed on our wide sea-bed,
and I may have indicated my wound, for as she slithered back
into my arms she murmured, "They're here to serve us."

This was a revelation. She grasped, Europeanly, the order,
the hierarchy, of society. Had it been Norma and I in bed, we
would have felt a confused egalitarian obligation to the Afri-
can-American maid in the hall, who no doubt had her schedule
and, a hundred blocks to the north, her private problems, the
products ultimately of slavery and racial prejudice, and we
would have guiltily dressed ourselves and vacated the room.
But Genevieve saw reality in its true fine shadings of obligation
and prerogative. Among the household duties she took on in
our room was the ordering of breakfast and tea; this thrilled
me, for I always vaguely imagined that it was somehow rude
not to patronize the hotel coffee shop with its smell of frying
fat and its garble of alien tongues. Mornings, there would be
a rap on the door, and she would vanish into the bathroom with
a flicker of flesh like the tail of a bounding doe, and I would
be left in my hastily donned trousers and last night's button-
down shirt to deal apologetically with the tinkling, ostentatiously noncommittal waiter, signing his bill with a clumsy
overtip. She knew the world, how it fit together and did its
business, eliciting rewards and punishments on a scale cali-

brated by tradition. Like all enthralled students, I tempered
admiration with resentment. The order she would create in my
life depended upon reifying people, reducing them to their
uses. If the chambermaid was thus to be disposed of, what
about me, when my mysterious use had been served?

Meanwhile, Chou En-lai was dying, and Paul Robeson and
André Malraux, and Howard Hughes and Martin Heidegger,
Agatha Christie and J. Paul Getty. From a sultry, sliding quality in these memories I wonder if they *are* from the summer
of the tall ships after all. In which case, the movie we saw, in
a cityscape decorated by fire hydrants painted red, white, and
blue, was not *Tommy* but *Cousin, Cousine,* the show not *The
Wiz* but *The Belle of Amherst,* and the topic of the conference
to which I played truant was "The Fruits of Revolution: Colonies into Competitors, 1776–1976."

[*Retrospect:* from this point on, my old ms. exists in a fragmentary state. Personal distractions and intrinsic difficulties de-
railed the project. Also, JB's life after 1820 basks more and
more in the glare of historical record—see Klein, Curtis, Auchampaugh, Nevins, Nichols, Catton, Stampp, etc., plus the
Works, edited by John Bassett Moore, that saint, in twelve
hefty volumes—whereas my tropism was toward the unlit, the
underside, the region of shades where his personal demon
teased our statesman, visiting embarrassment upon his dignity
and violence upon his peacefulness. A few dashed notations
will prick your own well-stocked historians' memories and fill
in the narrative gaps. Thus: JB takes seat as Representative in
seventeenth Congress in December 1821—admires above all
other members William Lowndes of South Carolina—made
member of Committee on Agriculture—within three weeks

has spoken on floor of House three times—writes home to Judge Franklin that it *requires great compass of voice to fill the hall. It is a very magnificent and very elegant chamber, but unless a man has stentorian lungs, he cannot be heard distinctly*—modestly allows of his own speeches, *I am told, however, that I can be distinctly heard*—within first month gives speech from notes by ill Lowndes in defense of Secretary of War John C. Calhoun which furthers his alliance with Southerners—gives speech against Bankrupt Bill (sponsored by friend and fellow Pennsylvanian John Sergeant) which shows partiality to states' rights and property rights—re-elected in 1822 after conducting evasive campaign, staying clear of actively supporting Federalist candidate for Governor, Andrew Gregg, in view of the rising Jackson-Democratic tide in Pennsylvania—enjoys Washington society as romantically tinged (by Ann Coleman tragedy) bachelor, keeping company with Mrs. George Blakes of Boston and (to quote Klein) *the Van Ness girls, Cora Livingston and Catherine Van Rensselaer of New York, the Crowninshield misses from Vermont, Priscilla Cooper, who became the wife of his friend Robert Tyler, the Caton sisters from Baltimore,* etc.—runs and wins unprecedented third term as Lancaster Congressman on "Federal-Republican" ticket in 1824 election, wherein Jackson sweeps Pennsylvania but whose 99 electoral votes against John Quincy Adams's 83, William Crawford's 41, and Henry Clay's 37 fall short of majority, throwing Presidential election into House—apparently takes upon self, as an already prominent Pennsylvania "fixer," the delicate task of sounding out General Jackson on the matter of his intentions if the House elects him—Washington's rumor mill claims that Adams if elected with Clay's help would make Clay Secretary of State, whereas Jackson would keep on Adams, who was already serving in the post, with great distinction, under President James Monroe.]

On the morning of December 30, 1824, young James Buchanan outstayed all the other guests at a gathering in General Jackson's apartments and was rewarded for his patience by an invitation to take a walk with the former backwoodsman, now the Senator from Tennessee. More than tall and lean, Jackson appeared emaciated, even skeletal; not since his impoverished boyhood had he been entirely well. His eyes were a glittering blue. Unruly locks of ashen-yellow hair framed his parched face. A greasy pigtail behind was tied with an eelskin. To Buchanan's nostrils Jackson smelled faintly rancid, and smoky, like beef hung too long in the curing, or like the warmed inside of dogskin gloves. In the open air, this unpleasant impression dissipated: Washington City on this bracing winter morning breathed, beneath its bare sycamores and locust trees, an atmosphere cleansed of the long summer's scarcely tolerable heat. The mudholes in the avenues wore a thin glaze of ice, and the ubiquitous sense of incompletion—of ill-financed starts at marmoreal grandeur thrusting aside the shacks wherein the negroes (then so styled) and the less fortunate class of whites found shelter, with occasional charred proofs of the savage British destruction in 1814 still permitted to stand—was softened by a picturesque mist come up from the swamps by the Potomac. Compared with Lancaster, it was a raw city, a grand design but as yet sketchily given embodiment.

The Hero of New Orleans did not waste much time on pleasantries. "You tarried this morning, Mr. Búchanan," he said, accenting the first syllable of the name in the frontier fashion, "with a gleam in your eye, as of one with a message to impart."

"No message, sir, but merely a question," the thirty-three-year-old politician answered, taken aback but locating courage in the sound of his own voice, a faithful friend, clear and untiring if a little high-pitched, which had seen him through many a court case and stump speech, and which carried even in the abysmal acoustics of the House chamber. "However," he went on, "before I trespass upon your forbearance in posing my question, let me petition in advance for a guarantee of your continuing friendship, which I value most highly among all my claims to public service, saving only my love of the Constitution and the great Christian people which it serves."

"That is nicely said, young man," said Jackson, little concealing his impatience but hoarsely letting escape the words, "You have your guarantee." Nowhere did Jackson fever run higher than in Pennsylvania, so this popinjay from the Keystone State must be allowed his rigamarole.

Still, Buchanan did not dare charge ahead. "My question would be asked on behalf not of my own curiosity but that of many others, all friendly to your interests, and concerns a subject upon which, typically, and to your great honor, you have expressed a determination to remain silent. I recognize that, deeming my question improper, you may refuse to give it an answer; believe me that my only motive in asking it is friendship for yourself, and anxiety that this Republic have as its chief executive the man best qualified to lead it—that is, General Jackson!"

In the midday foot traffic along Pennsylvania Avenue, with its rows of freshly planted saplings and its distant termini of an incomplete Capitol and a freshly repaired White House, a small negro urchin darted out and pointed at the two men's dusty boots, offering a fresh application of goose grease, to be polished on a much-trodden wooden box he carried as a tool of his humble trade. Jackson, with a visionary's sure sense of proportion, gave the little petitioner a quick glance relegating him to his place, a low and inconsequential one, whereas Buchanan felt himself inopportunely tugged by pity for the child, and by an irrational sense of obligation to him. The child's need to earn a penny seemed a claim upon him, as the baby's cry is a claim upon the mother and gets the milk to flowing in her breast. But he could hardly allow a shoe-shine to interrupt a verbal negotiation upon which the Presidency might hinge!

The General was urging, "Speak on, Mr. Búchanan. From your respectability as a gentleman and a Congressman, I do not expect you would lend yourself to any communication you suppose to be improper. Your motives being pure, let me think what I will of the communication."

Buchanan had not used the word "communication," with its implied insult of regarding the speaker as a messenger for higher-placed others, but thought it best not to contradict. Nor did he hear his avowal of friendship reciprocated. Nevertheless, he proceeded, with the words he had anticipatorily framed to the point of memorization: "We live, General, in times of intrigue and rumor; would that we lived in a better, but we do not. A report exists in circulation that, if—as I fervently hope and trust—you are elected President by the House, you will continue Mr. Adams in his present office as Secretary of State. You will at once perceive how injurious to your election such a report might be. It rises, I think you will also perceive, from the friends of Mr. Adams, as a reason to induce the friends of Mr. Clay to accede to their proposition—which has been distinctly forwarded, of that I have been assured—to the effect that Mr. Adams's election will bring with it the appointment of Mr. Clay as Secretary of State."

At the convenient pausing-place of the curb, where both men hesitated as the elegant equipage of the French Legation spun past in a coruscation of plumes, hooves, and ebony spokes trimmed in gold paint, Buchanan gathered himself to pose the obvious crux: could General Jackson, then, hold out to the friends of Henry Clay hope of the same office, in return for the votes of the Ohio and Kentucky delegations? With the safety of the opposite curb secured, he pitched his voice to a more meaningful, though still casual register, in saying, "I think you will not be surprised to hear that the friends of Mr. Clay do not desire to separate West from West." In case this was too subtle for the whip-thin apostle of backwoods America, whose wild pure eyes were surveying, above his interrogator's head, the transparent treetops and slate rooftops of Washington City as if gauging the limits of a cage in which he was held, the deferential young Congressman asked, "Do I mistake in supposing your view of the matter to be not unlike mine, which is that in this Republic there are many able and ambitious men, among whom Mr. Clay might be included, who would not disgrace the first Cabinet post?"

"Our views of the matter have some correspondence, Mr. Búchanan. Mr. Clay has considerable ability and is second to none in the ambition department. Was this the question you proposed to ask? If so, it seems unworthy of its long preamble."

Thus challenged and stung, Buchanan lunged, so to speak, at the exposed chest of the matter. "Senator, my question is merely this: have you ever intimated the intention ascribed to you, that is, to continue Mr. Adams as Secretary of State? If it could be contradicted, under your authority, by you expressly or by one of your confidential friends, that you have already selected your chief competitor for the highest office within your gift, then I have reason to believe that the Presidential contest can be settled within an hour." *The obstinate fool,* Buchanan thought, *the Presidency was his for a nod.*

The General, feeling his turn had come to speak, pulled himself erect, so that Buchanan had to twitch his head to keep his revered companion's face in focus. Their stroll halted beneath a scabby-trunked sycamore, near a bench of weathered slats where a negro in threadbare blue field clothes had fallen, with the aid of rum, into an oblivious doze, cold as was this, the penultimate day of the year. "I have not the least objection, Mr. Búchanan, to answering your question. I think well of Mr. Adams. He stood by me when the Indian-lovers would have had my hide for cleaning out the damnable Seminoles. But I have never intimated that I would, or would not, appoint him my Secretary of State." A fury of righteousness now stiffened Jackson's slender frame, as if there were an audience beyond his lone auditor, a ghostly vast audience stretching to the frontiers of the Republic. His talk became rhetorical, Biblical. "There are secrets I keep to myself," he said, the ever-latent fury of the man finding sudden vent. "I will conceal them from the very hairs of my head! If I believed that my right hand knew what the left would do on the subject of appointments, I would cut it off and cast it into the fire! In politics as in all else, Mr. Búchanan, my guide is principle alone. If I am elected President, it shall be without intrigue and solicitation. I shall enter office perfectly free and untrammelled, at liberty to fill the offices of government with the men I believe to be the ablest and best in the country!"

Buchanan could hardly suppress a sigh of disgust, at such peculiar and high-flown hypocrisy, such madly inspired ignorance of negotiation. He made a bow. "Your answer is such a one as I had expected to receive. I have not sought to obtain it, sir, for my own satisfaction; may I ask, am I at liberty to repeat your response to others?" For with only a little shift, Jackson's declaration that he had not *decided* to appoint Adams might be made to declare that he had decided *not* to appoint him. Still, Clay's men would want more, slightly more, so slightly much more that a twist of a word might close the breach, and the young Congressman's mission could be accounted an unqualified success.

But the breach resisted being closed. The General had mounted his figurative high horse, there in the lacy shade of the bare branches, next to the comatose negro, who would reap pneumonia for his repose. "Indeed you may, Mr. Búchanan," the General said, in a twanging voice as remorseless as the cut of a pit saw on the downward drag. "You may tell Mr. Clay and his friends that before I reach the Presidential chair by means of bargain and corruption I would see the earth open and swallow us all! Why, the Kentucky legislature has already instructed Clay to throw his support to me, and he has made them no response! He is defying them while he finagles! If winning half again as much of the popular vote as my nearest opponent is not enough to secure me victory, then the House will stand exposed as a nest of corruption, and those who profit by its corruption shall face public disgrace."

Buchanan repeated his bow, this second time suppressing a smile. "I understand you, sir. I thank you for your patience and frankness. Good day; duties await us both on Capitol Hill."

The glittering eye, perhaps seeing the impolitic smile, softened, and Jackson gestured, as they reversed directions and resumed their walk, for the heavier, younger man, also tall, to draw closer. His voice, becoming confidential, put on a thicker backwoods accent. "B'twixt oursel's, Búchanan. Ye have a future ahead, unless ye waffle it away. The straight path is always the high road. Them that travel the byways of compromise is the ones that get lost." This allusion to Clay, whose masterful engineering of the Missouri Compromise had won him the glorious title of "the great pacificator," was a warning Buchanan could inwardly dismiss, knowing the enmity the speaker carried against Clay for the Kentuckian's objections to the Tennessean's pre-emptory invasion of Florida in 1819; the operation had been equally ruthless toward Spaniard, Britisher, and Seminole, and only Quincy Adams's stout defense, in his capacity as Secretary of State, had saved Jackson from Congressional censure. West bore no love for West. The General now, as this morning's walk proceeded toward its termination through the motley sights of the new nation's ambitious and ramshackle capital, touched the area of, beneath his bulky greatcoat, his slender breast. "In here," he confided, "I carry Charles Dickinson's bullet, so close to my heart the surgeons feared to cut it out. I took his shot square in the chest and then I aimed. The villain couldn't believe his eyes; they had to hold him to the mark. He folded his arms across his chest, so I shot him down below, in the parts of his manhood. He groaned for days before he died: serve the snide fop right, for impugning my Rachel's honor. More savages and scoundrels have been dispatched by my hand than could be housed in Gadsby's Hotel. A father's protection I never knew; two weeks after I came into the world he lifted a log so heavy his insides burst. He was a laboring man from Ireland, back there in the Waxhaws."

Buchanan reflected upon his own father, a man from Ireland who also died violently, a scant three years ago, of striking his head on the iron tire when his carriage horse bolted. Violent ends were as common in the New World as in the Bible.

"Myself," his suddenly fatherly companion continued, "I should be dead ten times over. As a lad of thirteen I took my first wound; running messages for the Revolution, my brother Rob and me were caught and held prisoner. A swine of a British officer slashed his sabre at my skull—see this scar?— when I declined to clean the hogshit from his boots. Then they marched us forty miles to prison with open wounds. In the filth there we caught the smallpox. My sainted mother came and begged her boys' release and walked us home to the Waxhaws through a hurricane; my brother died of it. My other brother, Hugh, had already met his maker, courtesy of King George Three. Within the year another plague took off my mother; she had gone to Charleston to nurse two cousins on a prison ship of the infernal British. They tossed her body like a dog's into an unmarked grave, and sent me her clothes in a bundle. I have been alone ever since."

They were approaching an intersection where they might gracefully part, but Jackson, sensing Buchanan's wish to be elsewhere, gripped the younger man's upper arm and steered him further along the avenue, toward the then red, unporticoed Presidential mansion where James Monroe was sitting out in a stolid whiskey stupor the last months of his decaying Era of Good Feeling.

"Alone," the Senator pursued, "and never real well, young man. When in Nashville it came into my head to take a horse-whip to the Benton brothers, one of their bullets broke my shoulder like a china cup; but I pulled a pistol on the doctor when the rogue unsheathed his knife to amputate this arm. I crushed the British at New Orleans still bleeding from the wounds the Bentons gave me; I routed the Creeks and Seminoles so consumed with bowel complaint my fever fried the leather of the saddle. I've been there, Mr. Búchanan, and out the other side. You're still this side, and that makes a man gingerly. When I was a youngster in the Congress, as you are now, I didn't go around tiptoeing on errands for the likes of Henry Clay; I stood right up on my own hind legs and in a big voice voted Nay to a farewell tribute for that sanctimonious old mule General George Washington. Soft on redcoats and redskins, he was, and fancied himself a king besides, and I hated him for it."

Buchanan, whose mother used to put him to bed with pious stories of Washington's glorious deeds, took in breath to make a courteous protestation, but thought better of it. This other man's force was like that of a river which frothingly redoubles its fury wherever a rock would pose an obstacle. By choice, we Americans are not the enjoined and harmonized servants of a king who is God's earthly appointee but instead form a contention of free wills and selfish interests, set loose in a wilderness to survive or fail. General Jackson, out of some compassionate or edificatory impulse, was trying to urge upon his deferential inquisitor a guiding philosophy.

"Young man," he said, a wheeze beginning to declare a certain weariness, "ye mistake where the power in this country lies. It's not in the wits of the politicians, and never was in such a set of weasel holes. Mark my words: any bargain Clay and

Adams strike'll be the ruin of 'em both. When ye've passed through to the other side as I have, and slaked yer appetite for hollow flattery from those around ye, ye'll know where the power lies in God's own country: it lies in the passions of the people." With the vigorous arm once marked for amputation he thumped not his breast but lower down along the lapels of his greatcoat, toward the softer part of his abdomen. "It lies in their guts. They can smell ye out, false or true. With the people in yer belly, ye can do no wrong. Otherwise, wriggle as ye will, ye can do no right. Take your stand on principle, Mr. Bú-chanan, and never fear to make yerself enemies."

Seeing the Senator at last decided to leave him, Buchanan bowed, and ventured a pleasantry. "I shall not so fear, General Jackson, as long as you are never counted among them."

[But, as we historians know, in 1826, even as Buchanan in weasel fashion was attempting to slip the inconvenient Federalist label, under which he had won his fourth term in Congress, and to create in Pennsylvania a so-called Amalgamation party of Federalist German farmers from the east and Scots-Irish frontiersmen from the west, all strongly pro-Jackson, the "bargain and sale" controversy tainting Adams's Presidency mounted to include that open-air conversation with Jackson nearly two years earlier. Buchanan received in October a letter from Duff Green, John Calhoun's campaign manager, bristling with friendly menace: *The part taken by you on the occasion referred to, is known to me; and a due regard to your feelings has heretofore restrained me from using your name before the public. The time, however, is now approaching when it will become the duty of every man to do all in his power to expose the bargain which placed the Coalition in power. Will you, upon the receipt of this, write to me and explain the causes which induced you to see Genl. Jackson upon the subject of the vote of Mr. Clay & his friends a few days before it was known that they had conclusively determined to vote for Mr. Adams; also advise me of the manner in*

which you would prefer that subject to be brought before the people.
The people! Buchanan took four days to frame a circumspect
reply, fending off this inimical ploy by the pro-Calhoun, anti-
Clay, and anti-Jackson forces, which in his own state were
centered in the "Family" party, of rich and interrelated eastern
Pennsylvanians, who in their correspondence spoke vindic-
tively of *Mr. Buchanan, who has for some years past been fond of
being considered a Democrat in the liberality of his principles,
whilst he desired the support of the federalists as their Magnus
Apollo,* and who dreaded the possible day when *Mr. Buchanan
would have "bestridden our narrow world like a Colossus" with the
patronage and power of Pennsylvania at his feet.* His reply to
Green invoked the people: *I must therefore protest against bringing that conversation before the people, through the medium of the
Telegraph or any other Newspaper. The facts are before the world
that Mr. Clay & his particular friends made Mr. Adams President,
& that Mr. Adams immediately thereafter made Mr. Clay Secretary of State. The people will draw their own inferences from such
conduct & from the circumstances connected with it. They will
judge the cause from the effects.* But the issue of his conversation
as an aspect of the "bargain and sale" kept surfacing. The
following year, Jackson himself stated, in a public letter to
Carter Beverly of Virginia, that a Congressman had sought to
make a corrupt bargain with him in Clay's behalf. He did not
name the Congressman, but soon must, as Samuel Ingham of
the Family party gloatingly wrote to Buchanan in July of 1827:
*Shd Clay demand of Genl Jackson his author he will have no
alternative, nor could he have had from the first. . . . You will
therefore be joined into the battle under a fire,—but I see no difficulty in the case if you take your ground well and maintain it
boldly.* This was irony, no doubt, since Buchanan was not
known for boldness and from his point of view the case presented nothing but difficulty. His alternatives appeared to be
confessing involvement in a bargain attempt or calling General

Jackson a liar. A week after Ingham's letter Jackson was writing Buchanan, saying, *I have no doubt when properly called on you will come forth & affirm the statement made to Major Eaton,* * *then to Mr. Kreamer* [sic]† *& then to me, & give the names of the friends of Mr. Clay who made it to you.* Less than a month later Jackson named Buchanan as the propositioning Congressman in an address in Cincinnati, and Buchanan on the 8th of August composed for the Lancaster *Journal* a detailed account of his conversation that morning of December 30, 1824, upon which my own account above is largely based, save for the General's descant upon his life and philosophy, which is my invention. In that curious way of fiction and reality, it came to life as nothing in the reported conversation did, save possibly Jackson's sudden claim that *these were secrets he would keep to himself—he would conceal them from the very hairs of his head; that if he believed his right hand then knew what his left hand would do on the subject of appointments to office, he would cut it off, and cast it into the fire.* This leaps out with an unreal force,

---

*Major John Henry Eaton, Jackson's Secretary of War, whose marriage, at Jackson's advice, to Margaret O'Neale Timberlake, a tavern-keeper's daughter of considerable romantic experience even before her marriage at the age of sixteen to a navy purser whom the infatuated then-Senator Eaton used his influence to keep at sea while he comforted the lonely bride, failed to quiet scandalized Washington tongues, especially those wagging on the distaff side of the Calhoun camp: Buchanan had approached Eaton with the Adams-appointment question before approaching Jackson, and was rather curtly advised by the major to inquire of the general himself. And so he did.

†George Kremer, Congressman from Pennsylvania and Ingham satellite, whose letter to the *Columbian Observer* of Philadelphia the January after Buchanan's interview with Jackson claimed that Clay had offered to vote for whoever would give him the State Department; Clay's challenge to a duel was retracted after it was rumored that Kremer proposed to duel with squirrel rifles. Jackson's reference here assumes that Kremer's basis was a conversation with Buchanan describing the epochal interview of December 30th.

as vehement beyond the needs of the occasion. Composing history is like packing a suitcase with objects that persist in overflowing, or underfilling the space. Buchanan ventured to contradict the General only very mildly: *I do not recollect, that General Jackson told me I might repeat his answer to Mr. Clay and his friends; though I should be sorry to say he did not. The whole conversation being upon a public street, it might have escaped my observation.* His critical statement was: *I called upon General Jackson, upon the occasion which I have mentioned, solely as his friend, upon my individual responsibility, and not as the agent of Mr. Clay or any other person.* His letter to the editor continued, *I have never been the political friend of Mr. Clay, since he became a candidate for the office of president, as you very well know.* Jackson, accustomed to having soldiers risk death at his command, seems oblivious of the fact that to bear him out Buchanan would have to incriminate himself as a conspirator with the Clay forces. Contemporaries remarked variously upon the contretemps. *It places Jackson in a most awkward predicament,* said a letter received by President Adams. *But what surprises me more than anything else is the situation in which the General places his friend. . . . Buchanan is ruined if anything can ruin a man who is a partisan in party times.* William Rawle of Philadelphia confided to his diary that *Jackson appears to great disadvantage unless we discard all that is asserted by Buchanan.* Henry Clay avowed vindication and said, *I could not desire a stronger statement from Mr. Buchanan.* John Calhoun wrote that *Mr. B. it is clear feels the awkwardness of his situation;* hence his attempt *to give a character of innocency to the whole affair.* Buchanan vented his own irritation to Ingham: *You will have seen General Jackson's letter to the Public in which he has given up my name. It will at once strike you to be a most extraordinary production so far as I am concerned.* But his pacificator's temper strives for control: *I have not suffered my feelings to get the better of my judgment but have stated the truth in a calm & temperate manner.*

If General Jackson and our editors should act with discretion the storm may blow over without injury.

[It appeared to. In 1828 Buchanan, running as a Jackson Democrat, won his fifth term in Congress, and Jackson swept Adams aside in the Presidential election. In the spring of 1830, Buchanan, his Amalgamation party split by patronage disputes and threatened by the rising tide of anti-Masonry, while the Family party boasted control of the Governorship, both Senate seats, and, with Ingham Secretary of the Treasury, a post in Jackson's Cabinet, announced his retirement from politics—which he had entered, remember, ten years before only *as a distraction from* [his] *great grief, and because* [he] *saw that through a political following* [he] *could secure the friends* [he] *then needed.* But did he mean it? With the dissolution of the entire Cabinet—at Van Buren's suggestion, as a way to end the painful Peggy Eaton affair—there was talk of a Cabinet post for Buchanan, and even of him as Vice-President for Jackson's second term, now that Calhoun, like Spiro Agnew on the eve of the Ford era, had resigned this office. But what forthcame from Andrew Jackson was a poisoned sweet: Buchanan was invited to become Minister to Russia, *a distinct letdown,* according to Klein, *since this assignment was a sort of genteel exile for those political figures who could neither be ignored or trusted.*]

BETWEEN THE TWO ACTS of *The Belle of Amherst,* I seem to remember, Genevieve fainted: returning from the lobby where we had chugged down two three-dollar plastic cups of so-called champagne, she murmured to me, "Darling, I'm going to throw up." As I recoiled from her, she leaned all the more heavily upon me, so heavily that her body tilted like a motorcycle going around a curve and I had to hold her with both arms to keep her from falling beneath the trampling feet of the intermission crowd, anxious to resume its seats and see Julie Harris emote some more. I managed to drag her—she had become remarkably dense and inert, though petite; when we made love she felt as weightless as an acrobat or one of those newly idolized child gymnasts from behind the Iron Curtain— toward the ladies' room, against the exiting surge of perfumed, "freshened" women there. The painted eyes of these women flared with horror as I barged in with my burden, but then, like a swarm of ants adjusting itself to the sudden fall of a bread-crumb in its midst, they took over. Genevieve was laid upon a rose-colored couch in their facility's silken anteroom; I discreetly retreated to the doorway, where I could observe, over the shoulders of her multiplying caretakers, that the Perfect Wife looked magnificent—she had become her own effigy in glossy, colorless wax. Her precise, decisively marked features had been transposed to a plane of perfect peace. She was wear-ing a high-necked brocaded gray dress in the Chinese style, and she later claimed that it was the dress, and the claustrophobia-inducing qualities of Emily Dickinson's world, that made her faint. But in fact a medical exam, a week later, revealed that she was harboring a duodenal ulcer which had, under the accumulating stress of leaving Brent and waiting for me to disentangle myself from Norma, begun to bleed. No more champagne for her—Maalox and skimmed milk, rather. I felt guilty, of course. But at the moment I was struck by the grandeur of her sudden unconsciousness, so much purer than her restless, grabby sleep. Smelling salts were produced. In memory I lean forward, the more deeply to inhale their bitter ethereal scent amid the compressed perfumes of the other women, there in that silken foyer faintly redolent of female urine and fair bodies overheated by the excitements of the theatre. I am proud, I remember, proud of Genevieve, proud to be her escort. Frighteningly, I seem, bending forward, to dip beneath the anesthesia of daily events into the divine and dreadful gravity of life—this lovely woman laid low, and both of us far from home, matter in the wrong place, here in New York, if that's where we were.

Speaking of theatre, Wayward had a Drama Society that put on plays in the fall and spring. Let me, patient *Retrospect* editors, set the scene. *Time:* Spring in New England, with cleansing winds, and nodding jonquils and asphalt roads still whitened by winter's salt. *Place:* The Student Center, our newest building, erected in what retrospectively seemed the boom times of Lyndon Johnson, a five-story structure with a colonial-brick outside and a Bauhaus-cement inside. The ground floor was a kind of mall, with the campus bookstore, some shops offering such rudiments of attire and furniture as hadn't been brought from home, a combination grocery and drugstore, and a pizza parlor with six round metal tables that ventured out onto the cement paving in imitation of a European sidewalk café. On the second floor, reachable by several broad, neo-fascist flights of outdoor steps as well as by interior stairways and elevators, was the college dining hall, offering three square cafeteria meals a day, and on the third floor—the hot center of student nightlife—a combination lounge and amusement gallery, a central array of already exhausted and seam-split sofas and chairs surrounded, at a distance in the barren open space, by recreational resources—a darkened gallery of chirping video games, a coffee-and-snack shop that stayed open until midnight, a row of sleepless junk-food-vending machines, and a room holding abused Ping-Pong and billiard tables, both perennially short of balls. Our girls gathered here, not all six hundred at once but many, some with male dates but not many: even on Saturday nights the lounge was what my father's jocosely male-chauvinist generation would have called a hen party—a gynous concentration, in torn jeans, sloganned T-shirts, and grubby salt-and-slush-soaked sneakers, emitting a high-pitched babble and a subliminal scent that bombarded my pheromone receptors with as much radiation as if I were a Ukrainian peasant on the day Chernobyl let loose.

I can see, dear NNEAAH, how this last sentence above might misread in a scholarly journal, and if it offends your taste, or threatens your parsimonious subvention from the Granite State's pinched educational budget, of course strike it out; but I am trying at your behest to remember the Ford era, and the senses are Mnemosyne's handmaidens. The aroma of a hundred young females lying sprawled and jabbering, munching and straw-sucking and with loud excessive animation presenting their cases, their agendas, their hopes and disappointments to one another like so many amateur actresses trying out for the starring role—this scent is an avenue to truth, historical truth as it has become, with the passage of a decade and a half. A nobler teacher, it may be, would have sensed only their minds; his thoughts would have flown to what lay between their ears rather than between their legs and erected fantasies about their term papers and future professions. But it was not clear, in the Ford era, that Woman's proper destiny was to toil on Wall Street or fly a helicopter into Iraq—there was still in the air, left over from the lotus-eating Sixties, a belief that being, not doing, was the point of it all and that psychosexual fulfillment, in a practical form as vague as possible, was the aim of education.

At any rate, am I my reptile brain's keeper? I confess: I had no special reason to be passing through the Student Center; I was cruising it. My bachelor habits had come to include working late in my office in Harrison Hall—named after neither the quickly deceased William Henry nor his equally forgettable grandson Benjamin but after Georgiana Harrison, Wayward Junior College's militantly unwed founder and first President, who brought her father's mill-money, earned by the sweat of sallow maidens manning mechanical looms in twelve-hour stretches, across the river and sank it into the neo-Georgian apparatus of a liberating two-year education. Bleary from my attempts to breathe life into the tortuous career of James Buchanan, between nine and ten I would leave Harrison Hall to its ticking radiators or dripping air-conditioners, depending on the season, and walk toward the faculty parking lot on the far side of the campus. The bucolic randomness of our campus paths presented no unequivocal route; it was as direct as any other to walk through the Student Center, inhaling the aura and bringing a pause to the gabble of the students. They were, as young animals and as cloistered women, immensely sensitive; their pooled sensibilities rippled in the slightest breeze. To be fair to myself, there was something reassuring in passing in out of the damp dark through this cheery, shrill American scene—the video games chirrupping, the Ping-Pong and billiard balls clicking—on my way to my mobile cave of a car and thence to my modest rooms across the river, there to field a harrowing and hard-to-terminate phone call from either Genevieve or Norma, both sopranos (a mezzo and a coloratura, remember?—see page 148) singing, subtextually, the same aria: *Perchè devo dormire sola?* Why wasn't I with, both voices asked without asking, her or her? The Student Center was a kind of last port, gaudily commercial and communal, on the edge of my choppy personal sea.

The ground-floor mall was darkened and locked after nine. I climbed the wide Mussolini-style steps toward a bank of glowing glass doors where the silhouettes of hyperactive girls flickered in a frieze of shadowplay, and entered the young-hearted hubbub. Often I stopped at the third-floor snack shop for a tuna-salad sandwich or honey-and-raisin roll to tide me through the night in Adams. One night, inside the steamy door to this mini-eatery, next to a darkened chamber wherein slumped rows of frizzy-haired students were hooting at the Milwaukee imbroglios of Laverne and Shirley, I bumped into

Jennifer Arthrop. Not literally, luckily, for she was balancing a frail cardboard tray on which a scalding paper cup of coffee loomed above a jumbo-size chocolate-chip cookie. In the months, or was it years, since I had eased her from my digs and the vicinity of my bed, I had seen her in class and in the halls of our intimate institution, but encountering her at this nocturnal hour, when the juices of human contact flow thickest, set off a spark; I could see the shock in her near-sighted eyes and feel it, like the kick of an electric resuscitator, in my heart. Again luckily, she had eaten more than one chocolate-chip cookie since our parting, and her doughy overweight somewhat neutralized my nostalgic pang of appetite.

But I had underestimated the complexity of our encounter. "Professor Clayton," she mouthed, getting her social bearings, "I'd like you to meet my mother." Indeed there was, behind her, *her* cardboard tray holding a dainty can of apple juice and a healthful tangerine, an older version of herself. The two women's heads were at the same height, but Mrs. Arthrop's curls were artfully tinged a metallic bronze, to hide filaments of silver no doubt, and had a firmer, more settled look on her scalp. Her toothy smile, springing forward even before we were introduced, seemed too ready until I remembered, *She runs a gift shop.* "My mother's come up from Connecticut to see me in *Lysistrata*," Jennifer explained, with a touch of nasal petulance. "We've just come from dress rehearsal. She's staying upstairs."

The two top floors of the Student Center, I neglected to explain, were a campus hotel, with rooms for visiting parents, speakers, overseers, and salesmen of newly revised textbooks boasting a simplified and corrected canon.

"Jennifer has told me all about the course she took from you last year, Professor Clayton," Jennifer's mother gushed at me. "She loved it, the way you bring the Presidents to life."

"Well, Presidents are people, too," I snapped, my intense

little vision of a bean-sprouts-on-rye sandwich and a cottage-shaped half-pint carton of milk in a take-out bag slowly fragmenting under the impact of this encounter.

Jennifer's mother laughed as if I had said something rather naughty. Her teeth were remarkably large, and square, without being at all buck or false-looking; when her lips closed over them, it was an act of containment that gave her mouth a composed *presence* I found exciting. Her lips were full, and at the end of a long day away from home had lost lipstick on all but their edges, like a drawing of lips in red ink. Her round yet not fat face had the gloss and glow of youth, with an albedo higher than Jennifer's, who for all her youthful amplitude and thrustingness of figure had something unripened about her, something sullen and light-absorptive, whereas her mother's mature face gleamed with decades of moisturizer and anti-wrinkle cream. I calculated that Mrs. Arthrop, whose twenty-year-old daughter might have been born when she was herself twenty, need not be much older than I, who had celebrated my thirty-ninth birthday (falling in October—see page 159) by passing from a twilight supper catered by Norma and attended by the children in my old house, the cake arriving from the kitchen wearing a crown of candle-flame that three breaths by me, suddenly asthmatic, could not extinguish, so that dismay was kindled on the faces of Andy, Buzzy, and Daphne, who knew this meant bad luck and cancelled everybody's wishes—by passing, I say, with singed eyebrows from this ex-domestic feast of melting ice cream to a nocturnal celebration at Genevieve's, sneaking in the back door and accepting toilet-paper-wrapped presents (a Bic pen, a Magic Rub eraser) from the two little girls before my perfect almost-wife tucked them in and came back downstairs in a filmy black nightie to serve up, in deference to her ulcer, two champagne glasses filled with white milk—a rather stunning visual effect—and two ambrosial macaroons, a feast for dieting gods, consumed by the light of a single tall candle whose phallic hint was soon taken by living flesh. My mistress lay on her modernist, goosedown-filled sofa and let the folds of black film drift up her white waist so I could eat my fill of her musky slit; a few macaroon crumbs from the corners of my mouth were suspended like stars in her tingling pubic cloudlet. My prick kept tapping my belly like a door-knocker, it was so hard.

"Would you like to join us, Professor Clayton—is that terribly forward?" Jennifer's mother asked, two questions in one, rather breathlessly. It flashed upon me that she thought I had slept with her daughter and was slyly granting me a kind of honorary son-in-law status. How could she have gotten this idea? Only from Jennifer's sulky, embarrassed manner now, unless the girl was an outright liar, as even normal girls often are. They lie, they shoplift, they attempt suicide, all as part of their sexual development. I pictured my lonely room, my phone poised to shrill into life with the details of two unhappy women's lives, and figured that fifteen minutes of parent-child-teacher socialization could do no harm, and might do Wayward College, which was always looking to widen its support base, some good. Also, there was about Mrs. Arthrop an elusive likeable something—a bit of blankness, like an unmarked price tag, that signifies a woman who will sleep with you. Or is it that you want to sleep with them? The one becomes the other, in the shadowland where sexual politics defies the best attempts of legislators to clean up corruption and graft.

I joined the two Arthrops in a plastic booth, adjusting my hoped-for milk to a more sociable herbal tea and for the bean-sprout sandwich substituting one of those tempting, Christmassy tangerines Mrs. Arthrop already possessed. "Well, how did the rehearsal go?" I asked, turning myself toward Jennifer, steering away from the dangerous blank next to her, the glossy forty-plus face. Jennifer didn't have that blank; few of our students did. They were too full of ideas and uncertainties;

three-fourths of their lives were ahead of them, instead of a diminishing third. "Who are you?" I asked. "Lysistrata?"

This was tactless, actually. "I'm Cinesias," Jennifer said. "It's a little, man's part, but I have a big scene with this real cock-teaser."

Mrs. Arthrop blinked her daughter's language away and told me, "The girl playing the part is quite wonderful. As you probably remember, the plot is she keeps leaving him, in the throes of—how shall we say?—passion, to get one more thing to make it all perfect—a pillow, ointment. And of course it never happens."

"Marjorie Weisman," Jennifer told me, naming another student. "If you ask me, she gets too much into it. I began to feel sorry for myself. The guy."

"You were *won*derful, dear," her mother told her. "A real man couldn't have done it any better."

"You get to feel like raping her," Jennifer allowed. "Her roommate tells me she's a sadist in other ways. Marjorie."

I had a reprehensible itch to wink at Mrs. Arthrop, Jennifer was mulling things over so solemnly. The very air around us seemed to be winking, since the Student Center, for all its installed comforts, had the bare concrete frame of a multi-story garage, with such a garage's gloomy flicker of ailing fluorescent tubes. Jennifer's young mind for the first time seemed to be questioning the conventional binaries of male/female, sadist/masochist, desire/anger, war/love.

"Well, it's all in a good cause, isn't it?" I asked, none too brightly, explaining myself: "To end war. And it comes out happily, as I recall." I was being very much the teacher, focusing on Jennifer as a student, while being all too aware of her mother next to her as a crevasse of invitingness that might swallow my teetering eyes.

"Yeah, the women go back to being sex slaves," Jennifer said sourly. "I guess you and old Aristophanes would think that's a happy ending."

"*Jen*nifer," Mrs. Arthrop said. "What a way to talk to your professor!" She was my age, we had passed from class to class in the same corridors of time, so I could read in her motherly rebuke the subtext of flirtation, of more warmth than the social thermostat called for, of titillation based upon the (false) premise that her daughter and I had achieved the intimacy of lovers. In fact I felt distaste for doughy Jennifer; she was stale goods, touched by the loathed Brent Mueller intellectually at least, contaminated by his anti-canon deconstructionist chic, which flattened everything eloquent, beautiful, and awesome to propaganda baled for the trashman; Brent dwelt in an ideological Flatland from which I was endeavoring to rescue Genevieve, and Jennifer was his two-dimensional minion there, ostentatiously rounded though her dull flesh was.

"No problem," I said to my defender. "All that respect we were supposed to show our teachers was hierarchical crap. At Wayward we ask our students to be frank."

"*I am a woman, but I don't lack sense,*" Mrs. Arthrop surprisingly recited, in iambic pentameter, her eyes shut to get her started. "*I'm of myself not badly off for brains, / And often listening to my father's words / And old men's talk, I've not been badly schooled.*" She lifted her greasy-blue eyelids, exposing irises that indeterminate organic color called hazel, and broadly smiled, exposing those confident teeth. Her facial gloss had gone a degree higher.

"*O.K.,* Mom," Jennifer said, uncomfortably sensing that this was sexual display. To me she grudgingly explained, "*She* was Lysistrata in a school play once." *Big deal,* her tone implied.

"At Miss Porter's School, ages ago," Mrs. Arthrop modestly amplified. "Seeing Jenny's rehearsal brought that bit of it back. At the time, there seemed nothing wrong with her having to learn by eavesdropping on men's talk. What *did* seem daring, as I remember it, and offended some of the faculty and the chaplain, was the anti-war theme—it would have been in, oh, I was seventeen, '51, Korea was on, and though it was all right to be against war in the abstract, nobody *dreamed* of being against a war the United States was fighting."

"Yes," I agreed. "The war ended before I was eighteen, and I remember feeling slightly cheated." There. Our ages were on the table, if we could do the figuring. "How long are you here for?" I asked the woman—a *real* woman. The girls of Wayward insisted on being called "women"; their boyfriends, conditioned in puberty, had no trouble with it, but we older guys kept tripping up.

"Just this one night," Mrs. Arthrop said, with an enigmatic upturn of her face, as if toward a spotlight still shining upon her girlish performance as Lysistrata. She had been the star where her daughter had a bit part. The world can be cruel to the young. Think of all those newly hatched leatherback turtles, scrambling to get to the sea's safety while all up and down the beach the famished gulls are swooping.

Memory fails of exact recall, but we talked, Mrs. A. and I striving to keep Jennifer at the focus, though she kept slipping away, through a short and sullen or else unduly combative answer, while her mother's thumbs and mine dug into the soft hollow spot crowning our tangerines and undressed the furry segments, juicier than grapes, of their loose and stippled hides. I could not help but be aware of a certain mastery in Mrs. Arthrop's scarlet-taloned hands and of the way her plump mouth—plump but the lips flat to the face, like Jimmy Carter's—coped with the little masticatory indiscretion of ejecting the tangerine seeds as each segment was consumed, letting them find their way via her fingers to the cardboard tray. Her lips performed this awkward necessity with a fasci-

nating air of *accomplishment*, of self-appreciation, that produced, along with each ejected seed, a bit of a smile.

Jennifer at last slipped away entirely, seeing a friend leave
the television room—*Laverne and Shirley* having yielded up its
last tracked laughs and surges of theme music—and rising from
our booth to go outside and confer in heated whispers. Her
mother and I were left alone. The thin oily sting of tangerine
juice and the dull underfoot smell of many much-worn Tre-
torns serve in this episode as the aromatic accompaniment, the
half-heard sound-track music, like the ladies'-room perfumes
and smelling salts when Genevieve fainted. I asked, in Jennifer's abrupt absence, "How *are* the rooms upstairs?"

"Adequate," Jennifer's mother enunciated, letting me know
she was a woman of the world, who had seen her share of hotel
accommodations and was not automatically pleased. "Rather
minimal," she said, having complacently disposed of another
tangerine seed, and then added, as if not wishing to undersell
her room's charms irrevocably, "The window overlooks a
pond and a strange long brown sculpture."

"The students call that the French Fry. It won a competition
in the Sixties but keeps coming apart now. The welding was
poor, it turns out." My conversational attempts felt desperate,
an idiotic waste of Jennifer's absence. We could see her
through the snack-shop plate glass, whining on and on into this
other girl's—all right, woman's—ear. My sense of this real
woman's face across from me having attached to it a tag of
inviting blankness was succumbing to a sense of her extraordinary fullness; she seemed stuffed *full*, like a thoroughly studied
savage, of sociological data—Miss Porter's School pieties,
Northeastern-U.S. upper-middle-class courtship-and-marriage
lore, marketing techniques adapted to the small gift shop, standard post-Spock parenting trials and heartbreak—parallel to
my own. She, too, remembered the Korean Conflict, the ad-

vent of Elvis, the Kennedy assassinations; she, too, had sat in a darkened living room somewhere and watched Nixon blubberingly resign. Even her performance in *Lysistrata* (her round girlish legs exposed, in my mind's eye, by the unhistorically short chiton with which school-level producers of my youth shamelessly beefed up interest in Aristophanes' hoary and hieratic old farce) was more vivid to me than that of Jennifer's generation, overlaid with such Fordisms as feminism and androgyny. Mrs. Arthrop's little smooth feet would have been bare but for sandals like a web of gold thongs, her unbronzed hair upswept in a Claire Trevor do, her voice pushing out the speeches in a brave adolescent voice just on the edge of authority.

She was reading my mind. Cocking back her hand as if it held a cigarette, she asked me, "The students—do you do a lot of, how shall we say, *mingling* with them, Professor?"

"Not as much as people think," I told her, somewhat curtly. Her absurd conviction that I had slept with her daughter was making her eyes sparkle as if loaded with belladonna. She was back on stage, legs swinging, voice rising. Her hands were flirting in mid-air with an invisible cigarette. I said, "But you're not a student, Mrs. Arthrop. You don't have to keep calling me Professor."

"What *shall* I call you?"

"Alf. My parents called me Alfred, for political reasons. And you?"

She leaned forward slightly above the table in the booth, here in the steamy late-night student eatery. The high gloss of her face, the fetching little space between her large front teeth, the visible gamble in her bulging hazel eyes seemed to express some numbing animal truth, that my rudimentary brain stem had no word for.

"Ann," she said. She lowered the hand holding the imaginary cigarette to the silver-starred Formica tabletop, the same motion carrying her eyelids down as if she were fighting a blush.

Oh. Ah. "Ann," I repeated. That tore it.

BUCHANAN WAS WALTZING with the Czarina of Russia. Pleasantly plump in his arms she was, the back of her gown of dove-gray silk moist with imperial sweat beneath his hand, here amid the thousand mirrored and refracted candles of the Winter Palace, above the intricately parqueted ballroom floor, while the inflexible Russian winter immobilized, in white chains of snow, the world beyond the tall windows, which were steamed by the hard-breathing gaiety within. Since the days at Dickinson when he notoriously danced on tavern tables, Buchanan enjoyed the self-forgetful methodical whirl of dancing, whether in the stately strides of the polonaise or the looping interlocked triangulations of the waltz. "*Vous dansez très bien, monsieur l'envoyé extraordinaire,*" the empress confided to him, as the orchestra of Parisian musicians, bored and weary, pale and unhappy, with frazzled jabots and blue noses, here in this frostbitten extremity of civilization, lifted the melody to yet a higher plane of irresistibly urging rhythm, thrusting on every third beat "*Peu d'hommes aussi grands que vous le feraient avec une telle grâce.*"

Forgetful, in the ecstasy of the music, of the sacred dignity of the majestic person so plump and responsive in his arms, he ventured a small joke: "*J'ai appris à danser avec Andrew Jackson. Mon président fait ceux qui le suivent très agiles. Après l'avoir suivi, les pieds sont pleins de la grâce.*"

She perhaps did not understand so political a jest, though her life had been lived in palaces. Her father was King Friedrich Wilhelm III of Prussia, an uninspired monarch who, after the

crushing defeat at Jena (1806) and the humiliating Treaty of
Tilsit (1807), ruled, like royalty all across Europe, in terror of
the shades of Napoleon and Jacobinism. Her husband at the
time of their marriage, on July 1 (Old Style), 1817, was the
Grand Duke Nikolai Pavlovich, and had no prospects of being
czar, since, though his oldest brother, reigning as Alexander I,
was childless, another older brother, Constantine, stood next
in the line of succession. Nicholas, anticipating a life of luxuri-
ant aristocracy, with a smattering of military duty (for which
he possessed a certain grim aptitude), threw himself into the
joys of family life and, to assuage his wife's homesickness,
imported the Prussian paintings of Caspar David Friedrich,
amassing an unsurpassed collection of this exemplary Romantic. The future holds strange treasures; Constantine, having
married a Polish wife and taken up residence in Poland, secretly renounced the throne in 1823, so that when Alexander
died on December 1 (New Style), 1825, Nicholas became emperor without the fact's being widely known, Constantine
having not deigned to make a public announcement. Army
officers professedly loyal to Constantine, but in truth concerned to bring about the abolition of serfdom and the establishment of representative government, staged the Decembrist
mutiny, which Nicholas, known as a military martinet, stoutly
faced down and quelled. The new czar's regime thus got off
to a reactionary start, and continued by forbidding foreign
travel, founding the secret police (the notorious "third section"), and promoting the ideas of nationality *(narodnost)*,
autocracy, and Orthodox Christianity. *Nicholas was not blind
to the evils of Russian society,* one source tells us, *but he feared
that changes would be worse yet.*

The czarina, realizing that she was being, albeit in full propriety, flirted with, by this tall American in a well-cut but,
among the ubiquitous military uniforms glistening with brass
and braid, somber black suit, responded, *"Assez de grâce, peut-*

être, pour vous porter jusqu'à la présidence de votre grand pays, dans la manière du Général Jackson?"

Seven years younger than Buchanan, the czarina was to die seven years before him. She had the Germanic, faintly sallow and low-albedo complexion of the better-kept women of Lancaster County, though separated from these females by five thousand miles and twenty degrees of latitude; to this extent Buchanan felt familiar with her. And she with him, for at their very first encounter, upon his presentation, she *talked very freely,* as his dispatch to President Jackson declared: *She spoke on several subjects, and with great rapidity. Amongst other things she observed we were wise in America not to involve ourselves in the foolish troubles of Europe; but she added that we had troubles enough among ourselves at home, and alluded to our difficulties with some of the Southern States.* Her observations on this score must have struck Buchanan as reckless or unduly ominous, for he *endeavored in a few words to explain this subject to her; but she still persisted in expressing the same opinion, and, of course,* [he] *would not argue the point.* He was disposed to argue, for he goes on in his dispatch, with some feeling, *The truth is, that the people of Europe and more especially those of this Country, cannot be made to understand the operations of our Government. Upon hearing of any severe conflicts of opinion in the United States, they believe what they wish, that a revolution may be the consequence. God forbid that the Union should be in any danger!* Evidently, she foresaw another American revolution, and he did not; and she was right.

Her face, broad and smooth-skinned, was marked by distinct patches of rouge and a narrow, sharply tipped nose, *un peu retroussé.* The value of the diamonds at her throat and in her small tiara would have purchased, at a guess, a thousand serfs.

The miserable, snuffling, ill-clad band of imported French musicians changed from a Viennese to a Königsberg tempo— brisker, more military—and the alleged grace within Buchanan's feet was laggard, momentarily, as he framed a suitably modest yet sufficiently high-spirited response to the empress's probe in regard to his ambitions. A reflexive *"Mais non, non"* gained him time to offer her the explanation, *"La grâce seule ne suffit pas: il faut aussi—"* His brain, weary of groping in a second language, hesitated among "good fortune," "suitable friends," and "the people." None made quite enough sense, in French. He thought of General Jackson—met in many encounters from all of which Buchanan emerged feeling, as from an interview with his father, diminished if not rebuked—and finished simply, *"la force."*

"La force? La force de la personnalité? La force des alliances politiques?"

She was trying genuinely to understand, he saw, the workings of a system in which birth and inheritance are—inscrutably; blasphemously, even—not the crucial factor. The strange confluences of self-interest and moralism that foment events in a democracy were beyond her but not, as the Decembrists made vivid, beneath royal notice any more; her husband's personal inquisitions and the hanging of Colonel Pestel and the poet Kondrati Ryleyev would not rid this despotic frozen empire of the warm breath, from the west, of freedom. The pert-nosed empress's intelligent curiosity for a moment formed, for her partner, here amid the stifling heat and the dizzying whirl of braided uniforms, a small fogged window into the vast dungeon in which all women—Queen Victoria excepted—were condemned to political impotence in this century, constrained to move the levers of power only by moving their men, with charms and beguilements. Poor dear Ann had chafed at this, this natural powerlessness of her sex, save to command men's feelings and to order the domestic realm.

"La force du destin," Buchanan responded. *"Beaucoup des hommes américains sont capables, mais peu achèvent, dans les chances d'élection, la position plus haute."* He feared, from the

failure of her regal face to pounce upon his meaning, that he had lost her; perhaps *achever* was the wrong verb, and *position* imprecise. And yet, even in his uncertainty, and the possibility of inadequacy at the highest reach of his mission here in Russia, he retained a sense of masculine comfort with this woman, who had recently risen from her bed of *accouchement*, delivered of another Grand Duke. *She is remarkably fond of dancing in which she excels,* Buchanan wrote Hannah Slaymaker from his apartment on the north side of the Neva. The following year, he wrote John B. Sterigere, *I think I may say, I am a favorite here, & especially with the Emperor and Empress. They have always treated me during the past winter in such a manner as even to excite observation. I am really astonished at my own success in this respect.* Her doughy Germanic softness in his arms, the careful simplicity of her French, the silken patch of moisture beneath his hand, even the slightly puzzled look in her eyes, which were brown shot through with a honied pallor, all catered to his comfort, his feverish illusion, amid the swinging pressures of the dance, of mastery—of their two weights connected by an attraction kept taut. The empress's lips, thin but rosy, with a dent of latent smile—of self-appreciation—in the corners, were parted as if waiting for him to give her reason to speak. So Buchanan went on, adding a shrug of his arms to the conjoined movements of the waltz, *"Mais nous parlons des possibilités imaginaires. Je voudrais seulement que le traité de commerce et de navigation entre nos pays se conclure; donc, je retournerai à mon état natal de Pennsylvanie, où j'assumerai les devoirs and les plaisirs très modestes du citoyen privé. Ma carrière publique achève"*—yes, this was the correct use of the verb, but for emphasis he amplified—*"fait sa fin avec cette mission ici, en Russie."*

She smiled; her small round teeth glinted, and the disarming gap where an eye tooth has been pulled. Her jewels and eyes sparkled alike; her naked plump shoulders shone with their glaze of human sweat. *"Je pense que vous avez longtemps le mal du pays, de votre pays chaud et fertile, dans le Pennsylvanie, alors qu'il faut vivre dans notre royaume tellement froid, tellement vaste et vieux et barbare."*

"Ah, que non—pas barbare! Pauvres, peut-être—la plupart des gens sont pauvres et aussi, dans la vue d'un homme américain, très superstitieux."

"Dans les Etats-Unis, personne ne croit?"

"Au contraire, votre Majesté—tous les gens croient dans le bon Dieu, parce que—ça va sans dire—Dieu a les donné, a nous donné, tant de bonheurs. La terre si grande, les beaux temps, les bois, les fleuves, et, au-dessus tout, notre constitution sage et généreuse— toutes les choses, les dons du bon Dieu! Mais, en comparaison du Dieu russe, notre Dieu tient à distance sublime; dans cette manière, il met à l'épreuve notre sincérité, et nous donne l'espace pour l'exercice de la liberté!" Buchanan was not sure he had done justice, in these clumsy idioms, to the mighty subject of faith in his native land, but from a tension on the empress's face, like that on a bulging drop about to run down a windowpane, she was waiting her turn to speak.

"Votre pays est très curieux à mon sens—une Russie pleine d'Allemands! Mon mari," she went on brightly, *"attend beaucoup de votre pays."*

He was not sure he had heard correctly. *Attendre*, he supposed, in the sense of "expects." The czar, absolute ruler of the world's largest terrain, seemed implausibly miniaturized in the intimate phrase *mon mari*. Confused, Buchanan responded merely, *"Vraiment? Pourquoi?"*

"C'est simple, n'est-ce pas? La Russie a besoin d'amis, maintenant que la France et l'Angleterre ont conclus leur traité sur la question belge. Aussi, l'opinion publique et la presse européenne ont été peu aimables à mon mari concernant la question polonaise, et particulièrement les atrocités alléguées de la guerre, sa suppression héroïque de leur révolte méchante. Dans toute l'Europe, le mouve-

ment révolutionnaire naisse—ça bouillonne! Et quel pays est la source du mouvement, à l'origine? Le votre! Ainsi, s'il y soit ce traité maritime, l'empereur pourra dire, 'Voilà, mes bon amis, les américains, les gens les plus révolutionnaires au monde—ils ne résistent pas à ma politique polonaise!' "

"Je vous comprends, Majesté, et je vous remercie très sincèrement pour votre explication lucide." In fact her blithe words did help Buchanan better to understand why the commercial treaty, after years of surly inaction on the part of Russian officialdom, was now, with some prodding from Count Nesselrode, the Foreign Minister, and Baron Krudener, the Ambassador to the United States, making sudden headway against the objections of Count Cancrene, the Minister of Finance, and Monsieur de Bloudoff, the Minister of the Interior; certain tariff reductions (on hemp, sail duck, and hammered iron) in the proposed Congressional bill of 1832, together with a marked increase over the last year of Russian imports of, especially, American sugar, of course had helped, as had Buchanan's judicious and flattering remarks in those of his dispatches bound to be opened and read by the emperor's spies. But this insight, that a despotic government might relieve itself of revolutionary pressure by striking a trading deal with the most progressive power on earth, he owed to the empress, and the curious propensity of her feminine sun to shine upon him. His last official communication from Russia, an accounting to Secretary of State Louis McLane of his final days and his official farewells,* included this mysterious—almost romantically so—paragraph:

I had, on the same day, my audience of leave of the Empress who was very gracious; but what passed upon this occasion is not properly the subject for a despatch.

Buchanan's letter to McLane includes a number of passages

---

*Moore, ed. *Works*, Vol. II, pp. 378–82.

that deserve quotation. Emperor Nicholas, for instance, inquiring as to Buchanan's homeward itinerary, expatiated upon the worrisome French people. *The French were a singular people. They were so fickle in their character and had such a restless desire to disturb the peace of the world; that they were always dangerous. They had tried every form of government and could not rest satisfied with any. French emissaries were now endeavoring, every where, to excite disturbances and destroy the peace all over Europe.*

And Buchanan describes—with how conscious a parallel, one wonders, to Ann Coleman's death—the virtual suicide of Nicholas's oldest brother, the handsome, erratic, and in the end melancholy Alexander I. *Throughout his last illness, he refused to take medicine and thus suffered his disease which was not, at the first, considered dangerous, to become mortal. When Sir James Wylie, his physician, told him, that unless he would submit to medical treatment his disease must prove fatal; the Emperor Alexander regarded him earnestly and exclaimed, in the most solemn manner, "And why should I desire to live?" He continued to reject all remedies and his death was the consequence. On the truth of this anecdote you may rely. There was no foundation for the report that he had been poisoned.*

In parting, the Emperor Nicholas embraced and saluted the stout Pennsylvanian in the Russian manner, *a ceremony for which I was wholly unprepared,* and *told me to tell General Jackson to send him another Minister exactly like myself. He wished for no better.* The Russian manner was more fully described in Buchanan's diary of June that year: *Upon taking leave of Antoine, I submitted to be kissed by him according to the Russian fashion, first on the right cheek, then on the left, and then on the mouth. This was my first regular experiment of the kind.*

One wants to imagine Buchanan happy in Russia, amid the four-horse carriages, the gilt, the unmelting snows, the unending balls, the stately pace of court intrigue, the flirtatious ladies (some speaking English) of the royal circles. As with Benjamin

Franklin in the French court a half-century before, an American in the plain dark clothes of a democrat charmed the court like a dwarf, like a black-skinned Ethiopian—a delegate from a different sort of space. When the world was emptier, it was larger; there were blanks on the map wherein explorers could win fame, and travel skirted the realms of fantasy. The diary Buchanan kept of his trip to Moscow in June of 1833* seems happy, with its descriptions of pious monks and rascally muzhiks in tanned sheepskins. Of the Reverend Father Antoine, the archimandrite or abbot of Troitza Monastery, sixty-two versts north of Moscow, Buchanan seems almost enamored: *His long beard was of a most beautiful chestnut color, and made his appearance venerable notwithstanding his comparative youth. I shall never forget the impression which this man made upon me.* Bronze figures on the door of a church in Novgorod were *strange and barbarous figures not unlike those of Mexico.* He was far from home, and was amused when a Princess Ouroussoff in Moscow inquired *if the United States still belonged to England* and *whether they spoke the English language in America.* Conversation with another hostess, Madame S——, *would have been agreeable but for the constant interruption of a parrot which screeched as if it had been hired for the occasion.* Moscow, since its conflagration in 1812, *has lost, however, in a great degree, that romantic and Asiatic appearance which it formerly presented. The cumbrous and rude magnificence of palaces irregularly scattered among Tartar huts, has given place to airy and regular streets in all directions. It appears to be in a prosperous condition. That which chiefly distinguishes it from other cities is the immense number of churches. Their cupolas, in all colors and of all forms, rising above the summits of the houses and glittering in the sun, are very striking and imposing objects.* Also imposing, though less attractive, were the armies of peasant women offering themselves as

---

*Moore, ed., *Works,* Vol. II, pp. 348–63.

wet nurses to the directors of the Foundling Hospital, or Imperial House of Education: *It was quite a novel spectacle for me to pass through the long ranges of women, with infants in their arms, or in the cradle. Everything was clean and in good order; though the women were anything but good-looking.* He was more favorably impressed by the poor but noble children of the Alexander Institution, orphaned by such misfortunes as cholera, recruited from all over the empire, *250 boys and as many girls.* He was especially impressed by the girl students, collected at dinner, *all dressed alike, in green frocks and white aprons, which came over their arms. . . . Previous to taking their seats, they sang a hymn in Russian as a blessing. Their performance was excellent. Here the goodness and piety of the female heart shone out in a striking manner.* His escort, a Mr. Gretsch, editor of the *Bee* in St. Petersburg, made a speech in Russian, explaining that Buchanan was *the minister of the United States, a great and powerful republic. That the people there were well educated and well informed; but that every person had to labor. That their Government was a good one; but no paternal emperor existed there, who would become the father of orphans and educate them at his own expense.* At the Troitza Monastery, Buchanan was impressed not only by the chestnut beard of the young archimandrite but by the uninscribed tomb of Boris Godunov, by magnificent specimens of embroidery wrought by the Empresses Elizabeth, Anne, and Catherine the Second, and by a crystal in which the image of a kneeling monk was miraculously embedded. At Peterhoff, at an imperial fête,* he was enchanted by the extent and ingenuity of the waterworks—*they place candles under the shutes of the water and thus have an illumination under the water*—and by *a carp which has been in the lake for a century, with a collar round its neck. It, with others, comes to the edge of*

---

*Moore, ed., *Works*, Vol. II, pp. 368–9.

the water at the sound of a bell, every morning, to receive its breakfast.

Happiness! What is it? It can be breakfast. It can be a foreign country, where we are treated as a guest, and our ignorance of the language shields us from many difficulties. At the fête, the royalty in attendance and numerous dignitaries, including Buchanan, mounted *singular vehicles on four wheels and drawn by two splendid horses* which the diarist can describe no better than *by imagining a double sofa with a single back, on which ten of us could sit back to back comfortably, five on each side.* [Later,] *we slowly promenaded through all these walks, the sides of which were covered by immense crowds of spectators. The effect of the illumination was brilliant. The Grand Duke Michel was on horseback, and great precautions were evidently taken, on account of the Polish conspiracy.*

Yet it leaves, happiness, as little residue in the memory as pain. We have in the end only a few flat images painted in calcium on the wet stuff of brain cells, a set of signs no more enduring than a fresco sunk in crumbling plaster. We read in Young's *Night Thoughts* of *gorgeous tapestries of pictur'd joys!* Just following the three lines which Buchanan or Judge Franklin incorporated into Ann's obituary, the next three run

> *O ye blest scenes of permanent delight!*
> *Full above measure! lasting beyond bound!*
> *A perpetuity of bliss is bliss.*

And a bliss short of perpetuity, the implication is, is hell. We want life eternally, or else its joys are hopelessly poisoned; its tie to bliss *breaks at every breeze.* Buchanan was happy, whirling in the rosy rounded arms of Aleksandra Fedorovna. "*D'une santé délicate,*" we are told by the *La Grande Encylopédie* touchingly, "*elle dut souvent quitter la Russie pour aller vivre à l'étranger. Son souvenir est resté populaire chez les Russes.*"

*Mon souvenir de Madame Arthrop est imparfait. J'ai oublié beau-
coup, depuis cette escapade.* And yet we sought, in the approved
manner of the Ford era, to give each other happiness, for a
stolen interim. Before Jennifer's return to our booth, Ann
contrived, in the guise of resuming humorous denigration of
her "minimal" room above us, to let me know its number,
casually yet distinctly, "five oh eight," with an eye-flare—an
alteration of hazel iris as of Wendy Wadleigh's blue when
carnally entered—that left no doubt of the centrality of the
signal being given. That imaginary price tag fluttering near her
face had become the size of a flag of surrender. I remember the
number still, 508, each curved numeral plump with sexual
invitation.

When our little threesome broke up, as it shortly did—
Jennifer off with her girl-pals toward an attempt at nocturnal
study, her mother into the elevator to attempt a night's sleep
away from her chintzy Connecticut bedroom—there was
nothing for me to do but stroll outside, beneath the aloof and
scudding moon, skip diagonally down the fascist breadth of
stairs, chafe my hands and huff my breath against the spring
chill as if this would explain my behavior to a hypothetical
witness watching me, and rapidly stride through a well-worn
pondside grove where entangled young couples fell apart at
my passing like tapped chocolate apples. Then, a conspicuous
insouciance wrapped around my racing heart, I went diagonally back up the broad stairs, around to the other entrance to
the Student Center, which was populated by now with only
a handful of torpid stragglers, and sidled toward the elevators,
where in time, at the push of a button, a steel box appeared,
prepared to make me vanish like a rabbit in a false-bottomed
hat. My guilt at not being home on schedule, able to answer

the telephone with its torrent of needy nagging, I suppressed with the reflection that, as de Tocqueville was among the first to point out, Americans prize freedom above all other goods. Tied though I was, to two women, five children, a mother, and an unfinished book, did I have no rights of movement? Was this the Soviet Union, where one needed a permit to go from Omsk to Tomsk? Was this already 1984, with Big Brother's sister watching my every move? I flicked myself through the rubber-edged elevator doors, pushed the green number that spelled ascent and adventure and Ann, and with halting steps silenced by the orange carpeting made my way down the corridor. I had never been up here in this part of the collegiate dominions before. Arrows indicated odd numbers to the right, even to the left. 502, 504, 506, bingo.

Before Ann answers my sly little knock, a mere back-handed tap of the knuckles that chivalrously gave her the out of not hearing it, if her mind and mood had changed, let me, *Retrospect* editors, place the moment in a historical context. Gerald Ford, in his two years and five months of Presidency, presided over a multitude—dare we say millions? of so-called one-night stands; a tenet of this era was that you did not need to like someone very much to fuck him or her, or know them very well. Fucking was the way in which you got to know them, these hers and hims, and to decide how much you liked them. Even so, heterosexual contacts never attained the amazing facility and number of homosexual contacts in this era, when a mere hole cut in a plywood partition in a bathhouse created access enough. Between men and women, the old courtship dances were still enacted, but in wonderfully accelerated form.

Ann answered my knock instantly, as if poised by the door; she was already in a bathrobe, in a room where but one dim bedside lamp, its parchment shade decorated with a pointing Labrador, added its beige glow to the moonlight pressing on the drawn curtains. We tightly embraced in wordless relief. The bathrobe was a sensible flannel, but I soon noticed she wore nothing beneath it. I kept saying her name—"Ann! Ann!"—until she betrayed annoyance. My absurd name lent itself to no such betranced intonations.

"I've never heard it said that way," she at last protested. "My husband calls me Annie. Annie Sure-Shot. Because I always come."

Her husband, not hitherto evoked, borrowed a phantom reality from this jocose salute—he was thoroughly familiar with this hefty body and the direct, vital, possibly coarse personality inside it. He would himself be a big man, to kid her thus fondly. He wore a fake-gold collar pin beneath the knot of his necktie and white-collared shirts with a fine blue stripe and shoes that were solid-black wingtips in an extra-wide size. He was a bit of a dude, a bit of a gangster, a solid family man with some flings on the side—a man in love with all the angles life can be approached by, with no time for books, for history, for doubt. A single impulsive tug at the flannel belt revealed his wife's glories. Ann Arthrop had her daughter's pneumatic impressiveness, the curves of her affected by four decades, as an old river swings ever wider, but still a swaggeringly fine figure of a woman, who bestowed herself upon me with the amused efficiency of a suburban mother laying out a big tray of peanut-butter-and-jelly sandwiches for her children and their playmates on a Saturday afternoon. Hers was an overflowing femininity; her buttocks overflowed my hands, her breasts so swamped my mouth and nostrils I gasped for breath. "Ann," I could not help repeating, at the moment I entered her. I had turned off the bedside light—whose doggy shade was partnered with a ceramic base showing green-headed ducks taking wing at sunset—and could not see her eyes. She was matter-of-factly slick, accepting me with a certain somber swallowing motion of her shadowed eye sockets, yet revealing to my agitated, flurrying kisses upon her mouth the tension of a possible laugh.

She was one of those women who come forward for their serving; she flared her thighs and clipped her little penile homologue determinedly against my pelvic bone until, in rising tempo, she delivered herself of an orgasm and two faintly rote moans. In no hurry, I followed; a restrained, then released selfishness is the only path for love, purling downhill between narrow rocks on the way to pools of gentleness. Muted moonlight picked up gleams of dew on her temple; I stretched myself, craning my neck, to lick off the salt sweat. She mistook my motion and pressed down on my buttocks. "No," she said with husky despair. "Don't leave me yet." Her firm fingers pricked me with the cool touch of rings.

"Wouldn't dream of it," I said, but already an enlarging guilt was gnawing at my stomach—Genevieve trying to phone with some new legal twist the nefarious Brent had developed, Norma with word that Andrew had had a terrible accident in the Volvo, my mother crying out that her Clearwater condo was burning down. . . . The present is Paradise, yet our brain forbids our living in it long. Past and future conspired to diminish this treasure beached beneath me, lightly panting. She, too, began to get herself together. She permitted me to slide out of her and fall to one side, and propped herself up in the bed, so her tits bobbled like flotsam above my dazed face. She was smoking that phantom cigarette again, right elbow in left palm, right wrist cocked back. "When did you give it up?" I asked.

"Four months ago. I've put on weight, damn it."

"Very becoming. The weight."

She snorted and added, "The trouble is, when you stop, you're healthier. I'm horny all the time."

"That's nice, too," I said. "Nice for me, in this instance."

She snorted again, a cocky noise like a half-sneeze. "Well,

Professor," Mrs. Arthrop said. "Was I better or worse than Jennifer?"

"I've never slept with Jennifer, I swear it. Has she said I did?"

"Not in so many words, just the body language."

"I was saving myself for you," I said, adding, "dear Ann. *Dear* Ann."

"I'm not so dear," she said, glancing about as if for an ashtray in which to tap her lengthening ash. "Bit of a whore, actually. But it was just too mean, to make me come back to this dreary room alone. Also, frankly, I found watching Jen rehearse tonight very painful. She's no actress. How is she as a student?"

"Conscientious. Tries to deconstruct everything. Makes every issue feminist. A lot of the girls do." My answers were terse because I was fascinated by Ann Arthrop's body, clarifying and widening under my eyes as they, adjusting, saw more and more by the moonlight that pressed at the window curtains like blue cheese wrapped in burlap. In the ripeness of her flesh every big curve sprouted little curves, qualifications of minor muscle and fat-rumple, so that an endless Rubensesque activity of mortal pucker was inscribed upon the ideal large forms of the eternal feminine. She had not affected the phony old Hayes–Code Hollywood device of post-coitally tucking the sheets over her chest, and with silent amusement she let me roll the sheet down further, to the staring darknesses of her navel and pubic bush. The smell came off her that low tide releases from wet sand.

She kept talking. Coyly: "Are you going to want to fuck her now, now that you've had me?" In her Connecticut circles, they evidently called spades spades. Or was she casually trying to deconstruct my romantic, too worshipful mood? I touched her here and there, with tongue and fingertip. How nice that particular whiteness is, just above the pubic hair, where even the skimpiest bikini protects the skin. Her sweat was sweeter here than at her temple, a rarer honey.

"Of course not," I said. "Please. These girls aren't paying tuition to be sexually exploited by the male faculty. It's their minds that are given to us in trust."

"Good. My husband would kill you," she said pleasantly.

I looked up the many little crests and swales of her abdomen toward the Olmec impassivity of Mrs. Arthrop's face. Great stone lips, naked of lipstick but the rims. Swallowing eye sockets, all shadow, in which reptilian lids moved, and lashes jerked quickly, like spiders. "Do you and Mr. have affairs?" I asked her.

"I do. He doesn't. He's too busy, off in town twelve, fourteen hours every day, screwing other guys in his business. He's in communications technology."

"Does he know? That you do?"

"Of course not." She was now ready to put out the imaginary cigarette, and made a grinding motion on the little bedside table. The table, like the headboard, was fastened to the wall. "He thinks he adores me."

This was unpleasant, I felt, to both of us—the "thinks" to him, and to me the rubbing of my nose in the success of her marriage.

"This interest in your daughter's sexual conquests," I said. "Do you think it's quite normal? I wouldn't know, my own daughter's just barely adolescent, but I don't think my wife—"

"Probably not," she interrupted. "But healthy to admit it, don't you think? I'm phasing out, she's phasing in, I need to live vicariously. You know, Al, what I sometimes fantasize?"

I hope I suppressed an expression of disgust. Nobody called me "Al." This woman was getting to be too much. But out of elementary courtesy I had to ask, "What?"

"She and me," she said, "sharing a man, or a boy, I guess

he'd be a boy if she brought him home, I'd rather do a boy than see her worked over by a grown man." Noticing my silent abashment, she added quickly, "I just *think* about it, I'd never *do* it."

"You must have a lot of free time, for fantasizing, on your hands," I ventured.

"The shop is slow some days," she admitted. "Summer afternoons, when everybody is at the beach. And that dull stretch before Thanksgiving, when the weddings are over and the Christmas lights aren't up yet. You get maybe half a dozen people coming in. I'd love to rent at the other end of the mall, where the pizza places generate more traffic."

I've been used, I thought to myself, perceiving that my value to her had lain largely in her mistaken faith that I had seduced her daughter. But, then, what had been her value to me, the igniting impetus? Her name. A chance to rescue lonely Ann from the Hemphills' cold bedroom.

In the Ford era, one didn't hold a grudge long, in sexual matters. Nor was performance judged perfectionistically, as in the Eisenhower years, when the sleeping beauty was so hemmed about with thorn-bushes that only a peerless prince would do, wielding Excalibur. Under Ford, if one lay didn't work out, another would be along soon. "I got to run," I announced.

This rippling giantess, so confidently reclining within the largesse of her flesh, dismissed the threat lightly. "Why, Professor? It's not even midnight. I thought you were separated from your wife."

"I am, but . . ." Picturing the Perfect Wife, my mistress in transit, and her Gallic purity and intensity over against this sloppy, chatty piece of middle Americana, I felt an inner burning as if a handful of pepper had reached my stomach. Yet I remained crouched above the globe of Ann Arthrop's belly, with its high albedo and its umbilicus cut in careless Roosevelt-era style, a fold of flesh left like an eyelid.

"We could raid the refreshment bar," she said, "if this room wasn't too crummy to have one."

I tried to defend the Wayward College Student Center, saying, "Students rent these rooms sometimes—if they had refreshment bars the kids might empty them and not fill out the little honor-system tab."

"You got to run, *I* got to go *pee,* " she said, with an unnecessary emphasis, "and mop up a little," swaggering toward the bathroom with rippling buttocks and a touching two-handed tug on her mussed-up hairdo, pulling it back into a Psyche knot. She was determined, it seemed, to remind me at every turn that this was a carnal encounter, with the usual overflow of slime into the plumbing. She didn't bother to close the door. I heard her pee and rattle the toilet-paper roll ruthlessly. When, after a tumult of splashing and flushing, she re-emerged, her face and inner thighs shining wet from the washrag, she smiled to see me still present, waiting naked on the bed. "I thought you had to run."

"How would you define dirt?" I asked her.

She blinked, but nothing stopped her for long. "As matter in the wrong place," she said. Jennifer had been right.

"That's how I feel," I confessed, with my peppery stomach.

"My daughter doesn't understand," she told me bouncily in turn, "how I can know what shits men are, and love them anyway."

I was dealing, it seemed, with some kind of masochist, or bully, or combination, but her long-range psychological problems belonged to the lady's husband, daughter, gift-shop customers, pets, neighbors, and shrink, if she had one. To me belonged, as big as a thumb held up to the eye, her pallid moistened body with its thousand jiggles and many membranous apertures. Just the mental gloating, as she noisily pursued her ablutions, had reinvited nature's magic back into my loins. It was noticing this, perhaps, that had prompted her fond generic insult. Almost meekly she lay down beside me and let me pull up the wrinkled sheet. This time, I would endlessly gentle her. We had drifted into a zone beyond the reach of phone calls; we were passingly free. The campus noises below our windows had shrunk to a lone good night called out girl to girl, and to the lessening whisper of traffic on the riverside road and the bridge to Adams, where my bed was staring blankly at the ceiling. I hoped this time to lure her into a little fellatio, or at least to get her up on top of me. [*Retrospect:* trim this passage if space considerations dictate.] I love the passive position, the silken heavy sway above me of pendulous breasts, the tent of female hair formed when her Olmec face lowered majestically to mine, the earnest and increasingly self-absorbed grind of an ass too big for my hands. Being our second time, it took longer, giving me ample opportunity to keep moaning her name. "Ann. Ann! God, Ann. Oh Ann, Ann. Annnn"— the "n"s, the "a." She took it in stride by now, making no comment; she had slept with enough men to know we're all, one way or another, kinky.

[JB RETURNS FROM RUSSIA in 1833 by way of European tour—Lübeck, Hamburg, Amsterdam, Brussels, Paris, London, Edinburgh, Glasgow, Belfast, Dublin—hobnobs with Talleyrand, Esterhazy, Bülow, Palmerston—visits home of ancestors at Ramelton, in County Donegal—*There I sinned much in the article of hot whiskey toddy which they term punch*—back in Lancaster, takes possession of old Coleman house on East King Street, purchased for him in his absence by John

Reynolds and Nathaniel Sample—hires as housekeeper White Swan Hotel owner's niece, twenty-eight-year-old Esther Parker, who as "Miss Hetty" will keep house for him to the day of his death—buys, frees, and retains as servants two slaves, Daphne Cook, twenty-two, and Ann Cook, five, from Virginia family of brother-in-law Reverend Robert Henry, to save political embarrassment—pays court to unknown woman in Philadelphia household of Judge Thomas Kittera (pp. 110, 114), jesting in letter to Kittera, *be particular in giving my love to my intended*—elected by Pennsylvania legislature to seat in U.S. Senate vacated by William Wilkins, whom President Jackson appointed to replace Buchanan in Russian Mission—in 1836 re-elected to Senate, despite usual divisions among Pennsylvania Democrats—takes up lodgings in Washington with Senator William Rufus DeVane King of Alabama, the two of them referred to in gossip as "the Siamese Twins"—as chairman of Foreign Relations Committee quarrels with Van Buren's Secretary of State John Forsyth—on June 3, 1837, writes Mrs. Francis Preston Blair that before the next year *I expect to be married & have the cares of a family resting upon my shoulders*—in September delivers in favor of the Subtreasury Bill a speech that former President Jackson avers *must become a lasting monument of the talents that made* [it], yet is instructed by Pennsylvania state legislature to vote against bill, which he does, construing his alternatives as *to obey or to resign*—in 1839 Van Buren offers him the post of Attorney-General, which he declines—expecting Van Buren to run again for President in 1840, hopes to get roommate King nominated as Vice-Presidential candidate, placing self in position to run for President in 1844—but Whig candidate General William Henry "Tippecanoe" Harrison defeats Van Buren, then dies a month after inaugural, placing unpopular Southerner John Tyler, the first Vice-President to become President, in the office, where "Tyler, too" becomes "Old Veto"—Buchanan re-elected to

Senate in 1842—by this time deaths of sisters Jane Lane and Harriet Henry have placed five more orphaned children in his care, including future White House hostess Harriet Lane— breaks off romantic relationship with Dolley Madison's young niece Anna Payne with poem explaining in part *Blooming nineteen can never well agree / With the dull age of half a century. . . . Meantime, where'ere you go, what e're your lot / By me you'll never, never be forgot*—1844 Democratic convention settles after eight ballots upon dark horse and Jackson protégé James K. Polk—victorious Polk invites Buchanan early in 1845 to become his Secretary of State—JB serves full four years, though frequently differing with Polk in Cabinet meetings— Polk maintains diary in part to keep track of Buchanan's shifts and changes of opinion, writing, *If I would yield up the govern-ment into his hands and suffer him to be in effect President, . . . I have no doubt he would be cheerful and satisfied. This I cannot do*—yet Buchanan's divide-the-difference views influence the ultimate dispositions of the Oregon and Mexican questions, the last great enlargements of the contiguous continental Ameri-can territory—in 1845 asks Polk for Supreme Court seat, then declines it—in 1846 concludes treaty with New Grenada for right of transit across Isthmus of Panama, basis for later canal— toward end of term as Secretary of State develops nervous tic in leg and a painful nasal tumor which requires a series of operations—in March of 1848 writes correspondent, *I have wished 1,000 times that I had never entered this Dept. as Secretary. I have had to do the important drudging of the administration without the power of obtaining offices for my friends. I have no power. I feel it deeply*—loses out at 1848 convention to Lewis Cass, who loses to Whig candidate, Mexican War hero Zach-ary Taylor—Buchanan expresses wish *to return to private life and do some writing*—declines to run for Governorship of Pennsylvania, vacated by resignation of tubercular Governor

Francis Shunk—in December of 1848 acquires estate of Wheatland, a mile west of Lancaster—has become by now "rich uncle" to twenty-two nephews and nieces and thirteen grandnephews and grandnieces—renovates, gardens, entertains, advises Harriet Lane, *Never allow your affections to become interested or engage yourself to any person without my previous advice*—in 1851 negotiates peace treaty between students of Dickinson College and faculty after mass dismissal of junior class—becomes president of board of trustees of merged Franklin and Marshall Colleges and donates one thousand dollars—has leisure to read Jared's five-volume life of Washington and works of Byron, Scott, Dickens—according to Klein, *these days of temporary political retirement at Wheatland were to be the happiest and most carefree of his life*—Presidency still beckons—at convention of 1852, having positioned self against popular sovereignty provision of Compromise of 1850, which was endorsed by Cass, and strongly supported new Fugitive Slave Law provision and repeatedly decried abolitionist agitation, JB leads ballot for a time but due to refusal of New York's William Marcy to yield up his votes fails to secure nomination, as also do, in turn, Marcy and Stephen Douglas—Buchaneers (so-called), with votes of Pennsylvania and Virginia delegations, engineer selection of New Hampshire's Franklin Pierce on the forty-ninth ballot and collect their reward: the nomination for Vice-President of Senator William R. D. King, Buchanan's long-time roommate, even though King is so ill with tuberculosis that he has to be sworn in in Havana, Cuba, and dies back in Alabama one month after inauguration.]

W. R. D. King [I wrote] is one of those eminences whose strong impression on their own times has suffered a gradual erasure upon the tablets of history. Five years older than Buchanan, he was born into the planter class of Sampson County, North Carolina; he graduated from his state's university in

1803 and won admission to the bar in 1806. He served in the state legislature and was elected to Congress in 1810, at the age of twenty-four; he was one of the young "War Hawks" who voted, in 1812, the fledgling nation into another war with Britain. Presumably [*Retrospect:* unable to locate facts of military career and rank; will do further research if this section is used in your Ford issue (unlikely)], it was amid the scattered and unsatisfactory engagements of little Madison's little war that King earned the title of "Colonel" with which Buchanan in his letters and public addresses invariably honored him. In 1816, King was appointed secretary to the legation, headed by William Pinkney, to the Kingdom of Naples and then to the Court of St. Petersburg—those chilly parqueted halls constantly reverberant, it seems, with the tread of the thick boots of American politicians. In 1818 King moved to Dallas County, in Alabama, and in 1819 was elected Senator from that state. Thus he, thanks to faithful re-election by the sufficiently pleased voters of his adopted state, for fifteen years figured near the forefront of a golden age of the Senate, when the inexorably rising tensions of a growing nation divided by the slavery issue incited an epic eloquence from such giants of oratory as Webster, Clay, Calhoun, and Benton; King, like Buchanan, Silas Wright, and John Crittenden, must be counted in the second rank of these noble arguers of the nation's complicating case, but contemporary vision did not perceive a striking difference in stature. History buries most men, and then exaggerates the height of those left standing. King was president *pro tempore* of the Senate from 1836 to 1841, an office made unusually important by the erratic temper and rare attendance of Van Buren's Vice-President, Richard Mentor Johnson, a profligate Kentuckian whose hammerlock on celebrity was his slaying of the Indian chief Tecumseh ("Rumpsey, dumpsey," went his campaign chant, "Colonel Johnson shot Tecumseh") and whose fathering of two daughters by his mulatto mistress was so flagrant an indiscretion that even Jackson, who had pushed Johnson upon Van Buren, by 1840 admitted him to be a *dead wait* [*sic*] on the Democratic ticket. When, in 1850, Vice-President Fillmore became President upon Zachary Taylor's abrupt death, King was elected to preside over the Senate.

Now, did Buchanan love King? Fellow bachelors and Senators, they lived together from 1836 to 1844, when President Tyler appointed King Ambassador to France. In 1845 Buchanan became King's superior, as Polk's Secretary of State. King asked in 1846 to be recalled; after his defeat as the Union candidate for Senate from Alabama, he returned to the Senate in 1848, as Buchanan was retiring to his idyllic Wheatland interim. A visitor to Wheatland in 1856 wrote in a letter published in Buchanan's campaign biography, *I was much gratified in finding in his library a likeness of the late Vice-President King, whom he loved (and who did not?). He declared that he was the purest public man that he ever knew, and that during his intimate acquaintance of thirty years he had never known him to perform a selfish act.* American gays, having seized as theirs Whitman, Melville, and Henry James, among our crusty, straight-lipped Presidents must be satisfied with Buchanan, our only never-married chief executive, who in the heat of 1860 was characterized thus by a calumnious but not unpoetic pro-Douglas paper: *Mr. B. has a shrill, almost female voice, and wholly beardless cheeks; and he is not by any means, in any aspect the sort of man likely to cut, or attempt to cut his throat for any Chloe or Phillis in Pennsylvania. Nevertheless, and in spite of all these drawbacks, the portly figure and courtier-like address of Mr. Buchanan form very striking features at a reception. Like Dean Swift and Alexander Pope, he rather courts the reputation of gallantry; and his half-fatherly, half-lover-like attention to such ladies as are presented, rarely fails to flatter the vanity and elicit the gratitude of the fluttering and glittering victims.*

King was, history assures us, the epitome of a Southern

gentleman and an exemplary—dare we say, a perfect?—Senator. In Buchanan's eyes, it might be imagined, he loomed as a beau ideal, a masculine angel, conversant with the multitudinous ins and outs of Congressional politicking and the friendships whereby white political males maintained a network of interacting persuasions that up to the rupture of civil war extended from Maine to Texas, Michigan to Florida. The word *friend* occurs again and again in Buchanan's letters; one standard source *(The Dictionary of American Biography)* says of him, *His nature was adapted to friendships, and those which he made were lasting and gratifying to him.* Nineteenth-century men were more easily gratified short of orgasm than men of our time. Indeed, the pleasure and relief which male companionship afforded Victorian Anglo-Saxons was in large part the decided *absence* of physical interaction, with its demands of tenderness, expertise, hygiene, energy, and extensive preamble and follow-up. Men were simply not educated to cope with women. Ruskin, seeing his bride nude, with her healthy pubic bush, embarked on six years of unconsummated marriage, finally confessing, after much evasive sophistry concerning his non-performance, to his virgin wife that (in the words of a letter she wrote her parents begging an annulment) *he was disgusted with my person the first evening 10th April.* This same underappreciated woman, born Effie Gray, survived to enjoy a successful marriage, producing eight children, with the painter John Millais. Yet Millais, anticipating *the day* in a letter to his *close friend* Charles Collins, likened anticipation of his impending wedding to *the glimpse of the dentist[']s instruments* and, though he professed to be *not in the least nervous*, his bride's diary recorded that in the honeymoon train *He got very agitated and when the Railway had started the excitement had been so much for him that instead of the usual comfort I suppose that the Brides require on those occasions of leaving, I had to give him all my sympathy. He cried dreadfully.* Impotence at the moment of defloration was not uncommon; Charles Kingsley warned his fiancée, *You do not know how often a man is struck powerless in body and mind on his wedding night,* but he looked forward bravely to the coming time when he *had learnt to bear the blaze of your naked beauty.* Throughout most of history men love one another, yes, but as spirits, not bodies; only our coarse materialist imaginations seek to de-Platonize the masculine romances of the previous century. Does not every detail of masculine personal decor—the black stovepipe hats and trouser legs, the constant cigars and chewing tobacco with their residues of foul breath—declare physical unapproachability? Shared housing among bachelors was common domestic economy; witness Doctor Watson and Sherlock Holmes. [*Retrospect:* details needed here on incontrovertible homosexual contacts among Victorians; informed demographics on results of male sequestration in schools, jails, armies, and above all navies (CK Melville, Dana); probable sub-elite carryovers from looser and more physicalized Renaissance and eighteenth-century mores, etc.: a book in itself, and perhaps already written. Let's hope so.]

One surviving portrait limns King as a youthful Byronic beauty, but a photograph shows a King whose swarthiness, lustreless stiff hair, and high chiselled cheekbones convey a suggestion of Indian blood unexpected in a man who, writing from Washington to Wheatland in May of 1850, deplored the expansion of territory achieved by the Mexican War and warned against any expansion into Central America on the grounds that *its remote situation and degraded mongrel population would involve us in constant difficulties.* Mongrelization was much on these gentlemen's minds. The Ostend Manifesto of 1854, drafted entirely in Buchanan's hand, urged the acquisition of Cuba by purchase or force and asserted that by not interfering we would *be recreant to our duty, be unworthy of our gallant forefathers, and commit base treason against our posterity, should we permit Cuba to be Africanized and become a second St. Domingo with all its attendant horrors to the white race, and suffer the flames* [of black insurrection and rule] *to extend to our neighboring shores, seriously to endanger or actually to consume the fair fabric of our Union.*

One searches the correspondence of Buchanan and King for traces of homosexual passion, and finds little. Accepting, in his capacity as Secretary of State, King's resignation of the French Mission in August of 1846, Buchanan perhaps puns when he relates, of President Polk, *Whilst granting your request, he has instructed me to say, that he is deeply sensible of the patriotism, prudence, and ability with which you have performed the duties of your important mission; and I may be permitted to add that it affords me sincere pleasure to be the organ of his approbation.* The hypothetical lovers had been separated for two years at this point, with a cold ocean between them. Again, in the letter of 1850 quoted above, King flirtatiously permits himself, while discussing the British incursion into Central America, a self-characterization suggestive of a feminine yielding, to a pleasant end: *Now I am as you know a man of peace, and always disposed to adopt the most gentle course to effect an object however desirable.* But by and large the two men repress written allusions to their relationship, and in fact invariably include closing courtesies to Miss Lane on the one hand and on the other to a certain Mrs. Ellis who seems to be ever at King's elbow. Yet it is not impossible to imagine that Buchanan's Congressional speech of January 5, 1838, supporting Benton's motion to move to a select committee Calhoun's resolutions against intermeddling with slavery (*That the intermeddling of any State or States, or their citizens, to abolish slavery in this District, or any of the Territories, on the ground, or under the pretext, that it is immoral or sinful; or the passage of any act or measure of Congress, with that view, would be a direct and dangerous attack on the institutions of all the slaveholding States*), is, in its uncharacteristic keenness of feeling, a love song to King, sung in the intimate old Senate chamber, with its desks arranged in concentric half-circles around the speaker's rostrum, its red velvet drapes and mural paintings, and its semi-circular visitors' gallery set above the main floor like boxes in a theatre.

King's darkly handsome, smolderingly receptive face must have hung like an oval-framed steel engraving at the center of Buchanan's wavering vision as he orated. Launching his high, clear voice into the space of the chamber, the Pennsylvanian tilted the magnificent head whose gauzy crown of pale oak-colored hair already held, at the age of forty-six, more than a few white filaments. His arms gesticulated in stilted imitation of the Roman orators upon whose Latin effusions he and his colleagues had been schooled. "The fact is," he ringingly stated, having noted that the Senators from Delaware and his friend Mr. Wall of New Jersey had voted against the motion, "and it cannot be disguised, that those of us in the Northern States who have determined to sustain the rights of the slave-holding States at every hazard, are placed in a most embarrassing situation." He was pleading with the South like a man who, in love with his raven-haired mistress, yet still has a wife and children—those Pennsylvania voters in their pious, rural, tariff-hating innocence—to consider. "We are almost literally between two fires," continued Buchanan: "whilst in front we are assailed by the Abolitionists, our own friends in the South"—his voice cracked, piteously, and then rose higher to carry to the back rows of the visitors' gallery, where spectators of the fair sex, having troubled to obtain admission, now audibly conversed among themselves—"are constantly driving us into positions where their enemies and our enemies may gain important advantages."

Buchanan in his stirred imagination felt the rhetorical heat, fore and aft, like a systematically roasted side of beef at an Independence Day barbecue; Senator King's face, the sharp center of a wide-spreading vague radiance of listening faces, turned as the Alabaman murmured a word to his fellow Senator, whiskery Clement Comer Clay of Huntsville, a former state governor appointed to fill the place of John McKinley, who had been elevated by President Van Buren to the Supreme Court. Even in mid-peroration Buchanan felt a jealous pang that he was not privy to this murmuring, this political confidence between the two Southerners. The sight of King's profile with its swarthy half-breed sangfroid gave the Senator from Pennsylvania the illicit sensation with which we observe a love object unawares of our attention, as if we are stealing a sip from a sacred vessel. Buchanan felt giddy in the curious gulf between this glimpse, in so public and already, as it were, historical a setting, and the multitudinous private glimpses of King he enjoyed in the leathery, cluttered, cozy, tobacco-scented bachelor quarters where, emerging from separate bedrooms and returning from divided duties, they often shared morning bacon and evening claret. King was always impeccable, appearing clean-shaven even at midnight and his masculine odors skewered by a volatile dash of bay rum or Eau de Cologne. Righteous indignation strengthened Buchanan's clarion voice as it asked aloud, "What is the evil of which the Southern States complain? Numerous abolition societies have been formed throughout the Middle and Northern States; and for what purpose?" To vent New England's perennial Puritan spleen, he knew the answer to be, and to effect a diminution of the South's economic strength and prosperity relative to that of the North, with its industrial wage-slaves and miserable immigrant urban hordes. But he contented himself with a sop to the constituency at his back, that stew of Pennsylvania voters, heated by the national-bank issue and the hypocritical Philadelphia gang headed by Biddle and Dallas and the Quaker plutocrats: "It cannot be for the purpose of effecting any change of opinion in the free States on the subject of slavery.

We have no slaves there; we never shall have any slaves there."

King had a beautiful dark-eyed way of gazing, on the edge of anger, like Ann Coleman in the old days, as if a fathomless pool was welling up, and like Ann a spacious and strikingly white forehead, hers the effect of general feminine pallor and his the product of the broad-brimmed planter's hat faithfully worn against the Southern sun. That lustrous black gaze appeared to interrogate and then to confirm Buchanan as he informed the assembled Senate, "The object cannot be to operate upon the slaveholders; because the Abolitionists must know, every person within the sound of my voice knows"— the crucial paradoxical point, the justification for the path of moderation and patient forbearance—"that their interference with this question has bound the slaveholding interest together as one man against abolishing slavery in their respective States."

One man: King himself had often told his roommate how his views, barely distinguishable, when he was a youth in North Carolina, from those of a Pennsylvanian, favoring gradual emancipation followed by African resettlement in Liberia (of which hopeful young nation Buchanan's cousin Thomas was presently Governor), had hardened in Alabama, as cotton plantations overspread the state, to an adamant patriotic defense of the peculiar institution from the assaults of those who, not living with the negro, quite fail to comprehend him—his limitations, uses, and needs. Buchanan yearned to protect King and his fellow Southerners from the slanders of the North much as he had unavailingly sought to shelter Ann from those sarcasms of her unfeeling parents and brothers which had crowded and blighted the space their tender union had required for proper ripening, for arranging its mutual sustenances with delicacy and patience. Giddiness at the chasm of time that memory opened under him threatened to weaken Buchanan at his very moment of pronouncing an incontrovertible fact: "Before this unfortunate agitation commenced, a very large and growing party existed in several of the slave States in favor of the gradual abolition of slavery; and now not a voice is heard there in support of such a measure. The Abolitionists have postponed the emancipation of the slaves in three or four States of this Union for at least half a century."

King and his friends were, as Calhoun increasingly betrayed signs of not being, firm Union men, like Buchanan horrified by any attempt to rend the fabric of federal unity. Only madness, the madness of blood and fire and gunpowder that lurks in the wounded brains of some few marginal opportunists, could dream of destroying a fabric knit so circumspectly, with so cunning an interplay of checks and balances, rights and obligations. "They have, by their interference, produced such a state of public opinion that no man within these States would now be bold enough to raise such a question before any of their Legislatures." This fact, of doctrinaire extremism, given publicity by an irresponsible press, intimidating the voices of moderating reason, had been learned from King and other responsible Union men of the South. A certain pity for the black man, with the friendly images of his Daphne and little Ann Cook and Enoch the colored barber on Queen Street present to his mind, now shadowed Buchanan's voice, as King gazed unwaveringly upon him, seeming to ask a public show of loyalty that would enrich this evening's nightcap of claret.

"What, then," the orator asked, and even the ladies in the gallery seemed to rustle themselves into silence, and the negro attendants grew still as they lounged in the doorways and along the back wall, where on this bitter winter day an arc of fireplaces was all alight and dancing with flame, "is the purpose of these societies—I will not say the purpose, for I cannot, and do not, attribute to them such unholy intentions—but what is the direct tendency of their measures? To irritate and exasperate the feelings of the slaves; to hold out to them vague notions and delusive hopes of liberty; to render them discontented and unhappy, and, finally, to foment servile insurrection, with all its attendant horrors, and to cover the land with blood." Blood! He thought of his sister Jane spitting blood in Mercersburg. He thought of the misery wrought by last year's financial panic and widespread collapse of banks, and of the dangers of war wrought by the seizure and sinking of the *Caroline* on the Niagara, and of the old King William IV dead and his willful eighteen-year-old niece now queen in a world made perilous by Britain's bullying ships, and of his own sister Harriet and her husband, Robert Henry, wasting away in Greensburg with all their children, and when he thought thus death indeed seemed to be steadily scything through the field of the world and our poor attempts to forestall the angels of ruin and destruction as pathetic as a voiceless outcry of grasses.

Yet, it was crystal clear, the attempt at forestallment must be made, beneath God's heavy heel, while the Abolitionists ignorantly clamored for absolutes the Constitution had disavowed. "However devoted to the Union the South may be," Buchanan warned aloud, a pregnancy in his voice like a bulging tear about to overflow a lower lid, "the cup of forbearance may yet be exhausted. If the father of a family be placed in such a deplorable condition"—and the memory of his own father returned, his bulky shadow moving in the low dark log cabin at Stony Batter, moving swiftly as a bat flitting amid the sparks from the fireplace and the wavering candle over in the corner where baby Maria slept in her cradle, and little Jane on her trundle bed, their father moving things about just as he scrapingly moved barrels and boxes all day in the store, closing up the cabin for the night, against the Indians and wolves, the bears and drunken drovers and incited slaves—"that he cannot rest at night without apprehension that before the morning his house may be enveloped in flames, and those who are nearest and dearest to him may be butchered, or worse than butchered,"—the fair sex forced to submit, it might be, at an extremity of earthly misfortune, to the black man's untamed animal appetites—"the great law of self-preservation will compel him to seek security by whatever means it may be obtained." Killed, it is nearing twenty years ago, that vigorous shadow of paternal protection, by a bolted carriage horse, the old man's head striking the iron tire, and proving to be the less hard. Died without a will, leaving it to his overworked son, freshly elected to the Congress, to untangle the estate.

"Now, sir," Buchanan told the Senate in the singular, as if all the manifold personalities, participating and witnessing, within the chamber were in fact gathered within the attentive, receptive masculine face at the etched oval center of his fluctuating field of vision, his two eyes ever contending in their impressions rather than, as with most men, effortlessly harmonizing, "I have long watched the progress of this agitation with intense anxiety, and"—the confidentiality of his voice dropped to the pitch of earnest intimate conversation—"I can say in solemn truth that never before have I witnessed such a deep pervading and determined feeling as exists at present upon this subject among the sober and reflecting men of the South." Sober, reflecting—such was King. *He is among the best, purest, & most consistent public men I have ever known*, Buchanan will write fourteen years later to Franklin Pierce, a few months short of Pierce's inauguration and King's death, *& is, also, a sound judging and discreet counsellor.* Also in 1852 he will tell another correspondent, *I have written you such a letter as I have never written to any other friend except Col: King.*

What is it that enables us, in some few instances, to touch the walls of alien sensibility and inimical self-interest which surround us, and to discover a panel which yields to our faint pressure? The difference must be the intuition, backed by friendly evidences, that the other likes us. Not many did like Buchanan. *In his public life he elicited little warmth of friendship,*

Roy Nichols—freely given to *ad hominem* assertion—tells us. *One looks almost in vain among his legion of correspondents for any who used informal address. Vice President William R. King, who died in 1853, was almost the last of the few who wrote him as "Dear Buchanan."* In the year prior to his speech on the Calhoun resolutions, according to Klein, *Senator W. R. King had ribbed him during the early spring about neglecting his usual affairs from "the anxieties of love."* King was somehow amused by the country lawyer with his big pale dishevelled head tilted as if by the pull of a scar of an old neck wound, an old emotional bafflement; King presumably liked not least in the other the affection Buchanan awarded the men and women of the South, as possessing the opposite of that clangorous appetitive quality which had wounded him in his hardware merchant of a father, in the iron-forging Colemans, in the politicians of New England and New York, who were tools of the manufacturing interests. There were two broad currents in the national enterprise, agriculture and manufacture, which for a time flowed side by side, as for a stretch do, African explorers report, the White and Blue Niles. Like Lancaster County, the South changed slowly, its rolling black-soiled tracts dozing within the sun-soaked haze of a stable agrarianism. When Buchanan looked at King, he saw safety and civility, he saw life, a flutter of an invitation to live, to enjoy, to laugh, to gossip, to arrive at sound and pure conclusions. He saw Dr. John King, the Presbyterian pastor at Mercersburg who took young Jamie into his counsel, and William Lowndes, the representative from South Carolina whose legalistic thoroughness and personal moderation served as a model for the novice Congressman of 1821.

"They love the Union," he asserted aloud, of these sober and reflecting men of the South, "but if its blessings cannot be enjoyed but in constant fear of their own destruction, necessity will compel them to abandon it. Such is now the southern feeling. The Union is now in danger, and I wish to proclaim the fact." As if to soothe the gasp his assertion provoked in his audience, particularly in the feminine gallery, he announced, in prophetic echo of the critics of his own Presidency when it would come, "The brave man looks danger in the face, and vanquishes it; whilst the coward closes his eyes at its approach, and is overwhelmed. The Union," he told his roommate's staring face directly, as if foreseeing the day when even sober and reflecting men of the South might stand as his enemy, "is as dear to me as my heart's blood. I would," he ringingly avowed, "peril life, character, and every earthly hope, to maintain it."

Coitus is the model of all passion: it pursues a curve of rise and fall, and nothing will sustain it on the highest level forever. The tone of Buchanan's speech became less elevated, less heartfelt, more didactic and ominous. "And," he asked, "if the Union should be dissolved upon the question of slavery, what will be the consequences?" He answered himself: "An entire non-intercourse between its different parts, mutual jealousies, and implacable wars. The hopes of the friends of liberty, in every clime, would be blasted; and despotism might regain her empire over the world. I might present in detail the evils which would flow from disunion, but I forbear. I shall not further lift the curtain. The scene will be too painful."

And what, at the moment, might be done to forestall unbearably painful scenes? First of all, he proposed, the select committee might offer to the Senate a resolution affirming what the Constitution already grants, the right of slavery to exist in any state where it is recognized by law. Not even the Abolitionists denied this principle, which had been solemnly announced by the first Congress, and is most clearly the doctrine of the Constitution. "This, then," Buchanan stated, "is not a question of general morality, affecting the consciences of men, but it is a question of constitutional law." A second resolution, he proclaimed, might assert that slaves like any other sort of property can be transferred from state to state. And a third might insist that slavery be maintained and not abolished in the District of Columbia, ceded to the Union by two slaveholding states whose good faith would be betrayed if abolition were "to convert this very cession into the means of injuring and destroying their peace and security."

This language was rather far for a Northern politician, even a doughface like Buchanan, to go; the risk was his love offering. But King had turned his impassive, almost Seminole profile again, to murmur with his fellow Alabaman Senator Clay, a lesser Clay than the Great Pacificator from Kentucky—Clay the Whig, the anti-Jackson, with much of Jackson's mad mulishness and more brains and eloquence yet with not enough of the people in his belly. Buchanan, still on his feet, conjuring up the select committee and its projected resolutions ("Let the resolutions be framed in a most conciliatory spirit, and let them be clothed in language which shall shock the opinions of no Senator"), felt himself in the position of a man who, having mounted to the heights of ecstasy with his mistress, and performed heroic feats in the lists of the bedroom, finds her still with unsatisfied needs, and practical expectations, and what seems an inhuman indifference to his own delicate situation. King had ceased to listen. His hatchet face was buried in his close colleague's attending ear. "The Middle and North States are the field upon which this great battle must be fought," Buchanan concluded, his voice hoarse and exhausted. "I fear not, I doubt not, the result, if Senators from the South, where the people are already united, would but consent to adopt the counsels of those who must bear the brunt of the contest." Thus he ended, as many do, by begging mercy of those whom he had dared to love.

IN COMPOSING THIS SEGMENT of my never-to-be-completed opus, somewhere in the centennial-year struggle of Ford versus Carter, I had intended to model Buchanan's love for King upon mine for Genevieve, but in truth my one-night stand with Mrs. Arthrop kept intruding—that supernatural quality her face had at first blush, not only its high albedo (cf. the glow of King's planter's forehead) but the something immaterial attached, a ghostly tag declaring that she would "put out." Of course I entertained no such carnal notions of old Buck and Colonel King; nineteenth-century men, my belief was, loved one another with no more physicality than that of the companiable gourmanderie described by Melville in his "Paradise of Bachelors." What I sought to convey in the out-of-focus chamber as seen through Buchanan's mismatched eyes was the way in which the apparition of the beloved pulls an entire scene into life—like a sun in the sky, or like, perhaps, a live prey in the web. I remember, conversely, a party at which Genevieve's absence made a great sensible hole.

It was during the composition of the preceding scene, let me add for the benefit of my fellow historians, that I was cripplingly struck by the hopelessness, in an era when history has turned away from tales of kings to the common heroes of everyday life, the merchant and the peasant buried deep in the records of manor-house and guild-hall, and in this ever self-reforming New World nation to the rescue from obscurity of the women and slaves patriarchal historians had hitherto consigned to the shadowy margins of their establishment-prone accountings—the hopelessness, I repeat, of sympathetically animating the fussy, cagey discriminations of a pro-Southern strict constitutionalist whose timorous legalisms were all to be swept away by a bloodbath and Lincoln's larger, less scrupulous perceptions of the rights and duties of the high office to which he succeeded. American slavery *not a question of general morality, affecting the consciences of men*? In this utterance alone Buchanan forfeits the sympathy of all but the most perversely patient of historians, one who would try to comprehend deeds and opinions within the gloom behind the scenery, the dusty flats and rigging, the intricate weights and counterweights, rather than by the simplifying stagelight of retrospect. Present-day students, adolescents thrust from the jingling nursery of television into the bewildering forest of texts, have no patience with their ancestors and little interest in the erratic half-steps whereby a people effects moral change and whereby well-intentioned men of substance might seek amid agitation and a long stasis of contending equal interests the path of least general harm. Buchanan's own contemporaries, north and south, cried him down as a traitor. In his last decade his circle of warmth, of human approval, dwindled to a close few—a few Cabinet loyalists, Harriet Lane, Miss Hetty, Hiram Swarr, some servants at Wheatland. The analogies that come to mind, forgive me, are Jesus and Hitler. But, you say, we all come to our Gethsemane, our last bunker. Buchanan's, I say, came in full view, within history, or almost within it, and coincided with national policy. Never mind: my effort of, if not rehabilitation, reanimation, loomed as too much for me, for my poor powers, which were diffused by personal concerns, in the era of Gerald Ford's administration.

The party at which Genevieve was conspicuously absent but which I had to attend was the President's faculty party, given early each fall, when New England puts its best foot forward, a ruddy brilliance of foliage like the iridescence of a bubble about to burst. I have already mentioned [p. 53] the President's resplendent purple muu-muu, one of the many flamboyant costumes in which she boldly sought to assert her vast corpulence as a kind of beauty, and also her lilac-tinged crown of inflexible upsweep; I have not mentioned her minuscule husband, a dark-suited satellite of hers, one almost wants to write "parasite," whose inherited fortune and, considering his cretinous small face, surprisingly clever telephonic manipulation of securities had enabled her to pursue a triumphant though modestly remunerated progress up the ladder of educational administration. She had come to us from a deanship at a California football power located in one of those valleys fed by stolen Colorado water and worked by illegal Mexican immigrants. The languid cynics of our faculty called her the Pep Organizer. Not old, just further advanced in the decade of life wherein I would soon [see pp. 159, 198] find myself, she still affected the broad clattering bangles and mobile earrings of the Sixties, bedecking herself as if her big body were a year-round Christmas tree. Yet she could be a stern mama, with a West Coast high-tech management style. Like Ford in his Presidency, she had subdued the carnival spirit. She had whipped money out of the parents and the husbands of alumnae, turned Wayward back from ivied insolvency, and spoke winningly of making us a four-year co-ed institution, with presumably a football team fund-raisers could rally around. There was no excusing oneself from her back-to-school party. I had to go, and Brent Mueller had to go, and both the Wadleighs and even my unorganization-minded Queen of Disorder, as a part-time teacher in the art department, had to. But Genevieve, the care of her two little girls precluding even the most tenuous faculty connection when they came here five years ago, was not invited, and was too separated from Brent to be escorted. There were drinks, hors d'oeuvres served by doe-eyed scholarship students, background music tinkled forth by Ben Wadleigh's latest keyboard protégé, forced laughter, friendly faces, but no Genevieve. No life, no spirit, no point to the gathering. No bull's-eye beauty. No expectancy, no suspense. No sense of oneself as a towering sexual presence—Alf the Amorous, hero of one of the sagas that are sung the world over of lovers. Alf and Iseult, with their bed-sword and carbonated potion; Alf and Cleopatra, with the world well lost between them; Alf and Juliet, featuring the fadeout kicker of their double suicide. I felt guilty at Genevieve's absence, as though I were excluding her. As though, at some deep and (before Freud) inexpressible level, I were participating in her murder, or that of the child—our toddling love—that we had engendered, in these now more than two years of romance. To suppress the presence of her absence I drank more than usual.

The party. Oh, I could sketch a few of the faculty in attendance, having so jollily limned our Madame President, who drifted back and forth like a bright solid square cloud in her dress the color of the edge of the rainbow, as tan from her August at their cottage on Squam Lake as a Hawaiian queen greeting the missionaries, but you know, dear colleagues of the NNEAAH, how invariably academic narratives, like Hollywood novels, are populated by gargoyles, to show the writer's indignant superiority. So I will spare you our German professor's snaggly yellow teeth and crinkly eyes the bluish no-color of crazed glass, and the elderly body that his vanity kept as trim as a youth's through a fanatic regimen of bicycling, squash, and jogging; and his Jewish wife's pockmarked flat cheeks and soulful ursine eyes and aggrieved honk of a Bronx accent; and the head of the chemistry department's bald head fringed by a gray duckling's down combed upward as if electrified by a fit of terror; and the washed-out beauty of his wife's face as she flinched at the sound of his booming deaf-man's voice; and our tieless young mathematician with his asexual leathery leer that hinted of wholly abstract satisfactions; and our gleaming token, our professor of black studies, from Cincinnati, with a radio-quality elocution that could click into an unintelligible jive-talk when he felt hostile; and his elegant Antiguan wife, with skin the color of cocoa butter and teeth as white as coconut meat when she smiled; and our glum squat professor of physics, a drinker but never drunk, so sobering was the effect of his consignment to a scientific backwater like Wayward College; our contrastingly tall, pained professor of biology, pained by his bad back, his spine canted forward by a lifetime at the microscope; and their young and frisky tennis-playing second wives, one-time students who had weathered scandals to be the mothers of second families, their faces starry with the fine creases of actinic damage and flecks of flaking sunburn; not to mention our hippy lady economist, one of the few, a real catch, her body in its snug wool dress sweetly wearing what D. H. Lawrence called (referring to Constance Chatterley) *a certain fluent, down-slipping grace* but her face rendered eerie and alarming by myopia-correcting eyeglasses as thick as bottle bottoms; our pioneering professor of film studies, pale as a spectre, moving in startling optical jerks as if carelessly spliced; jejune boy deans groomed for PR in their studiously baggy Ivy League tweeds; stolid female athletic coaches with butch haircuts and wary, puffy stares amid the chatter; and all the others—associates, assistants, upwards of sixty of us to provide for the education of our six hundred young women. A hard core of twenty were my intimate colleagues and friends, co-survivors of a hundred midnights together, of a thousand mornings entering, egged on by coffee, our parallel cages of long-haired lionesses. More than colleagues, they were my life's witnesses, tracers of my pilgrim's progress, cannibal devourers of my vital flesh transmuted into gossip, as I of theirs. They knew I had been holed up two years in Adams and my academic burrow in Harrison Hall; they knew Norma, they knew Genevieve, they knew Brent the crackerjack deconstructor. With them, here, I had nothing to explain; I had merely to put on gray slacks, a button-down shirt, a narrow necktie, and a navy-blue blazer, and come.

Talk, we must have talked. Of what? There must have been

something, or sixty things—a topic for each mouth. The re
of party conversation hangs in my memory like a surge o
music I cannot hum, like a fog that kept me, one summer day,
from finding my way into Hampton harbor. A little research
reveals possible topics. The death of Mao Tse-tung on September 9th. The stunning defeat, in Sweden on September 19th,
of Olof Palme, the first time the Socialists had lost in forty
years; the great rightist rollback had begun, and Palme would
eventually fall to an assassin's bullet. Or perhaps we talked
sports: on September 12th, another Swede lost, Borg to Con-
ners, and Evert beat Goolagong for the U.S. Open title—an
American sweep. It was a great month for Americans: a Soviet
pilot defected with an advanced MiG-25, and Christo completed his two-million-dollar, twenty-four-mile *Running Fence*
environmental-artwork in California, and our Space Shuttle
was unveiled in the same state, which also enacted, on September 13th, the nation's first right-to-die law. That summer, the
Democrats chose Carter and Mondale, Viking I had landed on
Mars, the Israelis had rescued over a hundred hostages at En-
tebbe Airport in Uganda, Bruce Jenner won the decathlon at
the Montreal Olympic Games, and Renee Richards won his/
her first tennis match playing as a female. I cannot hear any of
this in the rumble of the party, though it all would have been
fodder for our swelling hilarity; what I hear instead is a certain
mid-Seventies disappointment that the sky had not fallen, that
we as a nation, a faculty, a circle of aging adults were obliged
to plod on. We had worn love beads and smoked dope, we had
danced nude and shat on the flag, we had bombed Hanoi and
landed on the moon, and still the sky remained unimpressed.
History turned another page, the Union limped on, the dead
were plowed under, the illegitimate babies were suckled and
given the names of wildflowers and Buddhist religious states,
the bad LSD trips were being paid for by the rich parents who
covered the bills from the mental institutions. Young Ameri-

can men and women, sons and daughters of corporation lawyers, had sinned against the Holy Ghost and got up the next
morning to take a piss and look in the mirror, to see if there
was a difference. There didn't seem to be. Everything was out
of the closet, every tabu broken, and still God kept His back
turned, refusing to set limits. A President had been shot, a war
had been lost, our empire had been deemed evil, our heavenly
favored-nation status had been revoked, the air had been let out
of our parade balloon, and still we bumped on, as we had in
1865, with wandering steps and slow, as out of Eden we took
our solitary way. Of course, we had bitten the apple of defeat
before—e.g., in 1812–14, up to Jackson's delusory footnote of
a victory at New Orleans—but living history is no older than
a living man's memory, and none of us under forty remembered the poster-plain despair of the Depression, when not just
rebellious youngsters but out-of-work workingmen believed
that the system was the enemy and Communism might save us.
A fellow historian called ours a culture of narcissism. When
Father leaves the room the mirrors on the wall begin to stare.
The Ford era was a time of post-apocalyptic let-down, of terrifying permissiveness.

Wait—there *was* a topic at the party. Flitting from group
to group, tête to tête. Sexual harassment. The term was novel,
the idea alien. A first-year Spanish concentrator had complained to the dean that Professor Alvarez—like Genevieve,
conspicuously absent from the party—had used his pedagogic
leverage to extract sexual favors from a nineteen-year-old student, herself. That she had complained to the authorities and
involved her parents (both of them, unhappily, lawyers) was
the scandal, not that she had been seduced. It cast a chill into
our seraglio, where consensual sex with starstruck maidens was
taken as one of the implicit perks for male instructors [see page
82]. Had not the younger wives among us made their way into
marriage along this same academic track? Were not the female

students at eighteen as legally adult as a grizzled guru of four decades? Was not the guru's power as giver of assignments and grades as legitimately a charm as the dewy youth of his pupil? Is not clout, in short, what men have instead of beauty? What did it mean—harassment, coercion—in the free and open erotic market where every trader must have an asset? Might not the young señorita—Lydia Biddle, to be exact, a nondescript blonde of very average appeal and ability, those who had had her in class agreed—be with equal justice accused of harassing the professor with the textures and perfumes of her fresh ripeness? We were still just emerging from an era when shrieking adolescent girls sexually assaulted rock stars right on the stage, risking electrocution amid the tangle of wires. A good fuck, one of that era's many gurus averred, never hurt anybody. [CK who? Abbie Hoffman? Bobby Seale? Timothy Leary?] Alvarez was a rather shy, slight man, with the usual Latin mustache and a large family he had left behind in Providence, where he had been an assistant professor at Brown, accepting the promotion in status and salary but not wishing to expose his children to the perils of New Hampshire's tax-free educational environment. No doubt he had been affected by his pupil's pallor and very Anglo name—aristocratic Nicholas Biddle, of course, had been Jackson's chief enemy when the President made war upon the national bank on behalf of the common man and the Western speculator. Lydia Biddle's charges portended the end of another era, the end of the free flow of love, fertilizing the tracts between races and classes and generations, and the arrival, heralded by the legalisms of the civil-rights battle, of society's crystallization into strident blocs, all seeking to extend their power with legal threats. Always, in America, with its emphasis on spelled-out rights, there is this final recourse to the law, which lets lawyers rule us, sucking the money from our economy like aphids draining a rose bush. Lydia's parents intended to sue for the loss of their daughter's virginity, if that's what it had been. A chill, I say, moved through the party. No less an evil presence than Brent Mueller sidled up to me, saying, "Didn't you have the Biddle girl in 'American Beginnings'?"

"Just in the 'Robber Barons and Trust Busters' seminar," I told him. Somehow, out of some craven kink in my psychology, I was grateful to have the victim of my own sexual aggression seek me out. As her husband still of sorts, he had for me the fetishistic magic of Genevieve's used underpants. Recklessly, even though he was my mortal foe and would have deconstructed me without a pang, I confided in him: "She struck me as asexual."

He squinted at me through a veil; always between us hung Genevieve, her body torn into its parts, sorrowful and obscene, a carcass we hyenas were snarlingly subdividing. "Nobody's asexual," he told me. "If Alvarez is nailed for this, it means a whole new ball game. These kids have us all over a barrel—the possibilities for blackmail! Damned if you do, damned if you don't."

I took up his tough-guy locutions. "I've never thought screwing these babies was a good idea. It fucks up your teaching—it *has* to. Stick to your own generation, that's where the resonance is." This was tactless, even for me, I realized— praising his own wife's resonance to him. Not that she or he were *exactly* my generation, as an occasional flatness in their emanations reminded me. The paddle wheel of ongoing history hadn't spilled us at quite the same angle: certain national moments, like Pearl Harbor, were legend to them and memory to me; certain prophets sacred to them, like Eugene McCarthy, had met in me a sensibility already jaded; and they took for granted certain freedoms that still excited me [see page 171]. I hastily backtracked. "These kids, they could be Martians, from the crap that's in their heads."

As I dizzily rattled on, impelled by my kink, which made me

love my enemy, Brent studied me with an alert and fishy eye. "Jennifer Arthrop," he said. "She was a Martian?"

"Never laid a finger on her," I boasted. "As she must have told you. Unless she's a more pathological liar than I think."

"A very responsible and sincere girl," he said, still watching my face with an alertness that made me wonder if my jaws were smeared with cheese-puff crumbs. "Her mother's her only problem," he ventured. His slant smile revealed his teeth one by one, like computer bytes emerging from the depths of an arduous number-crunching.

"Her mother?" I echoed. A pit opened up in the spot where, seconds before, my stomach had been innocently digesting a few of Madame President's piping-hot cheese puffs, on plate-lets of Melba toast. Ann Arthrop: her big naked body as pale and serviceable as a thumb, her slangy careless way of speaking about her life. Not a great keeper of secrets. Truly, our lives are like the universe: nothing is lost, only transformed, in the slide toward disorder.

"You've met her mother, I think," Brent insisted, his smile revealing in its left-hand corner a molar blackened by old fillings. There was a strange shiny knob of muscle at the hinge of his jaw, under his ear, like a nut that had been fleshed over.

"Briefly."

"But affectingly, perhaps."

That room of hers, 508, with its view of the French Fry. Its furniture, including that dim lamp with scattering ducks on its base, and the thunderously flushing john, and an oatmeal-colored wallpaper of vaguely "historical" design, arose from their tiny place of neural storage to swamp me, like a giant pair of earmuffs. He was saying things I could not hear. The muscle at the angle of his jaw, where it turns up toward the ear, kept bulging, I could see. It seemed as though his fluctuating smile was a small gray headline that one of those compulsive obligations in nightmares forced me to keep trying and trying to read. *He knows*, I thought, and my brain, accepting a belt of adrenaline, ran a series of lightning-fast estimates of possible damage. Great. Moderate. Non-existent. I still, aided by another vodka-and-tonic scooped from a passing silver tray, enjoyed a warm sensation of pervasive love in which Brent and I were immersed all rosily, all bloodily, like twins slithering down the birth canal.

"She seemed a pleasant enough woman," I fended. "She was with Jennifer, fresh from a *Lysistrata* rehearsal last spring. We sat at a table in the SC for a second. She conveyed, Mrs., the information that at Miss Porter's School in Connecticut she had had a more major role, in fact *the* major role, in the same play and suggested that she played it better." Women against war. Women at war. "What do you think *Lysistrata* is signifying really?" I asked him, hoping to deflect him into his specialty. "What values is Aristophanes *really* endorsing, showing these women bargaining with their cunts like that? My feeling is Aristophanes was a terrible misogynist. And loved the pants off of war."

Brent would not be deflected. "A very overpowering woman," he prissily went on, having been acculturated to a concept of personal fields of power that to my old-fashioned sense had too tactical and schematic a sound. "Flaunts her infidelities in front of the daughter, to keep the father in his place. Even sleeps with Jennifer's boy friends, to keep *her* in her place. The girl gets back the best way she can. She steals."

"Steals?"

"Shoplifts, you know. Not from her mother's store, that would be too directly hostile. But from other stores. Little things. And then throws them away."

"How do you know so much?"

"She tells me. I'm her faculty adviser. She tells me whatever I need to know to clear away her garbage." His unpleasant slant smile stretched to include one more molar. "That's my shtik, Alf. To cut through the garbage. Not you. You roll around *in* the garbage. Speaking of Jennifer, how's my Gen doing? How's her ulcer?"

I stiffened with something like nineteenth-century hauteur. "Genevieve is lovely, as always. A perfect woman, as you know."

"Nobody's perfect." Who else had I heard this from, within memory? "If she were perfect, she wouldn't have let you give her an ulcer." Brent nudged closer. "Aren't you curious, to know what Jennifer told me lately about her mom? There was this boy—"

"No," I told him, at last beginning to feel, through the cozy mist of metabolizing vodka, the clammy touch of true enmity. War happens. Forces compete. Death, so abstract in the grave-yard and demographic charts, will truly come for you. "I'm not interested in her mom, or in Jennifer, either. Little Jen, let's call her. First you had Big Gen, now you have Little Jen. Why ask me about Genevieve?" I asked him. "You see her. You visit the girls."

"We don't talk," he told me. "We're separated. We're not like you and Norma, pretending nothing has happened. But maybe we *should*. Talk. Maybe it's time. Yeah, I'd like to talk to Gen."

He was trying to scare me, only this was clear. "Go ahead," I said.

"You wouldn't mind?"

"She's your wife. Go ahead. Chat her up."

"What are you two talking about?" It was Norma, come up to the two of us out of the buzzing blur of the party. She looked a little pink beneath her freckles, flushed with alcohol. Her hair in its natural kinkiness was escaping her party coiffure and giving her a bushy youthful look, even if she was my genera-tion. She glanced from one to the other of us. "I thought I heard my name mentioned. Good evening, Brent. Hello, you."

We chatted. How strangely charming it was to be standing with one's estranged wife and one's mistress's estranged husband, all very civilized in our party clothes, in this provincial pocket of Western civilization, Northeast American branch, in a gracious brick mansion in the twilight of a lovely early-fall day, the sugar maples turning, the swamp maples turned, the oaks still holding their chlorophyll. The days and nights now were of equal length. Brent and Norma were the same height, their eyes—vermouth green, dead-fish blue—at the level of my worried, busy mouth. The pit within my stomach began to seal shut, and the work of digestion rumblingly to resume, now that Norma made our duo a trio. The effect of massing—in an airline terminal, say—is to give an illusion of safety. Surely so many casually, even clownishly, dressed prospective passengers, fussing with their baby slings and chewing on their newspapers, will not crash. Surely at a party like this the bottom cannot fall out of one's newly renovated life. The buried escapade with ample and appetitive Ann Arthrop—it seemed quite possible, as nonchalant, know-nothing Norma joined us, that it had never happened. After all, doesn't history demonstrate over and over how hard it is to say what actually *did* happen, so that even the Nazis' fanatically documented extermination of six million Jews and Lee Harvey Oswald's broad-daylight shooting of John F. Kennedy and (let's not forget) Patrolman J. D. Tippitt are still seriously debated?

I forget what happened next. Brent must have slunk off, muttering Iagoesque asides. I and the deeply familiar Norma were left alone, shyly islanded in the party like a man and woman just met. She looked tousled, with a silk scarf the size of a baby blanket arranged over her shoulders, but not unhappy—adjusting, my eye was eager to conclude, to the life single, the pink flush on her cheeks a sign of thriving, a sign that soon she could stand alone at last. I must have asked her how she and her lawyer were coming, now that his summer vacation was over, for I can see her in the mists of dim recall gazing into the distance beyond my shoulder, toward the Presidential mansion's egg-and-dart ceiling molding, and saying something like, "He keeps asking me to provide all these financial facts and figures, and I have no idea where they are, and I keep meaning to call you at your apartment, but you're never there when I *do* try, and then I keep forgetting."

I said, rather sternly, "Everything that's not in the safe-deposit box is in the middle right-hand drawer of my old desk on the third floor. There may be a savings-bank book in one of the pigeonholes up top."

"I think I've looked, and all the bank statements frightened me. Some of them should be thrown away, but which? It would be just like the tax people to want just the ones that aren't there. And it makes me too sad, to go up there and see your old desk, that you used to be at all weekend. I don't like the safe-deposit box, either. The last time I went into it, it actually made me cry—the children's three birth certificates and ours all together. We both have those old-fashioned kind of birth certificates hospitals used to give you, with the little baby footprints in ink, they don't do that any more. And our marriage license, and those life-insurance policies our parents took out for us, for a thousand dollars each, it seems like such a pathetic amount now, but I guess it wasn't then. And stacks of the slides you used to take of my paintings, in case the house burned down. The box even *smells* of our place in Hanover— remember that mousy smell when we came in the front door?"

"Norma, for God's sake, you *must* get organized. It's been two fucking years since I left, and you're mooning about baby footprints."

"You sound just like my lawyer. Except for him it's all time he can chalk up on his expense log. Speaking of sexual harassment, he's invited me out to dinner."

My stomach reclaimed its hollow spot, as if I were walking

planks across high steel and had inadvertently glanced down.

"Did you accept?"

She passed the back of the hand not holding her drink across one especially stray piece of hair, with no visible effect. "Why not? He's young and pushy and married, but those people have to eat, too."

"You'd actually *go*? Out to dinner with your married lawyer? Doesn't the invitation strike you as a bit unethical? He's taking ad*van*tage of you."

"Oh well," she said, "if you're a woman, you get used to that. Maybe, on the financial stuff, if you came back now you could show me the drawer and get me started."

"For God's sake, it'll produce just the same figures my lawyer already has. All your lawyer has to do to move this thing along is get on the phone to mine. He shouldn't be ex*pect*ing you to know anything."

"Also," the Queen of Disorder said in her gentle, unhurried voice, "Daphne has been running a fever."

"For how long? How high?"

"Oh, I don't know. Two or three days. Over a hundred, depending on how you hold the thermometer in the light. I can't get her to keep her lips closed when it's in her mouth."

"You *must* get her to the doctor!"

"I thought she was too sick to go out, and they never come to the house any more."

"I can't believe you're being so neglectful!"

"And Andy put a scratch on the Volvo maybe you should look at sometime. He says ever since the accident happened the car pulls to the left. Doesn't that mean the tires will wear unevenly?"

"When did this happen? Whose fault was it?"

"You don't have to yell, sweetie. At that corner where the river road meets 1A and there's a lot of traffic from the new mall. He says some blind old lady pulled out of the supermarket lot right in front of him, but I suspect he was going too fast. He drives very angrily now, now that he's confident."

I was nearly speechless, yet not entirely unhappy, still floating on the vodka and that cozy airport feeling the party was giving me. Her casual sideways approach to disaster felt familiar. A fresh drink, transparent and cold, had appeared in my hand. The lime slice was clinging to the rim by a clever effort, it seemed. "How long a scratch?"

Norma's eyes, the pale green of beach glass, flicked past my face. "Not exactly a scratch," she said. "More of a gouge. But the headlights still work, more or less. Alf, I don't understand why you're never in your apartment, the way you were at first, working on that book about that President whose name I keep forgetting."

"Buchanan. I'm stuck, momentarily. I'm in the library a lot, doing more research. The first half of the nineteenth century, the bastard was all over the lot. He virtually ran the country."

"Or at least you should be there at night, shacking up with your little *bijou*. Or do you two use the woods now? It's nice, isn't it? Like nymphs and satyrs."

"She has her little girls to take care of," said I stiffly. "She just can't wander off at night like you evidently do. We're fine. Don't you worry about us. Genevieve is still fantastic."

She didn't seem to hear, and said, after a pause, "I'm sorry you're stuck. You can have your old desk back if you want it."

Now the Wadleighs came up to us, Ben allowing his pupil to tinkle away on automatic pilot. Wendy had cut her hair short, just like the other athletic coaches, and in her frilly yellow frock looked like a pixie in a buttercup. Couples who stay together in spite of all have a curious merriment about them, as of daredevils shooting the rapids, or of defiantly healthy alcoholics. "You two shouldn't be talking," Wendy said gaily, adding with shining eyes, "Alfred *et ux.*"

"This entire gathering is scandalized," Ben assured us in his fruity choirmaster tones. I looked at him through Norma's eyes and saw that he was lovable—pompous but clever, fruity but massive, artistic as was she, and light, like her an adept of the unsaid and the ignored. The waterbug approach to life, merely dimpling the surface tension as you move along. Me, I had been naïve, perhaps, and coarse, to attempt to penetrate, to sink, to pearl-dive into the past. It was cheerful, standing here with the Wadleighs as if we were two couples, Ben taller than I and Wendy shorter than Norma. The Claytons, bracketed. The Wadleighs were pulling, plainly, for us to get back together again, and thus again be accessible. Their dyad loved our dyad. We mischievously buzzed together a bit, and noticed that the party was thinning around us, to the point that Madame President's husband came up and attached himself to us with suckers of small talk. We thanked the host and hostess and went our ways. Not quite our separate ways, for the Wadleighs had a shared home of glass and redwood, high above the river, and Norma and I moved together through the dark and the rustle of the first soft fallen leaves on the dried-out small-town grass (so different in quality from overtrodden city grass, or the untrodden grass of the country). Norma's body beside mine felt like a gentle revenant. I muttered to her that I'd like to see the Volvo's scratch and, sensing beneath her insouciance that this already rusting injury to her automobile brought her as close to tears as the inky baby's feet, offered to come home with her a minute, to check on Daphne's fever and search through my old desk. I might find some notes in it (ran my secret agenda) that would definitively unlock the mystery of James Buchanan. My practice of history was superstitious as well as unsystematic.

Stars, there must have been stars above the mansard roof—Orion's belted sprawl, the Big Dipper balanced on its handle, the whole heartbreakingly random array sparkling in anticipation of first frost. Did our breaths show white? Too early, perhaps. I do remember how, several hours later, after we had made love on our former bed, that redwood box bought at Furniture in Parts, the Queen of Disorder turned her head on the pillow and said casually, in her most merely observational voice, "You've gotten better at it."

A motherly remark, complimenting a child come home with a new prowess. My sword had been tempered in Genevieve's sheath, and my technique honed to something like her own sharp-edged perfection. Before, sex had been muddle and melt to me. Before, I had fucked with just my prick—the tingling glans, readying to spurt, eagerly pushing ahead. Now I used my entire pelvis, the whole lower half of my trunk, repeatedly lowering myself as if into an onyx bathtub, in cold control while I sweated like a gymnast. Sex is impersonal, a well-oiled machine that works best sealed into darkness. The Perfect Wife had taught me that, and the imperfect one responded. I was the piston, she was the cylinder. A deep hostility kept us slick, and slightly startled. When with two shudders—hers involuntary, mine deliberate, like driving home a nail—we finished, Norma looked up at me with resentful eye-whites and pinched the skin of my sides, where the ribs turn the corner, so it hurt. Then she let go and turned her face on the pillow and paid me her compliment.

I remember, too, before we went to bed, entering the house with her, the big house quiet, my nose wrinkling and twisting into a sneeze at the cat dander, and feeling that at this unaccustomed hour of visitation I had surprised the furniture—the butterfly chair, the foam-rubber sofa and easy chair with their scarf-patched worn spots, the paper lampshade globes from Taiwan—in a huddle of conspiracy, these inanimate things conspiring to reconstruct the past, to dam the flow of time with their fragile, obstinate shapes.

The time is strange—the party couldn't have gone past seven-thirty, and yet in memory it seems to be after ten.

Stealthily we had climbed to the second floor. Andrew had moved to the third floor, setting up an independent domain in the low-ceilinged rooms there, whence descended, at various times, the throb of rock tapes, the rhythmic rumble of his exercise bicycle, and the clunk of the weights he had taken to lifting. He was building his body into something beautiful. His mother was under orders not to disturb him, and though from the driveway, crackling to a stop in our separate automobiles, we had seen his lit windows burning like angry eyes in the mansard roof, we did not climb the second flight of stairs, which led twistingly up from the second-floor landing. Disapproval of us emanated from above.

Down the hall, Buzzy's unconscious breathing filled his little dark room, and the beam of hall-light when we pushed open the door revealed an obsolescing apparatus of boyhood—his telescope; his glass terrarium, whence all the lizards and scorpions had long since decamped; the posters of some rock stars, bare-armed men with stringy hair and leather vests, like muscular miners stripped to forage underground for precious metal; another poster, of a gleaming Italian sports car draped with the body of a young woman spottily clad in leopardskin; his silent boom box with its sleepless red light; a scuffed little bookcase holding a clutch of brave books by Tolkien and Frank Herbert and a curling heap of old school papers; and shelves filled by carefully spaced collections of plastic dinosaurs and tinfoil athletic trophies won at grade school, when he was yet younger, and his hopes for himself were untarnished. We eased shut the door as if on a treasury of sad secrets, leaving a crack of light to show in case a dream's turmoil awoke him.

Daphne's room was across the hall, which ended at our—Norma's—bedroom door. My daughter awoke, or had been awake, and shrieked at the second shadow beside her mother's. "Who are you?" she asked in the voice of one still asleep, or transported by fever.

"Your father, honey," I said, whispering to suggest she keep her own voice down, and moving to test her forehead with my hand. But she shrieked with such blank fright, like a stepped-on animal, that I stopped in mid-motion.

"Daphne, it's Daddy," Norma explained. "He's come to see how sick you are."

Daphne didn't hear. "You're an elephant," the child told me, in a voice that emanated from the whole white blur of her face but did not belong to it, like a voice in a séance. It hesitated, groping to shape a complex concept. "He ate a bad mushroom and got all wiggly and died."

"Babar," the Queen of Disorder explained softly behind me. As if it hadn't been I who had read those books to the children, more often than she.

"Go away," Daphne told me hollowly, betranced. "You hurt people."

"Not you," I told her, my own voice strange, dipping deep into the gravity of parental assurance, "not little Daphne," and did manage to stretch an arm (like a proboscis, actually) and rest my fingertips on her brow. Its taut curve felt warm and dry. "You have a bug," I announced.

She stared upward at me, and her fever of delusion broke. "It's you," she said, and fetched a mighty, shuddering sigh.

I sat on her bed's edge, and tucked the covers more neatly around her. "That was mean of you," I scolded, "to call me an elephant. You have a little bug that makes you hot and tomorrow if it's not better Mommy will take you to the doctor's to find out what it is. Now you go to sleep."

This firm instructional tone, which my old house and its many shadowy needs had called forth, revived after our (Norma's and my) lovemaking,* when I quickly dressed and

---

*Does it need explaining? A matter of opportunity and romance, let's say— the romance of the child's fever, the closed door at the end of the hall, the

hissed downward at my wife as she still lay naked in bed, *"Listen.* You've had over two years to adjust. Get moving on the divorce, for Chrissake, or I'll start suing on my own. For Ben and whatever else I can dig up. You're costing me my life, all this stalling and fucking around you've been doing."

FRANKLIN PIERCE'S PRESIDENCY brought William King the Vice-Presidency, Buchanan the Ambassadorship to London, and Nathaniel Hawthorne, who had written Pierce's campaign biography, the very remunerative post of American Consul in Liverpool. Hawthorne's journal for January 6, 1855, records a visit paid him by the Ambassador, who had come to Liverpool with his niece and hostess, Harriet Lane, because she was to be the bridesmaid at the wedding of an American girl resident there. The Ambassador called on his consul, who had abandoned the seclusion—first single, then wedded—that had nurtured his masterpieces in order to serve in this post of busy intercourse with men of all stations. One wonders how aware Buchanan was of the genius of his underling; *The Scarlet Letter* came out, with considerable praise and publicity, in 1850, one of the years when Buchanan, semi-retired at Wheatland, had leisure for reading. Certainly Harriet Lane had read some Hawthorne, for, having met her at a dinner in Liverpool on January 9th, the author rather dourly recorded in his diary, *She paid me some compliments; but I do not remember paying her*

---

look of the side yard from what had been our window, motionless in the blue night like a frozen garden of ferns. A sentimental carryover from the faculty party, where we had momentarily seemed again a couple. Don't ask, *Retrospect.* At some point history becomes like topography: there is no *why* to it, only a *here* and a *there.*

any. His impression, superficially favorable, of the vigorous, violet-eyed, twenty-five-year-old woman carries a note of reservation; one can feel the great dreamer's fine nature rather cringe: *Miss L—— has an English rather than an American aspect,—being of stronger outline than most of our young ladies, although handsomer than English women generally, extremely self-possessed and well-poised, without affectation or assumption, but quietly conscious of rank, as much as if she were an Earl's daughter. . . . I talked with her a little, and found her sensible, vivacious, and firm-textured, rather than soft and sentimental.* Viewed through the same silken weave of Hawthorne's sometimes feline style, Buchanan comes off rather better: *I like Mr. ——. He cannot exactly be called gentlemanly in his manners, there being a sort of rusticity about him; moreover, he has a habit of squinting one eye, and an awkward carriage of his head; but, withal, a dignity in his large person, and a consciousness of high position and importance, which gives him ease and freedom. Very simple and frank in his address, he may be as crafty as other diplomatists are said to be; but I see only good sense and plainness of speech,—appreciative, too, and genial enough to make himself conversable.*

Their conversation would have taken place in Hawthorne's office in the unprepossessing consulate housed in *a shabby and smoke-stained edifice of four stories high . . . at the lower corner of Brunswick Street . . . in the neighborhood of some of the oldest docks.* The gouty, top-hatted Ambassador would have had to maneuver his corpulent person up *a narrow and ill-lighted staircase* giving onto *an equally narrow and ill-lighted passageway* crowded, most mornings, with *beggarly and piratical-looking scoundrels . . . purporting to belong to our mercantile marine.* Dealing with *these specimens of a most unfortunate class of people* composed, according to the opening pages of the memoiristic sketches collected as *Our Old Home,* much of Hawthorne's duties—*the scum of every maritime nation on earth; such being the seamen by whose assistance we then disputed the navigation of the world with England. Not one in twenty,* he tells us, *was a genuine American,* but all looked to the American Consul for relief from their misery and indigence—*shipwrecked crews in quest of bed, board, and clothing; invalids asking permits for the hospital; bruised and bloody wretches complaining of ill-treatment by their officers; drunkards, desperadoes, vagabonds, and cheats, perplexingly intermingled with an uncertain proportion of reasonably honest men.* Through this crowd of brutalized unfortunates, most of them wearing red flannel shirts, Buchanan, in cravat and morning coat, would have eased his way, to reach the outer office manned by vice-consuls and clerks, and then the inner sanctum, *an apartment of very moderate size, painted in imitation of oak, and duskily lighted by two windows looking across a by-street at the rough brick-side of an immense cotton warehouse, a plainer and uglier structure than ever was built in America.* Buchanan's squinting eye was taken, it may be, by the large map of the United States on one wall, cartographed as it had been twenty years ago.

"Your portrait of our homeland lacks Texas, and all the California territory that we wrested from Mexico," he genially pointed out, once the initial civilities had been pronounced. The men had met before, at the end of last April, when the Ambassador waited in Liverpool for the arrival of his niece, Miss Lane. *I had the old fellow to dine with me,* the writer wrote his publisher, *and liked him better than I expected.*

"Were we to draw the map twenty years hence, I fear it might show even less territory than is displayed here," Hawthorne ventured, the mellifluidity of his voice to some extent masking the pessimism of the prediction. Since he regarded his rôle of Consul with a certain amusement, as something of an imposture, he did not greatly fear offending his superior. Further, the older man's manner had a holiday joviality—a holiday abroad from seeking his political fortunes, and a holiday in Liverpool from his London responsibilities. And people forgive a known writer a great deal, such forgiveness constituting an inexpensive form of patronage of the arts.

Buchanan had lit a cigar, and smokily tut-tutted, "Oh come, Mr. Hawthorne, not as bad as that. With a little connivance and compromise, we shall pull the Union through. If you would mute your vociferous friends the abolitionists, and we somewhat quench our friends the fire-eaters, the plain economics of it, as they emerge in the West, will render the slavery question obsolete."

"I fear, sir," said the darkly handsome, high-browed Consul (whose diffident manner yet hinted at a certain premature fatigue), "that the question has become a passion, on both sides, which there will be no quenching but with blood. Senator Douglas, in laying the Kansas territory open to squatter sovereignty, has created there a witch's brew, to which flock fanatics and madmen and all of Missouri's gun-toting riffraff."

"And yet, cotton will not grow in Kansas. The Missouri Compromise, I have always stated," Buchanan affirmed, leaning deeper into the creaking Windsor armchair that amid these worn furnishings did for the seat of honor, "should never have been revoked. Douglas thought to throw a sop to the Southern half of the Democracy and advance his Presidential prospects for '56, but in truth he has split the party in two, and in the bargain finished off the Whigs. The Know-Nothings are high in the saddle now, and opposition to Kansas-Nebraska has bred a new national party, I am informed, that calls itself by Jefferson's old name of Republican. So much for personal ambition, Mr. Hawthorne, when it entwines itself with matters of grand policy. Douglas will never be President now; he has awakened too much hatred." The old man's effortful gaze wandered to the top of the Consul's bookcase, where stood *a fierce and terrible bust of General Jackson, pilloried in a military collar which rose above his ears, and frowning forth immitigably at any Englishman who might happen to cross the threshold.*

The Consul followed his visitor's eye, gauged its speculative and even alarmed expression, and offered by way of agreement, "Senator Douglas is no Jackson, though he might hope to be. As an idea, squatter sovereignty has a Jacksonian ring."

"Jackson was a great hater," Buchanan sighed, amid a fresh effusion of tobacco smoke, "but he had the South with him. The curious condition of our Union is, no election can be won without the South, and none with the South alone. That is the bill, and the nation has few to fill it."

Hawthorne, though fastidiously aloof from most public enthusiasms, was in his consular capacity politician enough to know that the substantial old gentleman sitting before him was already being spoken of as the only possible candidate for the torn Democracy. [*Retrospect* eds.: the word is used of course in the old sense of the Democratic party. Footnote? Or generally understood among our learned readership?] "It was perhaps a fortunate wind, Mr. Ambassador," he rather wickedly suggested, the tone of address warning his guest of a construable presumption, "which brought you to service in London. Had you been still in the Senate, how would you have voted, sir, on this ill-begotten Kansas-Nebraska Bill?"

Buchanan, with a cool deliberation that the Consul had to admire, levelled his crooked glance upon his questioner, and stated, "Between us—I would have had no choice, but to vote, as would have you if in elected office, with our benefactor and chosen leader, General Pierce, who made support of the bill a point of loyalty to his administration. Nevertheless, the popular-sovereignty provision was a grave and needless mistake, hastily inserted in the late stages of working out the legislation. Douglas wished the territory to organize in the swiftest manner, to keep it from becoming Indian territory and blocking a railroad centered upon Chicago in his own state. In his haste to profit Illinois and himself, he upset three decades of precarious balance. Compared with Jackson, whose personal friendship it was my honor to claim, Douglas is an unprincipled dwarf—pardon my bluntness—who is frequently drunk, most harmfully upon the sound of his own voice." The old man settled back into the consular office's audibly protesting guest chair, smiling at his own indiscretion. Yet he judged it time to change the topic. "In art," he said, "I take it there is never this distinction, to be often found in political service, between formally assenting to a thing, and inwardly assenting to the wisdom of it."

"In art," Hawthorne admitted, "we are sometimes invited to trim our texts, for a general good. For instance, my preface to *The Scarlet Letter*, which with great good nature but excessive accuracy sketched my former associates in the Salem customhouse, made such a fierce local stir that I was urged to withdraw it from subsequent editions; but I resisted those pleas. A compromised work of art becomes on the instant worthless, since we look to art for an otherworldly integrity."

"If in politics we so severely rejected all compromise, I fear chaos would come to the affairs of men."

"As it yet may, in spite of much compromise."

"As it yet may," the old man agreed, to speed the conversation along, for he had another instance of scandalous muddle to cite. "Less than three months ago, I participated—most unwillingly, mind you—with the Minister to France, Mr. Mason, and the Minister to Spain, Mr. Soulé, in a conference in Ostend and then Aix-la-Chapelle, which had been convened to draft a confidential report to Mr. Marcy and General Pierce upon the matter of purchasing Cuba from a bankrupt Spanish throne."

"I have read of it in the news," Hawthorne said quietly. "The British press has been considerably indignant, and those on the continent more so."

"Oh, and the U. S. Congress, too—we have been mightily flayed," Buchanan avowed, "and not without justice! The entire business was instigated by two swashbuckling reprobates in our government's employ, Dan Sickles and Pierre Soulé— both of them hasty in temperament, and quick to take short cuts, whether with diplomatic channels or with other men's wives. I invited Sickles, at his request, to join the London Mission, thinking as compensation for his willful and pompous moods we would have the company of his charming young wife; but he left her at home in New York and brought along instead a young woman, Miss Fanny White, with whom his only ties appeared to be those of affection! As for Soulé, he has nothing of the temperament of a minister: come to Louisiana from France as a political refugee, having been jailed for agitation against the Bourbon restoration, he has continued his anti-monarchical activities in Spain, lending the diplomatic pouch to revolutionary letters and further distinguishing himself by shooting the French Minister to Madrid in a dispute over the latter's wife!" The old man rocked forward in the protesting chair, its legs and rungs and curved stick-back loosened by the squirms of untold unhappy petitioners; he coughed with smoke and laughter and took pause to dab at his eyes with a handkerchief produced from his black sleeve. "Well, these two hotheads, Sickles by going to Washington and stirring up the President with talk of an easy conquest and Soulé by demanding a bullying ultimatum to accompany our offer of a hundred thirty million to the Spanish queen, had put our Mr. Marcy in such a bind that he found himself instructing Soulé to 'detach that island from the Spanish dominion'—I use his very words. Meanwhile, Dan Sickles had returned to Europe spilling into every receptive ear what he had understood to be General Pierce's order for drastic action. Naturally, protest though I did, it fell to me and Mason—and Mason took the whole conference as a lark, and contributed scarcely his presence at the table—to frame a formal advisement that would draw the teeth from Soulé's threats while expressing, in some sort, their gist. Though I cannot claim your own pride of artistic authorship, mine was an ingenious composition, which achieved abeyance enough for Marcy to coax from Soulé his resignation this last December. In the case of Cuba as in many another, the best deed is doing nothing. The Young Americans and their hope of a filibustering expedition have been stymied, and Cuba will fall into our hands when the Spanish rot advances a little farther, as under Providence it is bound to. The public press, which understands nothing but crude sensation, accuses me of proposing 'sale or seizure,' when in truth it was I who pulled the administration back from such a disastrous option, which might well have given the European powers an opportunity to come forth and rattle our domestic peace with a Caribbean intervention! Britain is in a fighting mood, as you may sense. It has taken all the friendship I enjoy with Lord Clarendon to curb their reaction to our destruction of Greytown and, worse from the diplomatic point of view, our President's adamant refusal to disavow Captain Hollins' rash action! Luckily, not a life was lost in the bombardment, though a mass of mud huts were flattened."

Hawthorne silently wondered at the old fellow's ability to delight in the intrigue that the expediencies of power impose. The Ambassador knew his auditor to be the President's dear and loyal friend from their college days together at Bowdoin, and while seeming to rattle on freely, yet left to incommunicable implication any low view of Pierce's ability; neither Pierce, who had defeated him for the 1852 Presidential nomination, nor Marcy, whose stubborn retention of his New York votes helped deny the Pennsylvanian that same nomination, could be counted among Buchanan's friends, yet here he was (Hawthorne reflected), serving them both in this mostly ceremonial post, bereft of real negotiating authority, making the best of their erratic orders, yet serving with a curious relish. He had become, whatever his initial nature and its potential, a slave of public life, at home only among its formalities and nuances, which, like those of feminine society, seek to regulate with a touch and a word the masculine currents of force that seethe across the planet, and to put an acceptable face on the world's bloody business of birth and murder. Buchanan and Miss Lane cut considerable figures in high British circles, and indeed it was not infrequently rumored that the Minister's niece might soon make a titled marriage. Like all eager talkers, the man had something to sell or conceal. Yet, withal, something rustic and honest—a sunshot innocence aged in the barrel of long experience, an unspoiled aptitude for pleasure foreign to the shadowed psyche of New England—rendered the old functionary companionable, and indeed imparted a sense of his pleading, beneath the *consciousness of high position and importance,* for the less public and more reflective man's approbation.

The Consul, whose consciousness was divided between the deferences owed by his inferior office and his responsibilities as host, thought it wise, after so long an unburdening by his elderly guest, to introduce a topic where he might bear his share of the discourse. He took up the mention of the English mood, and expanded it to a question of the general English personality, as perceived by his fellow American, and discovered impressions not unlike his own, though on a broader plane. Buchanan felt the British willing to fight for their toehold on the Mosquito Coast, if maladroit and domestically distracted American policy provided an excuse for John Bull to exercise his bully tactics, and Hawthorne found the British personally overbearing and cold. *There are some English whom I like,* we might imagine him saying, in colloquial paraphrase of his words in *Our Old Home—one or two for whom, I might almost say, I have an affection; but still there is not the same union between us, as if they were Americans. A cold, thin medium intervenes betwixt our most intimate approaches. It puts me in mind of Alnaschar, who went to bed with the princess, but placed the cold steel blade of his scimitar between. Perhaps, if I were at home, I might feel differently; but, in this foreign land, I can never forget the distinction between English and American.* Buchanan nodded in eager agreement; when he did return from his English mission, he proclaimed to a crowd in New York City, *I have been abroad in other lands; I have witnessed arbitrary power; I have contemplated the people of other countries; but there is no country under God's heavens where a man feels to his fellow-man, except in the United States.* Emboldened by the warmth of his important guest's agreement, and by the second glass of morning brandy, from the consular cabinet, which the visit entailed, Hawthorne moved on to caricature English women, in implicit contrast to willowy American beauties both he and Buchanan had known. *As a general rule, they are not very desirable objects in youth, and, in many instances, become perfectly grotesque after middle-age—so massive, not seemingly with pure fat, but with solid beef, making an awful ponderosity of frame. You think of them as composed of sirloins, and with broad and thick steaks on their immense rears. They sit down on a great round space of God's footstool, and look as if nothing could ever move them; and indeed they must have a vast amount of physical strength to be able to move themselves.*

The Minister's response to this word-picture was so gratifying, forcing the gentleman to squeeze the mirth from his abdomen with several lurches of his large and well-upholstered frame, that Hawthorne added, to modulate the conversation back into sobriety, "They must exist, but I have not happened to see any thin, ladylike old women, such as are so frequent among ourselves."

His slender Ann would be one such, Buchanan thought, soberingly. A life with her at his side, as time worked its gradual way with their bodies, felt suddenly to have been within reach, and narrowly missed. He found himself, for the moment, unable to speak, to this handsome reserved Yankee with his deepset, heavy-browed eyes, *the wonderful eyes,* Elizabeth Peabody had once exclaimed, *like mountain lakes seeming to reflect the heavens.*

Hawthorne sensed the snag in the Ambassador's social flow, and motionlessly waited. He was not one of those men, those lusty Southerners given easy initiations in slave shacks and river-town brothels, who found Buchanan's failure to marry comic and odd. He knew from his own experience how easily a man might remain a bachelor, never gathering the energy for the leap, the days and years blending one into another, as they had in the Mannings' house at 12 Herbert Street, he writing his dim delicate tales in his little room under the eaves, his mother distant and discordant in her antique widow's weeds, his sister Ebe his only soulmate, little sister Louisa their only emissary to the people of the town, their shopper and gossip, his mother and Ebe and he venturing forth only at dusk for a walk along the wharves, skirting woodland and marshy pastures, strolling sometimes as far as Gallows Hill, where the witches had been hanged and flung into their graves, returning by way of proud streets lined with the red-brick mansions of Salem's China merchants. But for the energy of another family—the intellectual busybody Elizabeth Palmer Peabody and her two sisters—he might be immured there yet, in a kind of betranced obscure disgrace; Lizzie Peabody called him out into daylight, and little Sophia, the invalid youngest, seized him, no longer young, with the talons of love. That first visit, Sophia later told her husband, Lizzie had rushed upstairs, where her sister was sequestered with one of her migraines, and cried *Oh Sophia, Mr. Hawthorne and his sisters have come, and you never saw anything so splendid—he is handsomer than Lord Byron! You must get up and dress and come down.* Somehow certain of her prey even then, Sophia had laughed off the command: *I think it would be rather ridiculous to get up. If he has come once he will come again.* And this proved true. Like everyone else—the tale was folklore in political circles—Hawthorne knew that Buchanan's life had early taken a stain: the lovers' quarrel, the unexpected and unexplained death, the refused plea to attend the funeral, the grieving family's curse, and the survivor's curious escape into public life. No doubt it had been the making of Buchanan as a politician, just as those dozen closeted years had been his own making as an artist. *In this dismal chamber FAME was won.* Fortune warps us to fit its ends.

"In the same fashion, you never see a fat plowhorse in the United States. We work them too hard," Buchanan responded, apropos of American women, their thinness. The old man had shaken off his reverie, and now was attentive, cocking his white-haired head, to another ornament of the Consul's apartment, *a colored, life-size lithograph of General Taylor, with an honest hideousness of aspect, occupying the place of honor above the mantel-piece* and darkened, since his aborted term, by five years of oily smoke from the coal grate. "I hope, Mr. Hawthorne, your appointment calendar doesn't run as tardy as your Presidential portraits; you are two Presidents behind."

"We are a war or two behind as well," Hawthorne said, indicating another wall adornment, *some rude engravings of our naval victories in the War of 1812.*

"Old Zack," Buchanan mused. "Some say he was poisoned, by an agent of the South, when he showed himself to be a Free-Soiler at heart. Had he lived, he would have vetoed the Compromise of 1850, with civil war the likely result."

Hawthorne politically kept to himself his opinion, that the celebrated Compromise had been mere fiddle-faddle, a futile placation of the South's irrepressible fears, as it saw slavery crowded into an increasingly minor fraction of a country tripled in size since 1800. All of Cuba, with the Mosquito Coast thrown in, could not right the balance.

"I have always supported," Buchanan stated, "extending the Missouri Compromise line to the Pacific. All those territories below 36° 30', as they apply for admittance, to vote for or against slavery as they please. None will vote for it, and that includes Kansas. What the South needs from the North at this juncture is not lectures and pamphlets urging the slaves to massacre the planter and his sleeping babes, but indulgence, as we would show a man ill beyond recovery—as we show defenseless minorities in our midst like the Mennonites and the Jews." He may have heard in his own voice an unneeded note of lecture, for he became confidential and faintly apologetic again, shifting his weight forward in the rickety petitioners' chair to declare, "But by a quirk of fate my views have rarely been put to the test of a heated public vote: I was not yet in the Congress when the Missouri Compromise was passed, I was Minister to Russia during the worst of the nullification struggle, I was out of office and tending my garden in Lancaster by 1850, and I have been lifted above the vicious Kansas-Nebraska debate by my mission here."

"A charmed life," Hawthorne murmured.

"I was early wounded in life's lists," Buchanan confided, as if assuming his tale to be known, "and have been a peacemaker ever since. At times I had to differ with Jackson and Polk, and two flintier heads the country hasn't seen since the first John Adams, but I always avoided a break."

"It may be, sir, that fate has reserved you for a great task not far ahead."

Buchanan's color rose slightly. "Impossible, my dear friend. I have put in for my recall next October. Firmly and gladly, I intend to retire forever from public life. I am sixty-three years old, and have many familial responsibilities, though none of my own making; I possess a pleasant country estate that hasn't known my step for it will be upwards of three years, and, if I may dare say this to you, whose words have been graced by the divine breath, I have some writing I wish to do—a memoir of my times, especially the administration of Mr. Polk. Though never possessed of genius, I have been in my plodding fashion a man of the written word, who has preferred written communication to any other form. When Henry Clay wished to heap scorn on me, he would merely say, 'He writes *letters!*' Well, I admit it—many the night I have fallen asleep at my desk, writing. When passions have evaporated, and what we strive to achieve has been undone by history, the words we write remain, and will plead for us."

"For some blessed few," Hawthorne amended. "For the rest, books find a grave as deep as any. But your retirement, sir— will the people permit it? If our friend the General, who has conducted his duties under a stifling weight of personal sorrow and domestic pall, fails of renomination in the cry over Kansas—" He let the thought complete itself. Another thought crossed his mind: that he was meant to relay Buchanan's protestations of final retirement to General Pierce; but he dismissed the notion. *But it is a very vulgar idea,—this of seeing craft and subtlety, when there is a plain and honest aspect.*

The other's animation increased, and his pink color sharpened. "My mind is fully made up; I will never be a candidate; and I have expressed this decision to my friends in such a way as to put it out of my power to change it. I admit, I would have been glad of the nomination for the Presidency in 1852, and would not have refused it in '48 or '44; but now it is too late, I am too old. My time has come for reflection and repose, and to improve my relation with my Maker, for we shall shortly, I devoutly trust, meet face to face."

Hawthorne involuntarily cast down the famous lamps of his eyes at this flare of piety, and said so softly the other had to strain to hear, "I pray not shortly. Come what may, Mr. Buchanan, you are at this moment the only Democrat whom it would not be absurd to talk of for the office."

And the old man's blush deepened further. His lips parted and merely trembled, groping for an evasion that would yet do justice to *the high vision of half his lifetime.* The blush of excited ambition stained all his face, between the white linen of his old-fashioned stock and his crest of upstanding white hair. Visibly he calmed himself, pondering with his ungainly squint the one English object in the room, *a barometer hanging on the wall, generally indicating one or another degree of disagreeable weather, and so seldom pointing to Fair, that I began to consider that portion of its circle as made superfluously.* "Do you know any French, Mr. Hawthorne?"

"Un peu." There had been readings of Montaigne, Rousseau, Racine, Voltaire under the eaves, in books Ebe brought back from the Salem Athenaeum, and then, the weeks he stayed with Horatio Bridge in Augusta, his nightly conversations with Bridge's tutor and boarder Monsieur Schaeffer, a little blond, cross-eyed Alsatian who would return from a day of trying to drum French into young Maine blockheads with the cry *"Je hais les Yankees!"*

"There is a profound wisdom," Buchanan told Hawthorne, "in a remark of La Rochefoucauld with which I met the other day—'*Les choses que nous désirons n'arrivent pas*'—comprenez?"

"Thus far."

The accent that had served in the Court of St. Petersburg was carefully distinct, testing each word like a man advancing over thin ice. "—*'n'arrivent pas, ou, si elles arrivent, ce n'est, ni dans le temps, ni de la manière qui nous auraient fait le plus plaisir.' Oui? Comprenez-vous? C'est une vérité dure, n'est-ce pas?"*

"C'est dure, c'est triste, mais vrai. C'est la vie."

"La vie humaine depuis la Chute—depuis Adam and Eve, eh?" And the old fellow laughed, a high-pitched laugh wheezily withdrawn as soon as it was offered, mixed with a shriek from the tormented chair as if its runged and spindled wood were inhabited by the agonies of all the wriggling supplicants who had ever sat there in its hard embrace. Hawthorne felt on his

neck a chill of the uncanny—the shriek seemed to have arisen not within the fusty official chamber but within his own haunted, reverberant skull.

WHEN WAS IT? My memory wants to assign our exchange to a raw gray day of earliest spring, with soot-besprinkled tatters of unmelted snow huddling beneath the Muellers' bushes and against the northern side of their cellar bulkhead, but by the logic of sequential event it must have been fall—late fall, let's say—after Election Day. The Ford era is drawing to a close; Ford has lost, albeit narrowly; the leaves so ruddily, rosily, goldenly translucent on the day of the President's cock-tail party have fallen. More than fallen, they are raked and bagged or mulched and already rotting back into the sweet, misty earth. The maples and beeches and few surviving elms of southern New Hampshire—a woodsy state that like Penn-sylvania has in over two hundred years contributed but one son to the Presidency, a state too good, one might say, to make great men, who extract such a toll from the rest of us; a state where Mt. Washington, that bitter blowy dome of rock, has never been renamed Mt. Pierce—stood silvery-bare along the meandering Wayward River, which having once powered and cleansed a few mills to the north was now free to pour itself uselessly into the sea. *Live Free or Die* is our motto; low taxes, our boast. We are the Union's fourth most industrialized state. Though not so gothic as Maine, we have our pockets of rural poverty and sad fits of sex-motivated murder. Our highways have an honest tackiness; no curried Vermont, its green hills plump with New York money, this. No two streets of Way-ward were parallel, and half had no sidewalks. Genevieve's house, you will not have forgotten [see pp. 49–50], stood across the street from a great old elm and was *an early-nineteenth-century former farmhouse, clapboarded and painted pumpkin yellow with rust brown shutters and trim,* symmetrical and modest yet rendered majestic for me by its enclosing of her live body and ardent, orderly spirit. Lately, I rarely got inside it. Brent came and went, visiting their two daughters, and Genevieve thought it would be too confusing for them if another man made equally free with the front door and back door. Also, the neighbors would notice my car, a conspicuously aging old Corvair convertible, if it were frequently parked where her front lawn blurred into the asphalt street, and who knows what neighborly evidence her husband's lawyers might call upon in a pinch? In the Ford era, superstitious dread of lawyers and stockbrokers as potential sources of financial ruin had not been superseded by fear of failing banks and outlandish hospital bills, as in the present, Bush era.

The Muellers' front lawn looked not merely raked but scrubbed, and their azalea bushes were each wrapped in burlap. Standards were being upheld. The great old elm wore a blue plastic box on its side, dropping some kind of palliative into its poisoned capillaries, and its dead branches blended with its living in the seasonal leaflessness. The day persists in feeling like spring in my mind, one of those unnumbered dull days that carry us to our deaths, spring the least satisfactory of our New England seasons, the air suffused with the gray hopelessness of nature sluggishly rousing itself and endeavoring yet again to replace one generation of weeds with another, while winter's winds continue to blow in from the Atlantic.

Yet, once inside her house, having knocked and opened the front door in a single motion, I was heartened by the Perfect Wife's arrangements, her ubiquitous clarifying touch. The glass table with its ice-green edges on its sturdy chrome X. The Aubusson rug with its distinctly Seventies harmonies of salmon and washed-out lime green. The abstract prints on the walls, trying spottily to mirror my head, on the surface of their slashing blacks and whites. The clean panes of the living-room windows.* The ricochet of earth-tones off the square edges, with rolled seams, of her sofa and easy chairs. The dining room, where eight rush-seated chairs of stained beech waited on tiptoe for the next dinner party, around a polished table in whose center a turquoise glass vase with spiralled ribbing held a dainty spray of brown-and-yellow asters, the year's brittle last blooms. Everywhere, the glisten of cleanliness, the absence of clutter. Not a dog hair or dust mouse to be glimpsed; it was all as purely intentional as an architectural sketch, with human figures stylishly scribbled in to indicate the scale—ovals for heads, stick legs for men and triangular skirts for women, coded signs the lines of perspective pass right through.

Genevieve was wearing snug white Calvin Klein slacks, the hip pockets like tattoos stitched onto buttocks of bright cloth, and a black cashmere turtleneck in which her hair remained caught, as if she had just put the sweater on and not yet taken the moment to free and flip out from the elastic neck her silky black tresses. It gave her an electric androgynous look, as of a page in a modernist production of Shakespeare. Her feet—I don't think I misremember this—were bare, as if, again, she had rushed into this costume a second before making her appearance on stage. Perhaps my letting myself in immediately after knocking had rushed her. As I say, I was rarely invited

---

*I was reminded, possibly, of washing our windows in Hayes with my mother as a child—the running-down ammonia-tinted suds, the squeak of the slowly soggy-becoming cloth, the growing ache in the forearm, the sunny bite in the air, which in northern Vermont can be cool even in August. A child sees no difference between clean and dirty windows, so the ritual was for me, like so much adult behavior, a purely magical act, an ordeal invented to bring me to my mother's side and under her fond supervision. Through Genevieve's ideally transparent panes the outdoors seemed to have crept closer, like a beast about to pounce.

to her home, as our affair wore itself into grooves. She came to me in Adams, or we took little trips, and found a motel not too close to the highway, or too painfully seedy. Roadside cabins were not bad, with their quick electric heat and back view of laurel or lilac in the shelter of the pines; in Ramada Inns, the halls were too full of boozy salesmen's banter. My mistress seemed, in her Rosalindish costume, so perfect, so svelte and compact, I hesitated to embrace her; it seems an illusion—as if up-to-date computer trickery has enhanced my clumsy old memory-tape—that we did embrace. Her dear sturdy, wide-shouldered body, given a yearning athletic thrust by the tiptoe stretch of her bare feet, came tight against mine and clung with an ominous finality.

She had summoned me, by telephone at my office. Her voice had sounded especially humorless and direct. She was calling from work. She had taken a job, finding her academic husband's grudging dole inadequate, in a Portsmouth boutique founded by the sister of another faculty wife—the leaning professor of biology's tennis-burnished second bride. The shop was in Portsmouth's renovated wharf section, old brick warehouses refitted to hold the new commercial wine, in this case the post-counterculture tweeds, jumpers, and smart suits. Sensible, subdued clothes were back in style. Genevieve acted not merely as a saleswoman but, as the weeks elicited her flair and sense of fashion, an assistant manageress and advisory buyer. She was succeeding, but it meant she was gone most days, and in returning had to rush about, retrieving the girls from the neighbor or babysitter that had taken them in after school, and laying out a supper, and catching up on the tasks which when a mere housewife she had stretched to fill the day.

So it was not a gloomy afternoon after all, it must have been evening. Her cleaned windowpanes were black, but for the bleaching sweep of occasional headlights sweeping past. By the ebb and flow of those passing beams we had more than once made love, she lying belly-up on the down-filled sofa, my face bent to her black triangle or her round breasts with their hard dark tips, the lights coming and going on our bodies as if taking a series of photographs for a sentimental album of our love.

I had grabbed a bite to eat at some joint or other in Adams or else in the gynocentric Student Center, after hours spent at a desk somewhere with the by now quite baffling Buchanan. His life from the inside was a deal with God, like everyone's, but the outside kept complicating, the characters in his story kept multiplying, old backstage manipulators like John Forney fell away and new ones like John Slidell arrived, women continued to haunt his fringes, his letters and memoranda piled up, his career drifted toward its clamorous yet cluttered climax in the White House, his life had become an incubus stealing strength from mine. My life had at some unnoticed point peaked and passed into decline. My fortieth birthday had come and gone, scarcely celebrated. Everybody had been too busy, including Norma. I lay on the sofa wearily. Genevieve was upstairs again, singing her daughters to sleep. She had a touching voice when she sang, quavering but true, more childlike than her speaking voice. The songs were ones I didn't know; my mother for all her good qualities had not been a singer, and in our white Congregational church would stand with firmly clamped lips while the rest of us bumbled and whined through the hymn. To me it seemed Genevieve was always singing one song, that went up and down, and returned upon itself as music does, repeating, repeating more urgently, looking for that thing it never does quite find. In my bachelor digs, to banish silence and street-noise, I reflexively turned on my little radio as soon as I entered, and over two years of WADM had bred in me a certain contempt for music: it strives, it shouts, it whispers, it tries again, a half-octave higher, but it doesn't get anywhere, it doesn't escape, it eventually ends. The best you can say for it is that it's not silence.

Genevieve came downstairs looking as I have described. Perhaps by now she had put white clogs on her feet, or mules, thick-heeled and open-toed, so her painted toenails showed their black dabs, their punctuation spelling finis to the thrilling chapter of her body; but no, I think not, her feet were naked after a long day standing in tight shoes at the Portsmouth boutique. The boutique had a name, which I have just remembered: Fancies.

"Anything?" she asked, trying to kick her own weariness. "A beer?"

"What kind?"

"Löwenbrau, I think."

"Brent left some in the fridge again," I deduced. Löwenbrau was his brand. French ideas, German brew, anything imported. He aped Derrida and drove a Peugeot. No wonder we were becoming a debtor nation.

Bristling at my implied resentment, she said, "Why shouldn't he be here? He was filling in for me with the girls Friday, when the shop's open to nine. The Christmas season's begun."

"You poor thing. We got to get you out of that store."

She looked at me as if trying to gauge how much I meant that. In fact I had meant nothing, except sympathy. I saw us as fellow sufferers. That I was the cause of her suffering did not really occur to me. "Why?" she asked. "I like it. I like the human contact, I don't have much around here, everybody at Wayward cuts me dead. It distracts me from the mess I've made of my life."

"A Löwenbrau wouldn't be so bad," I admitted.

"Shall I have a glass of wine?"

"What about your ulcer?"

Was that a blush? She never blushed. But now, like Buchanan, she did. "I've been cheating on it a little."

"Wine sounds good. Make that two."

"There's only a little bit left in the bottle." She hesitated, then decided to say it, still blushing. "Brent drank most of it when he was here."

One mention of Brent I didn't mind, but two was too many. I sat up. "You and he seem to do a lot of drinking together. Come here. I'll give you the sofa and get you the wine."

"You want the wine."

"Not the last glass, when you want it."

"Oh, take it. You've taken everything else."

"What do you mean?" The electricity she exuded wasn't just my imagination. It touched me, made me slightly breathless. It puffed out her hair, caught in her black sweater's turtleneck.

"What do you mean, what do I mean?" she cried. "*Every*-thing. My respectability, my comfort. My self-respect. My girls still love me but in five years when they work out what happened they won't. I'm like a whore with you. I'll do any-thing to please you. I've never been like this with a man before."

"It's nice," I said, flattered.

"For you it is," she said.

"Not for you?"

"For me it's more than nice. It's madness, Alf."

"I meant of course more than nice for me, too. It's Heaven. You're Heaven, Genevieve." I spoke her name rarely. It was too long, and yet I couldn't bring myself to shorten it to "Gen," as Brent coarsely, jocosely did.

"It's not, and I'm not," she said flatly. "We live on earth. And not so very long, at that." My tendency to poeticize, to enlarge and elevate with words, to as it were *construct*, and her more practical nature had come into conflict before, as when under the budding elm she had announced our leaving of our spouses. I had done it, in a scene so painful I cannot bear to recall it even for you, *Retrospect*. I had paid my dues; I had secured her love; I was her white knight. But a disgust, or dissatisfaction, colored her tone as she said, "I'll get you the beer. The wine's probably acid by now anyway."

Returning with a round tray on which a wineglass and a beer glass stylized in silhouette a perfect heterosexual couple, Genevieve sat down not on the sofa beside me but in the matching easy chair, covered in pale beige, across the glass table. When she crossed her legs with a swift, narrow-ankled motion, the underside of her white-jeaned thigh flashed, and my mouth went dry with desire. I wanted to be there, between those clean thighs, the sweetly dirty furry moist place between them. She watched me take a golden swallow of Brent's beer and smiled. "Beautiful Alf," she said. "You're so innocently greedy."

"Thirsty," I innocently corrected. "I want to make love to you so much my mouth suddenly dried up just then."

Primly she uncrossed her legs and put her knees together. "Tell me about Ann Arthrop." Her large clear eyes, the dark irises riding high in the whites, stayed with mine as she took a measured sip of the wine. She grimaced, and made a French sort of sound that might be transcribed as *Yoog*, pronounced rapidly.

For a second, I had thought she was referring to somebody in the Buchanan saga, whose mists rarely lifted from my brain. The wife or perhaps unmarried sister-in-law of one of his Southern Cabinet members, dangled before the old bachelor as a distraction from their treachery. "I believe," I said carefully, "she's the mother of Jennifer Arthrop, a pet student of Brent's."

"Good, darling. That's what I believe, too. And when did you fuck her, exactly?"

"Who says I fucked her?"

"You deny that you fucked her?"

One of the innumerable things I liked about Genevieve was the way that she, once she found the word she wanted, would stick with it. She had no more use for idle, vain variation than a machine. Perfection is like that. "I don't deny it," I said. "I just want to know who says."

"Who cares who says?" she said.

"Brent says," I accused. "Bastardly old Brent says his bratty little pet cunt Jennifer says, because her mother told her because they have a sexual rivalry going. A mother-daughter combination like that should never be trusted."

You know, *Retrospect* editors, in animated cartoons, how the cat starts to slip on marbles the mice have spilled, first slower, then faster, so his legs become a windmill blur, and still the marbles keep feeding under his feet, while it takes him a terrified forever to fall? Our conversation had become like that, I desperately trying to keep myself in the air.

Genevieve had become relentless. "You're saying Mrs. Arthrop lied to her daughter? Why should she do that?"

"To annoy her. To create confusion. Why do people ever lie? Because people are perverse—to assert themselves over against totalitarian fate. Lying is a kind of vote; it's democracy in action."

"When did it happen, Alf?" Her tone was pointedly patient.

"Who says it happened? Winter." No, that was when Buchanan waltzed with the Czarina of Russia. "May, maybe. I met Mrs. Arthrop in April or May, with Jennifer over in the Student Center, after a rehearsal of *Lysistrata*, put on before final exams started."

Genevieve's lovely eyes, not buried bits of watchful jelly as with most of us but sculptural forms—slightly almondine, as I may have said, as if from a dash of Oriental blood, somewhat as Senator King had a slightly Seminole look—widened; her starry lids, the lashes so thick mascara muddied them, flared in cold fury. "Then you went with her. You fucked her that night and then the two of you like a dear old married couple went the next evening to see little Jennifer perform."

: 285 :

"It was an afternoon performance," I corrected her. "In Truman Hall. And I certainly did *not* go to the performance, with or without Mrs. Arthrop. What a shocking idea. I never saw her the next day; the woman got back in her car and went back to Connecticut where she belonged, to her husband, who sounded awful. He called her Annie, like in 'get your gun.' " The marbles had stopped rolling under me. Somehow, to my enormous relief, we had bypassed the moment of confession, and were safe on the other side. The Mrs. Arthrop episode was behind us, part of our pasts, upon which we could resume building our immaculate future.

"How do you know?" Genevieve asked, without any of the good and hopeful humor I felt within myself.

"Know what? That she got back in her car and went home to Connecticut? I assume so, because it's six months later and I haven't heard otherwise. A crash would have made the papers."

"That her husband called her Annie."

"Oh, I don't know. It must have come up at the table in the Student Center. I had a bean-sprout sandwich, she was eating a tangerine. Jennifer kept jumping up and down to talk to her buddies, leaving us alone at the table to make awkward chitchat." Why wouldn't this incident go away, sink into history? I had assumed we both assumed, by now, that I had slept with Ann.

"You're lying," Genevieve said.

"About what? About *Lysistrata*? I promise you, on a thousand Bibles I promise you, we did *not* go to the play together." Although she had got me to wondering if I should have—if it had been a lapse of manners on my part. "I might have run into Brent there, coming to admire his protégée. I don't like running into Brent." How much of my behavior, I thought as I supplied these sentences, was indeed innocent. Most of it. As much as ninety-eight percent.

: 286 :

Her wonderful eyes, like painted marble eggs, suddenly brimmed pinkly with tears. I was stricken. I would rather have watched Daphne cry. In a cracked voice Genevieve blurted, "I don't know when you're lying and when you aren't."

I must straighten this out; our relationship was cracking up over irrelevant details. "Genevieve dear, please listen. I did *not* escort Jennifer Arthrop's mother anywhere the next day. I have never heard boo from her since. She was a tough upper-middle-class broad. I *did* go to bed with her the night before. I'm sorry, it was—what did you say?—madness. It was nothing. It was like a footnote the reader can skip. It's you I love. It's you I adore. I want you to be my wife. I *feel* you're my wife already." Even in this moment of annealing truth-telling, I lied. It had not been nothing. It had been a magnificent regal bestowal of her plump assured body, towering with the solemnity of flesh above me like a thumb held out to eclipse the distant cool disk of the moon. Her multiple jiggles, her pendulous breasts, her minimal room with its view of the French Fry, the kitschy little dim bedside lamp that saw everything, above its sunset—I had often thought back upon it, with pleasure and pride.

"You fucked her," dry-eyed Genevieve stated, for clarity.

"Genevieve, *please*. Why do women keep saying 'fuck'? It was lovemaking, it was natural, like the tides. It happened only once." Ann and I came twice, actually, I remembered. I hoped my face wouldn't reveal this second thought, this scholarly qualification. The perfect woman's red-rimmed gaze was sharp as a hawk's; even her lips, never plump (like Sarah Coleman's, say), had thinned.

"Who else says 'fuck'? Who else have you been screwing, while I've been standing on my feet all day and telling everybody below the knee is what's in now and rushing back to feed Susan and Laura and tuck them into bed and tell them that Mommy loves them and Daddy loves them even though he's not here and God loves them even though their prayers aren't always answered right away? I don't ask them what their prayers are, I *know* what their prayers are, *I'm* the one who's denying them, not God. Then I go around and lock up and lie there and pray you'll call and try not to be too frightened and stop listening to the creaks and cracks and the way the refrigerator downstairs sounds like a man walking around and get some sleep so I can be fresh and charming in the shop tomorrow." I had never heard her talk so much, with so little self-censorship; I was at last getting the unabridged edition. "You don't know what it's like to be a woman alone," she went on, "you're a man, you're like a stupid bear, you just go off into some cave and if a warm body wanders in you jump on her. While I'm humiliated and scared, not just for my selfish self but for my poor dear little girls, you're preening in front of these adoring brainless Wayward brats and fucking anybody you please because it's cute to be perverse against totalitarian fate. Who's the totalitarian? Me, I suppose. Not sweet old Norma, she's too disorganized. She's just a big woozy maternal cloud of, of "—and with an impatient flick of her fingers she slipped into a language native to her marriage, her husband's Derridian—"*la dissémination.* "

For a slip-sliding heart-stopping second I thought she also had been told of my lapse with Norma after the President's party. Who would have told her? My nemesis Brent saw us talk together and maybe leave together. That bastard. He was all around me, cutting off my air supply. Like the smell of Norma's paints that night.

As I dipped into my chest for breath to defend myself, Genevieve asked, "What was the attraction?"

"With whom?"

"My God, Alf, how many floozies are there? With this Arthrop woman! Brent says she's fat and sloppy."

"How could he know?"

"Don't try to sidetrack me. He saw her somewhere the time she was up here, maybe at the rehearsal, maybe at the play. I don't pry into his life. She sounds awful. What attracted you to her?"

I resisted telling her; it was too intimate.

"What did she have that I didn't have? Bigger boobs? Dirtier tricks in bed? How did you know until you got there? Or can men tell ahead of time? Can men smell it? Did she want it up the ass?"

She was bringing out my prim side. I shuddered and said, "Don't be vulgar. She had nothing you don't have. You're perfect. For me, at least."

"Sure as hell sounds it." She was getting slangy, with her loosened tongue. I didn't like this. I had liked the rather formal way she had talked, as I had her old-fashioned, erect posture and correct, faintly severe clothes.

"Her name," I confessed. "Her name was Ann. Like Ann Coleman, the love of Buchanan's life."

"That's a laugh," she said. I hated the phrase. It sounded like Brent, in faculty meetings, the voice of today's thinking, debunking in a false demotic accent.

"It's the truth. What else is the truth?" I wondered aloud, using a trick I had developed with inattentive or unruly classes, of retreating into monologue, of delving into myself with an arresting honesty. "She was a woman. A different woman, a new woman, I don't know. Not to have responded at all would have shown a total lack of intellectual curiosity. The same thing for her, I'm sure. Human beings are intellectually curious. I've said I'm sorry, Gen, come *on*. It happened six months ago, it's over, it's gone. If it wasn't for goddamn Brent—"

She was crying again, more freely now, as if her precise, beautifully modelled face were getting the hang of it. Her lower lids overflowed; her lips trembled like a slapped child's; the faint shadow of a depression in the center of her shovel-tip-shaped chin flickered off and on like a defective light bulb. "It—it just makes everything so meaningless," she got out.

"Why meaningless? What do you mean by meaning? What meaning does any of this have, in the long run, when every-body is dead, and our children are dead, and their children's children?" I heard myself sounding like a taunting professor; it was the ghost of Brent I was combatting; he was possessing her, prompting her, whispering into her tender ear with that tightly hinged jaw of his, its masseters overdeveloped by years of clenching a pipe between his teeth. He was in the room, like smoke from a fire the campers thought they had extinguished, but that has been smoldering beneath the pine needles. For the first time, it came to me that the sofa I was sitting on would not likely be used for lovemaking tonight; we had gone too far off course; a transit in my stomach measured the widening angle of unlikelihood. Up to now, we had slowly but steadily plowed the waves of the society that upheld and tossed us; now our great white love boat was sliding more and more to lee-ward. To offer another metaphor, the cliff face I had been climbing was tilting outward at me. "I cannot believe," I pleaded, rather frantically but neglecting to shed my pontifical voice, "that this one utterly trivial incident should matter so much to you. Brent's been balling little Jennifer right along, it seems obvious, and then as you were kind enough to tell me he's been taking out Norma and God knows who else."

"I kicked Brent out." Her voice had recovered distinctness, though her tears still flowed, giving her face there in the dim-lit living room a shine, an albedo, that reminded me of somebody else—who? Perhaps Sarah Coleman, the night she so youth-fully went off to the theatre, where they had freshly installed gaslight. "I have no right to restrict or judge what he does. With you I thought I *did* have some right. I kicked him out for you."

"You kicked him out on your own—you told him without warning me. Our five children up in smoke—*poof!*"

"Oh, that again." With one of her incisive white hands she waved away my old resentment, which in spite of good intentions I had more than once failed to conceal. "If you're so obsessed with children, you should have stayed faithful to Norma."

"I didn't know how." The words came out of me a bit enigmatically. Did I mean I couldn't nail her to the wall, like Teddy Roosevelt and the currant jelly? Or that the Gerald Ford *Zeitgeist* precluded such knowledge? "Anyway, you weren't exactly a Barbie doll just sitting there on the shelf. Remember that time at one of the Wadleighs' parties, I was in the kitchen all innocent, looking at the notes and *New Yorker* cartoons they'd put up on the refrigerator door with magnets, and you came in helping Wendy clear away glasses or something and gave me this flat-out big French kiss and said to me, 'Don't be such a chicken.' "

"No," the Perfect Wife answered. "I don't remember that at all."

I was thrilled by this totalitarian ability to alter history; how much more creative and human it is, after all, than the attempt to recover the exact quiddity of events.

"I *do* remember," she went on, "the time you came to the house to return some book by Lacan or Paul de Man that Brent had lent you and begging you to stop, begging you right there on that sofa, it was in the middle of the morning and I remember there was snow on the ground, everything so bright, I felt so naked, I felt so used, such an adulteress—" She broke off, the tears overcoming her again, her lovely, slightly wide face hidden in her hands, her hair by now half-freed from her cashmere turtleneck and falling in forlorn hanks down past her huddled, convulsing shoulders.

Chastened, frightened, I told Genevieve, "Of course you have the right. I've loved being loyal to you—having somebody I *could* be loyal to."

Her hands dropped, her face lifted, her eyes flared: "But you haven't been!" As if this merely literal point bore repeating, when I had been speaking spiritually, in essence, in a large general sense, day after day: I had felt betrothed to her. She said, "I have no idea how many others there have been."

"Dearest, there haven't been any others." Not counting Norma, who was after all my legal wife, and Wendy, fucking whom I thought of as clearing up an old tension rather than creating new business, and the slim blonde woman, a guest speaker on transactional analysis here for two days, who cried out "I'm kissing my own cunt!" (which might have happened under late Nixon, to be precise), and semi-Platonic brushes with a few Wayward girls, students in their second year and soon to move on anyway. Never get involved with a first-year student; they hang around forever, becoming dependent and developing Electra complexes. I was having chronic trouble reminding myself of the seriousness of this conversation. Under our aggrieved words ran the thought of mine that even perfect couples quarrel, that like any long-established couple we were having a quarrel, that it brought us closer to being married, being able to quarrel. In the same way, it must be difficult for a man on his deathbed to take his own dying seriously; his son is asking to borrow the car, his wife downstairs is shrieking that the dishwasher is overflowing, his local sports team has lost four straight, his favorite sitcom is going to be on tonight at eight-thirty. All the time, he is truly dying, he will soon be light-years beyond all these concerns, but for now is still here, having to participate. For now, Genevieve was still before my eyes. I was in her immaculate living room, basking in the heightened sense of being alive that only she gave me, her peculiar beauty, earnestness, crispness, and composed energy bringing me to the edge of something like merriment, even as she wept, wept away our conjoined lives as if she had taken a bright wound no tourniquet could stanch.

My hands groped in air helplessly, to heal the hole. I rose from the sofa and went to her, huddled miserably in her easy chair, and put my hands on her wide shoulders, her firm back. "Forgive me," I said. "I love you. I want you. Norma's lawyer is getting back from a conference in Arizona and has promised to get in touch with mine first thing after the holidays. Things are moving along, honest."

Without turning her head, so my lips stayed at her ear, she reached up to her shoulder and put her left hand [see page 54] on mine, as if to quiet me. She got her sobbing under control. "Sit down, Alf. I have some things I must say to you."

"Oh, yeah?" It was as if the tiny seed of guilt inert and defiant in me was now flowering—cascadingly, its feverish soft blooms pressing into every crevice. [You know how it feels, *Retrospect* eds.: the slipping, the vast tilting, the panicky wish to backpedal, all mixed in with a certain irritation at being taken, by a woman's emotional violence, away from one's level-headed work.] I sipped my neglected beer. It tasted bitter, of arrested fermentation in Teutonic, glass-lined vats.

"You were right," she told me, a bit crooningly, as if the song she had sung her daughters were still in her throat, knitting her hands together between her white knees, in a gesture alarmingly gentle, as if wishing to restrain the blow she must give. Genevieve's head, I had sometimes felt, was full of poses—templates into conformity with which she was constantly bringing her body, face, and voice. It gave her glamour but also glamour's cruel and decisive imperviousness. "Brent *did* stay a long time the other night, and together we drank up almost all of the wine, as you saw. He made me a proposition, which I said I would consider, after talking to you. Now I *have* talked to you."

Though I have been a teacher for all of my adult life, I am not very good at being taught. I get restive; a certain hostility builds up during my respectful silence. I did not like her patient, instructive, motherly tone. A perfect wife should be motherly, but not so the husband notices.

"He said," she continued, "that Yale has made him an offer for the spring semester. There's been both a suicide and a pregnancy in the English department. The pay wouldn't be any better than here at first, and he would have associate status for at least three years, but he really can't say No. It would be like saying No to the Vatican if you're a priest. He has to go."

Genevieve, in bed or at cocktail parties, had a fine frontal directness—straight at you—so it was a striking deviation when she turned her head to a three-quarters view, her black hair swathed over her ear like that of a Brontë, its gleam mirrored in the framed abstract lithograph hanging behind her. She looked demure. She fluttered her eyelashes, not so much coquettishly as like a stutterer trying to blink away a laryngeal impediment. "He's asked me to come with him," she said. There was that ghost of a blush again. She peeked at me out of the corners of her eyes, then recovered her normal manner, gazing at me directly, even the hands on her knees perfectly symmetrical. "The girls would be *so* thrilled," she said.

"B-but"—myself battling a stammer of excitement—"you don't love him. You love me." Yet when I tried to picture our love I remembered an absolute darkness, and the primordial sound of her swallowing, and the malty brine of her breath afterwards. Except for our excursion to New York City, we had not been enough in the sunlight. We were underdeveloped film.

"I loved you very much," she said, in that same slow sing-song, neither emphasizing nor avoiding the fatal "d," "but you've worn me out, Alf. I'm tired of living in an unreal world.

I just need to rest now, and be normal, and watch my girls grow, and grow old myself." Is it by a trick of memory that as she said this she seemed to broaden, so her slightly wide face, with its dark brows and flat little proud chin-tip, became congruent with a housewife's placidly solid body, calmly sitting, the acrobatically supple waist thickened, the switchy lean legs on their way to a middle-aged waddle? "I feel ridiculous sometimes," she went on, "being romantic and passionate. It's not as if I'm twenty. I'm thirty three. I think the nuns did a job on me—they delayed my development. Well, if I *was* going to have such an episode, I'm glad it was with you, Alf. You really know how to keep a girl on her toes."

"But I *said*, Norma is moving. You and I can be married in six months, if the damn lawyers will stay in New Hampshire."

"Norma moves," Genevieve said, "but, oh, so slowly. Brent saw the two of you talking at the President's party and said you looked very cozy."

"Did we? I don't remember. She had a lot of bad news about the kids she had to dump on me." If I didn't stop, I would come to the car dent, and Andy up on the third floor, and Daphne's fever, and a betrayal beyond even Brent's ken. Not that, in the Ford era, going to bed with someone was the life-and-death matter it has become. But even then—to keep the historical perspective—it wasn't quite trivial.

The Perfect Wife smiled sadly. "Brent said the two of you looked just right for each other."

"Brent, schment," I snorted. "New Haven is a terrible city," I told her. "Beyond the Yale campus, it's all ghetto." Yet even as I spoke I felt how paltry, how touchingly bush-league, were the semi-rustic charms of Wayward and its environs.

"It can't be worse than your apartment in Adams," she said.

"We'll run away," I promised. "Now. We'll take the girls and stay in a New York hotel."

The sad smile persisted. The template was fixed. "New York hotels cost sixty dollars a night. What happens after the first week?"

"I'll get a job in advertising. I'll teach English to Japanese businessmen."

She shook her head, with a delicate metronomic precision, back and forth and back and forth, that gave her the terrifying relentlessness of the inanimate. "Sometimes things we want," she told me, "arrive too late. Two years ago, even a year ago, we could have forced the issue like that, and let the world pick up the pieces. It would have. It would have made allowances for us. It does, for lovers. But now—our case has grown stale, Alf. Mrs. Arthrop was no accident. There would be others, probably there *were* others—"

"*No,*" I lied, with a passion hollow but still expectant, still hopeful of being justified. Modern fiction—for surely this reconstruction, fifteen years later, is fiction—thrives only in showing what is *not* there: God is not there, nor damnation and redemption, nor solemn vows and the sense of one's life as a matter to be judged and refigured in a later accounting, a trial held on the brightest, farthest quasar. The sense of eternal scale is quite gone, and the empowerment, possessed by Adam and Eve and their early descendants, to dispose of one's life by a single defiant decision. Of course, these old fabulations *are* there, as ghosts that bedevil our thinking.

"Brent is willing to forgive me everything," Genevieve was saying.

"Big deal," I said. "What's to forgive? A post-structuralist bastard like that has no right to talk about forgiveness as if it has meaning. I'm the one who should forgive *him*, for marrying you first. But I don't. I don't forgive that smug ass-kissing shit, rushing down to Yale to find bigger asses to kiss."

Her smile had become less sad; a twinkle brimmed in her eyes like a new kind of tear. "Don't be so competitive. Brent's much more of a traditionalist than you think. He believes in family. I'll tell you a secret. His own true parents got a divorce when he was three, then his mother married her lover and they became ardent Lutherans. He swore he'd never do it to his own children. Get a divorce. He said if I'd come back he'd even let me have lovers, if he wasn't adequate for me sexually."

This was an agonizing prospect, his most fiendish ploy yet: a chain of licit lovers, of other *mes* enjoying her exquisite sex, her moist breathing, her sighs of satisfaction, while her beauty broadened and her sensuality deepened. The vision made me dizzy; I left the sofa and went down on my knees. As it happened, a nailhead in the dry early-nineteenth-century floorboards had lifted up in the area near her chair; I felt the stab and heard the gray flannel of my trouser knee rip.

My recollection snags on this irritating mishap; I forget what all I said; I had pretty well run out of promises. The ragged, burning tear in my knee may have impaired my eloquence. She was firmly in control now. She pooh-poohed as one would a child's fear my fear that she would with Brent's connivance take many other lovers. After me, after *us*, she assured me, they would be anti-climactic. No, fidelity to her husband would be her passion, her penance, her nunnery. How stunning, in my mind's eye, she would be in her habit, her wimple and winged headdress! She had been a nun all along, perhaps—that was the secret of her immaculate poise. The more extravagant my pleas became, the more gently adamant she grew; at last, trying to salvage something from this wreck of a tryst, I tugged at the zipper on her snug white Calvin Klein jeans and reached up under her black sweater—"*Ouf*, Alf!" she cried involuntarily, "your hands are *icy*!"—and proposed that we make love one last time. This, too, was refused, as too sad-making, the two of us knowing it would be the last time. There were things one shouldn't know. She was a realist, my perfect mistress, and I, I was that dying man I have described, unable to believe a blank white abyss drops off from the foot of his bed, that the film is within a few feet of running out and clattering in the empty projector, that there will be no tomorrow. We have trouble believing in yesterday, but believe absolutely in tomorrow. I could not believe this was the end. I was with her; I felt terribly alive, with that life she alone created in me; still in her presence, for these few more seconds, I was happy.

[RETURNS TO U.S. April 24, 1856, one day after sixty-fifth birthday—avoids public dinner in New York and in general avoids statements likely to offend one or another faction of agitated Democracy—says in Baltimore, *Disunion is a word which ought not to be breathed amongst us even in a whisper. . . . There is nothing stable but Heaven and the Constitution*—on May 22, 1856, Congressman Preston S. Brooks of South Carolina invades Senate and beats Senator Charles Sumner of Massachusetts, leading Abolitionist, insensible with gutta-percha cane—two days later, John Brown and sons slaughter five Southerners at Pottawatomie Creek in Kansas—in Cincinnati in June Democratic-party convention picks Buchanan on seventeenth ballot, over Pierce and Douglas, the South's favored candidate—platform asks for end to agitation of slavery question and recognition of *the right of the people of all the Territories . . . to form a constitution with or without domestic slavery*—in Pittsburgh the Republican party nominates its first Presidential candidate, the explorer John C. Frémont, and puts forth a platform prohibiting from the territories *those twin relics of barbarism, polygamy and slavery* and promising to bring all those responsible for the *atrocious outrages* in Kansas, including President Pierce, *to a sure and condign punishment*—Republican leaders in subsequent campaign speeches hope to *bring the parties of the country into an aggressive war upon slavery* (New York Governor William H. Seward) and *look forward to the day when there shall be a servile insurrection in the South; when the black man* [shall] *wage a war of extermination against his master* (Ohio Representative Joshua R. Giddings)—Buchanan makes no speeches during campaign, but stays at Wheatland copiously writing letters decrying the possibility of disunion, proclaiming, *We have so often cried "wolf," that now, when the wolf is at the door, it is difficult to make people believe it—*

[On October 15th, Democrats win Pennsylvania by narrow margin, assuring election for Buchanan—final tally shows 1,832,955 votes for Buchanan, 1,339,932 for Frémont (fewer than eight thousand below the Mason-Dixon Line), and 871,731 for American (Know-Nothing) candidate Millard Fillmore, the thirteenth President of the United States—electoral tally a comfortable 174 to 114 to 8—Buchanan's inaugural speech, delivered during debilitating siege of so-called National Hotel disease, while wearing a coat, tailor-made in Lancaster, lined with *a magnificent design of thirty-one stars representing the states of the Union, with Pennsylvania dominating the center,* in its one unexpected passage asserts that territorial issue *is happily a matter of but little practical importance, and besides, it is a judicial question, which legitimately belongs to the Supreme Court of the United States, before whom it is now pending, and will, it is now understood, be speedily and finally settled—*the Dred Scott decision, announced two days later, ruling that any law excluding slavery from a territory is unconstitutional, unleashes storm of protest in the North—officeseeker-harried Buchanan's disposition of patronage alienates former faithful political friends John Forney, David Lynch, and Dr. Jonathan Foltz—financial panic of 1857 leaves the relatively untouched South cocksure and crowing that *Cotton* *is King,* whereas in the depressed North hungry workmen chant *Bread or blood,* and industrialists and Republicans demand higher tariffs—

[Buchanan's insistence on submitting the technically legal but unrepresentative pro-slavery Lecompton Constitution to Congress for approval as condition of Kansas's admission to statehood splits Douglas off from Southern body of the party and results, after numerous strenuous and corrupt efforts of suasion, in return of Kansas to territorial status under terms of the English Bill compromise, passed April 30, 1858—Lecompton struggle generates impression that Buchanan is captive to pro-Southern "Directory" consisting of Secretary of Treasury Howell Cobb of Georgia, Secretary of the Interior Jacob Thompson from Mississippi, and Senator John Slidell of Louisiana, Senate whip and mastermind of the President's nomination and election—Howell Cobb once allegedly replies, when asked why he seemed troubled, *Oh, it's nothing much; only Buck is opposing the Administration*—at outset of the Lecompton affair Pierce's secretary, B. B. French, writes to his brother, *I had considerable hopes of Mr. Buchanan—I really thought he was a statesman—but I have now come to the settled conclusion that he is just the d—dest old fool that has ever occupied the Presidential chair*—

[April 1858 "Mormon War" ends happily as Buchanan, having dispatched troops under Colonel Albert Sidney Johnson, permits Philadelphian Thomas L. Kane to travel to Salt Lake City and reach peaceful agreement with Brigham Young, who submits to authority of federal government and the newly appointed territorial governor Alfred Cumming—in August Buchanan dispatches nineteen warships up La Plata River to win redress for Paraguayan wrongs against U.S. citizens—responds courteously to first official message over Atlantic cable, from Queen Victoria, despite patriotic furor in press over rude brevity of message, shortened in transmission by cable failure—in warming atmosphere of British-American relations, British abandon right of search of vessels on high seas—

[Summer of 1858, Lincoln-Douglas debates in Illinois Senatorial campaign keep national attention on slavery issue and widen Douglas-Buchanan rift—1858 election returns spell defeat for administration Democrats and rise of Republicans, though Douglas wins in Illinois—Buchanan writes to Harriet, *Well! we have met the enemy & we are theirs. This I have anticipated for three months & was not taken by surprise except as to the extent of our defeat. I am astonished at myself for bearing it with so much philosophy*—contentious Congress stymies Buchanan's foreign and domestic initiatives, failing by March 3, 1859, to pass routine Treasury bills—Postmaster General Aaron Brown dies four days after losing battle to win appropriation to cover postal deficit—Elizabeth C. Craig, widow and reputedly most beautiful woman in Athens, Georgia, who had come to Washington (with Cabinet wife Mary Ann Cobb) declaring her determination to snare the President, departs after living in White House for two months—Buchanan confesses to Howell Cobb he has spent restless nights dreaming of her—

[Spring of 1859, Southern excursion excites public ovations and newspaper report of President as *gay and frisky as a young buck*—takes annual summer fortnight in Pennsylvania's Bedford Springs with wealthy grass widow, a Mrs. Bass from Virginia, and her three daughters—they are placed in rooms next to JB's archenemy Senator Simon Cameron, and abolitionists persuade Mrs. Bass's black servant girl to run away—October 16–18th, John Brown's raid on Harper's Ferry is put down by forces under Colonel Robert E. Lee—

[Spring of 1860, at Charleston, Democratic convention collapses when Southerners, angered by Douglas's refusal to promise protection of "property" (e.g., slaves) in territories, walk out—in May, border-state moderates organize Constitutional Union party and nominate John Bell of Tennessee, and Republicans in Chicago nominate Abraham Lincoln of Illinois—in June Democrats re-meet in Baltimore and split again, Douglas nominated in main hall and seceders in separate hall nominating John C. Breckinridge, Buchanan's Vice-President —March–June, Covode Committee, established in March of 1859 to investigate solicitation of Congressional votes in support of English Bill, hears parade of anti-administration witnesses, though Buchanan in spirited rebuttal on June 22nd says, *I have passed triumphantly through this ordeal. My vindication is complete. The committee have reported no resolution looking to an impeachment against me; no resolution of censure; not even a resolution pointing out any abuses in any of the executive departments of the Government to be corrected by legislation. This is the highest commendation which could be bestowed on the heads of these departments*—also on June 22nd JB vetoes the Homestead Bill on grounds that *This bill, which proposes to give him* ["the honest poor man," earlier evoked] *land at an almost nominal price, out of the property of the Government, will go far to demoralize the people, and repress this noble spirit of independence. It may introduce among us those pernicious social theories which have proved so disastrous in other countries*—large delegation of Japanese to sign first commercial treaty between Japan and U.S. captivates Washington society and presents Buchanan with largest porcelain bowl in world—in August, at Bedford Springs, Buchanan approaches the Reverend William M. Paxton, rector of New York City's First Presbyterian Church, and questions him as *closely as a lawyer would question a witness upon all the points connected with regeneration, atonement, repentance, and faith.* At end of session says, *"Well, sir, I hope I am a Christian. I think I have much of the experience which you describe, and as soon as I retire, I will unite with the Presbyterian Church,* explaining, *I must delay for the honor of religion. If I were to unite with the church now, they would say "hypocrite" from Maine to Georgia—*

[In early October 1860, the nineteen-year-old Prince of Wales, travelling incognito as Baron Renfrew, visits the White House and at a state dinner JB permits card playing afterwards, for the first time in his administration—then the President discovers that all the White House beds have been taken by the royal party and he must sleep on a sofa—Abraham Lincoln wins November elections, polling a million fewer votes than his three opponents combined, and fifty-seven more electoral votes—in Columbia, South Carolina, Laurence Keitt orates, *South Carolina will either leave the Union or else throw her arms around the pillars of the Constitution and involve all the States in common ruin*—John Slidell writes Buchanan from Louisiana, *I deeply regret the embarrassments which will surround you during the remainder of your term—*

[*Retrospect* eds.: Speaking of embarrassment, what follows is fragmentary, unsatisfactory. After my break with Genevieve, I realized that my attempt to complete my book and my attempt to marry her had been aspects of a single vain effort to change my life.]

"Mr. Floyd, are you going to send recruits to Charleston to strengthen the forts?"

For a long time, things had not been right with Secretary of War John Floyd, whose middle name was Buchanan. A former Governor of Virginia, son of another governor, he had, like many men who have been born into a patrician eminence, that faint sleepwalking air of those who have not fully earned their lives. Dandified in dress, he wore his hair long, so it protruded from his balding skull in two crimped wings; his eyelids had a mournful droop and his mouth a maiden-auntish pucker; his furrowed and dry-skinned face testified to recurrent illnesses and intervals of exhaustion. A mere fifty at the time that Buchanan—on the advice of Slidell and his other friends Senator

Bright and Governor Wise, all three of whom had declined
Cabinet posts in deference to their own ambitions—had appointed him, Floyd had remained youthful in the President's
old eyes, and forgivably susceptible to the influence of harder,
hungrier men than himself.

The Covode Committee, in its perjurious and malice-moti-
vated workings, had uncovered disturbing bargains which
Floyd had indifferently struck with some of the New York
Hards [eds.: need explain Hards = Hardshell Democrats or
Hard Shell Hunkers (pro-Buchanan) vs. Softs/Soft Shell/pro-
Pierce faction, allied with old Barnburners?], John Mather and
Augustus Schell, the collector of the Port of New York, and
Schell's brother Richard: the purchase by the War Department
for $200,000 of a site for fortifications, at Willet's Point on
Long Island, which had recently been rejected by army engi-
neers at a price of $130,000, and, with some Virginia partners,
the purchase for a mere $90,000 of the eight-thousand-acre
Fort Snelling reservation in Minnesota, a site that had been
declared essential. Buchanan himself had intervened to prevent
the purchase of a California site at far too dear a price.

Floyd stood to profit financially by none of this, but he had
the air of a man whose honor was slumping away from him,
leaking away little by little, through one careless concurrence
after another. The Meigs affair this summer had brought disgrace upon the administration. Captain Montgomery Meigs, a
conscientious and efficient but abrasive official entrusted by
Pierce's Secretary of War Jefferson Davis with a number of
construction projects in Washington, including the completion of the Capitol dome and wings, had for long been feuding
with Floyd, whom he accused of using contracts as a means of
awarding political and personal favors; for example, Floyd
awarded the valuable contract for heating the Capitol to a
Virginia doctor who knew nothing of heating and was intend-
ing to sublet his concession. Meigs, of a prominent Philadel-

phia family, more than once complained to Buchanan, who attempted to keep peace in this as in everything else; the Senate, however, on the instigation of the rigidly principled Jefferson Davis, passed amendments to the appropriate civil-appropriation bill requiring, in one case, that the half a million to complete an aqueduct could only be spent if Meigs supervised; this frustrated Floyd's attempt, in January of 1860, to have Meigs transferred to a construction project in the Dry Tortugas.

So that when Floyd, looking languidly wan and bilious, appeared in the President's office, in response to an urgent evening note to discuss the condition of the federal forts in Charleston Harbor, and the likelihood that they would be attacked, Buchanan had little reason to expect reassurance.

[No—stopped here—too much like other people's history—Nevins and Nichols especially, full of pro-Northern, anti-administration innuendo. Floyd was more complex a case than a corruptible if not corrupt Tidewater aristocrat. Though a Southerner, he was against secession, and may have tried to warn Buchanan, after the election of Lincoln, against the influence of secession-minded Cobb and Thompson. Floyd was also the one Cabinet member somewhat sympathetic with Douglas, and anxious to heal the breach that brought on the ruin of the Democratic party. Philip Gerald Auchampaugh, in his *James Buchanan and His Cabinet on the Eve of Secession,* even thinks he wasn't a bad administrator: *Floyd was a man of real personality and ability, save perhaps in dealing with contractors. He was active, alert, always attending to his duties except when utterly unable to be about. The administration of his office force seems to have been able. The army was kept in as good state of fitness as the funds would allow.* Auchampaugh defends or dismisses the action that brought about Floyd's fall: his continuing endorsement, even after Buchanan ordered him not to, of bills presented by the Western contractor Russell, Majors, and

Waddell, who had supplied the troops of the Utah War while Congress was tardy with appropriations. These "acceptances" were then presented by the contractor to banks as securities on loans. However, the amounts mounted—by the calculations of the investigating House committee, Floyd's acceptances totalled close to seven million dollars—to the extent that banks ceased to discount them, and William H. Russell of the firm sought an illegal expedient: he connived with a minor clerk in the Land Office, Godard Bailey, a gambler and kinsman of Mrs. Floyd, to substitute these by now worthless acceptances for Indian-trust funds, locked in a chest, consisting of over three million dollars in unregistered, negotiable bonds. As Russell required money, Bailey substituted more, and eventually thus disposed of $870,000 worth. January 1, 1861, approached, however; the coupons on the bonds must be presented for payment. Bailey, panicking, wrote a confessional statement to his superior, Secretary of the Interior Thompson, and sent a copy to Floyd, who was lying sick of other causes. Thompson, a Mississippian with Snopesian energy, spent three sleepless nights tracking down Russell, who was then jailed with Bailey. This financial scandal, in which monies generated and absorbed in our Western expansion were cavalierly mishandled by Southerners, broke at the very time that the Buchanan Cabinet was wrestling with the explosive immediate matter of the Charleston Harbor forts and the ultimate constitutional conundrum of the states' right of secession—did it exist?—and the federal government's right to resist secession.

[Against the background of national disunion and impending fratricidal war, climaxing decades of mounting regional tension over the underlying moral question of whether or not this society should continue to include and protect black slavery in its fabric, Floyd's and Russell's and Bailey's malfeasances' coming home to roost is an irrelevancy almost comic. It was a great embarrassment to Buchanan and continues to be one to American historians, who in writing of these suspenseful last months of his administration must trouble to understand and explain what "acceptances" and Indian-trust bonds were. These economic details, though properly reminding us that our Manifest Destiny had a shaky and overextended financial underside, and that personal gain is the prime American mover, are a considerable headache to non-Marxians like myself. Yet the scandal was momentous at the time and cannot be isolated from the struggle within Buchanan's Cabinet, for it heightened the fever and clangor and finally compelled Buchanan to request the Virginian's resignation, though he was too cowardly or kind-hearted to do it himself, asking his fellow Pennsylvanian, Attorney General Jeremiah Black, to do it instead. Black refused, and then JB asked Breckinridge, who *did* approach his kinsman Floyd, who—but I get ahead of my story, thanks to the muddling Floyd, who kept a diary, by the way. I *hate* history! Nothing is simple, nothing is consecutive, the record is corrupt. Further, the *me* inside these brackets appears no wiser that the one outside them, though he (the former) is fifteen years older. I tried to begin again:]

President James Buchanan was in a severe and solemn mood. He had summoned his Secretary of War, John Floyd of Virginia, and asked him, "Mr. Floyd, are you going to send recruits to Charleston to strengthen the forts? What about sending reinforcements to Charleston?"

Floyd blinked his watery eyes, in equal parts languid and guilty, and responded, "Mr. President, I had not intended to strengthen the forts."

"Mr. Floyd," stated the President, "I would rather be at the bottom of the Potomac tomorrow than that those forts would be taken by South Carolina in consequence of our neglect to put them in defensible position. It will destroy me, sir. And if that thing occurs it will cover your name—and it is an honorable name, sir—with an infamy that all time can never efface, because it is in vain that you will attempt to show that you have not some complicity in handing over those forts to those who take them."

The utterance, in its length and urgency, left the old chief a bit breathless, his head, with its erect flare of fine white hair, cocked more than ever to one side, and *his* eyes, mismatching, glittering with fatigue and the bright wariness of a captive old bird, a pinioned eagle, as he imagined himself on the bottom of the Potomac. *Pearls that were his eyes.*

"Sir," said the Secretary of War, "I would risk my life and my honor that South Carolina will not molest the forts."

"That is all very well," responded the cagey veteran politico, cast in all his dignity of years into the maelstrom of heightening sectional tension. "But—pardon me for asking you—does that secure the forts?" *Into something rich and strange.*

"No, sir, but it is a guarantee that I am in earnest in the belief that they are secure. Governor Gist, advised of the conciliatory logic of your message to Congress to be delivered this December, has sent messages assuring me that, until the ordinance of secession is passed, everything is quiet and will remain so, if no more soldiers or munitions are sent on."

"I dislike," admitted the Chief Executive, "the way the Governor speaks as if matters all rest in his hands. And what do we hear from Major Anderson?"

"He has taken what I believe is undue alarm from the drilling of state troops in the streets of Charleston, amid public boasting of the intent to take Fort Moultrie. He prepared a requisition to draw one hundred muskets from the Charleston arsenal. Colonel Huger at the arsenal has asked the War Department for orders; I have informed him that authority to supply arms to the forts would be deferred for the present. I have replied to Major Anderson that any increase in the force under his command would add to the local excitement and might lead to serious results."

Buchanan appeared to absorb the information, but with a twitch of his head affirmed, as if to himself, in a kind of day-dreaming soliloquy the storm of events increasingly imposed upon him, "I am not satisfied."

Floyd thought it expedient to declare, "Sir, as you already understand, if Congress decides upon a course of forcible coercion, it will become my duty to resign."

"Nevertheless, it is your clear duty now to be certain that the forts are secure. But let us see what General Scott will advise. He should be telegraphed to come to Washington at once." The old hero of Veracruz and Chapultepec was in his dotage, and all but immobilized by his physical complaints. As Floyd had expected, any threat of resignation, of disruption within a Cabinet that Buchanan had pieced together as a model of the enduring Union, led the President to pull in his horns.

[Based upon a theatrical speech Floyd himself gave in Richmond, in January of 1861, after his resignation. Quoted in abridged form in Auchampaugh, *prev. cit.*, and refracted with various distortions in history texts. Stilted as it is, it comes as close as we will get to how these men talked to one another, and how the great shifts underfoot traced themselves in personal conversation. Auchampaugh dates this exchange *probably in the latter part of November* but Klein puts it definitely two days before the Cabinet meeting of November 9th. Well before, in any case, South Carolina's actual secession on December 20th. On November 27th a long dispatch arrived from Anderson reporting rising determination in South Carolina to take the three federal forts and asking for reinforcements—two companies for Sumter and Pinckney, and a reinforcement for his own Moultrie garrison. Each time the Cabinet discussed the forts, Black and Secretary of State Lewis Cass argued for reinforcement, and Cobb, Thompson, and Floyd argued against. Floyd was later quoted as saying to William Trescot, the South Carolinian Assistant Secretary of State, that he would *cut off his right hand* before signing any order to reinforce. Meanwhile, Buchanan's exquisitely balanced message to Congress on December 3rd, his fourth annual message, angered the South by refusing to grant a state's right of secession and angered the North by denying the federal government's power to make war on a state. *The fact is that our Union rests upon public opinion, and can never be cemented by the blood of its citizens shed in civil war. If it cannot live in the affections of the people, it must one day perish.* In this he was echoing Andrew Jackson's farewell address, in March of 1837: *the Constitution cannot be maintained, nor the Union preserved, in opposition to public feeling, by the mere exertion of the coercive powers confided to the General Government. The foundations must be laid in the affections of the people.* But would Jackson have taken this fatalistic tone in Buchanan's situation? Certainly he gave no encouragement to the would-be nullifiers of 1832. But you know all this as well as I, *Retrospect* eds.]

On December 8th, four of the Representatives from South Carolina were received by the President. The most voracious and radical of the fire-eaters, Laurence (he thus signed himself) Massillon Keitt, darkly handsome [a short Clark Gable, let's say], with a sensibility essentially literary and hence extravagant and ruthless, announced, striving to keep his tone respectful: "Sir: we are here as Congressmen from the sovereign state of South Carolina. In less than two weeks we expect that secession will be proclaimed in Columbia. When this occurs, we will send commissioners to treat with you over the future relations between our two independent republics."

Congressman William Porcher Miles, a former mathematics teacher at the College of Charleston, had come into politics by a curiously peaceable route: he had won such attention as a heroic volunteer nurse in a yellow-fever epidemic in Norfolk, Virginia, that he was elected Mayor of Charleston in 1855. Now, sensing a certain resistance in the old chief to Keitt's

implicit prediction of a diminished Union, Miles mildly interposed, "In the meantime during these dark and confused days,
Mr. President, we desire to reach some agreement with you
that will prevent bloodshed in Charleston."

A third Representative, John McQueen from Queensdale,
appealing to the President's well-known weakness for close
legal reasoning, pointed out that the forts occupied leased
property, and that only the improvements on the property—
the erected structures themselves—could be said to belong to
the federal government.

The delegation's fourth member, Milledge Luke Bonham, a
veteran of the Seminole and Mexican Wars, had been appointed to fill the place vacated by his cousin Preston S.
Brooks, who had died within a year of his honorably motivated
(Buchanan and all the South felt) assault, in May of 1856, with
a rubbery cane so fragile it broke in two, on Senator Sumner
as the Massachusetts abolitionist sat at his desk, inflicting three
cuts, two of which required two stitches each, in revenge for
Sumner's vile verbal attack upon Brooks' uncle, Senator Andrew Butler, who had been absent from the Senate that day.
Sumner, feigning lasting injury, was henceforth a greater nui-
sance than ever, for being a martyr, whereas poor "Bully"
Brooks, once considered the handsomest man in the House,
had curled up and died of the furor, at the age of thirty-seven.
Bonham told Buchanan, in one of those silky Southern voices
that soften every assertion to a pleasantry, "It is earnest token,
indeed, of our sovereign state's great good faith that, in anticipation of the sadly inevitable, we have come here today to
parley over what we could seize in a half-hour's fight. Major
Anderson has a single sergeant at Pinckney, two small companies at Moultrie, and a handful of engineers supervising the
work force at Sumter! At most a hundred men, counting musicians and men under arrest! The major is well loved in Charleston; nobody there wishes harm to a Kentucky boy with a

Georgia wife, and it is up to you, Mr. President, to prevent that from happening."

Buchanan sat at his desk stiffly, as if the pressure of events were inflating his clothes from within, and freezing his joints with arthritic discomfort. The eager petitioners surrounded him like a gelatinous, vested wall, smelling of male sweat and the fumes of good living. "Gentlemen," he responded at last, in a lawyerly voice squeezed up to an especially wheedling pitch, "put whatever you wish to recommend in writing. I warn you, I intend to collect the federal revenues in Charleston at all hazards. I am determined to obey the laws and fulfil the duties of the chief executive wherever these are unambiguously defined. I am bitterly grieved, let me confide to you, at your disposition to desert the Union before you have been in any particular injured, and when all the means of the defense of states' rights lie in the Constitution and in the legislature as constituted; though this election gave us a Republican President, the Republicans are minorities in both houses and powerless by themselves."

Keitt, impatient of passionless arguments he had heard a hundred times from the denatured wafflers of this artificial city, stepped forward to the edge of the President's well-used black-walnut desk and demanded, "Tell us this, then: do you intend, grieved or no, to use force in collecting revenues in Charleston?"

Stung by his tone, Buchanan tremulously replied, looking up at Keitt with a cocked head and uncertain focus, "I will obey the laws. I am no warrior—I am a man of peace—but I will obey the laws."

[This embroiders as much as was reported. But you and I know, *Retrospect* eds., how much more conversation, false starts and probes, idle courtesies and amiable chitchat, there must have been. Gone, gone into the air and the dust. The events of Buchanan's final months were lit by the glare of hyperexcited newspaper coverage and retrospectively by the memoirs of Buchanan, Black, Stanton, Holt, and Trescot— even relatively late and minor members of the Cabinet like Philip Thomas and John Dix left accounts. And still we don't know exactly what happened: Buchanan's state of mind varies from hysterical to coolly determined depending on the source and slant; a crucial document like the rejected final letter of the South Carolina Commissioners is missing; more basically, the quotidian fluff, the living excelsior in which every event is packed, has evaporated, leaving old bone buttons and yellowing papers nibbled all over by silverfish. The past is as illusory as the future, and we exist in the present numbly, blind to the cloud formations, deaf to the birdsong. Yet there is something sacred about life that leads us to keep trying to resurrect it.]

The visit of the South Carolina Representatives left the President rattled and depressed; later that same day, he sought comfort from his closest Cabinet associate, Treasury Secretary Howell Cobb, by saying, "The hottest fires burn out quickest. South Carolina has indulged herself in defiance before, and been isolated. What happens in Charleston Harbor little matters if Georgia holds firm—is that not so, my dear Howell?"

The short rotund man, with his appealing, well-oiled smoothness of movement and address, appeared uneasy, and wore the sallow glaze of sleeplessness. He began, "Mr. President, you know with what devotion I have furthered your advancement and advised your administration."

"And *you* know, Mr. Cobb, with how much affection I have received your support and enjoyed your company. Though I have been honored with an acquaintanceship as wide as half the world, intimacy has been a rarity in my life, and I have leaned perhaps too heavily upon your friendship. My spies tell me that Mrs. Cobb more than once complained of the long hours during which the President demanded your attendance. I believe it was even said that while she was in Athens no wife could have been more watchful of your time than I."

And yet, Buchanan acknowledged within, there had never quite been the magical fraternal affection—each speaking the other's thoughts, or leaving their shared thoughts unspoken— that had existed between himself and Colonel King. King had taken the rôle of the older brother, such a sheltering, guiding brother as Buchanan, elder in fact, had never known; and Howell Cobb that of a younger, whose dependent role was already overfilled by the never-grateful, ever-demanding Reverend Edward Buchanan. Though none of his advisers had been fiercer than Cobb in mocking Douglas and keeping alive the rift between Douglas and the administration, Buchanan now sensed in the man, emanating from him in palpable waves like those of heat from a pot-bellied stove, something of the Little Giant's egoistic, anarchic ambition—the ambition of short men, ever needing to prove themselves. Had Cobb not been unwilling to take the second Cabinet post with a man his own age in the first, Robert J. Walker instead of Cass could have had the State Department, a capable man instead of an obstructive relic.

Cobb responded graciously, "Mrs. Cobb knew that by serving you I was serving the nation, and with the nation our children's future. However, sir," he continued, at a lowered pitch, with an evasive sideways glance, "times are changed. Mrs. Cobb has returned to Georgia to await her confinement. My entire family there has mounted the blue cockade. My brother Thomas gives secessionist speeches that last for five hours, and my uncle John lets out that 'resistance to oppression is obedience to God.'" He tried one last jest. "Squire, you know kin, they're as hard to herd as chickens in a whirlwind."

Buchanan failed to smile. A spark of fresh calculation lit up his lopsided gaze. He cocked his head to give Cobb a terminal beam of attention.

"I had hoped," Cobb asserted, doing a small black-shod dance step on the Persian carpet imported by Harriet from London and already worn threadbare by the hordes seeking Presidential favors, "to persuade the people of Georgia to remain in the Union until March 4th, so that I could man my post in your Cabinet to the end. But—"

"But, Howell," Buchanan cut in, "opportunity calls, in the perfidious new nation that is breeding, and your financial embarrassments have been mysteriously eased by a spate of philanthropy from your disunionist brother-in-law."

Howell Cobb was impressed, as often before, by his chief's ability to obtain and retain gossip; those who have lived life the least, perhaps, have the freshest curiosity. "Sir, let me finish. I have long proclaimed you to be the truest friend to the South that ever sat in the Presidential chair. But as you dealt with those gentlemen from South Carolina, and refused them satisfaction, I saw that you and I have parted in policy, and so must part in fact."

Sea-change. On the wax-bedabbled desktop Buchanan saw his own hand trembling, like an unpleasant white animal, eyeless, with wrinkled white skin and an excess of feeble limbs. "The South has been a friend of mine," he stated, "and I have long sought to preserve for it and its institutions those guarantees which our wise founders wrote into the Constitution. I have leaned over backwards to keep the balance between it and the North in these fearful and unsettled times. But I cannot give away national property and my right to defend it." The President sighed, and removed his hand, suddenly ghastly in his eyes, from his field of vision. "Go, then, Cobb. I cannot bless your departure, nor can I prevent it."

"A word more. Attorney General Black more than once has to my face impugned—"

"No more words. Black and I are left to deal with the wreck of policies you helped create. I deeply trusted you. We shall not speak again," the President said, less as a threat than as a prophecy, uttered soliloquizingly.

On December 10th, the South Carolina Congressmen returned, with a fifth, W. W. Boyce, from Winnsboro, added to their number. As requested, they presented a written statement. It read, To His Excellency James Buchanan, President of the United States: *In compliance with our statement to you yesterday, we now express to you our strong convictions that neither the constituted authorities nor any body of the people of the State of South Carolina will either attack or molest the United States forts in the harbor of Charleston previously to the action of the Convention, and, we hope and believe, not until an offer has been made through an accredited representative to negotiate for an amicable arrangement of all matters between the State and the Federal Government; provided that no reinforcements shall be sent into those forts, and their relative military status remain as at present.*

Squintingly the old chief made his way through the verbiage. "I do not like the word 'provided,' " he at last said. "I cannot restrict the Presidential freedom with guarantees. Further, your delegation has no official status and cannot bind anyone to its terms."

Boyce said, "By 'relative military status' we mean that the transfer of the Moultrie garrison to Fort Sumter would be the equivalent of a reinforcement and would justify an attack."

Buchanan's squint narrowed, as if he were threading a needle eye. On the one hand, he devoutly wished to avoid tipping the South Carolinians into attack; on the other, he had a legal conception of the Presidency that was narrow yet vivid, a strip of prerogatives and duties the Constitution had left standing between the Congress and the courts. In his cracked wheezing tenor of a habitual compromiser's voice, he at last offered,

"Though I can pledge you nothing, I can state to you that it is my policy not to alter the *status quo.*"

McQueen stepped forward, like the paw of a predator instinctively shooting out. "May we have that in writing, Mr. President?"

But the old man was not to be so easily caught. Though weariness rested on his face like a veil of cheesecloth, he looked up with an alertness excited by technical parrying. "After all," he purred, "this is a matter of honor among gentlemen. You have no status, until South Carolina declare independence, and only Congress, not the President, has the power to deal with federal property. I do not know that any paper or writing is necessary. We understand each other."

Keitt stated in his barking baritone, "I doubt that we do. Mr. President, you have determined to let things remain as they are, and not to send reinforcements; but suppose you should hereafter change your policy for any reason, what then?"

Buchanan smiled, and tapped their written assurance on his desk. "Then I would first return to you this paper."

When the men had gone, he took their memorandum and wrote on the back his version of the meeting, and of a little meeting that followed it: *Afterwards Messrs. McQueen and Bonham called, in behalf of the delegation, and gave me the most positive assurance that the forts and public property would not be molested until after commissioners had been appointed to treat with the Federal Government in relation to the public property, and until the decision was known. I informed them that what would be done was a question for Congress and not for the Executive. That if they* [the forts] *were assailed, this would put them* [the South Carolinians] *completely in the wrong, and making them the authors of the civil war. They* [McQueen and Bonham] *gave the same assurances to Messrs. Floyd, Thompson, and others.*

The next day he wrote the brief memorandum *Tuesday,*

11th December, 1860, General Cass announced to me his purpose to resign. The same day, Senators Gwin and Slidell came calling. Slidell did almost all the talking. "Buchanan," he said, "I am astounded to be told that you refused the South Carolina delegation a simple promise not to reinforce the forts, after they had extended to you any number of manly and generous assurances!"

"Which they had no authority to extend. And they asked, Senator, for what the President cannot give."

"Your hand is weak, and growing weaker. Georgia is going, and the Gulf States cannot stay. Why stick at these forts, when a continent teeters?" [Slidell: The wily and unscrupulous political king of Louisiana, a native New Yorker with a tempestuous and irregular youth. Just two years younger than Buchanan, he displayed white hair, a red, whiskey-scorched complexion, and an occasional glint, above the sharp arched nose, of the steely-eyed glamour that had hypnotized the slightly older, more cautious and scrupulous man. Slidell by ingenuities of voter transfer had assured Louisiana for Polk in '44; in '45 had acted as emissary to Mexico from Buchanan's State Department, as the two nations approached war; in '53 he had seized upon the Senate seat impetuous Soulé had to vacate in accepting the mission to Spain. Pierce had won his enmity by prosecuting a henchman; in '56 he and Bright and Bayard and Benjamin had engineered Buchanan's nomination. Slidell will be appointed the Confederacy's Ambassador to France; he will be seized in the famous *Trent* affair aboard a British vessel heading out of Nassau; his machinations in the court of Napoleon III will not achieve French recognition or significant assistance; he will die in Cowes, England, in 1871, his request in 1866 for permission to return to Louisiana having been left unanswered by the first President Johnson.]

Buchanan adjusted the angle of his head to give Slidell a steady gaze, and said, "Sadly, Senator, do I perceive that you, too, would tip us toward disunion. That Keitt, and Rhett, and Yancy, and other discontented small fry seek to manufacture opportunities within upheaval I can comprehend; but that you, and Toombs, and Davis, who held sway over the Union's capital—no. I can no longer give ear to your advice. I regret that I needed it so long."

"That advice made you President."

"And would unmake me, as President, now."

"Buchanan, don't be an imbecile. Your interest has always lain south, and still lies there."

"*Mr.* James Buchanan, as a seeker of his own interest, is dead. There remains only the President of the United States. He has many duties to perform. Sir, you are excused. I thank you most gratefully for the favor of your views."

The next day, the 12th, General Scott at last was well enough to appear in Washington. He was informed by Senator Lyman Trumbull that Buchanan was planning the surrender of Fort Moultrie and ought to be gibbeted. He advised Buchanan to send a force of three hundred men to Fort Moultrie immediately. In his *Mr. Buchanan's Administration on the Eve of Rebellion*, Buchanan wrote: *It is scarcely a lack of charity to infer that General Scott knew at the time when he made this recommendation (on the 15th December) that it must be rejected. The President could not have complied with it, the position of affairs still remaining unchanged, without at once reversing his entire policy, and without a degree of inconsistency amounting almost to self-stultification.* Also, the army, hamstrung by Congress, scarcely existed: *Our army was still out of reach on the remote frontiers, and could not be withdrawn, during midwinter, in time for this military operation. Indeed, the General had never suggested such a withdrawal. He knew that had this been possible, the inhabitants on our distant frontiers would have been immediately exposed to the tomahawk and scalping knife of the Indians.*

Cass's letter of resignation, dated December 12th but not

delivered until the 15th, cited *his decided opinion, which for some time past I have urged at various meetings of the Cabinet, that additional troops should be sent to reinforce the forts in the harbor of Charleston, with a view to their better defence should they be attacked, and that an armed vessel should likewise be ordered there, to aid, if necessary, in the defence.* Reading this, Buchanan managed a bitter laugh. "Where was this fine bravado when he sat in Cabinet dozing off beneath his wig?" he asked Attorney-General Black, who as the storm mounted had drawn closer to Buchanan's side, like Edgar to Lear's. "When the Cabinet discussed my message to the Congress earlier this month, his only criticism was that I didn't emphasize strongly enough the *in*ability of Congress to make war upon a state; I strengthened it to suit him. I have often had occasion to remember what General Jackson said to me of Cass, when he sent him to Paris; he said, 'Cass decides nothing for himself, but comes to me constantly with great bundles of paper.' Well, Black, we'll no longer have to write his dispatches for him."

Black [harshly masculine; big-boned, shaggy-browed; ornate and avid in thought: Raymond Massey more than Jason Robards] said, "I understand he already regrets his resignation, and would like it retracted."

"Indeed? Quickly, then, write me a letter of acceptance full of courteous and patriotic flowers. I have a new Secretary of State: you, Mr. Black." Buchanan felt almost merry, at the thought of being rid of Cass. Though old himself, he disliked old men.

Black protested, "I pray you to reconsider. General Cass's resignation, which you can undo in a word, will give fuel to your enemies, as he is a Northern name of long-standing repute. He consented to serve your cause when he was past the age of usual retirement; now, on second thought, he wishes to serve with you to the end."

"He is a dropsical old dotard who spoiled the nomination for me in '48 and again in '52, with Cameron's wicked conniving. Let him go, and take his place. If all else desert us, we'll hold the fort with none but friends from the Keystone State!"

"Mr. President, if your determination is perfectly fixed, let me urge as my replacement as Attorney General my assistant, Edwin Stanton of Pittsburgh. He is incomparably informed upon the great land cases presently coming before the Supreme Court, and in my estimation his work as government counsel in California proved him the most brilliant lawyer in the land."

"But he is not well versed, I believe, in constitutional theory. He is an abolitionist, and his temper has made him many enemies. I have it from more than one source that Stanton is not to be trusted."

"An un-looked-for stricture, Mr. President, from one who so long trusted Howell Cobb, and who still trusts John Floyd."

Buchanan felt, as Black's excessively orotund and increasingly confident voice invaded his aural canals, undermined; his political constitution was being reformed, as if in the course of a cancerous disease, by these resignations and substitutions. His true substance had been left behind in John Passmore's Lancaster, in Nicholas's St. Petersburg, in the tobacco-brown and claret-red rooms he had shared with Senator King, in the glittering London he and Harriet had so charmed. "Floyd is a muddler, perhaps," he weakly admitted, "but not a villain."

"In his capacity as Secretary of War," said Black, "it is villainous to muddle as Floyd has done."

As always with these high-toned actors, Buchanan reflected to himself, there is overstatement, with the nuance of precise truth lost in the stampede of assertions and action. Floyd was a good man, but how tedious to explain in exactly what way! Wearily the President waved events onward. "Very well— Stanton is our soldier. My heart can just barely rise to this, Jeremiah. I approach the Biblical age, and should be composing myself to mingle my physical substance with the dust.

Instead, a fight beckons, against the very men whom I have counted first among my friends."

[Notes to myself, in late 1976:]

SHAME. Shame as the emotion of this endless December, creeping in, suffusing. Buchanan's need for silence, for peace, for space to pray. His prayers as a long soak in trepidation, hedged about as he is with bloody alternatives. His sense of layers peeling back, to reveal the shameful sinful incorrigible substance of the earth. His own life as one long trespass, beneath the gilt, gentility, success, etc. The odd sense of drawing closer to God through disgrace, terror, calumny, embarrassment. SHAME the taste of authenticity since *la Chute*, since Adam and Eve. Primitive chemical experiments remembered from Dickinson College days. JB's sense of soaking, tasting, this liquid substance. Gets drunk on it. Do a prayer for him?

[My text staggered on:]

The next day, December 16th, Secretary of the Interior Thompson [an energetic Mississippian, remember?] came to Buchanan and said his state had appointed him agent to visit North [*sic,* not South] Carolina, to discuss the secession movement. The President was much criticized then and later for granting permission for him to go, as if furthering the secession movement via a Cabinet member. But he had approved only in the belief that Thompson's mission was to prevent rather than precipitate secession, having been assured by Thompson as to the moderation of his views: Thompson believed, contrary to Buchanan's message to the Congress on December 3rd, that a right of secession *did* exist, but that this right came into existence only when there was sufficient cause, and sufficient cause did not *yet* exist.

December 16th, Buchanan wrote to George M. Wharton saying: *I have no word of encouragement to give you in regard to Southern secession. I still hope the storm may blow over; but there are no indications of it at present. . . . My information is not encouraging from any quarter. . . . The North are not yet impressed with a just sense of the danger. I have been warning them for years of what would finally be the result of their agitation; but Cassandra-like, all in vain. . . . P.S. I need not say that I consider secession to be revolution. This is the first letter I have penned upon the subject, & it is for yourself alone.*

On December 17th, Horace Greeley's *New-York Daily Tribune* ran an editorial [*not* headlined, as Klein has it] which began: *There is a rumor in town, apparently derived from responsible sources at Washington, to the effect that* President Buchanan is insane! *This is probably not true, though in view of his course through the last six eventful weeks, the confirmation of the report would afford no reason for astonishment. More lamentable imbecility, or more deliberate treachery, was never seen. At every step he has contributed to the disruption of the Republic; and if, as Mr. Cobb declared, he shall prove to be the last President of the existing Union, it will be due to either his own weakness or wickedness quite as much as to any other cause. Let him be pronounced a lunatic, and he may stand at the bar of history relieved of a crime with scarce an equal in the records of human frailty and depravity.* The editorial ended, *With* [General Cass's] *resignation the last vestige of dignity and of true patriotism seems to have left the Executive, and it would be a relief to the country and would alleviate Mr. Buchanan's own reputation in the future, if he could now be proved insane.* Henry Adams wrote from Washington to his brother Charles, of gossip from New York, *Toward the close of the day a report was circulated that President Buchanan had gone insane, and stocks rose. . . . Poor old Buchanan! I don't see but what he'll have to be impeached. The terror here among the inhabitants is something wonderful to witness.*

[Eds.: Could be shortened, but I put these quotes in to show what snide and supercilious pricks the so-called good guys, on the p.c. anti-slavery side, were. The entire Greeley editorial could be an appendix in 8-point, if you choose to publish. To get it I travelled all the way to the Boston Public Library—a little room at a corner of the musty courtyard where six of the crapulous homeless dozed; a plump omniscient girl of Asian ancestry behind the desk; a complicated call slip to fill out; a heavy spool of gray microfilm that sang in the projector like a missile homing in; then, Greeley!]

On the morning of December 20th, Buchanan received a communication from his old friend, the Palmetto State's new governor, Francis Wilkinson Pickens; it was delivered to the White House by the marshal for South Carolina, D. H. Hamilton, accompanied by William H. Trescot. Trescot, that same morning, had had his resignation as Assistant Secretary of State (a position enlarged in importance by Cass's limitations) accepted and was now acting openly on behalf of South Carolina. The letter asked that Pickens be allowed to *send a small force, not exceeding twenty-five men and an officer, to take possession of Fort Sumter immediately, in order to give a feeling of safety to the community. . . . If something of the kind be not done, I cannot answer for the consequences.*

Buchanan passed the letter to Trescot to read. Able, intelligent Trescot quickly sensed that the President was offended. He had been pushed too hard, too soon. Buchanan invited Hamilton to return tomorrow morning for his reply.

On the same day, Buchanan wrote the sympathetic James Gordon Bennett of the *New-York Herald,* in implicit riposte to the *Tribune*'s rumor, *I have never enjoyed better health or a more tranquil spirit than during the past year. All our troubles have not cost me an hour's sleep or a meal's victuals, though I trust I have a just sense of my high responsibility. I weigh well and prayerfully what course I ought to adopt, and adhere to it steadily, leaving the results to Providence. This is my nature, and I deserve neither praise nor blame for it.*

This same busy day, Buchanan attended the reception for the wedding of a Miss Parker to a Mr. Bouligny of Louisiana,

a very Southern affair, Auchampaugh assures us: as Klein tells
it, *guests at a wedding reception on December 20 which the president attended found him proclaiming that he had never enjoyed
better health and looking the part.*

Out in the hall, however, there arose such a commotion that
Buchanan asked another guest, "Madame, do you suppose the
house is on fire?"

But the incendiary commotion was being created by one
hot-blooded guest, Laurence Keitt, who was jubilantly leaping
into the air and brandishing a piece of paper. "Thank God! Oh,
thank God!" he cried. "South Carolina has seceded! Here's the
telegram! I feel like a boy let out from school!"

Buchanan called for a carriage and went back to the White
House. There, it seems, he composed an answer to Governor
Pickens, saying: *As an executive officer of the Government, I have
no power to surrender to any human authority Fort Sumter or any
of the other forts or public property in South Carolina. . . . If South
Carolina should attack any of these forts, she will then become the
assailant in a war against the United States.*

Meanwhile, Trescot, realizing that Pickens' demand might
lead to a rebuff and release the President from his informal
pledge to preserve the *status quo,* had talked with Slidell, Jefferson Davis, and South Carolina Congressmen Bonham and
McQueen, and all telegraphed Pickens to withdraw his letter.
By ten o'clock the next morning, Trescot called at the White
House with a telegram Pickens had sent—*You are authorised &
requested to withdraw my letter sent by Dr. Hamilton immediately*—and Buchanan's combative response was withheld.

This same day, December 21st, a Cabinet meeting considered the position of Major Anderson; Buchanan asked exactly
what orders had been forwarded to Fort Moultrie ten days
earlier, by way of Major Don Carlos Buell. Buell had had no
written instructions and he and Anderson had together composed some, which were sent back to the War Department and

authenticated by Floyd. Floyd could not remember what they were. A search turned up Buell's memorandum. Buchanan did not like the sentence which directed Anderson to defend himself *to the last extremity,* since this seemed to ask for needless sacrifice of life. Black wrote out a revised copy and Floyd signed it and sent it by courier to Anderson at Fort Moultrie.

Floyd was unwell but not idle. On December 19th he sent instructions to Captain J. G. Foster, at Fort Moultrie, to return to the federal arsenal in Charleston some forty muskets he had two days earlier removed under an unfilled order of the Ordnance Department dated November 1st. On December 20th Floyd called his ordnance chief to his sickbed in Washington and gave verbal orders to dispatch a large shipment of heavy cannon from a Pittsburgh foundry down the Mississippi to some uncompleted Texas forts.

What meaning did Floyd's actions—widely construed, by the Northern press, as an attempt to arm the South while keeping the Union disarmed—really have? None, or almost none, Auchampaugh argues. Floyd was a good man held up to too harsh a light. *Considering the things Floyd could have done and did not do, points to much in his favor. He sent nothing to Virginia; he knew the efficiency of the Southern cavalry, but sent not a sabre; he knew the Southern need of artillery, but sent not a gun before December, 1860.* And indeed, why should Floyd's actions have a meaning, if, as contemporary cosmologists virtually all agree, the universe itself has none?

An unusually inclement winter had set in, Nevins tells us, with the flair of a one-time journalist. *The white marble buildings were cold-looking, the ailanthus trees bare, the waters of the Potomac leaden-colored. As snow and rain smote the town, streets were alternately sheets of dazzling white, and stretches of viscid yellow mud.* This is history? This is word painting. *This* is history:

Christmas Day, 1860. Four events:

1. In the White House, James Buchanan pens a letter to William M. Browne of the runaway Washington *Constitution*, which, though founded and subsidized as a pro-administration newspaper, has come out stridently in favor of secession. *Private*, his tremulous but tireless pen traces in parenthesis, and then forms the salutation, *My Dear Sir*. The moving pen writes, *I have read with deep mortification your editorial this morning in which you take open ground against my message on the right of secession. I have defended you as long as I can against numerous complaints. . . . I am deeply sorry to say that I must in some authentic form declare that the "Constitution" is not the organ of the administration*. [The *authentic form* became the withdrawal of government advertising and printing contracts; by the end of January the *Constitution* had to suspend publication.]

2. Black tells Buchanan of Floyd's cannon shipment from Pittsburgh and the President instantly cancels the order. Floyd, still capable of taking offense, is offended.

3. Floyd is approached by Senator Louis T. Wigfall of Texas and others to join their plot to kidnap Buchanan and make Breckinridge, the Vice-President from Kentucky, President. Floyd refuses. [But what an episode in the history books that would have made! Old Buck would have become not just the only bachelor President but the only kidnapped President!!]

4. In Charleston, Major Anderson and his men attend a Christmas party hosted by Captain J. G. Foster [see page 326], giving no sign of the tactical surprise they had planned for the next night, that of the 26th; abandoning Fort Moultrie for the remoter, more defensible Fort Sumter.

Floyd [drat this ubiquitous, dilatory nonentity!], hearing the news on the morning of December 27th, said, "It is impossible," and telegraphed Anderson for an explanation. He received the reply *I abandoned Fort Moultrie because I was certain that if attacked my men must have been sacrificed and the command of the harbor lost.*

That same morning, the President was visited by a trio of Southerners—Senator Jefferson Davis of Mississippi, Senator Robert Mercier Taliaferro Hunter of Virginia, and the former diplomat Trescot, who in February of 1861 composed an account of the visit, as part of his often-paraphrased *Narrative*, which he revised for publication in 1870.

Colonel Davis asked the President, "Have you received any intelligence from Charleston in the last three hours?"

"None," was the cautious reply.

"Then I have a great calamity to announce to you. Major Anderson last night, under cover of darkness, spiked the guns at Fort Moultrie and moved his full force to Fort Sumter. Now, Mr. President, you are surrounded with blood and dishonor on all sides."

Buchanan, who had been standing by the mantelpiece crushing a cigar in the palm of his hand, sat down.* "My God," he

---

*Historians have generally treated this crushed cigar as a sign of great distress: e.g., Nichols has it that the Senators found the President greatly agitated. *He stood by the hearth crushing a cigar in his shaking fingers and stammered that the move was against his policy.* But Trescot, in the sentence that is the only source for the detail, takes the trouble to say that this untidy practice was a habit with Buchanan. His words are: *The President was standing by the mantelpiece crushing up a cigar into pieces in his hand—a habit I have seen him practice often.*

The punctuation and emphases for Buchanan's utterance considerably vary. Trescot's original, hastily jotted memoir gives it as *"My God are calamities (or misfortunes, I forget which) never to come singly. I call God to witness—you gentlemen better than anybody know—that this is not only without but against my orders, it is against my policy."*

Nevins dresses it up considerably: *"My God,"* wailed [sic] *Buchanan, who stood at the mantelpiece crushing a cigar in his hand, "are misfortunes never to*

asked, "are calamities never to come singly? I call God to witness: you gentlemen, better than anybody, know that this is not only *without* but *against* my orders; it is against my policy."

Other Senators—Yulee, Mallory, Bigler, Slidell—came calling, urging the President to order Anderson back to Moultrie and thus honor his gentleman's agreement to preserve the *status quo. Buchanan paced nervously,* Nevins tells us, *telling his excited callers to keep calm and trust him.* Amid the clamor and pressure his habitual indecision and elderly stubbornness served as a shield: he could not condemn Anderson, he said, without the facts. He must call a Cabinet meeting. "If our gentlemen's agreement has indeed been broken," he promised, "it will be repaired."

In the Cabinet session, Floyd, overwrought, took the offensive. "Anderson has betrayed us all! He has compromised the President, and made war inevitable! This catastrophic maneuver was totally against his orders!"

But Black said calmly, "On the contrary, sir, it was in precise accordance with his orders."

"Mr. Black, it was not. It could not have been."

"Mr. Floyd," responded Black, in a voice of iron, "I have sent to the War Department for these orders of December 11th, drawn up by Major Anderson and Major Buell and endorsed by you. I shall read. *The smallness of your force will not permit you, perhaps, to occupy more than one of the three forts, but an attack or an attempt to take possession of any of them will be regarded as an act of hostility, and you may then put your command into either of them which you may deem most proper, to increase its power of resistance. You are also authorized to take*

---

come singly? I call God to witness, you, *gentlemen, better than anybody,* know *that this is not only without, but against my orders. It is against my policy."*

similar steps whenever you have tangible evidence of a design to proceed to a hostile act."

Floyd said triumphantly, "Indeed so; I defy you to produce *tangible evidence of a design to proceed to a hostile act.*"

Stanton spoke up. Short, round, pugnacious, he sported the wire-rim glasses and pharaonic beard that would become famous during his term as Lincoln's Secretary of War. "Sir," he told Floyd, who, pale and ill, wilted a bit under this wind from a new direction, "a resolution has been publicly introduced into the South Carolina legislature for possession of all the forts! The Charleston *Mercury* insists on it daily! The very workmen employed at Fort Sumter openly sport the blue cockade!"

"Rumors and gestures, merely—not justification for a defiant military action," Floyd argued. "Anderson left the guns at Moultrie spiked and burnt the carriages; such warlike tactics utterly violate the solemn pledge given by this government."

Stanton asked, "When was any such pledge given? Where does it exist in writing?"

See pages 316–17.

Black stood to his lanky height and warned, "Mr. Floyd, you are impugning the honor of the President of the United States."

Buchanan attempted to defend his own honor. "I promised nothing certain. I said my intent was to preserve the *status quo.*" Had he said precisely that? It was so hard exactly to remember. Men's bellies and voices, pressing, pressing. He turned for relief to the silent members of the Cabinet—the Secretary of the Navy, little old Isaac Toucey of Connecticut, a colleague from Polk's Cabinet long ago, and pale, stocky Thompson, exhausted by his three days on the trail of the missing Indian bonds. The President mildly declared, "I agree that Major Anderson's maneuver, though unexpected, was justified by the discretion granted him in explicit orders."

Floyd, in a voice loud like that of a drunk or of an actor, stated, "If the letter of official orders is to replace honor among men, then one remedy alone is left, and that is to withdraw the garrison from Charleston Harbor altogether. I demand the right to order withdrawal. I will sit down here and write out the order."

Black shook the papers holding Anderson's orders in Floyd's face and, overtopping the Virginian's histrionics with his own, orated, "Mr. Floyd, there never was a moment in the history of England when a minister of the Crown could have proposed to surrender a military post which might be defended, without bringing his head to the block!"

Stanton added furiously, his excited spittle visible in the Cabinet Room gaslights, installed in 1848: "To accede to such a proposal would be a crime like Arnold's, and all the participants should be hanged like André, and a President of the United States who would make such an order would be guilty of treason!"

Buchanan lifted his hands and cried out, as if wounded, "Oh, no! Not so bad as that, my friend—not so bad as that!"

[How dismayingly, arriving at this climactic crisis of my tale and of Buchanan's life, did I find nothing but dried old words, yards of them strung together from accounts of suspect authenticity, concerning details that in retrospect seem ridiculously niggling—the exact terms of Anderson's orders, and the legal propriety of how to deal with the Commissioners from South Carolina, who had arrived in Washington and whose first meeting with the President had been postponed a day by the excitement over Anderson's move to Sumter. Are all great events as they occur hidden by details, first from the participants and then from us?]

The Cabinet meeting of the 27th wrangled on. They met again, after dinner, and into the night, while newspapermen waited for news and bands of Congressmen gathered to cast their weight into the battle for the President's mind. The *Tribune* reported that the Cabinet voted four to three (Floyd, Thompson, and Philip F. Thomas, a pro-Southern Maryland politician who had replaced Howell Cobb as head of the Treasury Department, and who was to resign after a month of uneasy service) not to order Anderson back, with Black, Stanton, and Postmaster General Joseph Holt, of Kentucky, successfully bringing pressure to bear on Toucey, the member closest to the President's extremely middling views. At last, midnight having come and gone, Buchanan decided to make no decision: *In this state of suspense,* to quote his own account, *the President determined to await official information from Major Anderson himself.* "He acted within the letter of his instructions," Buchanan wearily told the Cabinet, "though against the trend of my policy. If, upon receipt and examination of his report, it appears he took alarm without cause, then we might think seriously of restoring for the present the former *status quo.*"

Late as it was, Secretary Black lingered in the Cabinet Room. He said, "With some ingenuity, sir, we have brought ourselves to stand upon a very narrow piece of ground."

"It will suffice, if it serves to gain us time. Time, Mr. Black, time. Time is the great conservative force. We must buy it by the month, and it is sold only by the hour." He explained a secret thread he had been spinning beneath the tumult of these days. "Since Lincoln will not come to Washington, I have sent Duff Green to Springfield, to gain the assent of the President-elect to a new national constitutional convention. Such a convention would become the voice of the people, who are overwhelmingly conservative, and whose terror-stricken letters pour in upon me like a hurricane of tears. Extend the Missouri Compromise line, and enforce the Fugitive Slave law—that is all we need for peace. Hourly I await for Green to telegram Lincoln's reprieving statement."

"But," Black pointed out, in the face of the old man's pathetic hope, "the Republican party was born of repugnance for the Missouri Compromise. The party is the free-soil delusion's very child. Lincoln can scarcely disavow his own platform, when abolitionist fanaticism has at last secured in him its national instrument."

"But he will be *President*. If only he would come to Washington and smell the blood in the air! Seward now smells it, and was ready to assent to the Crittenden Compromise, until the radicals renewed their hold on Lincoln. Wall Street is panicking, and that will speak to the Republicans."

"But in no case will the Gulf States stay in."

"The tide runs secessionist now. But when Virginia and Tennessee hold fast, that tide will turn."

Black said, "I fear the ground where you stand is so narrow, not many will join you on it."

"The ground is narrow, as the gate to salvation is strait!"

Black said, with some tenderness for his old chief and sponsor, and with some condescension, "Mr. President, you need rest. These pressures bear upon you cruelly."

Buchanan brushed impatiently at cobwebs in the air. "They whittle, but there is still some stick left. All things pass. Sufficient unto the day. I say my prayers, and act by the light given me. The rest belongs to God."

Or "is God's." SHAME. LOSS. The *eternity* of life. The eternal non-returningness of it. His DOUBT, deeper and deeper. Byron was right. Ann was right. The gravity of time as it presses on us, shapes us, destroys us. So grave it makes us break into sweat, like a gravedigger who suddenly imagines the walls of clay collapsing upon him. At some point, maybe later, have JB look out window at frozen White House gardens and join Ann the night in Philadelphia she was struck by the horror of the colorless ferns in garden? He joins her then on the floor of things, in hopelessness. PRAYERS. In a letter to his brother, the

Reverend Edward Y. Buchanan, from Russia in 1833, we find this: *I have thought much upon the subject since my arrival in this strange land, and sometimes almost persuade myself that I am a Christian; but I am often haunted by the spirit of scepticism and doubt. My true feeling upon many occasions is: "Lord, I would believe; help Thou my unbelief." Yet I am far from being an unbeliever.* To the same, from Washington in 1844: *I think often & think seriously of my latter end; but when I pray (and I have preserved & with the blessing of God shall preserve this good habit from my parents) I can rarely keep my mind from wandering. I trust that the Almighty father, through the merits & atonement of his son, will yet vouchsafe to me a clearer & stronger faith than I possess.* Prayers return him to childhood prayers with his mother, in the log cabin lit by the brutal unsteady flare of resiny pine splints stuck between the fireplace stones. When they spark out, time to close eyes and sleep. SLEEP. We remain children, though we seem to become men.

Next morning, the 28th, brought the Carolina Commissioners: Barnwell, Orr, and J. H. Adams. *Men of parts,* says Nevins. *They had a natural sense of their dignity in representing a new republic, and came not to sue for terms but to treat as equals.* Buchanan told them, "I receive you as private gentlemen of the highest character, and not as diplomatic agents. As I stated unmistakably in my message of December 3rd, Congress alone has the authority to decide what shall be the relations between South Carolina and the federal government."

Former Governor James Hopkins Adams was the most extreme of the three: an old nullifier and ardent proponent of reviving the African slave trade, he owned one hundred ninety-two slaves on his cotton plantation in lower Richland County. He struck a note of high formality. "We have the honor, Mr. President, to transmit to you a copy of the ordinance of secession by which the state of South Carolina has resumed the powers she once delegated to the government of the United States."

"A well-worded document, no doubt," Buchanan said, but did not reach out his hand to accept it. Seated at his little walnut desk, while the commissioners stood, he was struck by the pendulous motion of Adams's watch fob, a chain leading into the pocket of his dove-gray vest and swinging in sympathy with the motions of his diaphragm as he spoke.

It was Orr's turn to speak. Buchanan liked James Lawrence Orr: a sound man. Like Buchanan himself, he had worked in his father's store and then turned lawyer; a former Speaker of the House, Orr knew the North's case better than most Southerners, and as recently as this past April had argued for the Union at his state's Democratic convention. Campaigning for the Senate in 1858, he had dared quote Daniel Webster on nullification, and been defeated for it. But now the secessionist tide was carrying him along. He stated, "Mr. President, in this very office, little more than a fortnight ago, you made a solemn pledge, as a gentleman, to maintain the *status quo* in Charleston Harbor. Major Anderson has violated that pledge, and unless restitution is made, a bloody issue is most probable."

The President permitted himself a wintry smile, and cocked his head to bring the other's large, flushed face into focus. "But, Mr. Orr, word has just arrived that the troops of Governor Pickens have now seized Castle Pinckney and Fort Moultrie, not to mention the post office and the customhouse. How can we order Major Anderson back, when the place to which he would return has been occupied by force?" Buchanan waited briefly for their reply, while contemplating their three vests. These men had been his friends and political allies a few weeks ago, solid congenial men with whom, save for a few trifling matters such as the sacred status of slavery, he had no disagreements. It now seemed that that had been an illusion. These men were willing to sink his Presidency and douse Anderson and his troops in blood. These groomed and well-stuffed bellies, these bulging vests and starched shirtfronts were hollow: there was nothing in there; nothing had ever been there but self-interest and expediency. The President added, in the face of their momentarily baffled silence, "I ask my question in a rhetorical sense merely, for it is not my office, nor my purpose, to negotiate with you. Only Congress can negotiate."

Barnwell, a Harvard graduate who had been President of the South Carolina College as well as Representative and Senator, bore down with a pedantic relentlessness. "Mr. Buchanan, sir, we came here as the representatives of an authority which could at any time within the past sixty days have taken possession of the forts, but which, upon pledges given in a manner that we cannot doubt, determined to trust to your honor rather than to its own power. We urge upon you the immediate withdrawal of all the troops from the harbor of Charleston. They constitute a standing menace; their presence poisons negotiations that should be settled with temperance and judgment. Remove them, Mr. President, to safeguard your own honor, and the welfare of the people who still accept your governance."

"My honor is not at issue," Buchanan said curtly. "I made no pledge; I distinctly recall stating that the President could not be bound by any proviso."

Barnwell insisted, "But, Mr. President, your personal honor *is* involved in this matter; the faith you pledged has been violated; and your personal honor requires you to issue the order. Withdrawal or war, sir. Choose. Withdrawal or war."

Buchanan then said, so memorably that Orr recounted it word for word in a letter written on September 17, 1871, "Mr. Barnwell, you are pressing me too importunely; you don't give me time to consider; you don't give me time to say my prayers.

I always say my prayers when required to act upon any great
state affair."

In truth, history testifies, the three Commissioners had been
badgering Buchanan for two hours. There is real time and
narrative time; if they were not different, it would take as long
to tell a man's life as to live it.

Perhaps it was this troubled day, or the day before, that
Buchanan had the agitated conversation with Senator Robert
Toombs reported in Trescot's *Narrative*. Trescot reports it but
provides as clue to the exact day only this opening remark by
Toombs. *"I am aware Mr President" said T "that the Cabinet is
in session and that today is the annual dinner to the Supreme Court
and that you have scarcely time to see me."* It would take a trip
to Washington City, I fear, and the dampest dimmest depths
of the Library of Congress, to ferret out the date of that Supreme Court dinner. [*Retrospect* eds.: Will make trip, if ex-
penses covered. Just airfare and modest hotel—will pay for
own meals and incidentals.] Toombs continued, *"But while I
apologize for the intrusion, it is an evidence what importance I
attach to the interview. I would ask Mr President whether you have
decided upon your course as to Fort Sumter?"* [Italics indicate
exact transcription of Trescot's telegraphic style.]

*"No Sir, I have not decided. The Cabinet is now in session upon
that very subject."*

*"I thank you Sir for the information that is all I wanted to
know," said T. retiring.*

"But Mr T. why do you ask?"

"Because Sir my State has a deep interest in the decision."

*"How your State—what is it to Georgia whether a fort in
Charleston harbour is abandoned?"*

"Sir the cause of Charleston is the cause of the South."

*"Good God Mr Toombs do you mean that I am in the midst of
a revolution?"*

"Yes Sir—more than that—you have been there for a year and have not yet found it out" and he retired. [According to Trescot, whom Nevins admires uncritically, calling him *the honest Trescot* and asserting of this secessionist Alger Hiss that *Few men had quicker insight than Trescot,*] *When the President returned to the Cabinet he seemed very much excited and said, "Gentlemen I really begin to believe that this is revolution."*

The Cabinet meeting of the evening of the 28th, a Friday, found Floyd, still ill, stretched out on a sofa between the windows of the Cabinet Room. The spotlight shifts to the other major Southerner, Jacob Thompson, as he argues soothingly, "Mr. President, South Carolina is a tiny state, with a sparse white population. The United States are a powerful nation with a vigorous government. This great nation can well afford to say to South Carolina, 'See, we will withdraw our garrison as an evidence that we mean you no harm.' "

Stanton—that pharaonically bearded pepperpot, that fiery Laertes duelling Buchanan's white-haired Hamlet!—expostulated, "Mr. President, the proposal to be generous implies that the government is strong, and that we, as the public servants, have the confidence of the people. I think that is a mistake. No administration has ever suffered the loss of public confidence and support as this has done. Only the other day it was announced that a million of dollars has been stolen from Mr. Thompson's department. The bonds were found to have been taken from the vault where they should have been kept, and the notes of Mr. Floyd were substituted for them. Now it is proposed to give up Sumter. All I have to say is that no administration, much less this one, can afford to lose a million of money and a fort in the same week!"*

---

*According to Thurlow Weed's account in the London *Observer* of February 9, 1862, Stanton's protest was even more elaborate and allusive:

"That course, Mr. President, ought certainly to be regarded as most liberal

Stanton's account, which has become history, claims that Floyd made no reply in his own defense. It seems unlikely—it contravenes all dramatic principles—that Floyd did not arise from his couch of infirmity and protest, with suitable broad gestures, "Mr. President, this attorney has shared our counsels a few brief days and he presumes to sit in judgment upon those of us loyal to you and this administration for four years! The truth of the matter of these acceptances is that, had I not signed them, our troops, through the negligence of Congress, would have been left unequipped in the wilderness of Utah! Not a dollar has been lost to the government through my department; the malfeasances of the Yankee contractor Russell and Mr. Thompson's appointee Bailey leave my honor untouched. And furthermore, to substantiate my loyalty, let me confide to you that, on Christmas Day, I was approached by a Senator from a state of the same latitude as Mr. Thompson's, and wherein disunionist views are likewise proclaimed in public daily; this Senator, I swear, invited me to join a conspiracy, sir, to kidnap *you,* and to place Mr. Breckinridge in the Presiden-

---

towards erring brethren, but while one member of your Cabinet has fraudulent acceptances for millions of dollars afloat, and while the confidential clerk of another—himself in South Carolina teaching rebellion*—has just stolen $900,000 from the Indian Trust Fund, the experiment of ordering Major Anderson back to Fort Moultrie would be dangerous. But if you intend to try it, before it is done I beg that you will accept my resignation."

Then, in Weed's spirited reconstruction, Black seconded the offer of resignation, followed by Holt and Dix, who did not join the Cabinet until the middle of the next month—which shows only that these rememberers get carried away, and history is built upon shifting sands.

*An allusion to Bailey (see page 306) and Thompson, who was right there, as we can see, and who in any case went to *North* Carolina, the previous week, leaving on December 17th and back in Washington by the 22nd, when the Indian-bonds scandal* broke.

*See pp. 306 and 322.

tial chair!" Smiling wanly at the sensation his words produced at the Cabinet table, the ailing, impugned, yet persistently aristocratic Virginian made a curt bow in Buchanan's direction and went on, "Of course, I indignantly refused; and from that same store of righteous indignation I hereby state that I cannot countenance your violation of solemn pledges respecting Fort Sumter!"

And then Black, that *emotional and sharp Scotch-Irish son of thunder from Pennsylvania's mountainous Somerset* according to Nichols, must have leaped up, and, with an ironical small bow echoing Floyd's, asked, "May we hope, Governor Floyd, to construe this lack of countenance, with its imputations of grave disrespect, as the long-delayed fulfillment of our expectations that you resign the post you have administered with such notorious incompetence?"

Stanton, his lipless mouth clamping on his words like a nutcracker, his eye sockets filling, now one and now the other, with blind ovals of reflected gaslight, would very likely have ringingly seconded: "You say incompetence; I say, with half the nation, treachery!"

In the event, on the next day, the 29th, Buchanan received a letter of resignation from Floyd. It read, *Our refusal, or even delay, to place affairs back as they stood under our agreement, invites collision, and must inevitably inaugurate civil war in our land. I can not consent to be the agent of such a calamity.*

I deeply regret to feel myself under the necessity of tendering to you my resignation as Secretary of War, because I can no longer hold it, under my convictions of patriotism, nor with honor, subjected as I am to the violation of solemn pledges and plighted faith.

With the highest personal regard, I am most truly yours.

When loved ones kiss us off, the question arises, did they ever love us? Or has it all been illusion and cool scheming? That blow job in the hotel. That panicked mating, once, right in her back yard, on the damp grass, ejaculation and absorption, while the girls waited to be tucked into bed with prayers, their docilely glowing windows rectangling the lawn. The voluptuousness of Buchanan's prayers. The floor of things: the worse things get, God draws closer, a sublime absence we conjure from the void, from beneath the floor. JB's *jouissance*, praying. Events, and the Buddhist something that is not-event. Work this in? [Among my working notes as of late 1976.]

That day Buchanan also received, as requested, the written statement of the South Carolina Commissioners —lost, alas, to history—and presented it, with a draft of his proposed reply, at a meeting of the Cabinet that evening.

Stanton brandished the papers in question and declaimed, "These gentlemen claim to be Ambassadors. It is preposterous! They cannot be Ambassadors; they are lawbreakers, traitors. They should be arrested. You cannot negotiate with them; and yet it seems by this paper that you have been led into doing that very thing. With all respect to you, Mr. President, I must say that the Attorney General, under his oath of office, dares not be cognizant of the pending proceedings. Your reply to these so-called Ambassadors must not be transmitted as the reply of the President. It is wholly unlawful and improper; its language is unguarded and to send it as an official document will bring the President to the verge of usurpation!"

Nevins has the grace to footnote this piece of oratory with the sly demur, *This quotation has the ring of truth even if not literally accurate.*

The ring of truth, too, attaches to Buchanan's placating answer: "I will allow the urgency of the days, Mr. Stanton, to excuse the heat of your words. I hold out to the Commissioners merely the hope of submitting a proposal from them to the Congress. If they will retreat from Moultrie, and guarantee our federal property immunity for the rest of our administration, I see no harm in considering the restoration of Major Anderson to where he was five days ago."

Thompson, now the last of the original Southern members of the Cabinet,* asserted, "The subject for consideration, Mr. President, is the removal of Major Anderson from Charleston Harbor entirely. I urge it upon you as the only sane and magnanimous course."

"For such magnanimity," piped up Stanton, "they carve gallows timber!"

When the flurry of shouts died down, Black said soothingly, of Buchanan's proposed response to the Commissioners, "Mr. President, the language of this paper is self-incriminatory. It appears to concede the right of negotiation, when the ownership of federal forts is beyond negotiation. It implies that Major Anderson might be at fault in regard to a pledge made by you, when any such pledge or bargain should be flatly denied."

Pledge, bargain, bargain and sale. A lifetime of tact, miscon-

---

*And yet he seems miscast as villain. In the photograph of Buchanan with his Cabinet taken by W. H. Lowdermilk & Co. of Washington, D.C., sometime between the death of Aaron Brown and the resignation of Howell Cobb, Thompson is on the extreme left, blurred, looking stolid and, with his short haircut and clean shave, oddly modern. He was self-made, a poor boy from North Carolina who, Nichols says, *in the young and growing state of Mississippi . . . amassed political power and a fortune.* A frontiersman, if we remember that much of the Deep South was frontier, torn open by the rapid spread of cotton—a terrain for entrepreneurs and arrivistes. Romantically, he had fallen in love with a poor girl of fourteen, married her without consummating the marriage, and sent her off to Paris for four years of schooling; she was Kate Thompson, one of the social ornaments of Buchanan's Washington, a special favorite of the old chief, and the author of lively letters that form an important illumination of the era and administration. When Thompson at last resigned (*I go hence to make the destiny of Mississippi my destiny*) Buchanan wrote a warm letter saying, *No man could have more ably, honestly, & efficiently performed the various & complicated duties of the Interior Department than yourself. . . . I regret extremely that the troubles of the times have rendered it necessary for us to part.* This billet-doux as late in the day as January 11, 1861!

strued, crushed in the world's iron gears. What did Jackson say? *Them that travel the byways of compromise is the ones that get lost.* Only the Secretary of the Navy, little timid Toucey, his appointment a sop to the Pierce contingent, liked the President's reply just as it was.

Stanton was stridently saying, his metal-framed spectacles flashing awry in his fury, "Major Anderson is a hero, who saved the country when all else were paralyzed!"

Black, more gently: "Mr. President, you reiterate the Constitution's failure to specify a right of coercion, when what is meant is the right of our government to make war upon a state considered as a foreign country, *not* the right of the chief executive to defend federal property, or to put down those who resist federal officers performing their legal duties. You have always asserted the right of coercion to that extent. In your anxious, and laudable, desire to avoid civil war, you promote in these Carolina rebels dangerous illusions of power."

Thompson protested, "I resist, sir, the imputation that any rebellion has taken place. South Carolina's dissolution of its contract with the other states was carried forward with strict legality."

Buchanan pleaded, in a voice grown wheedling and quavery, "Time, gentlemen, let me gain a little time. Time is the great healer."

Stanton contradicted, "Time does not preserve, it destroys. *Men* protect and preserve, Mr. President, when their nerve does not fail them!"

Black agreed: "Time is not their enemy but ours. We speak of Congressional prerogatives, but Congress has no clear will; the extremists paralyze every attempt at resolution; this fall's Democratic victories have hardened the Republican minority to the point that they are en*cour*aging Southern secession."

Holt pointed out, "Even the conservative press in the

North rages against our failure to show force. General Scott urged reinforcement months ago; but Sumter can still be saved. Two hundred fifty recruits can sail from New York tomorrow!"

Buchanan resisted. "You speak of the forts as though they possessed real value. But their value now is chiefly symbolic."

Stanton said, "Precisely, sir. Send troops to Sumter, send guns; and the Unionists even within the Palmetto State will rise up and scatter the secessionist illusion to the winds!"

ETC., ETC. BIFF. BANG. POOR OLD BUCK. There was a seriousness here, a bottomless depth, that Buchanan felt no one but he apprehended. "Such reinforcements will give the South a rallying cry. I *did* affirm the *status quo* as my policy. . . . If war is to come, we must not appear to strike the first blow." He again remembered General Jackson, that frosty morning in 1824. The black man dozing on the park bench, the old soldier slim as a kindle light, skeletal, as if the heat of life was burning him to a frazzle. *With the people in yer belly, ye can do no wrong.* It had been exactly this terminal time of the year. Buchanan told his Cabinet, "Power does not flow from the government, in a nation constructed such as ours; it flows upward, from the people. If the people are to rally, it must be to a flag that is wronged. I will not reinforce Anderson, nor will I withdraw him. There let us leave the matter, and convene again tomorrow, after our Christian devotions."

He had become an old man, the oldest man ever to serve as President. Next April, he would be seventy. Making his way up to his bedroom, he felt his body dragging on his spirit. He felt a taunting emptiness in things. A bitter rain mixed with streaks of quick-melting snow muttered on the black panes of the second-story windows. Oblong imperfections in the glass added to the effect of waver and blur. Squinting through the wet glass, Buchanan spied only scattered lights in the apprehensive city—the lamps of a few carriages threading their way on midnight errands through the dark and the mud. Gleams pale as glowworms bobbed beneath the lanterns, reflected from icy puddles. He could not see, at the far end of Pennsylvania Avenue, the Capitol waiting for its dome or, beyond the foot of the White House grounds, on the far side of Tiber Creek and its pestilential swamp, the ghostly marmoreal stub of the Washington Monument, uncompleted and perhaps now never to be, mutual sectional hatred having dried up all appropriations.

The coal-burning furnace Pierce had installed indifferently warmed the upstairs. Harriet was asleep, and all the staff. No longer was her cousin and the President's long-time secretary, James Buchanan Henry, under the White House roof; the boy had last year resigned, gone to New York, grown a large black mustache, and impudently married without his uncle's consent. Buchanan did not feel exactly well: his throat had never ceased to twinge beneath its scars from the operation when he was Secretary of State; a life of rich meals and ample drink weighed on his lungs and abdomen; his hard-working eyes felt tender and grainy; the endless disputations of the last weeks had robbed his system of sleep and left him light-headed. Yet neither was he exactly ill: as he lifted the warming pan from the Presidential bed and fitted himself, in checkered nightgown and wool sleeping cap, between the sheets—scalding hot here and chill as ice there, like opinion in the newspapers—the old functionary sank into his weariness with something like voluptuousness. The thin partition between war and peace had held for another day. The Congress, with Lincoln's concurrence, might yet arrange a constitutional convention, and the South Carolinians pull in their horns, as Pickens did the day after secession. And if not . . . if the worst befall . . . well, he had gone the extra mile with the men of the South, and the war would be on their heads. They would be crushed, as poor dear Ann had been crushed.

He sleepily prayed, and the silence into which his brain poured its half-formed words, the sense melting like wax at the edge of the flaming wick, tonight seemed itself a message, tuned to his great weariness. He saw for a moment through not his own mismatched eyes* but through God's clear colorless ones; he saw that *sub specie aeternitatis* nothing greatly matters: not his own life, his ambitions, his patient intricate craven search for power, nor, cruel as the thought might appear from a wakeful perspective, the lives of the nation, the millions as they strain toward him for rescue. The hordes of Sennacherib invaded Israel, and the Temple was destroyed stone by stone, and yet within the beautiful dispassion of God these cataclysms had been cradled, and now slept unremembered but by a few. While Buchanan had been Ambassador to the Court of St. James, British educated opinion had been considerably agitated by the apparent discoveries, within geology, of tracts of time vaster than any the Bible disclosed: Buchanan now perceived a cause for serenity here, a vastness that dwindled all our agitations to a scarcely perceptible stir, and our mountains and chasms to a prairie smoothness, a luminous smoothness like that of Greenland, or of the unexpected southernmost continent first sighted by Captain Cook. Having been long troubled by the silence into which his prayers seemed to sink without an echo, Buchanan in his majestic fatigue appreciated that the silence *was* an answer, the only answer whose mercy was lasting, impartial, and omnipresent. Just so, Lincoln's silence

---

*One hazel, one blue, according to Nichols. He cites no ophthalmological source. It's hard to believe, but magical to picture. The portrait by Jacob Eichholtz, done when Buchanan was about to go off to Russia, is chromatically inconclusive. The one by George P. A. Healy, in the National Portrait Gallery, shows his eyes as both blue, with a slight cast (strabismus) in the left. Opposite this portrait in *The American Heritage Pictorial History of the Presidents* the unsigned text parenthetically claims *one eye* [was] *nearsighted, the other farsighted.* See Kierkegaard, *Journals*, December 10, 1837.

from Springfield, was an answer, of a certain grandeur, after all the clamor of the Cabinet meetings. As if through the gimlet eye of an eagle soaring in God's silent winds Buchanan saw the nation beneath him, a colorful small mountain meadow scurrying with frantic life; its life would perish but infallibly renew itself in the turning of seasons, in the great and impervious planetary motions. Thus reassured, the old man sank on a sustained note of praise into the void and woke with surprise into a still-stormy world where it seemed all but himself had tossed sleepless through the night.

The morning brought a note from General Scott, saying, *It is Sunday, the weather is bad, & Genl. S. is not well enough to go to church. But matters of the highest national importance seem to forbid a moment's delay, &, if misled by zeal, he hopes for the President's forgiveness.*

Will the President permit Genl. S., without reference to the War Department, & otherwise as secretly as possible, to send two hundred & fifty recruits, from New York Harbor, to reinforce Fort Sumter, together with some extra muskets or rifles, ammunition, & subsistence stores?

It is hoped that a sloop of war & cutter may be ordered for the same purpose as early as to-morrow.

Their clangor muffled by the storm, which on long legs of visible, wind-swept sleet strode through the toy houses and monuments of Washington City, church bells called secessionist and abolitionist alike, master and mistress and thinly clad slave, to worship. Buchanan, content with his religious experience of the previous midnight, stayed dry at home, and enjoyed a perfect Union breakfast: Carolina hominy grits and Philadelphia scrapple drenched in Vermont maple syrup. An agitated Toucey, looking fluffy and alarmed, like a bird tossed from its nest, arrived at the White House, saying that Black and Stanton and probably Holt would resign if the President sent his reply as drafted to the Commissioners.

So Buchanan sent for Black, who, after what his reminiscence calls *the most miserable and restive night of my life,* was reluctant to appear, *for I knew the temper of the appeal he would make to me. I felt that he would place his demand that I remain by his side upon such grounds of personal friendship that it would make it impossible for me to leave him without laying myself open to the charge of having deserted a friend who had greatly honored and trusted me at a time when he was under the shadow of the greatest trouble of his life.* Having failed to respond the first time, Black answered a second summons.

Buchanan greeted him, "Is it true that you are going to desert me?"

"It is true that I am going to resign."

This terrible light of day has brought back all the terrors, the seriousness, the precariousness, the unfathomable *shame,* the daily small losses that mask great loss. [Cf. my first winter after Genevieve's kiss-off: I woke up every morning feeling hollow, inwardly sore with a desperate sense of having misplaced some huge thing.] He said, according to history, "I am overwhelmed to know that you of all other men are going to leave me in this crisis. You are from my own state, my closest political and personal friend; I have leaned upon you in these troubles as upon none other, and I insist that you shall stand by me to the end."

After listening to more of such pleading, Black replied, working up to a charming metaphor: "Mr. President, from the start I had determined to stand by you to death and destruction if need be. I promised that as long as there was a button to the coat I would cling to it. But your action has taken every button off and driven me away from you."

Buchanan appeared genuinely puzzled. "What do you refer to?"

"Your reply to the South Carolina Commissioners. That

document is the powder that has blown your Cabinet to the four winds. The Southern members will leave because you do not concede what they ask, and your conclusions make it impossible for them to stay. The paper is even harder upon the Northern members of your political household." Black and Stanton's exact objections to the draft, which has not been preserved, can be roughly reconstructed. Black himself, interviewed by the Philadelphia *Press* in September of 1883, denied, as had been speculated, that *Mr. Buchanan's letter acknowledged the right of Secession.* [Black's] *objections to the paper were that it dallied with the enemies of the Government, implied certain diplomatic rights of South Carolina that could not exist, and yielded points that were unfair to the President's position.*

Can we believe that, when Black had stated his objections, Buchanan replied, "*Judge, you speak the words of my heart. I recognize the force and justice of what you say. The letter to the South Carolina Commissioners my tongue dictated, but not my reason. But I feel that we must not have an open rupture. We are not prepared for war, and if war is provoked, Congress cannot be relied upon to strengthen my arm, and the Union must utterly perish*"?

No. We can more easily believe Black when he says, *The President seemed surprised that I took this document so much to heart.* Almost flippantly, like a hardened gambler folding a hand, Buchanan told him, "Your resignation is the one thing that shall not be. I will not—I cannot part with you. If you go, Holt and Stanton will leave, and I will be in a sorry attitude before the country. This is the greatest trouble I have had yet to bear. Here, take this paper and modify it to suit yourself; but do it before the sun goes down. Before I sleep this night I must know that this matter is arranged to your satisfaction."

Black went to Stanton's office and in a long memorandum the two men revised Buchanan's reply to suit themselves. Nevins, rejoicing in this hardening of the administration line, crows, *Seldom if ever have the advisers of a President administered, even by implication, so severe a rebuke.*

The softer-hearted Auchampaugh says of this period, *No President in American history ever spent so terrible a ten days.*

This same Sunday, Senator Robert M. T. Hunter of Virginia, on the turncoat Trescot's advice, made one more Southern appeal to the President, proposing that Pickens abandon Moultrie so that Anderson could be restored. Hunter emerged from the interview and reported to Trescot, *Tell the Comm*[issioners]: *it is hopeless. The President has taken his ground—I can̲t̲ repeat what passed between us but if you can get a telegram to Charleston, telegraph at once to your people to sink vessels in the channel of the harbour.*

Buchanan rewrote his letter, mostly by editing out sections that Black and Stanton had resisted, and dispatched it to the Commissioners the next day, the last day of this fateful year. The message rehearsed the circumstances of the harbor and the unofficial negotiations and concluded, more ringingly than Buchanan's usual style, *It is under all these circumstances that I am urged immediately to withdraw the troops from the harbor of Charleston, and am informed that without this negotiation is impossible. This I cannot do; this I will not do.* Always a strict accountant, the President cited the seizure of the arsenal by South Carolina, estimated the worth of the arsenal as half a million dollars, and stated it as his *duty to defend Fort Sumter, as a portion of the public property of the United States, against hostile attacks, from whatever quarter they may come.*

The next day, Buchanan held his customary New Year's Day reception at the White House, braving assassination rumors and enduring snubs from secessionist guests. For the last time, the Southern flower of Washington society savored what Nevins evokes as *the contrast between the tall, snowy-haired, black-garbed old President, standing with head slightly awry, and the statuesque, golden young woman by his side.* On the second day of the new year, a reply was received from the Commissioners which the Cabinet, even Thompson concurring, found *violent, unfounded and disrespectful.* There had been a number of unpleasant letters in Buchanan's life—that from Dr. Davidson to his father concerning his misbehavior at Dickinson College, for example, and the lost letter from Ann Coleman breaking their engagement, and the preserved letter of his own, begging to attend her funeral, which was returned unopened, and the letter from Duff Green in 1826 asking, *Will you, upon the receipt of this, write to me and explain the causes which induced you to see Genl. Jackson upon the subject of the vote of Mr. Clay & his friends a few days before it was known that they had conclusively determined to vote for Mr. Adams; also advise me of the manner in which you would prefer that subject to be brought before the people.* That letter had had to be answered; it was Buchanan's pleasure to return this one to the Commissioners, with the endorsement, *This paper, just presented to the President, is of such a character that he declines to receive it.*

Philip F. Thomas, the Marylander who with Thompson composed the dwindling Southern contingent in the Cabinet, remembered in 1881 Buchanan's saying, of the letter, "Let it be returned" but did not hear him say, "Reinforcements shall now be sent." Holt, Toucey, Stanton, and Buchanan himself (in his letter to Thompson of January 9, 1861) testified that the President, once the decision to return the letter had been reached, then said audibly, "It is now all over, and reinforcements must be sent." But Thompson, like Thomas, didn't hear him say it, and resigned with considerable show of indignation when he discovered, on January 8, 1861, that the light-draught (in order to pass over the sunk vessels blocking the harbor) steamer *Star of the West* had, to quote his letter of resignation, *sailed from New York on last Saturday night with Two Hundred and fifty men under Lieut. Bartlett, bound for Fort Sumter.*

"It is now all over, and reinforcements must be sent."
It was now all over. The South and Buchanan had parted.

THE LAST THING I remember about the Ford Administration is sitting with my children watching, while a New England January held us snug indoors, a youngish-seeming man walking down Pennsylvania Avenue with one hand in his wife's and the other waving to the multitudes. Washington City was bathed in telegenic white sunlight and Carter was hatless, in pointed and rather embarrassing echo of Kennedy fourteen years and four Presidents ago. A hundred years after the end of Reconstruction and the one indisputably fraudulent Presidential election in American history, a son of the South had risen, without benefit of (cf. Truman, Tyler, and the two Johnsons) another President's demise. The youngish, hatless man's smile was broad and constant but not, absolutely, convincing; we were in a time, as in the stretch between Polk and Lincoln, of unconvincing Presidents. But Polk and Lincoln, too, had their doubters and mockers and haters by the millions; perhaps it lies among the President's many responsibilities to *be* unconvincing, to set before us, at an apex of visibility, an illustration of how far short of perfection must fall even the most conscientious application to duty and the most cunning solicitation of selfish interests, throwing us back upon the essential American axiom that no divinely appointed leader will save us, we must do it on our own. Of all the forty-odd, handsome Warren Harding was in a sense the noblest, for only he, upon being notified that he had done a bad job, had the grace to die of a broken heart.

In the three fuzzy heads around me—no, I miscounted, there can be only two, Andy is off at college by January of 1977, he is eighteen and in his freshman year; he chose to go to Duke, to put a bit of distance between himself and his wayward parents—there was, if I can be trusted to read the minds of children, a dubiety not unlike my own at the sunny spectacle being beamed to us from the District of Columbia. No other President had ever seen fit to walk back from the inauguration to the White House. It made him, we felt, a bit too much like the circus clown who, with painted smile, jesting now in this direction and now in that, leads the parade into the big tent— the acrobats and the jugglers, the solemn elephants of foreign policy and the caged tigers of domestic distress.

"Showoff," Buzzy said, in his manly baritone, which I was still not quite used to.

"Suppose he gets shot?" Daphne asked. She had been in my lap, up in our apple-green home at Dartmouth, a few months old, the Sunday that Lee Harvey Oswald had been plugged for his sins on national television. She had been weaned, you might say, on assassination.

However much Carter wanted to be liked, we could not quite like him: the South couldn't quite like him because he was a liberal and an engineer, the Northeast liberals couldn't because he was a Southerner and a born-again Christian, the Christians were put off because he had told *Playboy* he had *looked upon a lot of women with lust*, and the common masses because his lips were too fat and he talked like a squirrel nibbling an acorn. Blacks liked him, those blacks who still took any interest in the national establishment, but this worked in his disfavor, since the blacks were more and more seen as citizens of a floating Welfare State concealed within the other fifty, and whose settled purpose and policy was to steal money from hard-working taxpayers. Carter and the other liberal Democrats were white accomplices to this theft, this free ride. Furthermore he told us things we didn't want to hear: We should turn our thermostats down and our other cheek to the

Iranians. Our hearts were full of lust, we were suffering from a *malaise*. All true, but truth isn't what we want from Presidents. We have historians for that.

Forgive me, NNEAAH, and editors of *Retrospect;* I've not forgotten it was Ford you requested my impressions of, not Carter. But what did Ford *do*? As I've said, I was preoccupied by personal affairs, and had the radio in my little apartment turned to WADM—all classical, with newsbreaks on the hour of only a minute or two.* As far as I could tell, Ford was doing everything right—he got the *Mayaguez* back from the Cambodians, evacuated from Vietnam our embassy staff and hangers-on (literally: there were pictures of people clinging to the helicopter skids in the newsmagazines in my dentist's office), went to Helsinki to meet Brezhnev and sign some peaceable accords, slowly won out over inflation and recession, restored confidence in the Presidency, and pardoned Nixon, which saved the nation a mess of recrimination and legal expense. As far as I know, he was perfect, which can be said of no other President since James Monroe. Further, he was the only President to preside with a name completely different from the one he was given at birth—Leslie King, Jr. "President King" would have been an awkward oxymoron.

There was a picturesque little layer of snow in Washington on television, so there must have been mounds of it in New Hampshire, and ice in the river, black and creaky, and bare twigs making a lace at the windows. Twigs. Our nest. Where

---

*Not, in fairness, that I was entirely oblivious to popular music. It was the Ford era that saw the rise of Pachelbel's Canon in C on the charts; I know because the tune, with its low, slow, trickling theme of infinite forestallment, became something like our, my and Genevieve's, romantic anthem, along with *The Divine Miss M*, a cassette I gave her on our affair's first Christmas, for its terrific one-two punch of "Do You Want to Dance?" followed by Midler's ding-dong belting-out of "Chapel of Love." *Going to get ma-a-arried . . .*

was Norma? My still regnant Queen of Disorder? Not within the frame of this memory, somehow. She could have been painting in her alluringly odoriferous studio, or drifting through one of her do-it-yourself lectures on art appreciation over at the college, but my memory places her in the kitchen, tossing together a meal for us all as she sips her lucid green vermouth, the same tint as her eyes. But wait—the 20th of January was a Thursday, according to my perpetual calendar, so Buzzy and Daphne must have been at school, puzzling their way through the post-noon lessons, or gobbling up the beef-barley soup and American chop suey the school cafeteria provides on Thursdays. Perhaps we were all watching Carter's stroll on the evening-news rerun, and Norma was in the kitchen, cooking our dinner. She wandered in to join us. She held against the bib of her apron a curved wooden sculpting tool, with a serrated edge, that she used as a stew stirrer. She looked over our shoulders and said, "After Watergate, I don't see how the Republicans will ever elect another President."

This may have been the only thing I ever heard her say that was not even somewhat true. Now memory jump-shifts us to the kitchen, just the two of us, amid the soft sizzle and bubble of a meal minutes from consumption. I possibly whispered, "How do you think they seem?"

"Who?" The hand, winter-chapped and rather red and broad compared to Genevieve's, that was holding the gravy-stained modelling tool pushed a bothersome wiggle of hair back from her forehead, and to keep it in place—an ineffective trick of hers I had forgotten—Norma blew sharply upward, from a protruded lower lip.

"The *chil*dren, of course," I said. "Now that I'm back. They don't seem especially grateful."

"Oh, Alf, they *are,* they're thrilled. They just can't express it all the time, every minute. But Daphne is very happy, and is sleeping much better. All the time you were gone, she had insomnia. She was worried you'd get robbed and murdered over there in that slum."

"It wasn't a slum. It was an old-fashioned blue-collar downtown. And Buzzy? Are his marks going up?"

"Don't be ridiculous, it's too early to tell. They just got back from Christmas vacation."

"And you? You, dear Norma?"

She sensed my need and came a step closer to me, there among the sizzling and bubbling. "Of course. Very happy," she said, but with an undercurrent of diffidence, I thought. "You've made an honest woman of me again." Meaning she had stopped sleeping with the men who had moved into the vacuum I had left. "Though I must say" (like Carter, she was a touch too honest) "it takes some readjustment after all that— what did the existentialists call it?—dreadful freedom." When she and I and our generation are all dead, who will remember the existentialists? Who will break their eyeballs on Heidegger and Sartre and try to grasp the priority of existence over essence and the towering, eggplant-colored mystery of *Dasein*? What generation will ever again frame these basic questions in non-electronic terms? "One *does* adjust, awful to admit," Norma concluded, meaning, I took it, to sleeping around.

"Well," I said, indignantly, "if you'd adjusted a little faster I wouldn't have had to give up Genevieve."

"Oh, so that's my rap, is it?" Her hair against the light from the kitchen windows (it has become afternoon again) showed a rim of the palest apricot color; her green eyes, rounded in anger, held thin flecks of gold in their green. "You two did it to yourselves. I didn't ask you to come back. Love us or leave us, you had your choice. Alf, you were so dithery she had to take measures to protect herself. Brent made her an offer she couldn't refuse. If he'd have asked *me* to go to Yale with him, I might have said yes, too."

"With that anti-intellectual intellectual shit? Now you're

kidding me. Now you're *trying* to hurt my feelings." To show this was a joke, I laughed.

Thus we patched it up, again and again, until the ground became tired, trod into dust, beneath further discussion but not, really, ever not there.

In truth I was disappointed that my family didn't rejoice more loudly over my return. I could not quite fill the vacuum I had created when I left, as if I had grown smaller while away. And the days, the interminable dailiness of my being back, dulled the shining edge of my re-emergence on the domestic scene. Real life is in essence anti-climactic. *Star of the West*, for instance, whose dispatch to Sumter with reinforcements climaxed a long struggle within the Buchanan Administration, arrived at Charleston Harbor the day after Jacob Thompson resigned, and failed to return cannon fire from South Carolina batteries on Morris Island. The *Star*, unlike the warship *Brooklyn*, for which General Scott, against Buchanan's better judgment, had substituted the *Star*, had no guns on board and could not fire back. Nor did gunfire come from the *Brooklyn*, which had followed, at exactly what distance history does not record; objects bigger than a battleship can slip through its fingers. Major Anderson, who had received no orders and heard only rumors of the *Star*'s approach, did not answer with Fort Sumter's batteries. The *Star* returned to New York; an informal truce between Governor Pickens and Major Anderson took effect; and the flashpoint in Charleston Harbor was left unignited until after Lincoln had taken office and for a full month had sustained Buchanan's policy of not supplying Anderson until he asked for aid. On April 12, 1861, as we of the NNEAAH all know, Brigadier General Pierre Gustave Toutant de Beauregard gave the order to fire, and fanatic old fire-eating Edmund Ruffin pulled the lanyard for the first cannon-shot, according to a debatable but indelible legend. Although Major Anderson after thirty-three hours of bombardment surrendered without losing a man, the great blood-bath was on. Buchanan was back in Wheatland, and stayed there, defended by his brother Masons from local threats of violence, and defending himself with his pen against journalistic assaults on his Presidency. Crawford [see page 361] in his 1887 edition reproduces, with the photographic means of the time, a letter Buchanan wrote to a John Griffin in June of 1862, stating in his always legible hand,* *It will not be long before the public mind will be disabused of the slanders against me & I have not the least apprehension of the award of posterity. I would be the happiest old man in the country were it not for the civil war; but I console myself with the conviction that no act or omission of mine has produced this terrible calamity.* I love that: *the happiest old man in the country were it not for the civil war.* When Lee's troops invaded Pennsylvania in 1863, Buchanan sent Harriet Lane to safety in Philadelphia but himself remained at Wheatland, awaiting what evil the day might bring. Unlike Black, he supported the necessity for war from the start; unlike Pierce, he never spoke ill of Lincoln. Upon Lincoln's assassination, he wrote a friend, *My intercourse with our deceased President, both on his visit to me after his arrival in Washington, and on the day of the first inauguration, convinced me that he was a man of kindly and benevolent heart and of plain, sincere and frank manners. I have never since changed my opinion of his character.* Harriet Lane married Edgar E. Johnston, of Baltimore, on January 11, 1866. James Buchanan died, at Wheatland, on the morning of June 1, 1868, at the age of seventy-seven. His last words were

---

James Buchanan, who served from 1857–1861, is said to have had the neatest handwriting of any President. This encomium from *Facts and Fun About the Presidents,* by George Sullivan, illustrated by George Roper (New York: Scholastic, Inc., 1987). The same valuable source informs us that *Three American Presidents were left-handed: James Garfield, Harry Truman, and Gerald Ford.* Since 1987, the voters have added a fourth.

reported by Miss Hetty [see p. 225] to be *Oh Lord, God Almighty, as Thou wilt*. An accommodator to the end.

Brent Mueller, as you doubtless know, although he is now a member of *SNEAAH*, the *Southern* New England Association of American Historians, has done well at Yale, publishing that short but trenchant deconstruction of Whitman's and Emerson's optimism entitled *Other People's Facts*,* delving up from stray phrases the two Protestant white men's awareness that American expansionism was fuelled by black slavery, child labor, domestic oppression of women, and government-sponsored swindling and slaughter of Native Americans. They knew all this, the sublime scribblers, and achieved optimism by dint of suppressing it, while dark hints leaked out in Melville, Hawthorne, and Poe. Are things now any different? AIDS, famine, boat people, ghetto hopelessness, children by the millions born to misery. If a man had half a heart, he'd drown. Optimism isn't a philosophical position; it's an animal necessity, like defecation. As I sat and read Brent's book, my vision blurred by envy, it seemed a flip negative of my unwritten own, with a perfect title. Brent wrote his book and Genevieve gave birth to two more children, twin boys. Hearing the news back in Wayward, I wondered if, had we married, such double-barrelled fertilization would have been demanded of me. I had been so anxious and guilty about my own children, and to a lesser extent about hers, that I had never actually considered the possibility of *ours*.

Ours. Would we have named them Ronald and George after the winners, or Jimmy and Fritz after the losers? The idea of

---

*Derived, of course, from that callous passage in Emerson's essay "Experience" which states, *I have learned that I cannot dispose of other people's facts. . . . A sympathetic person is placed in the dilemma of a swimmer among drowning men, who all catch at him, and if he gives so much as a leg or a finger, they will drown him.*

pushing a duplex stroller, both sons squalling, through the narrow aisles of the supermarket over on 1A intimidates me. There comes a moment when we cease creating ourselves. *I have come to lay my bones among you,* Buchanan told the assembled folk of Lancaster upon his return home in March of 1861. *What I have done, during a somewhat protracted public life, has passed into history.* My attempt to bestow upon Buchanan *the award of posterity* collapsed when I, having imagined an eagle's-eye view that would make of his life a single fatal moment, found myself merely writing more history, and without the pre-postmodernist confidence of Nevins and Nichols and Catton, yarn-spinners of the old narrative school. My opus ground to a halt of its own growing weight, all that comparing of subtly disparate secondary versions of the facts, and seeking out of old newspapers and primary documents, and sinking deeper and deeper into an exfoliating quiddity that offers no deliverance from itself, only a final vibrant indeterminacy, infinitely detailed and yet ambiguous—as unsettled, these dead facts, as if alive. Where, really, *was* the *Brooklyn,* when the batteries of Morris Island fired on the *Star of the West?* Can it be true, as Klein offhandedly asserts, that *Stanton had not opened his mouth during the tense meeting of December 29—the one obviously referred to by Weed?* Surely Weed meant the meeting of the 28th, since Floyd had resigned early on the 29th. And could Stanton—he who later contemptuously described these constant meetings debating the President's course as *a fight over a corpse*—ever have sat through any meeting without opening his mouth? And can it be true, as Buchanan asserted both during these hectic weeks and afterwards,* that he was

---

*In a letter of October 21, 1865, he replied to a correspondent, a Mr. Faulkner, who had supposed that the former President might admit, in retrospect, some mistakes, *I must say that you are mistaken. I pursued a settled, consistent line of policy from the beginning to the end; & on reviewing my past*

serene, and self-convinced, that he felt no shame and terror as he descended at the head of his nation into the coming abyss of battle and blood?

And can it be, by the same token, true that Genevieve and I made love that left us both gasping, a melding so absolute we thought it expedient to stage a revolution, to overthrow our existing marriages and marry? Little trace of our attempt remains—a false start or two in several lawyers' files, some love letters lost in an attic or turned to ash, a few displaced calcium molecules in my deteriorating memory cells. Our heaving spirits displace little matter; the past, insofar as it consists of human feelings, mostly vanishes, less enduring than recycled nitrogen.

I have found no place, *Retrospect* editors, in these memories and impressions for the blameless bliss of settling, in my bachelor bed as midnight crept past, under an L.L. Bean puff and a reading light placed just where I wanted it, into the two propped pillows redolent of the Adams laundromat, with a nice musty old book—the abovementioned [p. 358] Crawford, for instance, with its chummy long title, *The History of the Fall of Fort Sumpter,* [*sic,* on the spine] *Being an Inside History of the Affairs of South Carolina and Washington, 1860–1, and the Conditions and Events in the South Which Brought on the Rebellion,* and its line engravings and yellowing letterpressed pages and sturdy marbled boards with corners and spine of red leather. Crawford was a young military surgeon who had been there, at Moultrie and Sumter in late 1860. How innocent, as I read, scribbling on a pad of yellow paper notes whose meaning I would soon forget, facts seemed; how sweet the clear water at the bottom of the well of time!

Another memory of the Ford era that returns to me now

---

conduct, I do not recollect a single measure which I should desire to recall, even if this were in my power. Under this conviction I have enjoyed a tranquil & cheerful mind, notwithstanding the abuse I have received.

concerns the same bed, the same time, but Genevieve is with me. Susan and Laura must have been spending the night with the diabolically patient Brent, or else with a non-teen-age baby-sitter who could stay past midnight, for we had allowed ourselves the luxury of drowsing and dozing after intercourse. Usually, one or the other of us had to jump up and rush to the next appointment. I can fix the date exactly: Tuesday, October 21, 1975, edging into October 22nd, at around quarter to one. We had fallen asleep, sated and drained by sex and guilt, and were awoken by a tumult on the streets below, of blaring car horns and shouts of drunken jubilation from the throats of men pouring out of the bar whose neon sign fizzled a few doors down from my windows. Carlton Fisk had won the hard-fought, extra-innings sixth game of the World Series between the Cincinnati Reds and the Boston Red Sox, by hitting a home run off the left-field foul pole. It was called the Greatest Game Ever Played in the papers next day and Fisk later contributed his account to history: *Freddie Lynn was on deck. He was hitting after me that game for some reason. I don't know why, but he was and I can remember standing in the on-deck circle before the inning started, and you just had a feeling something good was going to happen. And I told Freddie, "Freddie, I'm going to hit one off the wall. Drive me in." And that was the way it ended.* Genevieve and I, locked into our own black-and-white blend of hell and paradise, were far from following baseball that fall, but the hullabaloo below my two windows united us with a celebrating New England at that wee hour. Then, as I recall, she got out of bed, her wonderful white body stamped on my retinas like a pulsating after-image, and dressed herself. Feeling drugged, I dressed, too, and we walked through the litter of broken beer bottles and fallen maple leaves to her car parked over on Federal and she drove alone back across the river. *And that was the way it ended.* The next day, we lost the seventh game and the series to a broken-bat single, 4–3.

What I had not quite counted on: the children left me, one by one, after I had returned to the nest.

Andy did Duke and found history as an area of concentration too fussily factual and English too theory-ridden and both too "political" in some sense that had come along since my own collegiate days. But he fell in love with French, of all things, and took two graduate years at the Sorbonne, finished his Ph.D. at Michigan State, and wound up teaching Racine, Simenon, and the conditional subjunctive to the blond and blue-eyed children of Texas oil money at a trim college called Trinity in San Antonio. He brought back a French wife from the Sorbonne years and now my grandchildren stare at me semi-trustfully (they only see me once or twice a year; Andy and Nathalie spend summers near her parents in Grenoble) with Genevieve's dark precision, beneath decisive, no-nonsense eyebrows.

Buzzy flunked out of UNH—not easy to do—and has become a successful auto mechanic in Portsmouth, with a beer belly, a scrawny wife from Seabrook, and a twenty-five-foot power boat with which he thunderously churns the waters of the Piscataqua and Wayward rivers, cruises the Maine coast, and circumnavigates the Isles of Shoals. He loves that boat, with its endless engine troubles. Though they have been working at it (so to speak) for years, he and Ruth Ann cannot seem to conceive. Norma blames nuclear radiation, but the plant didn't begin to operate until Ruth Ann was twenty, and living in Rye Beach. Furthermore, she had an abortion in high school, thanks to a broken condom and the captain of the track team. Buzzy is now thirty, and though he is the closest child to us geographically, he is the most remote culturally, and when we sit together, he and I, while our wives are cooking up something in the kitchen or having one of their fertility powwows, the silence, not quite comfortable but full of mutual forgiveness, returns from those nights when I used to visit his room, not knowing how to apologize for living a mile away, across the bridge, beyond the range of his telescope. We see few signs in us of my being his father and he my son, but our love is the stronger, and the more awkward, for that, like sexual attraction between strangers.

As to Daphne, I assume she is happy in her second marriage, though with people who live in New York it is difficult to tell: the high energy level they must maintain acts as a mask. Geoff, her husband, works on Wall Street, or near it, glued between a secretary pool and a computer screen, pondering how to milk still more lucre from the staggering old cow of American capitalism. I seem to be enough of a liberal to dislike these money men, who have turned Roosevelt's willingness to take on debt in a national emergency into, a half-century later, a game, the debt game, a numbers racket. I try not to let my dislike show, but Norma says it does and that Daphne is very hurt, and they spend most of their holidays with his parents in Greenwich. Daphne has produced a daughter, a little milky miracle with a wisp of pale-apricot-colored hair on her broad blue scalp and hands with the repellent texture of wilted gardenias. I preferred her first husband, a shaggy ex-hippie from Maine, ten years her senior. He was running a secondhand bookstore, mostly student texts, in Middletown, Connecticut, where she had gone to Wesleyan, after two years of living at home with us and attending Wayward. He had a touching stammer, as if the words he wanted to say were suddenly too brutal, or revelatory, for utterance. The divorce came within a year, on the grounds of mental cruelty, and cost as much as their wedding. Norma says the trouble with Ralph was that he was too much like me—a typical closed-up Yankee. I don't feel closed-up to myself—just to other people.

Wayward in the early Eighties went co-ed and became one more third-rate four-year college. I've thought of leaving but, frankly, nobody wants me, with no major publications to my credit. [*Retrospect* eds.: You can change all that! Excuse this end-of-the-tale sentimental tone; I've been responding to your query so long I feel we're old friends. Cut, trim, chasten my prose *ad libitum,* as suits your editorial requirements.] Since males were admitted (up to 43 percent of student body, at last fall's enrollment), the tone of the college has changed—louder, coarser, more naïve, less serious, more like the world outside. The girls—women—have lost something: if nothing else, the chance to take on male rôles, like Jennifer Arthrop as Cinesias And we males of the faculty have lost a part of our rôle as educators, the need and opportunity to be chivalrous, mounted as we were on the caparisoned stallions of our manhood above the unarmored mob of questing young females. Just the sound, in chapel, of the massed female voices on the hymns and responses, so open and silvery, vulnerable and strong, would drive me to near-tears and the thought that perhaps the old anthropologists were right, we *are* half-angels after all.

Norma and I are fairly content. College people acquire a certain grim yet jaunty expertise at aging, at growing grayer with each year's fresh installment of ever-young, ever-ignorant students. We roll with the annual punch. Alone in this big house (which we couldn't sell anyway, in the depressed present market), she and I at moments feel as shy with one another as honeymooners, without a honeymoon's great icebreaker. The children gone, we haven't replaced the cats as they've died off, so there is less dander and hair, and we're able to afford a once-a-week cleaning woman now. When my mother died in 1978, she left the Florida condo free and clear and a surprising number of CDs and tax-free municipals, plus a lot of AT&T and John Deere my father had bought when the shares were a few dollars apiece. Once males were enrolled at Wayward, Norma's approach to art appreciation was thought to be a bit too indirect and intuitive, and the President—herself a woman, you will remember—in the nicest possible way let her go. So my former Queen of Disorder has more time for housework. She has given up smoking and put on thirty pounds. We see a lot of the Wadleighs. Wendy was also let go, as hockey-and-dyslexia coach, when the boys flooded into Wayward. Norma spends whole afternoons over there, in that redwood house above the river, with all its pianos. Wendy is "into," as my generation can't stop saying, the body—she bicycles in spandex shorts and walks with dumbbells in her fists and at well over fifty has the waist of a nineteen-year-old. She drives all the way down to Boston twice a week to take a course in how to be a therapeutic masseuse, and gives Norma long backrubs that leave my wife languid and (she humorously complains) achy.

Where have these last fifteen years gone? What a quick idle thing a life is, in retrospect. How quickly we become history, while wanting always to be news. When you make the mental effort to lift yourself a little off the planet, and you see our particular species gobbling up all the land, so that soon there won't be any other big animals left, just rats and ants and poisoned mussels, all that earth and oxygen and airspace to give *Homo sapiens sapiens* room to breed and eat and starve and build and war and watch TV and listen to the radio, you see that the human race is just one immense waste of energy. The lifeless surfaces of Mars and Io must sigh in relief.

The Ford years. What else can you say about them/him? Or, really, any of them? These men, our Presidents, do their confused best, toward the end of their lives usually, and there's no proving that different decisions would have produced better results. They were constrained by invisible walls, assumptions and pressures that have melted into air, that were always air—*Zeitgeist, Volksgeist.* Time was on the North's side, and as Trescot said in his account, *Besides, like the Northern members of his Cabinet, he [JB] was a Northern man. If this revolution was checked he and they would claim credit for their firmness, if it succeeded they were to remain at the North and must be supported by Northern opinion.* The half-degree between Lancaster and the Mason-Dixon Line was, in the end, crucial. Perhaps I would have succeeded if I had tried a book about Pierce, but his administration was relatively dull (not one Cabinet change in four years!) and his household gloomy and Nathaniel Hawthorne and Roy Nichols had already written creditable biographies. I was drawn to the unknown—the unpossessed—in scholarship as in love. I loved Buchanan because he was a virgin.

Gerald Ford, it remains to say, is the only non-assassinated President whose name ends with "d," the only Nebraska native and Michigan politician to attain the office, and the only skier. Oh, perhaps Kennedy and Roosevelt in the course of their privileged boyhoods strapped on some boards, but only Ford flashed down the slopes while President, creating a wholly new protection problem for the Secret Service.

I remember (this is the end, *Retrospect,* and remember, you asked) taking a run under Ford, on I forget what mountain. At the top, at the clattering terminus of the upper lift, where the pines were stunted and ice was prevalent and the trails were narrow, a taste of fear made the high air hard to breathe as I buckled on my skis, bending over to fasten my safety straps in this era before retractable ski brakes, my only companions on the dazzling windswept summit seeming to be whooping adolescent boys and leather-faced ski bums whose tans stopped at their goggles. Nervously I picked my way down the first glazed turns, trying to stay to the edges where the snow could still grab, the whole purple-blue valley yawning in the tree-gaps like a view from an airplane, and then I gathered looseness and confidence on the broader middle slopes. I began to swing from side to side as if striding through air, singing to give myself rhythm. I had discovered as a boy on the tilted fields around Hayes that singing helped your skiing, almost any tune, strangely enough, if you shifted weight—boot to boot, edge to edge—on the beat. This day, as I remember, the tune was a Beatles oldie, but not such an oldie then; "*Yes*terday," I sang, "all my *troub*les seemed so *far* away," keeping my chest to the valley, "now it *looks* as though they're *here* to stay," my knees bent and thrusting, my mittened black hands in front of me as the poles pricked the snow alternately, elbows in. "I be*leeeve* in *yes*terday!" The held notes gave the ski tails time to turn and say *swish*. I felt weightless, and seemed to be carving a swanky great signature in the moguls and swales of the middle run. A quickening of tempo forced me to wedel: "*Why* she *had* to *go*, I don't *know*, she wouldn't *say*. I said something *wrong*, and now I *long*, for *yes*terday-ay-ayy-ayyy." Then came a flat lookout at the top of the beginner's slope, and I rested my trembling legs a moment, the lodge as small beneath me as a matchbox, its vicinity crawling with colored dots. I shoved off, and gathered speed, my knees and feet absolutely together, the whole trick of it absurdly simple, a matter of faith and muscle memory, and, as I with one concluding wiggle-waggle swooped to a stop in a plume of slush, there they all were, my life's companions, at an outdoor picnic table, their parkas off and jumbled with the wine bottles and picnic hampers: Norma and my children in woolly sweaters cats had napped on, and Genevieve looking terrific in her white cashmere and black headband, and Brent smugly polluting the mountain air with pipe smoke, and the Wadleighs in typically jolly matching Day-Glo yellow high-waisted ski pants with red suspenders, and assorted pink-cheeked children, their lips flecked with relish and mustard, and some other adults, the German professor and his Jewish wife, he still skiing in knickers and long-thongs and she togged out in a camel loden coat as if to go shopping at Bloomingdale's, and a pair of freckled second wives, and poor elegant Mario Alvarez before his disgrace and abashed return to Providence.

There were smiles on their ruddy faces; they had been waiting for me; they were pleased to have seen me ski so well. In those years I was a fabulous creature, wiry and rapacious, racked by appetites as strange to me now as the motivations of a remote ancestor. I was slender, the result not of exercise but of nervous energy, and my hair was still mostly brown, and like animal fur to the touch, bouncy and soft, not brittle and white and thinning. I wore a ski cap on only the coldest days. Today was not one. It must have been during the Washington's Birthday weekend (before it was dissolved into Presidents' Day) or perhaps even the Easter break, because of the strengthening sun; it was picnic weather in the lee of the lodge. But what mountain could it have been? Gunstock and Sunapee don't have outdoor tables, and Cranmore and Wildcat don't have run-out slopes the way I remember this one. Could it have been Pleasant Mountain, across the state line in Bridgton, Maine? How could Norma and Genevieve, rivals for my hand, have been there both at once, beaming at me from above the Chardinesque tumble of welcoming food? Perhaps my vivid mental picture derives from the winter before our *crise* began. Or perhaps we had all patched things up for appearances' sake, for this holiday outing, one big falsely happy family. I had descended the mountain into bliss; this lengthy response to your provocative query seems to have delivered me into darkness. The more I think about the Ford Administration, the more it seems I remember nothing

Brief Bibliography

Auchampaugh, Philip Gerald, *James Buchanan and His Cabinet on the Eve of Secession* (Lancaster, Pa., 1926).

————, "James Buchanan, the Bachelor of the White House. An Inquiry on the Subject of Feminine Influence in the Life of Our Fifteenth President," *Tyler's Quarterly Historical and Genealogical Magazine*, XX, no. 3, January 1939, 154–166, and no. 4, April 1939, 218–234.

Buchanan, James, *Works*, collected and edited by John Bassett Moore, in twelve volumes (New York, 1908–11).

Catton, Bruce, *The Coming Fury* (New York, 1961).

Craven, Avery, *The Coming of the Civil War* (New York, 2nd ed. 1957).

Crawford, Col. Samuel W., *The History of the Fall of Fort Sumter* (New York, 1887).

Curtis, George Ticknor, *Life of James Buchanan*, in two volumes (New York, 1883).

Furnas, J. C., *The Americans: A Social History of the United States 1587–1914* (New York, 1969).

Gay, Peter, *Education of the Senses*, vol. I, *The Bourgeois Experience: Victoria to Freud* (New York, 1984).

Klein, Philip Shriver, "James Buchanan and Ann Coleman," *Lancaster County Historical Society*, LIX (1955), 1–20.

————, *President James Buchanan* (University Park, Pa., 1962).

Lestz, Gerald S., *Historic Heart of Lancaster* (Lancaster, Pa., 1962).

Nevins, Allan, *The Emergence of Lincoln*, in two volumes (New York, 1950).

Nichols, Roy, *The Disruption of American Democracy* (New York, 1948).

Trescot, William Henry, *Narrative*, edited by Gaillard Hunt, *American Historical Review*, XIII, no. 3 (April 1908), 528–56.

Updike, John, *Buchanan Dying* (New York, 1974).

About the Author

JOHN UPDIKE was born in 1932, in Shillington, Pennsylvania. He graduated from Harvard College in 1954, and spent a year in Oxford, England, at the Ruskin School of Drawing and Fine Art. From 1955 to 1957 he was a member of the staff of *The New Yorker*. He is the father of four children and the author of more than fifty books, including collections of short stories, poems, essays, and criticism. His novels have won the Pulitzer Prize (twice), the National Book Award, the National Book Critics Circle Award, the Rosenthal Award, and the Howells Medal. He lives in Massachusetts.